AS LONG AS
I HAVE YOU

CHILDREN OF THE PROMISE

·CHILDREN OF THE PROMISE·

VOL. 5

AS LONG AS
I HAVE YOU

· DEAN HUGHES ·

DESERET BOOK COMPANY · SALT LAKE CITY, UTAH

Library of Congress Cataloging-in-Publication Data

Hughes, Dean, 1943–
    As long as I have you / Dean Hughes.
        p. cm. — (Children of the promise; v. 5)
    ISBN 1-57345-800-7
        1. Mormon families—Fiction. I. Title.

PS3558.U36 A8 2000
813'.54—dc21

                                                        00-055473

Printed in the United States of America   18961-6688
    10   9   8   7   6   5   4   3   2   1

FOR ROB HUGHES

I

Wally Thomas sat on his hospital bed with a couple of pillows propped behind his back. A nurse had given him a *Life* magazine full of photographs of the impromptu celebrations across the nation on V-J Day. But Wally couldn't concentrate. Everything in the magazine was foreign to him, a reality he could hardly imagine, and besides, he was too worked up. He glanced at the clock every minute or two, but it wasn't until after ten o'clock in the evening that a stout young nurse named Myrna looked into his ward and called, "Okay, Thomas. Come with me. You're up next for the telephone."

Wally slipped off the bed. His excitement had instantly turned to nervousness, although he couldn't have said why. It would be after eleven in Utah, and surely his parents would be home, even if he did get them out of bed. He pulled his slippers on, grabbed a robe, and followed Myrna down the hall. She told him to sit down outside an office door. "We can only give you five minutes," she said. "When the fellow on the phone comes out, go right in, and the corporal will place your call."

Wally did sit down, but as soon as Myrna walked away, he stood again. He watched the door. What should he say first? How should he use his five minutes? All evening he had been thinking of things he wanted to say, and ask, but he needed hours, not minutes.

Finally the door opened. The man who stepped out was far too thin not to be another released POW, but he was no one Wally knew—not anyone from his camp. Wally stepped forward a little too quickly, brushing against the man. The corporal was sitting at an oak desk in a tiny room. He was holding a telephone receiver in one hand and a pencil in the other. "Give me the number and then step in there," he said. He pointed with his thumb but didn't look up. Wally recited his parents' phone number—which he had never forgotten—and then stepped into the larger inner office and sat down. The office, except for a desk and chair, was empty, with stark white walls. The air smelled of something strange, sour—maybe some sort of salve or dressing from one of the men who had been there ahead of him. When Wally picked up the phone he could already hear the ringing on the other end. In a moment he heard a click, and then his mother's voice, breathy, anxious. "Yes? Hello."

"Mom, it's Wally." Then his voice broke, and that was all he could get out.

"Oh, son," his mother said, and she too began to cry. He suddenly felt like a little boy. He wanted to be there, to let her take him into her arms. "Wally, are you all right?" she finally managed to ask.

"I'm fine, Mom." Wally swallowed and tried to get control. He couldn't waste any more of this valuable time. "They've put me in a hospital, in San Francisco, but that's just to check me out. I'm doing great."

"When will they let you come home?"

"I don't know. I hope it won't be too long—maybe just a few days."

"Oh, Wally, you must have been through some terrible things."

"Well . . . yeah. But I'm doing fine now, and I'm putting on weight. I'm feeling pretty good. Did you ever get any of the letters I sent?"

"No. Sister Adair got a card from Chuck, and he wrote on it that you two were together, and you were okay. But that's the only thing we ever heard—and that was a long time ago."

Wally had always feared that, but it hurt to think that not one letter had reached them. "I didn't get any letters from you, either," he said. "I got a package a couple of years ago."

"Oh, honey, I'm sorry. We wrote all the time, and we sent you lots of packages."

"I know." But the thought of it—all those letters and packages he would have loved—was agonizing. "Well . . . it's over now." He bent forward and looked at the floor, the gray tile. It really was over, and he wanted to be home, really home.

"It sounds so good to hear your voice, Wally. I always told myself that you were alive, but sometimes I wondered if it was really true." She was still crying, even harder now. "I'm just so thankful."

And then Wally heard his father. "Wally. Hello."

"Hi, Dad. Sorry to get you out of bed. My turn on the phone didn't come until now." He couldn't think of any of the things he had planned to say.

"It doesn't matter. It's just so good to hear you. Are you really all right?"

"I am. I got awful sick over there a few times. But I didn't give up." He wanted his dad to hear that, to know that.

"We haven't heard anything, Wally. We don't even know where you were."

"This last year I worked in the coal mines in Japan. I'll tell you all about it when I get home." But Wally knew he wouldn't do that. He was never going to tell his family *all* about it. He pressed his eyes shut. He hadn't realized how difficult this was going to be. No one except the other POWs would ever understand what he had been through.

"Listen, Beverly just came running in here. She wants to talk to you."

"Okay, Dad. We'll talk when I get home. There's just a lot I need to say to you."

"Sure, sure. I understand."

"Well . . . maybe not. But I can't be on the phone very long tonight."

"Of course. When you get here, we'll sit down and have a long talk about everything. Let me put your sister on for a minute."

"Wally, Wally. Hello," Beverly was suddenly squealing.

"Hi, Sis. How are you?"

"I'm fine. I'm fine. Are you okay?"

Wally laughed. "Yeah. I'm great. All I do is eat and take it easy. I've got it made."

"I want to see you. When will you get here?"

In Wally's mind, Bev was a little girl in pigtails. He couldn't make a picture now of this teenager shouting into the phone. "It might be a couple of weeks. I'm not exactly sure."

"Do you want me to wake up LaRue and—"

"No, you'd better not. I don't have much time."

"Okay. But Wally, I wanted to tell you, I prayed for you every single day while you were gone—twice every day, at least."

"I knew you were doing that, Bev. I knew the whole family was. And it helped me, even just knowing it."

"But I was scared."

"I know. I was scared too."

"Come home soon, okay?"

"As soon as I can."

"Dad wants to talk to you again."

"Wally," Dad said, "I was just talking to your mom. We're thinking about driving to San Francisco. We could leave in the morning and—"

"They say they might transfer me to another hospital. I might be gone from San Francisco by the time you get here."

"And you don't know where they'll send you?"

"No. Everything is just rumors so far. As soon as I know something for sure, I'll let you know. But I think I'll be released quite soon. And, actually, I sort of want to come home to you. That's what I've always imagined."

"I understand what you're saying. We're just anxious to see you."

"I know, Dad. Let me find out where I'm going—or if I'm staying here—and then I'll call again and let you know."

"All right."

"And write me. I need to find out about everyone. Is Bobbi married? Or Alex? Are they in Salt Lake, or—"

"Bobbi's not married, but she's . . . well, it's kind of a long story. She's in the navy. She's a nurse, on a hospital ship. There's a fellow here who wants to marry her, and . . . but we can talk about that later, too. We just keep hoping she'll get her release before long. Alex is still in Germany. But he's married. His wife is in England."

"England? Did he marry a Brit?"

"No. He married Anna Stoltz—the German girl he met on his mission. They have a baby boy. They named him Gene."

All that was a little too sudden, too much to digest. Wally felt the rightness of the name, but hearing it, he felt the loss all over again—almost as powerfully as when he had first received his father's telegram. He was almost home, but Gene wasn't going to be there. "Well, that's good," was all he could think to say, and now he was straining not to cry again.

The door to the office opened, and the corporal said, "I'm sorry, but your time is almost up. You have thirty seconds."

Wally struggled to find his voice. "Dad, I've got to go. I'll talk to you about all this as soon as I can. But I'm so sorry about Gene. I've had a hard time with that."

"I know. We all have. But we've had time to get used to the idea, and you haven't."

"I've seen so much death, Dad. I lost so many friends."

"I hate to think of all you've been through, Wally. But I hope you know how proud I am of you. We all are."

"Thanks, Dad." Wally couldn't stop himself. He moved the phone away a little, tried not to let his dad hear how hard he was crying.

"Wally, I've got a job for you at our plant. So don't worry about that. You'll have work, and we'll help you get back into the swing of things."

"All right."

"We love you, Son."

"I love you, Dad. I love all of you. Tell Mom."

But Bea had taken the phone back, and she was the one who responded. "Oh, Wally, we love you too. I hope they'll let you come home right away."

"I think they will, Mom. I'm in pretty good health—better than a lot of the guys."

"Your time is up," the corporal was saying, but Wally clung to the phone. The sound of his mother sobbing softly, the connection to his home, the picture that was in his mind—his house, the phone on the dining-room wall, his mom and dad and sister standing together—it was all something he didn't want to let go. He was really close now. He was going to be there before much longer. What he had dreamed about all these years was within reach, and his dad was actually proud of him—he had said so.

* * *

A week later Wally still didn't know what was going to happen to him. Most of the POWs from their ship had been sent by train to Madigan General Hospital at Fort Lewis, near Tacoma, Washington, but Wally and Chuck kept insisting that they were healthy and doing fine. They just wanted to go home. Wally had met with a psychologist twice, and nurses had poked him a dozen times for blood tests or to give him vaccines. Doctors also questioned him extensively about his medical history, the various diseases he had suffered, and they x-rayed him and checked him over until he felt like some sort of medical experiment. Life was not so bad, with plenty to eat, but he spent every day in his pajamas and robe, wasn't allowed to leave the hospital, and had little to do most of the time. And all that was beginning to make him nervous.

One evening, after dinner, Wally and Chuck stayed in the hospital cafeteria and lingered over a pie-and-ice-cream dessert. Wally had dreamed about pies and cakes and cookies so many times during his years in the camps. It was hard, still, not to eat everything he could stuff into himself. He had gained back a lot of weight, but he had been little more than skin and bones by the end of the war, so he still looked slim. What he knew, however, was that he had to start backing off the food. He couldn't afford to keep gaining so fast, at least not for much longer.

Wally had called home a couple more times in the past week, and he had remembered to ask more of the questions he'd had on his mind. One thing he had learned was that Lorraine Gardner was not married. He had experienced a moment of joy when he'd heard that, but his mother had finished by saying, "But, Wally, she is engaged. I'm not exactly sure when she plans to get married. I suspect, now that the war is over, that it won't be long."

Wally had asked whether her fiancé was someone in Salt Lake and had learned that Lorraine had met a man in Seattle, where she had been working for Boeing, and that Lorraine was still living there. Wally wished, in a way, that she had been married for years, had a couple of children—that sort of thing. It hurt all the more to think that she was "almost" available. After hearing the news, he had lain awake in his hospital bed that night, and he had run through his favorite memories— especially the night at Lagoon, when they had danced in the parking lot. He even let the old tune run through his head: "I get along without you very well. Of course I do."

But then he had stopped himself. He would start over, meet someone new, and that was something to be excited about. He was happy for Lorraine, and he would always remember her friendship at such an important time in his life. The sun was going down behind a hill, a row of buildings creating an uneven silhouette. Wally could also see his face reflecting back from the window. He knew he needed some dental work, but otherwise he hoped he didn't look too changed, too worn. For a long time such things hadn't seemed to matter much, as long as he survived, but now he wondered about going back into the world he had left behind. What would the girls back home think of him?

"What are you going to do when you get home?" Chuck asked. "Have you figured that out yet?"

"Dad wants me to work with him. He's making washing-machine parts now. He said he needs someone to run the place, sooner or later, so maybe I'll have the chance to do that. Of course, I don't know what Alex will want to do. He was in charge of the company at one time."

"Sounds like you've got it made, Wally."

"Well, I don't know. Some things are still up in the air, but at least there's something I can do. It just scares me a little." He laughed. "Right now my only skill is shoveling coal."

Every time Wally thought about all this, he felt sick to his stomach. He had gained a lot of confidence among the prisoners, had learned how to survive—but now he was facing a world he could hardly remember.

"My dad told me I ought to go to college now," Chuck said. "He said there's some kind of government money that vets can get to use for their education."

"Yeah, my dad told me about that. They call it the GI Bill. That sounds like something we ought to take advantage of."

"Sure. No question."

But Wally heard the hesitancy in Chuck's voice, and he knew that he wasn't admitting to all he was feeling any more than Wally was. They had both told the psychologist that they were fine and didn't need time to adjust, but that was only to get themselves out of the hospital. The fact was, Wally's legs ached constantly, severely, and twice now he had awakened in the night to a dreadful dream in which he was being taken prisoner all over again, knocked down and beaten by Japanese soldiers. He told himself it was only natural to experience some bad memories for a while, but he was sure he could deal with all that and get it behind him.

"I never was a great student in high school, Wally. I hadn't planned to go to college. I'm not sure how I'd do."

"You're disciplined now. You'll do great."

"I've forgotten everything. I don't know any math or history . . . or any of that stuff."

"You can get it back. We both can. We can do *anything*. We proved that already."

Chuck looked away, not saying the obvious: that the new challenges were not so focused—maybe, in their own way, even harder. Chuck had lost a lot of his teeth, and the ones that were left were badly decayed. At one time he had lost most of his hair, too, but now that he had been eating better, most of it had come back in. The only problem was, he still didn't look healthy. His skin was pale, and he hadn't gained his weight back as well as Wally had.

Wally finished the last of his pie, and then he pushed the plate away, leaned back, and looked across the cafeteria. The tables were mostly empty now. A thin little man with gray hair was scrubbing the floor, a metal edge on his mop scraping the tile in a steady rhythm. Wally could smell the soap— like the Dreft dish soap his mother had always used. He loved the cleanliness of the hospital, the neatness, the quiet, kindly way that people talked to each other.

"I think the Japs robbed me of something, Wally," Chuck

said. "I don't feel sure of myself the way I always did when I was a kid."

"I know what you mean. It's like we lived in a cave for three and a half years and someone just let us out. It's going to take us a little while to get used to everything again. We'll be okay once we do."

"Some of the guys are really broken down, Wally. They seem almost crazy now that we're back with normal people. Some of them won't ever get their health back. You can see they're too far gone."

Wally knew that was true. Some had been kept in hospitals in the Philippines, and they were not in good shape; others had come this far and still looked hollow and pale, weren't gaining any weight. "Chuck, we're some of the lucky ones. We're in pretty decent condition."

"I know."

But Wally was worried about Chuck. He had been such a strength to his friends all through the hard days at Cabanatuan and, later, in Japan, but he didn't sound like himself now. "Let's stick together, back in Salt Lake," Wally said. "A lot of people won't understand what we've been through, but we can help each other get going again."

"I'm glad you said that, Wally. That's what I want. It sounds stupid to say, but I've depended on our group so long, it scares me to have it all broken up."

"Well, you and I won't have to split apart. We'll still be together. We'll help each other."

"Okay. That's a deal." Still, Wally could see the nervousness in Chuck's eyes, and he felt it in himself. He wanted to get out of this hospital and get on with life—not just worry about everything.

* * *

Bea was sitting in the living room, reading, when President Thomas came out of his office at the back of the dining room. "Are you ready to go to bed?" he called to her.

"Not yet. You go ahead." But then she added, "Get ready, and I'll come up in a minute to have prayers with you."

President Thomas almost always went to bed earlier than Bea, but they rarely missed having their prayers together. For so long, prayer had seemed the only hope against all the dangers that were stalking the family. Now, Bea prayed a hundred times a day, just quickly, silently, saying, "Thanks, Lord. Thanks so much." It was her response every time she thought of the war being over and of her remaining children all alive. Wally really would be home soon. Bea had heard his voice, and now she knew his return was real. Bobbi should be released from the navy before too many more months passed. And Alex might not get home until next year, but at least he was not being shot at any longer. President Thomas had written to the Stoltzes, in London. He wanted to sponsor them, help them immigrate to Salt Lake. They were hesitating because they still hadn't located their son, Peter. But Bea now had hopes that her little grandson, Gene, would be near her at some point, and that Alex would come back too.

Bea finished the page she was reading before she put her book down on the end table, next to the couch. She was halfway up the stairway when the front door opened and LaRue stepped in.

"Did Wally call tonight?" she asked. LaRue had not talked to Wally yet, and she had been disappointed about that.

"No. But he would have missed you, even if he had. I thought you were coming home earlier."

"I meant to. But . . . well . . . anyway, I'm glad he didn't call. I'll stay home tomorrow night."

LaRue looked pretty with her dark hair set off against a deep red sweater, but Bea could hear something in her voice, a certain flatness that wasn't typical of her. Still, Bea knew better than to ask. LaRue would open up and admit what she was thinking at times—when the mood struck her—but if Bea probed at all, she always retreated. So Bea said goodnight and

then continued on up the stairs. When she reached the bedroom, President Thomas was already in his pajamas. He
stepped to the bed and glanced at Bea, and without saying a
word they knelt next to one another. He took hold of her
hand, and tonight he prayed. He usually called on Bea on alter-
nating nights, but sometimes he seemed to want an extra turn.

"Our Father in Heaven, we are so very thankful," he
began. "So many blessings have come to us. Our son Walter
has returned to his homeland from his imprisonment, and he
seems to have become a better, stronger man. It is what we
have believed could happen, what we prayed for, and what
only thy Spirit could grant him. We sense in him that he has
passed through a refiner's fire and has been made into steel."

President Thomas had said something of this sort in all his
prayers since Wally had first called, but Bea understood her
husband well enough to know that these thoughts were on his
mind tonight, probably after reading his scriptures, and he
wanted to make sure he had expressed his thankfulness as fully
as he felt it. Bea was touched, even though Al's prayers made
her laugh sometimes. They were a little too lofty for her taste,
as though he were praying at stake conference.

After the prayer they continued to kneel, and each said a
silent, personal prayer. Bea poured out her own thankfulness
once again, and she enjoyed thinking of all the good things she
could thank the Lord for. She was only a little annoyed when
Al prayed twice as long as she did. There were nights when he
prayed until her own knees ached and she was tempted to
sneak away quietly, but she knew he had many matters of the
stake to concern himself with—matters he kept to himself—
and this was his chance to talk to "someone" about those
things.

When he finally got up, he pulled back the chenille bed-
spread and sat down to take off his slippers. "Are you coming
to bed?" he asked.

"I will in a minute. I think I'll go down and read just a little longer. I've hardly made any headway on this book. I've been letting my mind wander all evening."

"Bea, I'm excited about the way things are falling together for our family."

"What do you mean, 'falling together'?"

"It sounds like Wally wants to be part of us now. And Alex already got his feet wet at the plant before he left. By the time he gets home, you can have Wally up to speed, and we can—" He stopped. "Don't get me wrong. You can stay on for a while, if that's what you want. But you'll have the option, and you won't have to work so hard, with those two at your side to help you. We could expand our operation right now if we had the right managers. Once those boys are working for us, I don't see why we couldn't go after a lot more contracts. We'll need more space, but we could build on, or maybe even buy out that lot to the north of us. I've already talked to—"

"Al, slow down just a minute. Alex never did like working in that business. And there's nothing that says he's changed his mind."

"Oh, I think he will. He's got a family to raise now, and he'll never find a better opportunity than I'll offer him."

"Be careful, Al. Okay?"

"Careful? What do you mean?"

"You always tell me that you've learned your lesson, but then you jump right back in. You can't run these kids' lives for them."

President Thomas's head came up. "I haven't said anything about running anyone's life. All I'm doing is offering these boys the chance of a lifetime. I'm talking about turning the business over to them, gradually. Does that sound like I'm *controlling* them?"

"All I'm saying is that you can offer them an opportunity, as you put it, but if they turn you down, you'll have to accept that. And if they do come to work for you, you'll have to let them do things their own way. If they feel like you're looking over their shoulders all the time, they're not going to be happy about it."

Al leaned forward and put his elbows on his knees. Bea knew that she had taken the wind out of his sails, and she was sorry about that, but Al did need to be careful. He should know that about himself by now.

He took a long breath, and then he said, "You're right, Bea. I know it's bothered me sometimes when Dad's given me the impression that he thinks he knows more about running a business than I do."

"What father doesn't feel that way?"

"Well, I don't know. But I am proud of these boys and what they've survived. Alex is a decorated hero, Bea. If he wants to get into politics, with his looks, his speaking ability, the sky's the limit for him."

"Careful." She grinned.

Al smiled. "The trouble is," he said, "I *do* know what these kids ought to do. My dad just *thought* he did. If Bobbi were as smart as her father, she'd work things out with Richard, pronto, and not let him get away from her."

"Oh, certainly. And now admit the truth. You have your eye on him as another one of your managers, so you can expand all the more."

"And why not? What I see is a whole generation making a decent living and doing good things with their lives—serving the Church and raising fine families."

"And all of your grandsons named after you."

"Not all of them. Just the first son in each family."

Bea rolled her eyes.

"No. I'll be careful. I promise. I promise myself every day."

"Good."

"There's something else I wanted to talk to you about." Al took hold of Bea's hands. He was wearing his light blue cotton pajamas that were almost threadbare, but they were the ones he liked, the ones he wore year-round. The truth was, they pulled a little too much in the middle these days, although Al didn't like to admit that he was gaining weight.

"Now what?" Bea asked, and she winked at him.

"I've been thinking—let's go on a trip somewhere."

"Really?"

"Yes. Really."

"Where would we go?"

"I'm not sure. We could go on a driving trip somewhere— maybe up to Lake Louise, in Canada. I've always wanted to drive up that way. It's got to be pretty up there in the fall."

"Fall? Al, it's almost October. We'd have to go right away, and I want some time with Wally when he gets here."

"If he gets here soon, we could spend a week or two with him and then get away for a while. We wouldn't have to go all the way to Canada."

"What about the girls? They're in school."

"I'm not talking about a family trip; I'm talking about you and me. We need to spend some time together. Maybe we could head off to England and see our little grandson."

"Now?"

"No. But we could start planning."

Bea had to think about all this. She patted Al on the chest and smiled at him. She liked that he was thinking about such things, but it also worried her. "Al, the girls have never been anywhere. The war took all those things away from them. Maybe we ought to wait until next summer and then take them to Canada, or something like that. We could stop in Yellowstone on the way. Bev hardly remembers our trips up there."

"That's fine. We could do that, too. But you and I could take a trip this fall and then take the girls next summer. And maybe plan a trip to England, too—maybe fly on an airplane."

"But I think the Stoltzes will be coming here before long."

"Maybe. Maybe not. But we need to start thinking about

things a little differently. The war is over, and we have the means. We need to enjoy ourselves a little more."

Bea hated how practical she could be sometimes. She had always blamed her husband for being the stick-in-the-mud, but when he started sounding extravagant, the change made her nervous. What would the neighbors think of them if they ran off on three trips, all in one year? But that's not what she said. "Al, the kids are all coming home. That's what I want—all of us together. I don't want to go away. I want to be here this year and just enjoy the time with everyone."

"I couldn't agree more. But you and I could slip away at least once. We've needed to do that for a long time. The last couple of years, with you working and both of us putting in so many hours, I feel like we hardly see each other."

"But Al, I've never gotten the impression you care much about that."

"Well, I do."

She leaned closer, looking directly into his eyes. "I think you say to yourself, sometimes, 'I've made a bunch of money, and my life is still the same. What can I do to prove to myself that all the work has been worth it?'"

"No, I don't—" But he stopped himself. "Well, maybe I do that a little. I want to build a house, and yet I like this one just fine. And maybe that's because I want something to show for what we've done. But that's not what I've been thinking about lately."

"So what have you been thinking? Where did this idea to start taking trips come from?"

Al didn't move. He looked toward Bea, but still not into her eyes. "Bea, I'm not sure my family likes me. I'm pretty sure you and the kids all have some reservations about the kind of man I am. LaRue is the one who makes me feel that way the most, but maybe she just says what the rest of you think. I'm afraid we'll have a bunch of grandkids someday, a really nice family, and they'll all come home to you, not to me, and I won't be part of anything."

Al had never said anything of this sort before. Bea knew she had to say the right thing, but she wasn't about to lie to him. "Al, I do think you can do some things to be closer to everyone. That's what I was talking about when I told you to be careful. If they think you want to make their decisions for them—especially as they start having their own families—they're going to resent you."

"I know." He looked up at her. "And what about you?"

"What about me?"

"What do I have to do to keep you?"

"I'm not going anywhere."

"I know that. But we're going to be alone here one of these days. And I'm not good at doing the things that a woman likes from a man. I listen to the news and read the paper, and . . . I don't know . . . you know the things LaRue says about me. I'm wondering what we could do to spend a little more time together. That's why I was thinking that a trip might be good for us."

Bea slipped down to her knees. She leaned toward Al and rested her arms on his lap. "A trip would be good," she said, and she touched her hand to his cheek. "A little ride once in a while, now that we have gasoline. We could go dancing. Go out to dinner. All that would be good. But Al, I love you just the way you are. Don't ever doubt that for a minute."

Al nodded. "I love you, too, Bea," he whispered.

"We're coming into a strange time in our lives," Bea said. "Every day I tell myself I want to get away from that plant and stay home, but then, when I think of being home all day in an empty house, that scares me too."

"That's right. That's the same thing I worry about."

"I guess we can sit around the house and worry about our kids all day."

"I do worry about them—more than I need to, I'm sure.

Sometimes I just wish they were all little kids again, and right here with us—not spread all around the world."

"I know," Bea said. "But I think we've got some pretty nice worries ahead. Education and weddings and grandchildren—not war, for a change."

"Well . . . that's right." Al leaned forward and kissed Bea—something more than his usual little peck. Bea held him for a time, loving the closeness, and she decided that she wouldn't go back to her book, that she would go to bed with her husband.

2

Alex Thomas was sitting at his desk one morning late in September when Sergeant Barr, his staff assistant, stuck his head in the door. "Lieutenant Thomas," he said, "I just got a call I think you'll be interested in."

"What is it?" Alex asked.

Sergeant Barr stepped all the way into the room. "Someone spotted a man with a scar across his face and lip. He's working on a farm over by the Luxembourg border. The local police haven't gone to check him out yet, but they say he fits the description of this Kellerman guy you've been looking for."

Alex stood up. "Tell them to hold off," he said. "I'll leave right away and get over there. I can go in with the local people and make sure it's him."

"I don't think you have to do that. These guys can pick him up on suspicion and interrogate him. You could drive over later if you wanted to, and—"

"No. I want to be there." Alex was surprised by the surge of emotion he was feeling. He told himself he would act like a professional, simply make sure that justice was done, but it was not easy to fight off an urge to take revenge on this man. It was Kellerman who had inflicted so much misery on Anna and her family—all for reasons that had more to do with personal power than Nazi philosophy. "Contact the police. Tell them I'll bring in a team. I want some numbers—and surprise. I don't want to miss this chance to get him."

But it was four hours later when Alex finally reached the little village of Roth. He had with him a team of twelve American military police who had traveled from Bitburg in the back of a deuce-and-a-half truck. "All these officers will not be necessary," the local policeman told Alex, in English.

"I will make that decision," Alex told him in firm, clear German. "Lead us out there, and we'll take over. Stop your vehicles well back from the farm so we can get some men around the area without being noticed. I want to move in from all directions."

The policeman was one of only four in the village—a young man named Kammler who walked with a decided limp, probably from a war injury. He clearly had no great love for "Amis," and he didn't like being told what to do in this case. But Alex didn't care. He usually preferred to let German officials deal with arrests, but this time he was not going in short-handed.

The entourage set off, Kammler and his partner on an old military motorcycle with a side car and Alex in a jeep, with the truck behind. In a low, green valley, just a mile or so out of town, Kammler stopped. Alex pulled his jeep over as much as he could on the narrow dirt road, and then he walked to the motorcycle. "The farm is over this next hill," Kammler said. "It's the first one you will see, but it's quite large. If you want to surround the area, some of your men will have to work their way along this stream and follow it as it bends south around the farm."

"That's good. We can do that."

But the process was slow. Alex gave four of the men time to work their way to the north and west. He left two more at the south end of the farm and then drove to the east gate, where he stationed two more. Then he headed down the lane into the farm itself. The two German policemen wanted to go in, so he took them along with the four remaining MPs. They drove quickly to the farmhouse, and as they did, they watched the barn and outbuildings, but they saw no one. Alex sent the MPs to surround the house and buildings, and then he and the policemen went to the front door and banged on it. In a moment an older woman appeared, dressed in black, a scarf over her head. "What is it?" she demanded. "What's all the noise?"

Alex stepped quickly into the house, holding his .45 caliber pistol. It was a dark little house, full of the smell of cooked cabbage. "You have a worker here. He has a bad scar on his face. Where is he?"

"He left."

"When?"

"This morning."

"Who else is here?"

"My son. My daughter-in-law. The children are at school."

"Where's your son?"

"In the barn, I suppose, or out—"

Alex was already striding out the front door. He was sick to think that he might have missed Kellerman. As he trotted around the house, he saw two of the MPs coming toward him, a man between them. The man was dressed in rough, black clothes and was wearing high rubber boots. Before Alex could speak, he said, "He's gone already. Why didn't someone come a week ago, when I first reported this?"

"A week ago?" Alex asked.

"Yes. I saw the picture in town, in the post office. I knew it was him."

"Where did he go?"

"I can't say. He didn't show up for breakfast. But his bed had been slept in."

"What scared him off? Who warned him?"

"No one that I know of. It might have been his plan all along."

"What plan?"

The farmer lifted the hat off his head. He was a balding man with straggly, fine hair. "He came here quite desperate, or at least that's what he said. He told me he had gotten that scar in the war, that he had fought in Russia. I needed help, and he told me he only wanted a roof over his head and food to eat."

"What *plan* were you talking about? I don't have time for all this."

"Why would he want to be so close to the border? If he's a Nazi, as you say, then he must want out. Maybe he needed papers. Maybe he was searching to find a way to cross the river. I don't know. But my guess is that he's headed into Luxembourg and wants to keep going to some distant country."

Alex turned toward the two local policemen. "Should we search the farm? This man could be hiding him."

"It was Herr Kauffman who first contacted us. Why would he want to hide the man?"

"Then why didn't I know sooner?"

"We made our report instantly," the policeman said. And then he began some sort of excuse about bureaucratic bungling. Alex didn't care. He was heading for his jeep. He had to gather his men and get to the border. But he was furious, ready to kick something—ready to slam this policeman to the ground if he didn't stop talking.

Alex blasted the horn on his jeep—the signal for the men surrounding the farm to assemble. And then he spun back to the farmer. "Where would he try to cross?"

"The river is not easy. My guess is that he had papers of some kind. He would try to cross at the bridge, at Roth. Maybe he paid someone off. He could have been staying here long enough to find the right man—someone who would take a bribe."

That made sense to Alex. And Roth was an out-of-the-way

crossing, not as busy as many places. Kellerman might have found an advantage in that.

The men were coming now, some trotting, others taking their time. Alex screamed at them, "Come on. Let's go. Let's go." He felt as though he were back in battle, felt the old fury. "Pile in that truck. Follow me. We're heading back to Roth. Meet me at the bridge that crosses into Luxembourg."

Alex didn't wait. He jumped into his jeep, started it, and then gunned the engine as he popped the clutch out. His wheels spun in the loose dirt and then caught, and the jeep lurched ahead. An image had come to Alex's mind—a picture of Kellerman resting easy somewhere, in some foreign land, never paying for what he had done.

Alex drove hard, spraying gravel as he slid around turns on the road. He drove through the village and then, when he had spotted the military guard station, raced straight toward it. He hit the brakes hard at the last second and jumped out. An MP stepped back a little, as though frightened, and then remembered to salute. Alex threw a quick salute and said, "Did a guy come through here this morning—about forty-five years old with a big, ugly scar across his face?"

"Yes, sir. Within the hour. We checked his papers, and he—"

"How was he traveling?"

"On foot."

"You say he had good papers?"

"Yes. He was from Luxembourg City. He was over here on official business of some kind. He had a letter and passport—all of that. Our German guy checked it all out, and it looked fine."

"What are you talking about? Why would a man like that be traveling on foot? You'd better see how much money your German has in his pockets."

"I think he said his car broke down—or something like that. Someone was coming to the border to pick him up."

"Was someone waiting for him on the other side?"

The MP looked a little confused for a moment. He was a

big kid, and young, surely someone who had been sent over-
seas after the war. "I didn't see anyone. He walked across the
bridge, and then . . . I don't know. I didn't pay any attention.
Dieter said his papers were all right, so I just figured he was
okay."

"Why don't you try *thinking* next time, soldier? If you've got
a brain." Alex stopped himself, took a breath. "I'm going across.
There's a deuce-and-a-half coming right behind me, full of
MPs. Send them over. The guy with the scar is probably try-
ing to get to Luxembourg City. Tell them to head that way.
How long ago did you say he went through here?"

"Well, let's see . . ."

Alex had no time for this. He ran back to his jeep and
jumped in. Then he shot across the bridge. The road on the
other side continued straight to a tiny village—Vianden—but
Alex had no idea what Kellerman might do from there. He
might have headed off into the woods, but the going would be
difficult in the dense forest, and Kellerman had no reason to
think that anyone was after him. He was more likely to stay on
the road and head south. Luxembourg City was within a day's
walk, and once he got there, the city was big enough for him
to disappear into for a while.

So Alex sped on to Vianden and then turned left down the
little road toward Luxembourg City. But this was a gamble. If
he had guessed wrong, and Kellerman had chosen any other
route, or had headed off through the countryside, the man
could be free and clear. Alex kept watching the road ahead as
he flew over the tops of hills. The road was paved but chewed
up pretty badly by the tanks and trucks that had passed over it
in recent years.

As Alex crested a hill, he saw a man ahead in the valley,
walking along the road. He seemed big enough to be
Kellerman, even had that arrogant style, his arms swinging like
a soldier in a parade. Alex kept pushing hard, scared that the
man would turn out to be some local fellow, out for an

afternoon stroll. But the man looked back, saw the jeep, and suddenly bolted off the road into a wooded area along a stream. And Alex had seen for sure: it was him.

Alex braked hard and skidded when he came to the spot where Kellerman had turned off. He jumped out of his jeep, pulled his pistol from his holster, and shouted, in German, "Stop now. You can't get away from me. I'll shoot you." He fired his pistol into the air, almost without knowing he was going to do it, and then he charged into the trees. Kellerman could be armed, but it didn't seem to matter at the moment. Alex sloshed through the stream and then ran up a little hill, breaking his way through underbrush, wondering whether Kellerman would keep running or try to find a place to hide.

Alex knew that he was doing this wrong, following his passion, not his head. He should get back to his men, bring them in to surround this area. Beyond these woods was nothing but open fields, and Kellerman would have no way to cross them without being spotted. All Alex needed to do was contain him, get help, and then flush him out. But that wasn't enough. He wanted to take the man himself, let him see who had captured him.

He reached the top of the hill and then stopped, listened. He could hear someone thrashing through the bracken ahead of him, on down the hill. But no man that big could outdistance Alex. Kellerman was a fool.

Alex hurried toward the sound, followed the broken branches and trampled grass. He made up the distance quickly and then yelled again. "Kellerman, stop. You can't get away. Don't make me shoot you."

But now all sound had stopped. Kellerman had finally decided to duck somewhere, go into hiding. This was no time to walk blindly into a trap. Still, Alex couldn't stop himself. He kept moving ahead slowly, listening. And then he heard the man drawing breath, in spite of himself.

"All right. I know where you are. I can hear you. Come out now or I'll shoot."

"No, no. I'll come out."

"Right now."

Kellerman stood up and stepped from the ferns and under-brush he had found to hide under. "Don't shoot. Don't shoot," he said. He was heavier than he had once been, and his big cheeks were flushed from his run. The scar was healed and old but still obscene, angling across his cheek and splitting his lip.

"Take off your coat. Throw it over here. Then empty your pockets."

Kellerman complied, slowly, and he continued to mumble, "Don't shoot. I'll do what you want."

It was clear by then that he had no weapon, and Alex felt something close to disappointment. He wanted a fight, had wanted the man to give him an excuse. But Kellerman dropped everything he had in the grass, then stood with his hands raised. "I have no idea why you've stopped me," he had decided to say. "I was just walking down this road. My papers are in order. I can show you who I am."

"You don't recognize me, do you?"

Kellerman looked more closely, but Alex saw no sign of realization. What he saw was fear.

"You once demanded that I make the Nazi salute. I was a missionary then."

And then Alex saw the change, the panic. "Oh, yes. But, sir, I was only a functionary. I was told that I had to enforce such things. I denounce Hitler now for all he did. We were all taken in by him back then."

"You still don't understand. You don't know the whole thing. I married Anna Stoltz. She is my wife now. I believe you remember that name, don't you?"

Alex saw Kellerman take a long, deep breath, saw the color leave his face. "What are you going to do?" he whispered. "Please don't—"

"Shoot you?"

"Please don't."

"And why not? Do you remember what you did to my wife? To her family? And now I have you here alone. You've even made a run for it. I can shoot you, file a report, and that's the end of it. One more Nazi punished. There's not a man in this world who wouldn't tell me that you got what you deserved."

"Please. Don't shoot me. I beg you."

Alex thought of aiming to one side and firing his pistol, just enough to send terror through this coward, but he didn't let himself do that. Instead, he picked up Kellerman's coat, and he said, "Put your things back in your pockets. Then walk ahead of me, back over this hill."

"You're a decent man. A Christian," Kellerman said. "Tell me your name again."

"Thomas."

"Oh, yes. Now I know it. And I remember the other one. A big fellow. Mormons, aren't you?"

But Alex would not allow this. He wouldn't shoot him, wouldn't torture or beat him, but he didn't have to treat him as though he were a decent human being. "Be quiet," Alex said. "You'll be tried as a war criminal. And I will be a witness against you."

"But you understand, Thomas. I was only—"

"You tried to rape my wife, Kellerman. Now shut your mouth before I do what I've longed to do all these years."

"Yes, yes. I'll say nothing."

* * *

On the following Sunday Alex was back in Frankfurt. It had not been a good week. He was experiencing a troubling uneasiness that he didn't really understand. One of his goals, to see Kellerman apprehended, had finally been achieved, but Kellerman's behavior had fired a disgust, a hatred in Alex that had left him ambivalent about what he had done. In a way, he wished he had let go a little more, had at least denounced Kellerman more profusely. Or perhaps, rather than let the confusing court system take over, he should have pulled the trigger and let justice be done. He wasn't at all sure that wouldn't have been the fitting end to all this. Kellerman would probably sit in jail for a time, but he would never be sufficiently punished, nor would he ever gain the slightest insight. The man was a coward, willing to beg, but he was anything but repentant. He clearly had no conscience.

At the same time, Alex was uncomfortable with the memory of his rage. He had been working so long to put the war behind him, to remember the goodness of the German people. Now, just when he thought he had been making some spiritual headway, he had felt a viciousness in himself that he had hoped was gone forever. That, too, he wanted to blame on Kellerman, but he didn't think the confrontation was adequate to excuse what he had felt.

Something else was also plaguing Alex. He could let the Stoltzes know that he had apprehended their old enemy, and they would take a certain satisfaction in that, but it was nothing to them compared to finding Peter, and Alex had had no luck with that. Almost every week he visited camps or checked Red Cross records, did something to try to locate him, but camps were being emptied, and nowhere could Alex find any record of Peter's existence. If he had been captured by the Russians it might be impossible to learn anything, and Alex wondered whether the boy would ever get back. The fact was, Alex was beginning to believe that Peter was dead.

At church that Sunday Alex listened to President Meis speak about the basic principles of the gospel: faith, repentance, baptism, and the gift of the Holy Ghost. So many of the members had lost touch with the Church during the war, and President Meis taught them now almost as though they were investigators. Actually, some were. Many Germans had lost their faith during the war, but others were searching for an answer, and they came along to church with their Latter-day Saint friends.

But Alex was left empty by the sermon. It was fine to talk of repentance, but someone like Kellerman could mouth the words of regret and mean nothing. There was something sick at the very soul of these Nazi party leaders Alex had been searching for all summer. Americans talked about the "denazification" of Germany, but how was that really possible? There were people with Nazi hearts all over the world. Every country needed to be ridded of such attitudes, and no country ever would.

After the meeting, President Meis came over to Alex. "Don't leave until I have a chance to talk to you," he said.

Alex didn't mind that at all. He hated going back to his quarters on Sundays. The rest of the day always seemed so long. It was the one day of the week when he had time to think, to wish he were in London with Anna and little Gene. What he had hoped at first was that staying in Germany would give him time to adjust, to get the war out of his system before he returned to his family. Now, he was beginning to feel that he needed to stop thinking and simply move on with life.

The Gasthaus where the branch held church always cleared slowly after services. People stayed around to chat, to enjoy the company. Alex knew that the members often felt lonely and hopeless these days. Germany was trying to clean up, but mostly that meant clearing away debris; it didn't mean rebuilding. There were no finances for that, no plan. And with winter not too far off, many of the shelters that people were living in were not going to be adequate. The ration of food the military supplied to Germans was minimal—not really enough to sustain life, and certainly not enough to create much energy. Most people scrounged for additional food—selling off possessions on the black market or bargaining with farmers—and all too many German women had turned to prostitution as their way of getting at some of the cash the foreign soldiers possessed. At least Mormons could turn to each other for help, and they did that as much as possible, but no one had enough to supply all those in need. There was a lot of talk of the Church shipping food and clothing, but no shipments had been allowed into the country yet. What members could give each other now, more than anything, was friendship, and there was plenty of that in the branches.

Alex chatted with some of the members until President Meis finally said, "Come over here, *Bruder* Thomas. I can speak with you now."

President Meis walked to a table near the windows at the front. He sat down and Alex joined him.

Sister Meis said, from across the room, "Ernst, we'll start walking. Catch up, if you can, or meet us at home."

"Yes, yes. I won't be long," President Meis told her. And then he looked toward Alex, hesitating for a moment, checking him over. "How are things going for you now?" he asked.

"Fairly well."

President Meis nodded but seemed a little concerned, obviously picking up on Alex's lack of enthusiasm. "*Bruder* Thomas, the Church is trying to get organized and fully operating once again. We're using the same leaders who were holding positions before the war, as much as possible, but we're trying to fill in where so many are missing."

"That's good. You certainly need some help in this branch."

"I do. I need you."

"*Me?*"

"Yes. You're the most experienced priesthood holder in the branch. I'm wondering whether you wouldn't be willing to serve in the branch presidency. This is not an official call I'm making, but I want to turn your name in to President Huck for approval, and I thought I'd talk to you about it before I do that."

"I may not be here more than a few more months, President Meis."

"I know that. But I could use you for that time."

Alex looked at the table, the worn edge. He didn't want this. "President Meis, I'm not ready yet."

"*Bruder* Thomas, you tell me you need to feel the Spirit again. That won't happen if you run from the Church. You've got to take part. That will help you more than anything."

Alex looked out the window. It was a hazy morning, clouds still strewn about after a hard rain the night before. "We finally tracked down Kellerman, President. I caught him myself. He's in jail."

"Good. I'm glad to hear it."

"I went after him like a police dog. I smelled his blood, and I wanted, more than anything, to spill some of it."

"No one can blame you for feelings like that. But did you hurt him?"

"No."

"I didn't think so. We all have desires like that at times. But when the Spirit speaks to us, we know better than to give in."

"I didn't feel any Spirit. That was the last thing that I felt."

"I don't believe that. You knew right from wrong, and you chose the right."

Alex thought about that. He looked at President Meis's shirt, gray and frayed around the collar and too big around his thin neck. How did the man keep going—and keep everyone else going? Alex knew he needed to help, and yet he knew what he had been feeling all week. "I've been wishing I'd killed him, President. The idea keeps going through my mind."

"The only thing you're telling me is that you're human. Many men would have taken revenge. Just be pleased with yourself that you turned him over to let justice take its course."

But Alex knew there was more to it than that. "I just don't know whether I'm any better than Kellerman. Maybe there's not that much difference."

"*Bruder* Thomas, we all want to think that the world is divided into two great armies—good on one side and evil on the other. But good *and* evil are in all of us—and sometimes the evil is only held back by a thin thread. Still, it's that thread that makes all the difference."

Alex continued to stare out the window. He knew everything that President Meis could say, but he didn't feel the change of heart he wanted. It wasn't the killing he had done during the war that bothered him the most; it was the loss of himself. It was the corruption he felt inside.

"*Bruder* Thomas, we have both done things we didn't want to do. Let's put that behind us now and serve the Church. Serve our brothers and sisters. That's the best way to let God back inside. We need to forget ourselves and think about others."

"I'll try. I'll accept the calling."

"Good."

And Alex did feel he had made the right decision. What he didn't feel was confident that he could forget about the things he had seen and done. He still woke up almost every night, his head full of clashing, wild scenes. And now he had something new to remember: Kellerman pretending to repent, when in fact he cared about nothing but himself. Maybe that was the real heart of the human, of every human, when all the pretense was stripped away.

3

Bobbi Thomas's ship, the *Charity*, was docked in Tokyo Bay. For several days it had been filling up with American prisoners of war, who were arriving by the truckload. The men were dressed in new fatigues, but their bodies were filthy underneath, full of lice and disease. Some of them walked like zombies, and some couldn't walk at all but had to be carried. Those who had been eating for a time, having received supply drops into their camps, looked much better, but their hair was often splotchy, their skin covered with scaly filth, their teeth rotten. And there were still many who couldn't hold down much food. They were sick, suffering with diarrhea, and many seemed empty, as though devoid of emotion.

Most of the men responded quickly to better food, to cleanliness, to medicines that killed their parasites or healed their open sores. But some died hours or days after coming on board, and each time Bobbi heard that, she felt the pain. Many of these men had survived the death march in the Bataan Peninsula, had been held in miserable camps for over three years, and had suffered through backbreaking work, with little food. It seemed unfair for them to come this far only to die now. And, of course, each death made her wonder about her brother Wally. She knew he was "alive and well," from his own report. But she hadn't seen him yet, or talked to him. She wondered how much damage had actually been done to him. What she saw in the eyes of the POWs was that most were fighting to recover, to be themselves again, to feel human, but some were very far gone. It was hard to imagine, at least in the worst cases, that these men could return to their hometowns and pick up with their lives. She wondered whether she would ever really get her brother back, the one she remembered.

Bobbi also went on shore one day and rode in a jeep through "Tokyo." But there was no Tokyo. The city was a wasteland, charred and almost flat. No atomic bomb had been dropped there; fire bombs and explosives had done the damage. The city was much larger than Hiroshima or Nagasaki, but it was equally devastated. Bobbi wondered how many civilians had died in the bombing raids: children and old people, babies and expectant mothers. She wondered how humans could sink this low. How could the Japanese treat the American POWs with such viciousness, but also, how could Americans deliver death on such a grand scale?

Bobbi came back to the ship that night, knelt by her bunk and prayed for a long time. When she had watched the prisoners come on board, she had felt resentment and disgust with "the enemy," but after seeing Tokyo her disgust had turned toward the war itself. She wasn't thinking about politics, not even of right and wrong; she was simply alarmed that humans were capable of such things. She knew all the arguments for the bombing, even believed them, but it didn't change how she felt. So she told God she was sorry. She didn't know whether she had the right, but she apologized for *all* God's children, for everything they had done, and she wished that everyone in the world would feel the same way. Sorrow seemed the only answer—and repentance—and yet it didn't seem the likely result of this war.

Bobbi also prayed for Wally, for her parents, for Alex and Anna, for Afton and Ishi, and she prayed for both Richard

Hammond and David Stinson. She didn't know what to expect now, whether there was any chance that she would marry either one of them, but she had loved them both, still loved them both, and she knew that they were struggling. Richard was trying to adjust, accept the changes in his life, deal with his memories, and David, the last she had heard, was struggling for his life. She longed to see them healed. She wanted to make a decision based on the right questions, not all these matters of survival, but she didn't know how to do that, so every morning and every night she asked for direction. Was one of them right for her? Couldn't God tell her—and make the decision so much easier?

Bobbi was still assigned to the area of the ship that had once been the burn ward. It was now filled with former prisoners. As the men arrived, the medical staff had to learn how to treat them. Most of the POWs were eager for all the foods they loved and remembered, and the staff wanted to reward them for their courage, so they fed them well. But it soon became obvious that many of them were not able to eat the rich foods they craved. Broth soups were all that some could hold down.

Bobbi tried to check on every patient, supervise, and direct her corpsmen on what to feed each man—then, in many cases, to see to it that they were fed by hand. She and her corpsmen were also trying to treat all the sores and skin maladies, and that kept them busy too.

One day as Bobbi walked past a lower bunk, she saw a patient sitting by one of his buddies, talking softly, holding a spoon in front of the patient's mouth. "Come on, Wilford, you've got to eat," he was saying. "You can't give up now. We're going home."

Bobbi stopped and looked at the men. The one who was trying to feed his friend was probably only twenty-eight or so, but he looked older, looked used up. The man he had called Wilford was probably a couple of years younger. His cheekbones and jaw, his eye sockets, formed the shape of his face, with only a blue layer of skin to cover them. His arm lay next to his body, thin as a broomstick.

"Won't he eat?" Bobbi asked.

"Not much. A corpsman tried, but he didn't have much luck. I'll stay with him. I'll keep giving him a little at a time."

"Is he drinking water?"

"A little."

"He needs that, too."

"I know. The corpsman told me what to give him. I'll stay right here all day. The medicines should start to work before long. I just have to keep him going until then."

"What's your name?" Bobbi asked.

"Max. Max Jones. Plain as a mud fence." He looked up and grinned. He had blue eyes—strong and clear—but he was squinting, hard, and Bobbi wondered whether he needed glasses.

"Are you two friends from home?"

"No. We met in prison camp. We've sort of looked out for each other."

It was hot in the ward, down on this lower deck, and sweat had darkened most of Max's shirt, down his back and under his arms. Bobbi could imagine that it was anything but pleasant to sit here all day, not to go up on deck for some air. "I've noticed that most of you men formed little groups of three or four," Bobbi said. "Did that help you get through?"

"That's how we made it. You have to keep each other going."

Bobbi nodded. "Well, stay with him, Max Jones, plain as a mud fence. You might be his only chance."

"I'll tell you right now—he's not going to die. I won't let him. If things were turned around, he wouldn't let go of me."

Bobbi was surprised when her eyes filled with tears. One man fighting for one life: the idea seemed to reverse everything she had concluded about the state of humanity. She patted

Max on the shoulder again. "I'll check back in a little while. Keep talking to him. Keep feeding him."

"I will."

All day she did keep checking, and she never came back to the bunk without finding Max alongside his friend. "I got him to drink some water," he would say, or, "I think a little color is coming into his face."

Bobbi wasn't sure about that, but she found that Wilford's vital signs were holding steady, and that meant he had a good chance. She also found that her own vital signs were on the rise; she even told Max that she owed him something for that.

The *Charity* took several days to fill up, but it was eventually brimming over with men, so it put out to sea, headed for the Philippines first, and then, if scuttlebutt had it right, on to Honolulu and California.

By the time the ship docked in Manila Bay and a few critical passengers were dropped off at the hospital there, Wilford was sitting up at times, taking more soup, even eating a few solid foods. Bobbi couldn't get Wilford to say much, but Max never stopped talking to him. What she heard when she caught a bit of the running monologue was Max telling Wilford about all the great times they were going to have when they got back to the states. Or Max would say, "We've come a long way, buddy. But all the bad stuff is behind us now."

Bobbi was pretty sure that that was not exactly true. She was seeing some things in the men that they probably didn't recognize in themselves. She would try to fluff up a pillow and find a few slices of bread hidden away in the pillow case. And when she asked the man why he was sticking food in his bed, she would get nothing more than embarrassed excuses. But she knew what was happening. The men were still scared that the food might stop coming. It was hard for them to trust in the steady flow of such plenty, such luxury, so they held something back, hoarded it like wary animals. And that was not the worst. These men who had eaten their first ice cream with the joy of little boys were now getting restless and even impatient. Some were wondering how long it would take to cross the ocean, why they hadn't been flown—as some men had been. Bobbi understood that they wanted to get home, but she also saw a growing anxiety that came out in odd ways. It was as though they were starting to realize what had been done to them, and the depth of their resentment was finally starting to register. For all these years they had needed to survive and they had concentrated on that, but now some of them were getting angry that such a thing could ever have happened to them. She wondered how bitter and disillusioned some of them might end up.

One afternoon, as the ship was nearing Honolulu, Bobbi saw her friend Kate Calder out on the main deck. Her fatigues were soaked with sweat, and she was leaning over the rail with her eyes shut. She was obviously trying to let the air flow over her, cool her.

"Kate, have you been in surgery all day?" Bobbi asked.

Kate opened her eyes for only a second, closed them again, and then nodded. She had taken her glasses off, was holding them in one hand.

"I thought you didn't have much of that to do now."

"We've got some strange cases. Some of these guys had broken bones that were never set right. It's a mess to try to fix them now."

"Are you okay?"

"Sure. Just tired." She smiled a little. She looked pretty without the thick glasses magnifying her eyes. Her hair had been rolled up in back and pinned, but it was breaking loose, the strands blowing about her neck. "How are you doing, Bobbi?"

"All right. We're busy, of course." She took a step away and then stopped. "There's something I want to ask you, Kate. Do you have a minute?"

"About five. Then I've got to go back in there."

"Well, my question might be more complicated than that."

"I can stretch it to maybe seven." She laughed.

Bobbi knew she shouldn't do this. But there was no one else Bobbi was close to. "You believe in God, don't you, Kate? I mean, not the same as me, maybe, but . . . you do believe."

Kate turned, leaned against the rail with her hip, and then smiled, more fully than usual. "This could possibly take *ten* minutes."

"But you do believe. You've told me that, more or less."

"Let's say I cling to a certain hope. Nothing I've experienced in life convinces me that I should continue with such silliness, but I do. A little."

"Do you think God can give you directions or answer questions for you—that sort of thing?"

"I don't know, Bobbi. Probably not."

"Why just 'probably'?"

"Well . . . I do get these little glimmers of insight that I sometimes wonder about. Every now and then, during a surgery, I seem to know what I ought to do, and it seems to come from somewhere outside myself. Or at least it's just there all of a sudden—and it's nothing I've been taught. A couple of times, those little hunches, or whatever they are, have saved lives. Do you know what I mean?"

"I do."

"So what's God been saying to you, Bobbi?"

A couple of sailors walked by, and Bobbi had to step closer to the rail to let them get by, but she didn't want to block the air from reaching Kate, so she stepped back again, tucked her hands into the pockets of her skirt, stood with her feet set rather wide apart so she could keep her balance as the ship slowly rolled in the rather heavy sea. She didn't look at Kate directly when she said, "Yesterday I got a letter from Richard."

"Now there's a good example," Kate said, seeming serious. "When I looked at Richard's picture the first time, I thought I heard God whispering in my ear that that man, in all fairness, ought to be mine."

Kate was smiling again, and Bobbi knew it was time to let this drop. Kate would never really understand, never even take her question seriously.

"Hey, I'm sorry," Kate said. "Go ahead. I won't smart off again."

Bobbi watched the waves, the horizon, didn't look at Kate. She just wanted to say all this out loud once and see whether it seemed to make sense. "Richard wrote the letter the same day that he and I talked on the phone—the day back in Hawaii when I got so mad at him. Remember, I told you about that?"

"Of course."

"The letter was really sweet but so mixed up. He told me he was sorry, and he said he loved me and wanted to marry me. But half the letter seemed to be setting me free. He seems to have his mind made up that that's what I really want—that I could never love him after all the troubles he's had about his hands and everything. I know what's happening. He admitted his fears to me, and his confusion about the war, and now he thinks he's not a man in my eyes."

"And what *do you* think of him?"

"Kate, I don't think I've ever met a man who's so gentle and patient. He's good. He's strong. He's smart. He's everything I've ever wanted."

"Then how come you sound like you're trying to convince yourself?"

"Do I?"

"You certainly do."

"Well, I don't know. But here's the thing. I was almost finished with his letter, and then this feeling came over me, and all of a sudden I was really sure. I *knew* he was the one I should marry. There wasn't even any question in my mind about it. I just knew."

Kate nodded, slowly, waiting for the rest. But Bobbi didn't

know what else she wanted to say. Finally, Kate said, "You said you wanted to *ask* me something. You haven't asked."

"It's just . . . Well, I just wonder, would you decide that way? If you got a feeling like that, and you thought it came from God, would you think that was the end of it? That the case was closed?"

Kate reached for Bobbi, took hold of her shoulders. "Bobbi, do you hear what you're asking me? You're saying, 'If God told you to do something, would you do it?' "

"Well . . . would you?"

"You're the religious one. How can you even ask such a thing?"

"I don't know. I just . . . wonder."

"No, Bobbi. You still love David, and you're a little put out that God wants to get in the middle of this."

Bobbi had told herself the same thing a couple of times, but she didn't want to think about it that way. "Kate, I love them both in different ways. But I know Richard is right for me, and David isn't."

"God knows the same thing. Apparently. So where's the problem?"

Bobbi had come to this point fifty times in the past twenty-four hours. And she didn't understand the problem either. She had wanted an answer, had asked for one—over and over—and for those first few minutes after she had felt that overpowering confidence that she finally knew what to do, she had been relieved and thankful. And then her brain had started to clank into action, and what she had felt was the loss of David, the most exciting man she had known in her life. "Oh, Kate, I don't know. I don't know how to explain it."

"I do. You're not so sure you trust the source. No matter how religious you tell me you are, you're just not sure that feeling came from God."

"I was absolutely sure when it was happening."

Kate nodded. "Well, I do have to get back to work, Bobbi.

But here's what I've got to say. First, if I ever have a chance to choose between two guys of that quality, I won't pray, I'll just flip a coin. Because they both seem *mighty fine* to me."

"I know, but—"

"Just listen. Here's the second thing. If God ever speaks to me—and it's that clear to me that he has—I'm going to do *whatever* he tells me, no questions asked. Just once in my life I'd like to be that sure of *something*, even if just for a few minutes."

Bobbi ducked her head and nodded. "That's right, Kate. That really is right."

"God must love you, Bobbi." She rested her hand on Bobbi's shoulder. "But then, who doesn't? I'm a much harder project—for God or anyone."

"Not to me, you're not."

"Well, then, mention that to God. Tell him to send a man to me. Just one would be enough."

She patted Bobbi on the cheek, and then she walked away. What Bobbi felt was ashamed. She had gotten her answer, and it was actually only a confirmation of what she had known all along. So why did she struggle so hard to accept it?

When the *Charity* docked at Pearl Harbor, Bobbi was eager to help the patients who were being transferred from the ship to the navy hospital—the place that had been her home through most of the war. When she got inside, she took care of the paperwork she had to do, got the patients settled, and then hurried to the operating room. But Afton had the day off, so Bobbi walked to the nurse's quarters and found that she wasn't there, either. Bobbi was afraid that the ship would continue on the next day and she wouldn't see Afton at all. But in the morning the *Charity* was still at dock, and Bobbi pulled a few strings to get another couple of hours on shore. She hurried back to the hospital and this time found Afton on duty. When she spotted her in the recovery room, she ran to her, and the two hugged each other, but Afton didn't respond with quite as much enthusiasm as Bobbi had come to expect, and

Bobbi wasn't sure why. "Did you get my letter?" Afton asked, as soon as the two stepped back from one another.

"No. I haven't had any letters from you."

"That's what I was afraid of. Listen, Bobbi—I need to talk to you. Give me a minute or two and then I can get out of here for a little while."

Bobbi heard the tone, and she guessed what this might be about, but she didn't want to think it. Maybe Afton was still struggling with her parents—some of her usual concerns. This didn't have to be anything terrible.

Afton hurried to take care of a patient, and she then stopped at the nurse's station and made a notation of some sort. When she was finished, she said, "Bobbi, come with me." Without saying another word, she walked down the hall and then outside, out to the bench where Bobbi had sat so many times before—with Gene, with Richard, by herself.

"What's wrong, Afton?"

Afton sat down. "Sit here next to me," she said.

Bobbi was suddenly angry. "No. Just say it. It's David, isn't it?"

"Yes."

"Didn't he make it through the surgery?"

"Bobbi, he never made it that far. He died on the airplane, on the way over. But I didn't hear about it for a while. I wrote to you as soon as I got word. I'm sorry you didn't get the letter."

Bobbi had stopped listening. She was trying to think what had happened to her life. She knew that the sorrow would set in, that the mourning would have to begin, but she wasn't that far yet. She had felt the words, like a slap, and now she was waiting for the anguish to begin. She did sit down, but she didn't let Afton pull her into her arms, and she didn't cry.

"Were you still thinking that he might be the right one for you?" Afton asked.

"No."

"Are you sure of that?"

"Yes. I wouldn't have married him. It never would have worked. That's not what I've been worried about."

"What do you mean?"

"I was afraid I would always love him—more than Richard. And I'm going to marry Richard."

"Oh, Bobbi."

"David and I understood each other. We loved the same things. We thought the same way. I never have felt as close to Richard."

"Bobbi, I didn't really know David—not very well—but I know Richard, and I do think he's right for you. You're more alike than you want to admit. And I don't think you and David were at all alike."

Bobbi understood that. David had been more what she wanted to be than what she was. He had brought out a side of her that both pleased and scared her. Richard was careful and tentative, and the truth was, Bobbi's impulses were much the same, but that was a side of herself that didn't excite her.

Still, all this talk was wrong. It wasn't fair to David. It wasn't right to let Afton say, in effect, "Don't feel so bad; you still have the other one," or even, "The other one was better for you anyway." What Bobbi wanted to think about, for the moment, was the friend she had lost. "David loved life. He found *everything* interesting," she told Afton. "We need more people like that, not fewer. It seems like the earth ought to be moaning right now, just for the loss of such a man."

"Bobbi, you can cry."

"I know. I will cry." But the tears weren't coming yet. What she saw in her mind was David at the front of his class at the University of Utah, pacing and talking with his hands, loving his own ideas, stopping sometimes as though he enjoyed his own language so much that he wanted to savor his last sentence before he spoke another one. He was the sort of man Bobbi's father would never understand and wouldn't want to, the kind of person Salt Lake City didn't really welcome. But at the moment, Bobbi felt sorry for all the people who couldn't love David, hadn't loved David.

"Why in the world did he join the Marines?" Afton asked. "It was the wrong place for a guy like that."

That certainly seemed to be true. It was what Bobbi had told him. But it was like him to wonder about every experience, and to fear that the war might pass him by without letting him in on some secret that only combat soldiers understood. It was even like him to secretly enjoy the idea that he was more patriotic than he let on. He would have been embarrassed to spout the clichés of nationalism. It was just more like him to love the whole world than any one part of it, but it was also like him to love the rocks and rills—the idea—of America. It didn't seem like him to kill for those things; it did seem possible that he would die for them.

Bobbi didn't answer the question. Instead, she said, "In class, when he would give a lecture, I would always know that he was talking to me. He knew how fascinated I was—with the literature, and with him—and he loved it. It turned him into a performer. He would talk to me, and I would feel the way a girl does when she's walking down a hallway and some boy's eyes turn to watch her go by. Do you know what I mean?"

"Sure. Every girl knows about that. But I never had a teacher look at me that way."

"It was more than just having a guy look you over. I always knew that it was my brain that excited him."

"That doesn't sound very romantic."

Bobbi didn't answer that, but she wondered whether Afton knew the first thing about romance. It was actually one of the most enticing things Bobbi had ever known. The kiss, finally, in his office, had only been the natural result of all the brain tangling they had done in the classroom. She had felt that with Richard at times, too, that way in which they could embrace with their words and their thoughts, get close without touching, but Richard was so afraid to let go, and David didn't know how to do anything else.

"You're taking this so well, Bobbi. I didn't think you would."

After all the days Bobbi and Afton had spent together, Afton still didn't know Bobbi. That had never been more clear. "Once, when I went to Chicago, David came to my hotel room. He was very proper about everything, but when he was leaving, we started to kiss, and after a while, I didn't want him to go. It was one of those times when I could have done the wrong thing."

"Sam and I know all about that," Afton said. And then she added quickly, "But we've been good."

"David was the one who decided to leave. He didn't want to hurt me. He knew how I would feel, after, if I did something I believed was wrong. Then, the next day, he sent me home for the same reason. He didn't want to take my religion away from me, and he was afraid he would. He loved me that much."

"I think he'll accept the gospel in the next life," Afton said.

Bobbi was stunned by the response. "Afton, what do you mean?" she said. "That *is* the gospel." And finally, she began to cry.

4

When President Thomas came home from his Sunday morning church meetings, he seemed distracted. Mom always said that he had to deal with lots of problems in the stake and had things on his mind. Maybe that was true, but LaRue wondered whether he didn't like that excuse. It helped him stay out of conversations with "the girls," as he called Bea and Beverly and LaRue.

Today, however, when the four sat down for Sunday dinner, Dad did have something to say. He offered the prayer himself and dwelt more than usual on the past, on all the blessings that had come to the family through his opportunity to serve as stake president, and, as usual, he thanked the Lord for Wally's return to the States from prison camp and for Alex and Bobbi's well-being. After the prayer, he picked up a plate of boiled potatoes and cooked carrots, scraped some of them onto his plate with a serving spoon, passed them on to Beverly, and then said, quietly, "President Smith called me this morning."

There was nothing all that surprising in that. President Thomas talked to the president of the Church fairly often. The two had known each other for a long time, and President Smith tried to stay in contact with his stake presidents. What was obvious in President Thomas's voice was that he was trying to act more unaffected than he really was. LaRue heard a hint of emotion in his voice, but she didn't know whether it was excitement or concern.

Bea held a bowl of creamed corn in front of her, as though she had forgotten what she was going to do with it, and asked, "Really? What did he call about?"

"I'm going to tell all of you something, but it absolutely cannot leave this house."

It was Dad's usual proclamation. LaRue rolled her eyes and said, "Bev and I like to go upstairs and shout everything you say out the windows. All our neighbors sit in their yards, summer or winter, and just wait to get the latest word."

"I'm serious, LaRue."

"I know you are. We won't do it this time . . . we'll only tell a few close friends." But when her father stared at her sternly, she said, "For crying out loud, Dad, I'm just kidding. We won't say anything."

President Thomas leaned forward, his elbows on the table. He looked across at Bea. "I'm going to be released as stake president," he said. He glanced at LaRue and Beverly, then looked back at his wife.

"When?" Mom asked, her breath almost gone.

"At stake conference. Second week of December. Six weeks from today."

"My goodness," she said. A little shock had set in. LaRue could hear it in her mother's voice, saw it in Bev's eyes, but Dad was stone-faced.

It was hard to imagine. LaRue could still remember when her father had first become stake president, but it had been a long time ago, when she was a little girl. What she wondered, immediately, was what life in her home would be like now.

"Why is he releasing you, Dad?" Beverly finally asked. Bev's cheeks had turned red, as though she took this as some sort of insult to the family.

"It's a big scandal," LaRue said. "They found out that Dad's a Republican."

Dad actually smiled a little. "That might be it," he said. But then he added, rather seriously, "More of the Brethren are coming around to my way of thinking these days. Don't be surprised if we don't have more Republicans than Democrats in the Quorum of the Twelve before long."

"Dad, I'm serious," Bev said. "Why would President Smith release you?"

"There's no *reason.* It's just time. When I was growing up, stake presidents used to stay in office twenty or thirty years, but it's gotten to be a harder job, with all the things that go on in our world these days. President Smith said that he felt he'd asked enough of me, and it was time to let someone else carry the load."

"How do you feel about that, Al?" Mom asked, and LaRue could tell that she was a little concerned. LaRue knew why, too. Dad's church work had been the center of his life for such a long time that it was hard to imagine him around the house more, the phone not ringing all the time, the family living like other people.

"It's fine with me," Dad said. "The timing seems right. With our kids coming home, it's a good time to move back a little from all the busyness. I'll still have a church calling of some sort—you can be sure of that—but if it's something that doesn't keep me quite so on the go, and if I can cut back a little on my hours at work, I think that'll be very nice for a change."

"You say that, Al, but are you sure you won't be at loose ends, wondering what to do with yourself?"

Everyone had stopped passing food, but Dad reached for the roast, took a slice, and passed it to LaRue. She could see how hard he was trying to act normal, to hide what he was really feeling.

"I'm not old enough to retire. I don't mean that," he said. "But I can involve myself in some other things a little more than

I've been able to in the past. Wally will be home one of these first days, and I want him to start carrying some of the load down at the plant. I want to break you loose from the place a little more—and me too."

"To do what?" LaRue asked.

"I've talked with my dad about some other business interests, for one thing, and I'd like to give more of my time to politics, one way or the other."

"What business interests?" LaRue asked.

Dad hesitated, looking stern. "It's just an idea right now—something we chatted about the other day."

"Just tell me a little about it—so I can tell all my girlfriends."

Dad was obviously about to deliver another one of his little rebukes when Mom said, "Weren't you going to tell me about it?"

Dad was trapped, and LaRue could see him squirm. "Of course I'm going to tell you." Again he looked at LaRue. "Girls—all kidding aside—this is something you *absolutely* cannot talk about."

"Not even on the party line—with Sister Aiken listening in?"

"I'm serious, LaRue."

"I know."

Dad cut off a bite of his roast and forked it into his mouth, and then, after a couple of quick chews, he said, "This area out here in Sugar House, especially south and up into the foothills, is going to boom in the next few years. Dad has a chance to buy some of the farms and orchards out that direction. The prices have jumped pretty high, but they're going to go a lot higher. If we get in now, buy up some of that land, and then parcel it out into building lots, we can do really well with it." He looked toward Bea. "This is a *big* opportunity for us. It's a lot of money to invest, but we could get a bigger return than we've gotten on any of our other business interests."

"But what about that camel, Dad?" LaRue asked, and she waited for him to look at her again.

"What camel?"

"You know—the one trying to get through the eye of the needle."

Dad took this more to heart than LaRue had expected. She could tell he had already thought about it. "LaRue, there's nothing wrong with wealth in and of itself. It's what you do with it. I don't like the direction a lot of things are going in this country. John L. Lewis and these labor unions have way too much power. Between the coal miners and the auto workers, they can shut down the whole country any time they please. Look at all the strikes we're having—and we've got more coming, that's for sure. But if I want to do anything about it, I have to have a voice, and it takes money to be heard. That's just the way our system works."

"So what are you saying—that truth wins out as long as you've got the money to pay for it?"

Dad was absolutely stopped. He stared at LaRue. "No," he finally said, but he added rather weakly, "The truth will win out, but you have to let people hear it. And getting the word out can cost money. Part of it is getting the right people into public office, where they can have some influence."

LaRue knew that it was time to stop, had actually known before she had made this last remark. "I'm sure that's true," she said, and went back to her dinner. And she took a little pride in backing off. A year before she would have kept pushing until an explosion finally occurred.

Dad began to eat much more resolutely, even quickly, after that, and then he did something LaRue had never seen him do before. He left almost half his food on his plate, pushed it back, and said, "I'm sorry, Bea, but I have to run. I've got to spend some time in my office at the stake house this afternoon. Before they release me, I've got a thousand things to put in order." He slid his chair back from the table.

LaRue was sorry now, as usual. She had only meant to tease him a little. She hadn't expected to get him upset. "Dad, you've been a good stake president," she said. "Everybody always tells me that."

He hadn't stood yet. And once again, he was clearly taken by surprise. He seemed unsure how to take the words. "Thank you, LaRue," he said. "But what do *you* think?"

"I told you. You've done a good job." But LaRue didn't really know how good he had been, and her voice registered her uncertainty.

"I've worked hard at it," he said, and yet the words sounded like an apology.

"You've helped a lot of people. That's what people tell me all the time—how much you helped them when they were going through a hard time."

"Well, that's what I've tried to do," he said, and now his sadness was much more evident.

"You're one rich man who'll get through the needle."

"I have no interest in being rich, LaRue. I want my children to have a way to make a good living, and I want to do some good. That's all."

"Dad, I was only kidding."

"I know." He got up, however, and he walked back to his little office off the dining room. He was only there a minute or so, and then he came out, carrying his old leather briefcase. "I'll be over to our ward for sacrament meeting," he told Bea. "I'll see you there." And then he left.

"Mom, I was just teasing him," LaRue said.

Bea had finished her meal. She leaned on the table with her elbows, her fingers laced together over her dinner plate. "I know," she said. "But I doubt you have any idea what he's going through right now."

"Why, Mom?" Beverly asked. "He said it's a good time to be released."

"That's what he's telling himself. And I'm sure he knew this was coming. But Al has loved being stake president. That's who he is now. Everyone in Sugar House knows him. He can't walk three steps through this part of town without someone saying, 'Hi, President.' I think it's going to be hard for him to turn all that over to someone else."

"Won't he be glad to have all the problems off his mind?" LaRue asked.

"No. I don't think so. There's nothing he loves more than identifying a problem and then doing something about it."

"Maybe so. But he's a lot more patient with other people's problems than he is with ours."

There was a long silence, and LaRue knew she had said the wrong thing again. It was Bev who finally said, "LaRue, he's a good dad," as though she felt someone had to defend him.

"I didn't say he wasn't."

"LaRue," Mom said, "it's always hardest to solve your own problems. But I think you kids are turning out pretty well, and a lot of that is because of him. Maybe he preaches more than you like, but sooner or later, the things he tells you have a way of sinking in."

LaRue didn't know about that. But she hadn't intended any big insult. She really believed that her mother had more to do with keeping the family running than Dad ever did, but she wasn't about to say that now. She didn't want an argument—or to get Bev all upset. "I do okay with Dad now," she said. "Most of the problems we had were my fault. I've admitted that to you—and to him."

"And all I'm saying is that this is a very hard day for him, whether he lets on or not. We all need to understand that. Just when all the good things are about to happen, and we're getting our family back together, he has to make another big adjustment in his life."

"Maybe he'll get called to be an apostle," Beverly said.

"No. I just can't picture that," LaRue said. "Do you think that's what he was expecting, Mom?"

"No," Bea said. But then she added, carefully, "I think at one
time he did imagine that possibility. He was called to be bishop
when he was very young, and he's been stake president quite a
while for a man his age. Plus, he knows all the Brethren, and I
think they all think very highly of him. But—I don't know—
raising you kids, as much as anything, has changed him. This is
just my idea, and I don't know if it's right, but I think he felt, at
one time, that he pretty much had this world figured out. But
you kids have each been different, and you've each given him
some challenges. I think it's taken some of the starch out of
him."

"You've knocked him down a few rungs, too, Mom," LaRue
said.

Mom didn't like that. LaRue saw her head swing around,
saw the little twinge of hurt in her eyes. "LaRue, he's gained
some humility along the way. He's a better man than ever. I
think he'd be a wonderful apostle."

"I'm just saying that we aren't the only ones who've
humbled him. You have too."

"LaRue, I've always supported him, but I've asked him some
hard questions. And to his credit, he hasn't just passed them off.
He's changed the way he thinks. He's made some difficult com-
promises with all of us." She looked at Bev, and then back at
LaRue. "And there's something I want you two to know. I love
him more than ever. I respect him for doing what he thinks he
has to do to be a good father and a good husband. He may not
get everything right, but who does? I certainly don't."

LaRue smiled. "Maybe so, Mom. But he needs to learn how
to love a little more and preach a little less. That's all I've ever
wanted from him."

"Well . . . yes. That's pretty well put," Bea said, and she
reached out and patted LaRue's hand. "I just hope you kids will
understand how hard the job is when you have your own kids
to raise."

LaRue noticed, though she rarely thought of it, how pretty

Mom was. She was wearing a royal blue dress, and her eyes looked very blue, set off against her graying hair, and even when she tried not to smile, her big dimples had a way of appearing. LaRue couldn't help but wonder what all this would mean to her. "Mom, you may love Dad, but what are you going to do if he ends up being home a lot more than he has been? He'll drive you crazy."

There was a moment when LaRue thought she had said the wrong thing again, but her mom began to smile. "Do you think I don't know that? This is a hard day for me, too."

The girls all laughed. And even Bev said, "He'll be checking with me every five minutes to see if I've done my homework."

"I wish you hadn't said that," LaRue said. "I've got some I've got to do."

"Don't run off just yet," Mom said. "Help me get these dishes done before you hide away."

So Bev and LaRue helped their mom, and they got the dishes done quickly. Then LaRue headed upstairs. But she had hardly cracked her American History text before Beverly showed up at her door. "LaRue, I need to talk to you," she said.

"Could you wait until after I—"

"I heard something about you at church this morning."

"Now what?"

"Virginia Graves told me that you broke up with Reed Porter."

"How would she know?"

"Her big sister is friends with one of Reed's friends. He's telling people that you gave Reed the brushoff without so much as a thanks-for-the-memories."

"That's not true. I was very nice about it. And I don't think Reed even cared all that much."

Bev walked over to LaRue's bed, where LaRue was sitting up, leaning against the headboard with a pillow behind her back. She had taken off her church dress for now and was wearing her old plaid robe. "Why did you break up with him, LaRue?"

"You know why. The boy drove me crazy. He's got the brains of a doorknob."

Bev laughed, in spite of herself. "But he's *really* cute, and he's always nice to everyone—even me."

"I know, Bev. But even that started to drive me nuts. You can only eat so many pancakes drenched with syrup before they start to make you sick."

"Is that what he is—pancakes with syrup?"

"Sometimes he's just straight syrup. Try to drink a gallon of that."

Bev was laughing again. "So who are you going to go out with now?"

"No one."

"Are you serious? If I had so many boys after me, I wouldn't scare them all away." She turned and lay across LaRue's bed, at her feet, and she kicked off her shoes, as though she were going to settle in there for a time.

LaRue needed to study, and even more, she didn't want to talk about this. She remembered that first year of high school when she had wanted so much to have boys pay attention to her—the way Beverly obviously did now. But she was tired of all that business now. Most of the boys she knew had nothing to say. They couldn't carry on a conversation that interested her for ten seconds.

"Reed thinks you like Cecil Broadbent."

"Virginia said that?"

"Yup."

"That's stupid. I do like Cecil, but not as a boyfriend."

"Cecil's so creepy, though. Why do you like him?"

"I've told you before, Bev. He's interesting. He's smart. He understands things. He can talk about something other than sports."

"He's never kissed you, has he?"

"No. Of course not. And he never will. That's one of the best things about him."

"But you kissed Reed, didn't you?"

LaRue took a long breath. She had to end this conversation soon. "Bev, don't worry about kissing. Just don't let guys start all that."

"I don't. I just dance at church dances. Blair Handley likes me, I think, but he's never asked me on a date."

"Don't worry about it. Just play with dolls or something."

"LaRue! I'm not a little girl."

"Maybe not. But wait until you're older to start all this boy stuff. I got way too interested in boys when I was your age. It was the only thing I ever thought about."

"I'm not like that. I just—"

"But Bev, you're thinking about it too much. And that does something to you. I wanted to go with Reed just because all the girls swooned over him. It was like I'd won the biggest prize. I did everything to get him, but as soon as he started asking me out I was mean. I did rotten things to him just because he'd let me get away with it. The whole time I went with him, I didn't like myself."

"If I had a boyfriend, maybe I wouldn't be mean."

"No, you wouldn't. But you'd fuss and worry about it all the time. You're just better off to wait until you're older."

That seemed the end of the conversation, but Beverly was still lying on the bed. LaRue wanted to ask her to move on and was even thinking of the best way to say it when Bev said, "Virginia said something else. Something bad."

"What?"

"She said that Reed told some of his friends that you don't believe in Heavenly Father."

"*Reed* said that?"

"Yes."

"Oh, brother. That guy is so dumb."

"Why would he say that, LaRue?"

"Because he makes these *stupid* statements about religion—and I would tell him how silly they were. He wasn't even smart enough to know what I was talking about."

"Like what?"

"Oh, I don't know. I don't remember any examples." Actually, she did, but she didn't want to talk about such things with Bev and upset her. The truth was, Beverly thought a lot the way Reed did.

Beverly rolled onto her side and propped up her head with her hand. "I told Virginia it wasn't true. I told her about how you prayed about Wally that one time."

"Don't tell her things like that, Bev. You don't have to. It's none of her business."

"But I know you *do* believe in Heavenly Father."

"Well, then, forget about it."

"But it worries me that people are going around saying things like that. I don't understand why Reed would think it."

LaRue had slipped a little too far down, and her back was hurting. She pulled herself up straight. "Okay, I'll tell you how this all got started," she said. "But then I need to do my homework."

"Okay."

"I used to go with Reed to his sacrament meetings sometimes. And one night we were in his ward and this woman got up and said she was sure that God had saved her life. She said she was walking home from the grocery store, carrying a bag of groceries, and she came to a corner. She waited for the light, and she was about to step out into the street when something made her hesitate. This car came buzzing through right then. It would have hit her if she had stepped out when she first started to."

"What's wrong with that?"

"Nothing. But after the meeting, I just said that I'd read in the paper about a little boy who got hit by a car, on his bicycle, and got killed. Then I said, 'I guess God didn't love him as much.' Reed got all upset about that."

"LaRue, in Beehives, Sister Jenson, our Beekeeper, told us it's not God's fault when things like that happen. Maybe the boy turned right in front of the car."

"I know that. But this woman was about to step in front of a car, and she said that God told her not to—or the Spirit did, or something. I just wonder why people get hit by cars and killed all the time, and God steps in and saves this one woman and not the others."

"Why *do* you think he does?"

"I don't know, Bev. That's what I'm saying. People talk like they understand everything, but Cecil and I talk about this kind of stuff all the time, and it's not as simple as everybody makes it sound. People stand up at testimony meeting and make it sound like God is in control of everything, just running the whole show. But then they turn around in Sunday School class and say that everything is up to us. The way I look at it, if God is in control of everything, he has no right to judge us. But if everything is in our control, why would he jump in and tell that woman not to step off the curb?"

"Maybe it wasn't her time to die?"

"So is everyone supposed to die at a certain time? If I wander down the street and step out in front of a truck, if it's not *my time*, is God going to send a wind to blow me out of the way?"

Beverly sat up, seemed to consider, but what LaRue caught was a whiff of the sweet perfume Bev was wearing. It was like flowers, rather annoying, but something Bev loved, and suddenly LaRue realized that she was planting questions in poor Bev's head that would plague her forever—and the girl wasn't the sort of person who could let such things go.

"Look, Bev, there's probably a good answer to all of that. God knows it. But we don't. I just don't like it when people think they have all the answers when they don't."

"But LaRue, it does sort of sound like you don't believe in Heavenly Father."

"I don't see why. There are lots of things we don't understand in this life. Think of all the boys who went off to war. Most of them had parents at home praying for them, but some got killed and some didn't. No one knows why exactly. Maybe God wants certain people on the other side at certain times—or maybe it's just the way it works out. We just don't know. There's nothing wrong with that."

"But everyone said that Gene was needed to do missionary work in the spirit world. Don't you believe that?"

LaRue took a deep breath. "That could be right, Bev. I'm just saying that I don't know. And I don't think anyone does."

"Dad said that."

"It's a nice thing to believe."

"That's all it is? Just something nice to believe?" Beverly stood up and turned toward LaRue. "Is that what you think?"

"No. We believe there's a spirit world. And we believe that people do missionary work there. So that's what Gene is doing, I guess. I'm just saying that we don't know why God needed Gene and not Wally, or something like that. And we don't need to know."

"Dad always says that the Spirit can tell us things. Maybe the Spirit gave Dad the answer—told him why Gene was needed."

"Okay. Maybe it did."

"And maybe that woman, too. The one in Reed's ward."

"Maybe so." LaRue was going to let this go. Beverly was standing almost stiff, her arms straight down. She was like a little iron rod—straight, steadfast. It was wrong for LaRue to make her bend.

"Has the Spirit ever said anything to you, LaRue?"

"I don't know, Bev."

"Don't you have a testimony?"

That was something that LaRue had thought a great deal

about lately. But she was much more confused than she wanted
to admit. She chose her words carefully when she said, "I
thought I felt the Spirit at Gene's funeral. When President
McKay spoke, and he told us about Christ giving us peace and
everything, I felt all tingly and good, and I thought that was
the Spirit. I hope it was. But other things can make you feel
that way. That's what Cecil keeps telling me, anyway. So I don't
want to claim I know something that I'm not exactly sure
about. I do believe in things, but I'm not sure I have a
testimony—or at least a really strong one. But that's my fault,
not God's."

"Sometimes I feel the Spirit really strong, LaRue. I did that
day when we found out Wally was all right and we all prayed
together."

LaRue had felt something that day too. But she wondered
now. She wasn't going to tell Beverly this, but Cecil had told
her that anyone would feel relieved and happy at such a time.
That didn't prove that God was out there sending messages.
Cecil wanted *proof* that there was a God, and he couldn't find
one. "I'm not saying there isn't a God," he had told her. "I'm just
saying that I don't see any evidence that convinces me. Most
of what people say on the subject is just a bunch of hocus-
pocus."

"I felt something that day, too," LaRue told her sister. "We
all did."

"LaRue, that was Heavenly Father. Wasn't it?"

"I'm sure it was." But LaRue wasn't telling the truth now. She
wasn't sure. She just didn't want to pass her doubts along to her
sister.

Bev walked to the door and stopped. "LaRue," she said, "it
worries me to hear you talk that way."

"I know. But don't let it upset you. Maybe my faith will get
stronger. I think it will. We're still young."

"But my faith *is* strong."

"I know. You're a better person than I am."

"Don't say that."

"It's true, Bev. It really is. But don't worry about me. I'm not falling away from the Church. And don't say anything to Mom or Dad. Okay?"

"Why not?"

"Because you'll make it sound like I'm an atheist or something."

"What's that?"

"Never mind. Just don't say anything."

"Okay. But do you say your prayers every night?"

"Not always. Mostly I do."

"Say them *every* single night, LaRue. And read the scriptures. That helps me."

"Okay, Bev. You're right. I do need to do that."

"Are you going to try to get your Golden Gleaner award?"

"I don't know that either."

"You need to, LaRue. That would help you. Will you promise to try?"

"No, *Dad*, I won't."

"What?"

"You're more like him than any of us."

"But you do need to pray. And you do need to read the scriptures."

"I know. But I need to do it on my own—not because someone pressures me."

"Okay. But please do it." She finally smiled.

LaRue smiled too. And she was surprised to think how much she loved her little sister—even if she was too much like her dad.

5

It was almost four o'clock in the afternoon when Wally's bus pulled into the Greyhound station on South Temple Street in Salt Lake City. He hadn't told his family what day he would arrive because he didn't want them to pick him up at the station. He had imagined thousands of times the way he wanted to return: he would walk into his house the way he had always done when he was a kid, just open the door and stroll in, as though he had been playing outside for an hour or two and hadn't been gone for all these years. He didn't want to see everyone at once, either, or get stuck in the middle of a big celebration. He just wanted to find his dad sitting in his big chair reading a newspaper, or meet one of the girls out playing hopscotch on the front walk. He wanted to feel that it was a normal day, and he wanted everything to look the same, smell the same, *be* the same as he remembered.

So Wally didn't call home for a ride. He grabbed his duffel bag and walked to the corner of State Street, and he caught a bus home. Riding up Twenty-First South he saw the changes, some new buildings, some old businesses that were under new management—that sort of thing—but what surprised him most was the sameness of everything, how very familiar everything was. In San Francisco he had gotten used to the idea that

America was alive and busy, not at all like Japan, but something about the mountains, the angle of the afternoon sun, even the people moving about on the streets suggested that life had continued much the same at home. It was strange how safe he felt here, how consoled—even welcomed, although he didn't really talk to anyone.

Wally got off the bus at Eleventh East, by the old World War I Memorial, right in the center of Sugar House. As he walked north toward his house, through his old neighborhood, he recognized all the details of the place: the old cracks in the sidewalk—ones he had avoided stepping on as boy—and the elevated spot where the roots of Larson's big silver maple tree bulged the concrete. He remembered roaming through these streets, playing hide-and-go-seek among the homes and vacant lots, building snow forts in winter or sweating in the August sun. Each front porch or tree or fence jumped back to his mind—all surprisingly clear, part of him, and at the same time dreamlike. He had lived here as a boy, as a teenager, and then for so long he had lived here in his mind. Now, to be back, to feel it all again, brought back a sense of himself that he hadn't felt for a long time.

He remembered a summer day when he was maybe eight or nine, and he and Alex had been riding their bikes, going hard, and somehow, in turning a corner—this corner, right in front of him—they had bumped wheels or something, and both of them had crashed and flipped over on top of each other. Wally had come up crying, his pants torn, his knee bloody, and Alex had told him, sounding like Dad, "Your skin will grow back. It's your pants you need to cry about." And they had both laughed. Alex had seemed a giant then—so much older and braver and stronger, and Wally had known then that he would never catch up, that Alex would always be the king of this neighborhood, the star.

A block or so from his house, Wally saw Brother Shaw, who had been his Scoutmaster, but Brother Shaw was watering his roses, holding a black garden hose and crouching a little, as though he were bending over a baby in a crib. He didn't seem to recognize Wally, or maybe notice him, and so Wally said nothing. He wanted to see his family before he talked with the neighbors.

When Wally turned the corner and saw his big white house across the street and halfway up the block, he slowed. He wanted to savor this. He looked all about, trying to recall everything. What he felt was that it was all sacred, blessed, part of a beauty he had carried within him in his darkest days. Up on the mountain the fall colors were already fading, the red and bronze of the scrub oak turning gray. The air was cool and burnished, the sun lowering in the west. The two big spruce trees in front of the McKinnons' house had fattened, it seemed, grown a little taller, and the flowering plums in front of the Fairbankses' house had grown up considerably from the little braced-up sticks they had been. But most things were unchanged. The houses, the hedges, the telephone poles— everything was just as it was supposed to be, and his house, gleaming white in the softening light, was perfect, unfazed.

He thought of Bobbi, remembering one spring afternoon when he had walked home from junior high and found her there on the porch, sitting on the top step, reading a book. "What are you doing out here?" he had asked her, because the air was still quite cool, but she had said, "It's too nice to go in." That was all—just a strange little memory, but he could remember her saddle shoes and her ankle socks, her plaid skirt, and her face—her freckles and the way she rolled her eyes up and off to one side as she smiled. She had been a little harsh with him now and again, back then, but he had never feared her, never tried hard to please her—not the way he had done with Alex.

Wally stopped across the street, stood under the Archibalds' chestnut tree and looked for a time. He had imagined this moment over and over, and now it was finally going to happen: he was going to step in through that front door, and life would begin again. He didn't want to hurry one part of the experience. He looked at the lilac bushes out front, the love seat on the porch, the old black screen door . . . and then he saw the stars in the front window. On a field of white cloth were four stars: three blue, one gold. And, of course, that was the change, that gold star. This was not perfect, not entirely the return he had imagined all these years, and Wally realized why he had felt as much sadness as joy as he had walked through the old neighborhood. Gene had almost always been with him in these streets, tagging him, imitating him, granting him the deference a little boy gives his big brother.

Wally was still standing on the sidewalk when he heard voices—two people talking somewhere nearby. He didn't want to see anyone yet, so he walked on across the street, but he slowed again as he reached the sidewalk. He approached the house hesitantly, prolonging his steps, still taking everything in, and then he climbed the three steps to his front porch. He wondered who was home, how this would all happen, but he knew he didn't want to knock. So he set his duffel bag on the porch, pulled the screen door open, and turned the big brass doorknob. The door seemed to resist a little and then came open with a bit of a scraping sound—the way it always had. He stepped inside, where all was quiet, pushed the door shut, and then stood and looked at it all. The light filtered through the lacy curtains on the front window, and the stained glass in the upper window panes cast red and gold across the carpet. Everything inside the living room, just off the entrance, had been left the same: the old gray couch, the Philco radio next to Dad's chair, even the knickknack shelf in the corner, with the ceramic kittens. Wally knew this was a kindness, was sure that the room had been kept that way for him, and he was touched. He looked up the stairs, thought of his old room, felt it all, smelled the flavor of home. He thought of days after school, running in, shouting, "Hey, Mom, I'm home," of lying on the carpet with a new train set on Christmas morning, of all the family meetings. He stepped into the living room and looked toward the dining room: the big maple table that had always been stretched out long, with all the extra leaves, for Thanksgiving and Christmas dinners with the family. Off the dining room, in the kitchen, he could hear someone moving about, heard a pan touch the stove and make a tiny scraping noise on a burner. How could it all be so familiar, so reliable, so unchanging?

"Who's home?" someone called. Mom.

Wally wasn't sure how to do this, so he took a breath, and then he said, his voice soft in the quiet house, "It's just Wally."

Footsteps moved across the kitchen floor, and then the door swung open, and there was Mom, a little in the shadows, the light from the front windows barely reaching her. Her hair was grayer, her shape a little stouter—that much he could see—but everything else was the same. She was wearing an apron over a house dress, gray in the shadows. She stood fixed, as though shocked, but her hand came up, clapped across her mouth.

Wally didn't hurry to her. He walked slowly, enjoying every second of this time, and then he took her in his arms. "Hi, Mom," he said, but that was all he could get out before he began to cry.

Wally clung to his mother, felt her shake with sobs, and then he heard footsteps on the stairs, someone coming down. He stepped back enough to turn, and just then a girl stepped into the living room, still at a distance from him. He knew that this had to be Beverly, and yet it couldn't be. It was someone else.

She stood still for a moment, looking curious, not excited, and then the realization struck her and she shrieked, "Wally!" She ran a couple of steps and then jumped at him, threw her arms around him, knocked him backward. Wally still had hold of his mother with one arm; he wrapped the other one around Beverly, and the three held onto each other. "I can't believe it," Beverly squealed. "I can't believe it."

The sound of Beverly's little scream had apparently reached upstairs. Wally heard steps again, this time harder, quicker, and he heard a shout: "Is it Wally? Is Wally here?"

This was LaRue, of course, but she had turned the corner now, and she was so grown up and beautiful. Wally had tried to imagine what his sisters would look like, but he had never gotten the old image out of his head: two little girls in red velvet dresses.

Mom and Beverly both stepped aside enough to let LaRue get through, but they all ended up in a cluster, clasping each other, all crying, and still Wally hadn't said anything. The reality of all this was almost frightening. He had pictured seeing them, being home, but he hadn't thought of what to do after that. He didn't know where to start, how to tell them all the things he wanted to say.

Finally everyone stepped back, and Mom said, "How did you get here? Why didn't you let us know?"

But it was too prosaic a thing to talk about first, and Wally couldn't get himself to answer. "I can't believe I'm here," he said. "It's all the same. Everything has been here all that time I was gone—just the way I pictured it." He took his mother back into his arms, bent to hold her tight, and he couldn't stop crying.

"Dad wouldn't let us change the house," LaRue said. "That's why it looks so worn out. I keep telling him, 'Let Wally get one good look, and then throw all that old stuff out.'"

Wally looked over his mother's shoulder, and he laughed. "LaRue, you look like a woman," he said. "I can't get used to you. And look at Beverly." He stepped from his mom and took the girls into his arms again. "It's too good to be true," he whispered. "I just can't believe I'm here."

"Five years, Wally," Mom said. "It's been *five* years."

"Wally, you don't look so awful as everyone said you would," LaRue told him.

"LaRue!" Beverly said. "He looks great! Really great."

Wally knew he did look more like himself than he had

expected he would. He had filled out considerably more during his four weeks in San Francisco, and the color had come back to his skin.

"Come into the kitchen, Wally," Mom said. "Are you hungry?"

"I don't know. Probably. I haven't thought about it."

They all walked into the kitchen, and Wally looked around again. He saw the same wallpaper with the little yellow flowers; the same old white oven with the black handle; the same linoleum on the floor, if a little more worn. But it was the smell he remembered best, loved the most. He caught a whiff from the gas stove, but there was also the good aroma of bread—yeast—and something meaty, like simmering gravy—not cooking now but lingering in the air. "I was just starting supper," Mom said. "I'll call your dad. He can be home in ten minutes."

"No. Don't do that. Let me just talk to you three for now. I don't want to do this all at once."

Bea raised her apron and wiped the tears from her cheeks. "I don't know what to do," she said. "I've been trying to think what to say to you, what to do for you when you got here, but it just hasn't seemed real until now."

"Let's make him a good supper. That's the first thing," Beverly said.

Wally kept watching Beverly and LaRue. He wanted to get them into his head, accept who they were now, but it bothered him that they seemed such strangers. "Why don't we all just sit down," Wally said. "I'm not hungry yet. Really."

"Well, all right, but let me get some potatoes boiling. I was about to do that when you came in."

She walked to the sink. A half-peeled potato lay on the cabinet by the sink, next to a paring knife. She picked them both up, but she didn't start to peel. She watched Wally as he sat down at the kitchen table. He could see how much it meant to her, just to see him there.

Beverly moved in next to Wally, slid her chair up close.

LaRue sat down opposite him. "You can't believe how much we've talked about you during the war," LaRue said. "Bev would ask me a thousand times, 'Do you think Wally is all right? Where do you think he is?' Everything like that. And Mom would always tell us, 'He's alive. I know he is.'"

"Is that what you thought, Mom?" Wally asked.

She was still holding the potato and the knife, still not peeling. "I did. We only got word about you that one time, but I did believe you would make it back—most of the time, anyway."

"There were lots of times I didn't know whether I would make it," Wally said. "Lots of times."

"Was it really awful, Wally?" LaRue asked. "Did the Japs treat you really bad?"

"Sure. It was bad," Wally said, but he didn't want to say any more than that.

"Why did so many of the men die?" LaRue asked. "Did they starve you?"

"Well . . . they didn't feed us much. A lot of guys got sick, too, and we didn't have much in the way of medical help."

"What did they get sick from?"

Wally looked at LaRue, wondered how he could give her some concept of what it had been like. What did she know of beriberi or typhoid fever? How could she imagine the degradation and filth he had lived with? And why should she? "The guys just caught different kinds of bugs," he said. "There's lots of stuff to catch in the Philippines—especially if you aren't eating right." But he could see more questions coming, so he asked one of his own: "What's happening at old East High these days?"

"The football team isn't so hot this year," Beverly said. "But at least we can have more dances now. During the war we couldn't have nice decorations or even punch and cookies and stuff like that—because of the sugar."

"We still can't get much sugar," Mom said. "But they have taken the ration off meat and fat."

Wally nodded. He kept trying to get a feel for what life had been like, but it was hard for him to think that anything had actually changed. "I'll have to go to a football game one of these days. That sounds like fun to me."

"If you go, they'll probably have you stand up and wave to the crowd. They'll announce that you played football for East and that you're a war hero and everything."

"Oh, I doubt that," Wally said. "When Chuck Adair gets back, they ought to do that for him, though. He was a star player—and he *was* a hero. He kept me going a lot of times."

"When will he be home?" Mom asked.

"I don't know. They said he hasn't gained enough weight yet. I think they might send him to another hospital somewhere. He was really disappointed when they let me go and kept him in San Francisco."

"I saw his mother the other day," Mom said. "She said he sounded awfully nervous when she talked to him on the phone."

"Yeah, he is. There's a lot to get used to all at once."

"You aren't nervous," Beverly said.

"Well . . . every guy handles things a little different," Wally said, but he knew that he wasn't as calm as he might seem to them. Once he feasted on these first pleasures, he knew that lots of decisions were waiting.

"I saw Lorraine's mother at the grocery store," Mom said. "I guess Lorraine is quitting up at Boeing and coming back to Salt Lake."

"When is she getting married?"

"I don't know. I didn't ask."

Wally nodded, tried not to show any reaction, but he could feel his mom and sisters watching him. What he wondered was why Lorraine was coming home. Was it to get ready for the wedding? He wanted to see her if he could, just to talk to her, but he thought maybe that wasn't actually a wise thing to do. "I can't believe we're sitting here talking like I never left home," Wally said. "I keep thinking that I ought to be more excited."

"I was just thinking the same thing," Mom said. She had finally started peeling. "But I like that. I like how comfortable it feels to have you here."

"You don't seem the same to me," Beverly said.

"Really? How have I changed?"

"You're nicer, I guess."

Wally laughed, and then he slid his arm around her, pulled her close to him. "I did tease you girls a lot," he said. "I'll start doing that again—tomorrow—so you'll know it's me."

"No, you won't," LaRue said. "You're older. You seem more like a man to me now—not so crazy as you always were before."

"I'll tell you what you are," Mom said. "You're good. That's what I feel from you. I noticed it on the phone. You're a deeper man now, more in tune with the Spirit. You seem humble to me."

"Well, I hope so."

"Do you feel changed?" LaRue asked.

"I guess I do. I know that in San Francisco I got myself a Book of Mormon, and it was the greatest thing in the world to have one again. I read it all the way through in a few days, and then I started over. I read a lot of the New Testament, too, and it was like I was thirsty to get more." He grinned. "As you may remember, that was not exactly my attitude when I left this house."

"So maybe being a POW was a good thing for you," Beverly said.

"Well . . . yeah. In a way." But that was something Wally knew he would never believe. He was happy for some of the results, perhaps, but he could never pass the experience off as something to be thankful for. He just hoped that the bitterness he had known for so long would never come back to ruin his life.

.

"It wasn't a good thing, Bev," Mom said. "But Wally is taking something terrible and turning it into something good. That's to his great credit."

"I'm just glad it's over," Wally said. "Reality may not be *quite* as good as the dreams I used to have of being here. But it's *darn* close." He looked around the kitchen again, hugged Beverly a little tighter, tried to fill himself up with all the memories of this room: breakfasts at this table, cinnamon rolls with Mom after school, jigsaw puzzles with Bobbi and Alex when he was the little brother. "I hope you three know how much I love you," he said in a soft voice. "How much I kept loving you all the while I was gone. There were times when I thought I might die, just from not seeing all of you, just from being so far from home."

"Oh, Wally," Mom said, and she walked back to him, bent and kissed his cheek and then held her face next to his. "This is all better than I even dared to hope. I longed to have you back, but I was always afraid. I thought you might come home angry, or broken. I hardly dared to think that you would be a better man than ever."

Wally stood and took his mother into his arms once again. And life did seem as good as his dream. He couldn't imagine that he would ever be happier.

He was still hugging his mother when he heard the front door open. "Dad's home," Beverly said.

Wally was surprised by the twinge of fear he felt. He wanted to see his dad, but he also felt that this was the moment when he had to account for himself. His dad had always asked plenty of him, and that no longer bothered Wally, but he didn't want to be a disappointment.

Wally turned toward the kitchen door. By then he heard his dad call, "Bea, I'm home."

Wally pushed the kitchen door open, stepped into the dark dining room. Dad had turned the light on in the entry. As he walked into the living room and turned, Wally could see his face. "It's me, Dad. Wally."

Wally saw his father stop, take in air. He nodded. "I saw your duffel bag," was all he said.

The two stepped toward each other, and Dad was the first to spread his arms wide. He took Wally in. Wally remembered the Old Spice smell of him, felt the wool of his suit coat, remembered that too. "Oh, Son," he said, and he began to cry—audibly.

"I took the bus up here. I just wanted to walk in."

"Sure. I understand."

Wally took a long breath and then he said it. "I love you, Dad."

"I love you too, Son. Welcome home."

But now what? Wally stepped back. He had things he wanted to say, but he couldn't think of them now. "I've been here a little while. I've been talking to Mom and the girls. If you have a minute, I'd like to talk to you alone."

"Sure."

"Could we go into your office?"

Dad laughed, and both of them knew why. So many times Dad had called Wally there, and it had always been Dad who had wanted to "talk."

Wally turned and saw that his mother was standing in the kitchen door, the girls right behind her. "You two go ahead," she said. "We'll finish getting supper ready."

Dad led the way, stepped into his office, and flipped on the light. He was wearing a navy blue suit, almost black, with a blue tie, only slightly lighter. It was all the usual uniform, but Dad looked older, a little heavier, and somehow different in a way that Wally couldn't put his finger on. Some harshness in his face seemed gone. Either that or it had never been there, except in Wally's mind.

"So what's it going to be like not to be stake president?"

Dad had told him on the phone that his release was coming up soon.

"Life should be a lot easier," Dad said, but he didn't sound convincing. He had pulled a white handkerchief from his pocket, and he was wiping his eyes, his cheeks.

"I'll bet you'll miss it."

"In some ways, sure."

"You've been a great stake president, Dad. Everyone in Sugar House loves you. You'll always have that to hold onto."

"Well, I don't know. It's always a little more complicated than that. I've offended some folks along the way. I'm a little too set in my ways—as you used to point out to me—and some people will probably be more than happy to see me released."

"I don't know, Dad, but I doubt it. People always knew your heart was in the right place."

"You're a fine one to say that. You questioned my motives more than anyone." He laughed, and then he added, "No. I take that back. LaRue has outdone even you."

Wally sat down on the straight-back chair—one of two across from his father. Dad took his familiar seat behind the desk. But he leaned back, seemed more relaxed than he ever used to.

"Wally, this is as fine a moment as I think I've known in this life. It's like . . ."

"The prodigal son coming home?"

"Well, you read my mind. That is what I was going to say. But you never caused so much trouble as all that. You were just—"

"No, Dad. I like the comparison. Mom's in there cooking up a fatted calf."

"Or a meat loaf, anyway."

But this was not what Wally wanted, just to joke everything away. "Dad," he said, "there's something you need to know."

"What's that?"

"Right after I got taken prisoner, we had to make that march in the Bataan Peninsula."

"The death march."

"Well, yes. That's what everyone calls it back here, but we didn't have a name for it—and I don't suppose we would have chosen that one."

"I'm sure you wouldn't."

"But right from the beginning I knew I was in big trouble—the biggest trouble of my life—and it was going to take more power than I had. You know me. I hadn't been much of one to stick with things."

"But I was harder on you about that than I needed to be. I've often thought about that whole business with the track team and wished I hadn't said some of those things to you."

"I'm not sure about that. You had me pegged about right. But when that march started, I knew I didn't have the strength to do what I *had* to do, just to stay alive, so that's when I started to ask the Lord for help. What was strange, though—I prayed to God but I would think of you. After all the complaining I did about you being too hard on me, the first time I was really up against it in my life, I knew that I had to turn to you to survive." Wally leaned forward, his elbows on his knees. Tears began to drip from his cheeks onto the carpet.

"Not to me, Wally. You turned to God." But Dad was crying too.

"I know. But you're the one who always taught me to do that, and it felt like I was turning to you. And then later, when I came close to dying—more than once—you won't believe what I would think about."

Dad shook his head. "I don't know. What?"

"Those talks you used to give us. You'd tell us about our forefathers, how strong and noble they were, and how we had to live up to our heritage. And I'd say to myself, 'I'm a Thomas and a Snow. We're people who keep on going, no matter what kind of test we have to face.'"

"Did that help, to think that?"

Wally was crying too hard to talk. He waited, cleared his throat, and then he said, "It got me through, Dad. You got me through. I thought about you and Mom, and about our family, and I thought about your strength and all the things you believe in—everything you and Mom taught us—and I made myself keep living when it would have been a lot easier to die."

Tears were running down President Thomas's cheeks, but he let them run, let them drip onto the lapels of his suit coat, darkening into little spots. "I told your mother a thousand times: When that boy gets tested, he'll show what he's made of. I believed that, all through this thing."

"Did you, Dad? Really?"

"You bet I did."

"I wouldn't have guessed that. I thought you'd be surprised if I made it." And the idea that his dad had believed in him all along was almost more than Wally could accept. He put his hands over his face, cried against them.

Dad waited for a time, got control of his own voice, and then said, "Wally, one of the great sorrows of my life is that I knew, all the while you were gone, that I had made you feel that way—that I expected the worst from you. I never should have let you leave this house with so much of my doubt hanging over your head."

"I earned the doubt, Dad. Now, I just want to earn your trust."

Dad got up and walked around the desk, and Wally stood up too. "You have my trust, Son. But you didn't have to earn my love. It should have come without any strings attached. I regret that I didn't show you that."

President Thomas wrapped his big arms around Wally again. The two of them clung to each other and cried. And Wally knew he was home.

6

It was November, and Bobbi Thomas was being transferred back to her earlier assignment in the naval hospital at Pearl Harbor. The *Charity* had carried its load of POWs to Seattle, as it turned out, but it was not returning to Japan as she had thought it might. Hawaii was still receiving war casualties from all around the Pacific, many of whom were recovering from mutilating burns, and she was being returned to where the navy said she was most needed. She would head up the burn ward where she had once been a raw beginner in the Nurse's Corp.

Bobbi flew from Seattle to Hawaii with a crew that was shuttling seriously wounded patients to hospitals on the mainland. Her hope was that the Pearl Harbor hospital would be more or less emptied out during the next couple of months and she would be able to obtain her release. But if she had to stay in the navy a little longer, at least she took solace in the idea that she would be back with Afton and all her friends in Honolulu. What she learned on arrival, however, was that Afton had received her discharge just a few days before. She had been able to give her commanding officer a specific date for her planned marriage, so the navy had processed her papers, and now she was a civilian. What she had chosen to do first was to take a trip home. She was going to spend a couple of weeks back in Arizona, and when she returned, she and Sam were finally going to be married—in early December.

The *Charity* was being sent to the Philippines, where it would be anchored and then function as a station hospital. The ship wouldn't receive many burn victims now, nor many surgeries, so Kate Calder had been discharged and was heading back to Massachusetts. The last night before Bobbi and Kate had separated, they had had a long talk about their futures. Bobbi had tried to explain her complicated feelings about David. She had made her choice, had decided to marry Richard before she had known that David had died. But it was David's death that was filling her thoughts now, taking first claim on her emotions. And that felt wrong, as though she were being untrue to Richard.

"Bobbi," Kate had told her, "David was a wonderful friend. But he was more of a pen pal than a prospective husband. You always knew that. It's okay to miss him. Just don't let that interfere with your love for Richard."

"I'm trying not to," Bobbi told her, "but I doubt that I'll ever know anyone like David again. I'm afraid I'll look for David in Richard and never find him there."

"Bobbi, don't do that to yourself. You sound like a spoiled little girl. Just consider yourself lucky. You've had three different men want to marry you. That's something I may never experience. I had little hope for companionship in my life before the war created a shortage of men. What can I expect now?"

"It won't be that way, Kate. When you find a guy, he'll be something special. That's the only kind of man who'll have the confidence to marry you."

"You make me sound *formidable*. And I don't think that's what most men have in mind. I'll tell you this: if someone like Richard were in love with me, I wouldn't complain about anything."

During her hours on the airplane on her way to Hawaii, Bobbi had a chance to think about that. She told herself that Kate was exactly right. But when she tried to raise her own spirits, to feel lighter inside, she felt only the hollowness she had been living with since she had learned that David had died.

At church the first Sunday back in Honolulu, Bobbi had fun saying hello to so many of her old friends. And then after sacrament meeting she and Sam walked out together and strolled toward her bus stop. "What day are you getting married?" Bobbi asked him.

"December seventh," he told her. "I know that sounds a little strange, but it's a Friday, and that was the best day for us. We didn't choose it because of Pearl Harbor. But maybe there will be another disaster. Maybe she won't come back."

"Sam, you can't be serious. Of course she'll come back." Bobbi stopped on the sidewalk, turned and looked at him, touched his arm. He was wearing a white shirt and a dark brown tie. He looked like the missionary he had once been.

"I don't know that, Bobbi. Her parents will work on her the whole time. They still don't want her to marry me."

"They won't change her mind. They might have a year or two ago, but not now."

"Maybe." Sam began to walk again, slowly. "Or maybe at home, everything will seem different. They'll tell her that she'll have brown babies, that our children will have trouble. You know all the things they'll say."

"Sure, I do. But it won't matter. Afton isn't the little girl who came over here. She knows what she wants now."

"I hope you're right."

Sam had a delicate quality that Bobbi loved—a gentle voice, higher pitched than one would suspect, and kindly eyes, long eyelashes. He was not as massive as some of the Hawaiian men, but he was strong and good, and he could offer Afton the things she needed. He had a good job as a grocery store manager, and he had a head for business. Bobbi had a feeling he would own his own store someday and do very well with it. But the important thing was, he was crazy about Afton, treated her as though she were made of porcelain. There was also an evenness about him, a reliability, that would give Afton a stability that didn't come naturally to her.

"I got a letter from her," Sam said. "She promised she would be back. But she talked about her home and how much she liked being there. That worries me. What if she comes back and then misses the mainland?"

"She'll be happy here, Sam. And I'll tell you something else. Someday her parents are going to see those brown, beautiful babies you're going to have—even if it's just in a snapshot—and they'll fall in love. They'll be here any time they can. And you'll go there. I wish the Storys would come over and meet you now; they'd change their minds in five minutes."

"I don't know. Haoles only like Hawaiians when we stay in our place. We're supposed to wear grass skirts and play the ukulele. But we're not adults to them; we're children."

"I know that's how it's been. But the war has changed some things. People have gotten to know each other better. Some of those old prejudices are breaking down."

"Maybe. But everything changes too slow. I'm not as patient as my parents. I get angry when I see the way *my* people look at us."

"But I'm glad it hasn't stopped you—either one of you. You're two of best people I know. You *should* be together."

"Thank you, Bobbi. I wish we could always be close to you—you and Richard. I like him, too. He doesn't say very much, but he says things that are worth saying. I like that."

"Then how can you love Afton? She says *everything* she thinks."

"I know. And I like that too. There are all kinds of people. We can love them for different reasons."

"I'm glad you said that, Sam. That's good for me to think about."

Bobbi rode the bus back to Pearl Harbor. Fortunately, the number of personnel at the hospital was dropping and she had a room of her own at the nurses' quarters. But that was not so great at the moment. It was a lonely Sunday evening, and she was missing everyone. The war was over, and she wanted to go home to her family. She wanted to see Richard, to find out what would happen inside herself when she could spend some time with him again. She also missed Afton, and Kate. And tonight she missed Gene again, the way she did from time to time. She didn't want to think about David, knowing she should start to control those thoughts, but she missed him, too.

So Bobbi did what she always did when life got a little too much for her. She went to bed early and escaped into a long night of sleep. And she awoke to a beautiful morning that didn't feel quite so empty. Work was not easy because the remaining patients in her ward were severely burned, and often depressed, but at least the crisis days were over, the over-crowding in the ward, the long hours. And that night, when she finished her shift, she found a letter from Richard waiting for her.

Bobbi opened the letter with some hesitancy. His letters had been so awkward lately, as though he didn't want to pre-sume anything, was tiptoeing around their difficulties. But this letter was surprising:

Dear Bobbi,

I talked to your mother today. She told me about David Stinson. I'm sure this is a difficult time for you. I hope you're doing all right. I'm not sure what to say about it, except that I'm sorry. I know that at least in some ways he was a man more suited to you than I am, and maybe that will always be a problem between us. But that's not the most important thing right now. He was someone you cared for, and he's been taken, and I'm very sorry.

Bobbi, I don't know what to do. I don't like what's happened between us, and I'm afraid you need some time to deal with this loss. But I've needed to make some decisions, and I've done that now. You don't have to decide about me right away, but I want one thing to be clear in your mind: I still want to marry you. I know I haven't sounded that way lately, but these last few weeks, feeling like you've slipped away from me, have told me that I'd better speak up for what I want or lose you forever. Maybe David would have turned out to be your first choice, and that bothers me more than I like to admit, but it doesn't change the fact that my life will never be what I want it to be if I can't have you.

Bobbi, at one time it seemed that you had chosen me even though David was still available. What I fear is that I fouled everything up between us. I know the troubles I've been going through have had a lot to do with that. But there were things going on in my mind that I didn't know how to deal with. Something happened to me in the war—something that has been bothering me and making me act a little strange. It happened after my ship went down in the Leyte Gulf. But that's all I want to say. I just can't tell you anything else about it. I'm sorry about that, but I don't want to think about it or talk about it ever again. I know you think that isn't the right approach, but it's what I have to do. That's not such a negative thing as you might think, because I've made up my mind that I have to move ahead and put all that behind me. I've talked to some friends who were there, and we all feel the same way. A guy can come home from the war and worry about certain things the rest of his life, maybe have some real psychological problems, but he can also choose to let all that go and get on with his life. He just has to be a man about it. And that's what I've decided to do.

Here's one of the things I've made up my mind about. Your dad has offered me a swell job, a "position," you might say. It's just too good to pass up. I know I talked a lot about going back to college, but I have to tell you, the things I wanted to do in college weren't really going to get me anywhere. A lot of what I wanted to study was stuff that won't solve any problems— not for me, and sure as heck not for the world. What I'm a lot better off doing, I think, is getting on with my life, making a good living, and being in a position to get married and start a family. A good, busy life will solve more personal problems than anything.

Your dad isn't making my position contingent on you marrying me. He says he needs people like me, and he's willing to hire me whether things ever *work out between us. All the same, that could get real awkward, I'm sure, so I guess we could cross that bridge when it comes, but I doubt I'd stick around if that turned out to be a problem. But what I'm trying to say is, I would like to think we're still engaged. I would hope we could get married soon after you are discharged. My hands are not too bad, so the navy is about to let me go, and I just think it's time to be happy the war is over, happy I found someone like you, and not so dreary as I've been sometimes lately.*

Bobbi, I haven't said the most important thing. I love you. I've never known a girl I like a tenth as much. When I think about you and remember the closeness I've felt with you, I just want to grab you in my arms and hold onto you forever. I feel like a real idiot for letting other things get in the way—a lot of things that aren't as important as they seemed at the time. I'm going to be healthy now. I'm choosing to get on with things, and you're the one I want to share the rest of my life with. I got feeling sorry for myself when I first heard about David, and then, when it seemed like I had lost you, I told myself I was going to fight for you. Maybe I've said all the wrong things, and you're about to rip this letter up and throw it away, but I don't want to give up without your knowing that I love you and want to marry you, and without promising that I'll do everything I can to make you happy. I know I need to talk more, and express myself, and I think you can teach me how. Or at least I'll try.

So anyway, think about all this. And then come home. If our engagement is over, and you aren't interested in me now, just tell me that, but if you think we can still work things out, just know that I'm ready on my end. This is the worst letter I've ever written in my life, and it doesn't even make a lot of sense to me, but I'm going to send it anyway, because I'd rather try to say what I'm thinking about this than keep my mouth shut, the way I usually do. So just let me say it one more time. I love you and I still want to marry you, and I'm hoping that you still feel something for me. Please write back and give me some idea what you're thinking about all this.

Love,
Richard

Bobbi felt like crying and laughing, and a couple of times she had even felt the impulse Richard had talked about: to tear the letter up. But she was touched. None of this even sounded

like Richard, but he was trying so hard to do what she kept asking of him—to say what he really thought. The only trouble
was, the heart of the letter was a defense of his desire never to
tell her the very things that would be hiding away in his heart
and head forever. How could that work? Still, after she read the
letter a second time, she found herself happier than she had
been the past few weeks, happy to be loved, and happy that he
would say it with such strength. And happy that he had made
up his mind to fight for her.

She was also worried. What bothered her most was that
she saw her father at work, trying to make sure the two of them
ended up together, still building his little industrial kingdom
and placing his sons and sons-in-law where he wanted them.
Bobbi wasn't sure that was good at all. She thought Richard
really ought go back to college and do the things he had told
her he wanted to do. Somehow, Richard just didn't seem like a
businessman.

Bobbi waited a couple of days so she could think about
everything before she wrote back. Her letter must have
sounded as reticent as some of Richard's had sounded in the
past. She told him that she, too, still considered herself
engaged to Richard, but she wanted to spend some time with
him again when she got back—and just "let their love rebuild,"
whatever that meant. She also warned him. He should do with
his life what he wanted to do, not let her father make his decisions for him. What she didn't tell him was that she had her
answer, that she had prayed and gotten a response. She had
meant to do that, to tell him, but the words wouldn't come. She
needed to see him and find out what she felt when she did.
Even God should understand that.

* * *

Afton returned from Arizona after Thanksgiving, and the
week after that, she and Sam were married in the temple in
Laie. That evening the Nuanunus put on a luau reception in
their backyard, and most of the members of the Waikiki ward

came, along with other friends and neighbors. Bobbi loved the atmosphere, and she was pleased to see Afton so happy. Bobbi and Afton had had a couple of long talks that week, and Afton really was resolved now. Her time at home had been good for her. Her parents had not been willing to come to the wedding, and probably were not able, but they had softened a little as they had listened to Afton. She felt now that she could take her husband home to Mesa someday and that her family would relent even more once they got to know Sam. But she had also found the desert less appealing now after these years in Hawaii, and she had missed Sam every minute. There was no doubt in her mind that she was doing the right thing.

"I thought I was going home," she told Bobbi, "but this is my home now. What I love most is here. I feel more Hawaiian than haole."

"Who would have thunk it?" Bobbi said, and she laughed. "Just think of us when we first got here."

"Thank heavens for the war," Afton said, but then she added quickly, "No, I shouldn't even joke about that. But it is strange how such good things can come from a bad time. And a lot of good things did come out of the war."

Bobbi hated to admit it, but she felt the same way. And she was reminded of the thought at the reception. Afton, in her simple wedding dress—shapely and not at all like a muumuu—got up before everyone and danced the hula with her friends. And she did it very well. If the hula was supposed to speak to a man, it was obviously saying volumes to Sam, who looked as happy as anyone Bobbi could imagine. Bobbi remembered the day so long ago when she and Afton had tried to do the hula, and Bobbi had felt so self-conscious. That had been the last time she had tried it, but Afton had embraced the dance along with everything else she loved about Hawaii. Now, among the people in their aloha shirts, their muumuus and leis, she seemed to fit in as well as anyone.

Bobbi was watching Afton and the others when Sister

Nuanunu approached her. "I told you that night, way back two years ago, that these two were watching each other, didn't I? Now look what's happened." Sister Nuanunu laughed in her big, rich voice.

"Which one is more Hawaiian, Sam or Afton?" Bobbi asked.

"Oh, Afton is, to be sure. My Sam, he spent too much time with the haoles. He's a store manager now, a man of business. But dear Afton, she's more my child than Sam is. She's as natural as our flowers. And just as pretty."

Bobbi thought that was true. Afton wasn't deep, but she was clear, like the streams in Hawaii. And she was good. She would love Sam, and she would never hold anything back.

"Bobbi, when do you and Brother Hammond get married?"

"I don't know, Sister Nuanunu. Nothing's settled."

"What do you mean?"

Bobbi didn't want to get into all that. Sister Nuanunu had a way of asking more questions than Bobbi felt comfortable answering. "We need to see each other again and spend some time together—make sure we know how we feel. We've never really had a chance to do that."

"You're talking foolishness. You know that, don't you?"

"What's so foolish?"

"This man is beautiful. And he's very kind. You are beautiful—and lovely in your heart. So what's to think about?"

"I don't know whether we're enough alike. Our personalities are just so different."

Sister Nuanunu leaned her head back and laughed. She was wearing a wonderful muumuu, with big purple flowers and green leaves, and she had flowers in her hair—an orchid and some plumeria. She was a big woman, and beautiful herself.

"Don't laugh at me," Bobbi said. "You know how I am. You told me yourself—I think about things too much."

"Yes. But I thought by now you might learn something

from us. You're still a haole, through and through. You tell me now, what's so different about you and Brother Hammond?"

Bobbi tried to think what she could say. "Brother Hammond is a very private person, Sister Nuanunu—not at all like you."

But Sister Nuanunu was laughing again.

"What's so funny about that?"

"Because that's just how you are. You're both haoles, down to your toes. You're not too different—you're too much alike."

"That's not really true. When I'm with him, I open up. I tell him how I feel about things. He doesn't like to do that."

"No. No, Bobbi. You try to understand yourself. You think about it, try to say it. And it takes you forever because you use so many words. But you're not open—not really. You don't let yourself feel, and then do something about it. You don't listen to your heart. You have to *consider* everything, think about it for a year or two, take one little step at a time. You must be careful or God will turn you into a pillar of salt. You spend your whole life looking behind you."

"But a person has to make wise decisions."

"Sometimes. And sometimes a person has to *know*—and then do something."

That sounded a little like Richard's letter, and the idea startled her. Maybe that's what Richard was trying to do, and she was the one being reticent now, the one holding back.

"Look at me, sweetheart." Bobbi turned and looked straight into Sister Nuanunu's eyes. "I'm going to ask you a question."

"All right."

"What's better—happiness or unhappiness?"

"Happiness."

"Ah, you say that, like it's easy. But then you *consider* when the choice comes. When a beautiful man—a good man—wants to marry you, it's time to say yes. It's time to be happy. There's nothing to think about."

That sounded right in Sister Nuanunu's mouth, but what

about all the terrible marriages Bobbi had seen? Was it really that simple? "But if two people are not right for each other—beautiful or not—they can make each other very unhappy."

"No. That's more haole talk. Two good people can choose to make each other happy. They don't have to think so much about themselves all the time. They don't have to think about being happy. They can *be* happy. The worst silliness I can think of is to be loved by a good man, a fine man, and to turn him down because you think too much."

"Sister Nuanunu, there was another man. Someone I liked very much. He wasn't a member of the Church, but he was a good man. But he was killed in the war. I keep wondering whether he wasn't more the kind of man I should have married."

"Bobbi, you make no sense at all sometimes. *Most* of the time."

"But won't I always—"

"Bobbi, listen to me. Can you marry this man, the one who is dead?"

"No."

"Can you marry Brother Hammond, this beautiful and good man?"

"Yes."

"Okay. Now you know your answer."

Bobbi laughed. "I'm sure that's right," she said. "And I'll admit something else to you. I feel almost sure that God feels the same way—that he wants me to marry Richard."

"No question about that. I see God in all of this. He sent you here, sent Brother Hammond here, to find each other."

"Maybe so. It seems so, doesn't it?"

"It is so."

Bobbi felt happier. And she found herself moving about the party, talking with people, not dancing but letting the music fill her, the laughter. And she was delighted when she saw Ishi and Daniel arrive, with Lily and David. She had seen Daniel at church on Sunday, but she hadn't had much chance to talk to him, and so she went to the Aokis as soon as she spotted them.

Ishi had told Bobbi that Daniel was self-conscious about his limp, but now, as Bobbi watched him walk across the lawn, she could barely detect it. She was not sure she would have noticed, had she not known. "Ishi, Daniel," Bobbi called, but it was Lily and David who heard her, and they both ran toward her. She knelt and grabbed them, each in one arm. "You little sweethearts," she said. "It's so good to see you."

"Why haven't you come to see us yet?" Lily asked. She was wearing a white dress, and her black hair, glistening in the sun, fell down over her shoulders, lush and beautiful.

"Oh, I don't know. I will." But she stood then, and said to Ishi, "I'm not sure you want me popping in the way I used to. Things are a little different with a *man* around the house."

Ishi laughed. "Don't mind him," she said. "He doesn't get in the way much."

"How are you doing, Daniel?" Bobbi asked. "Is it a little strange to be home?"

He nodded, but the question seemed to catch him off guard. He was so much more formal than his wife. "A little, I suppose," he said. "But it's very nice, as you can imagine."

Now it was Bobbi who hardly knew how to react. "You can't imagine how often we've talked about this time, when you would come home. It's so good to see all four of you together."

He nodded again, even bowed just a little, seeming more Japanese than Ishi ever did.

"Have you gone back to work at the bank?" Bobbi asked.

"No. I haven't."

"Oh, Bobbi, it's so awful what they did. They told him that his position no longer exists."

Bobbi looked at Daniel, saw the tension in his face, and knew that he didn't want to talk about this, but still she said, "Oh, Daniel, that's so unfair. You're a hero. You've received all those medals. How could they do that to you?"

"It will all work out," he said. "I'll find something else." He looked off across the lawn. "I'll get us something to drink. Come with me, kids. You can help me." He walked away, and Lily and David followed.

As soon as he was gone, Bobbi said, "Ishi, I'm sorry. I said the wrong thing, didn't I?"

"No, not really. It's very hard for him. He took the train across the mainland before he sailed back here, and people called him 'Jap,' wouldn't let him eat in some of the restaurants. He had his uniform on, with all his ribbons, and they still asked him to leave. Then he gets home, and he can't find a job. He feels it as a shame to him—and to all our family. He doesn't blame anyone. He's just embarrassed to say he doesn't have work."

"But has it been nice for the kids to have him back?"

"It will be. He's very kind to them, very tender. But they don't really know him now, and he doesn't know them. He can't seem to let loose with them yet. He's more reserved now than he used to be, and I'm not sure why."

"When he gets a job and gets back into things, he'll be himself again. Don't you think?"

"Yes. I think so. I hope so."

"Is he in pain?"

"I don't know. He says he isn't. But he doesn't want to admit anything. When I ask him about the battles and what he did, he only tells me about the places he saw and the friends he made, not what happened to him."

"So many of the men are like that. But he'll tell you when he's ready. I wouldn't worry too much about it. Sister Nuanunu has just been telling me that we have to *choose* to be happy and not worry about everything so much."

"She's been telling you that for as long as I've known you," Ishi said, "and you haven't listened yet."

"That's not true. I always listen. I just can't do it."

"That's the same for me."

"I think we have to try this time, Ishi. We got what we wanted, and now we need to be thankful for it."

"I am, Bobbi. I am. At night, I wake up and hear him breathing next to me—snoring sometimes—and I touch him with my hand or foot just to be sure he's really there. I knew he would have to make some adjustments when he got back. I can live with anything like that as long as I have him with me. And he has been lovely with me, Bobbi. He's such a tender man."

Bobbi did like to think of that, of having Richard close to her. Maybe this time she would not only listen to Sister Nuanunu; she would also learn. She would actually try to be a little more Hawaiian.

7

Alex Thomas was sitting in front of the little branch of Church members that had gathered in a Frankfurt *Gasthaus* for sacrament meeting. It was December 9, 1945, and he had been set apart as a member of the branch presidency along with a young brother named Theodor Studdert. This was only Alex's second time to conduct the meeting, but he wasn't nervous about that. The branch was small, with only about thirty people usually attending, and by now Alex was well acquainted with everyone. The congregation sang *"Sehet Ihr Völker"*—"Hark, All Ye Nations!"—a favorite hymn. After the opening prayer, Alex told the members, "We still have great need for blankets and coats, with the weather so cold. If you have old coats that need mending, we have members in the branch who would be happy to do what they can to repair them. I was able to get several spools of thread." He smiled. "It's not always in the best colors, but it will still help."

Sister Hirschberg, seated at a table near the front, asked, "Where should we bring these coats, if we have something?"

"You could bring them here next week," Alex said.

But President Meis was quick to say, "I'll stop by your apartment, Sister Hirschberg, perhaps even later today. We need coats immediately. There are people who are not with us today because they have nothing. Children's coats are especially in short supply."

"Come today then," Sister Hirschberg said, and two others raised their hands, saying they would have something if someone came.

"I was also able to secure a few blankets from the military base," Alex said. "If you are short of bedding—or if you know of anyone in the branch who is—please let me know today. I'll see what I can do to obtain more. I have no way to get feather ticks, but these army blankets might help someone." Alex waited and looked about, but no one admitted to a need. He knew they very well might talk to him afterward, however. "Brothers and sisters, we all know that food will be in short supply throughout the winter and spring. The rations you receive will keep you from starving—but they'll do little more than that. I'll bring anything I can get. In fact, today I have a bag of rice. If you can carry a little in a pocket or a purse, there isn't much, but perhaps enough for a meal or two for each of you."

Alex saw the delight on the faces of the people. He knew that having rice, as a change from the rationed food they received from the American food stations, would be more than welcome. He wasn't supposed to carry food off the base, but he watched American soldiers waste their meals every day, dump what they didn't like into garbage cans. He couldn't imagine that it was a sin to bring, from time to time, a bag or can of food to hungry people.

"We will now sing 'Näher, Mein Gott, zu dir,' after which we will partake of the sacrament." The branch only had two hymnals, one of which the music conductor used, so the best practice was to stay with familiar hymns, ones the members could remember.

Alex sat down on a wooden chair next to President Meis. Off to the left one of the Gasthaus tables had been set up for the sacrament. Sister Walter had donated a linen tablecloth for that purpose, even though the cloth might have bought her a good deal of food on the black market. Rudi Fichte, the only young man in the branch who held the Aaronic Priesthood, broke the bread, along with Brother Studdert. The members didn't exactly sound like a choir, but they sang with full voice and with a conviction Alex didn't remember hearing back in his home ward. It seemed that the German members felt "nearer to God" in these hard times than they ever had before. After the hymn, and after Rudi blessed the bread, Brother Studdert and Rudi also passed it to the members, who were seated at the heavy, dark-stained restaurant tables. There was still no electric power in the building, and with a cover of clouds outside, the windows didn't provide much light. The members sat in shadows, bundled up, their faces hard to see.

As the bread was still being passed, Alex saw a young man enter the *Gasthaus* and slip into a seat at a back table, close to the windows. He was dressed in a heavy wool coat that had seen a great deal of wear. He took off a battered cap, and a cluster of hair flopped onto his forehead. Alex suspected that the man had heard the singing and come in off the street. It was not uncommon for that to happen. Many people lived in the streets these days, and the singing—or even just the chance to get inside, out of the cold—often attracted strangers. Even though the branch couldn't afford to heat the building as much as might have been comfortable, members would contribute a few lumps of coal when they could, or a little kindling, and that was enough to take the chill off the room.

Alex took the bread when it was offered to him. It was grainy, dark and rich, and to Alex it symbolized the body of Christ as he had always known it in Germany—as something more substantial, even more wholesome than the fluffy white bread he had always received in his Salt Lake ward. He chewed this bread and tried to concentrate on the meaning of the sacrament. He was working hard these days to feel the Spirit. What he had found most meaningful, so far, was working with the members, visiting them in their homes—or shelters—and bringing them what help he could. The less he thought about the war, and the more he concentrated on serving people, the better he felt about his life.

And yet, the language of the prayer was difficult for Alex. He tried to concentrate on Christ's sacrifice, the idea of it, but if he wasn't careful the references to Christ's blood and his broken body brought pictures to his mind—pictures he had been trying hard to forget. Today, an image forced its way into his consciousness, a memory that had come back to him many times: it was the face of a German boy lying in a glaring white field of snow. Alex had seen the boy in the Ardennes somewhere, after the battle for Foy. The young soldier had stepped on a land mine, probably one placed by his own army. He had bled to death, and the dark stain of his blood had saturated the snow in a half circle around him. The boy had been thrown from the explosion, tossed into the whiteness, without his legs. He had lain on his back and bled the snow red, his arms spread wide, like a cross. It was almost artistic, the picture, the way it would return to Alex now, probably made symmetrical, perfect, by his memory. This particular broken body was only one of hundreds that he had seen in the Ardennes, and Alex had paid little attention—or at least thought he had. It was not until the war was over and he had returned to his brothers and sisters in Frankfurt that Alex first thought of it again: this Christlike boy, dead by sacrifice—but an enemy.

Now that boy was back, once again asserting himself into Alex's mind, as though waiting to be accounted for. At the time, Alex had experienced the kind of relief and satisfaction a soldier feels in knowing that a body on the ground is one of "them," but the sacrament prayer didn't allow for that interpretation. So Alex mourned the loss of the boy, remembered his peaceful blue-glazed face, and he wondered whether he needed to recall all the boys, one at a time, and mourn for each one. If he could do that, complete the whole process, find every one of the images of mutilation hiding in his head, maybe he could finally take the sacrament and not feel unworthy. But he actually feared that he might go crazy if he kept allowing these lives back into his mind, and he knew the opposite approach was the only one that worked. He had to rid his mind of them and think about better things, the future.

As *Bruder* Studdert and *Bruder* Fichte passed the water, Alex watched, kept his eyes open, tried not to see anything but the members in front of him. For the first time he looked carefully at the young man at the back, the one who had come in late. The boy was looking at Alex, leaning forward, as though he were straining to see better. And then he turned his head a little, and the light from the window made a clear silhouette. Alex knew the profile, he thought, was even certain for a moment—but then he doubted himself. It couldn't be. It was too good to be true.

Alex watched, stared, and then the clouds moved, released a little more light. Alex saw the boy more clearly again, and he saw a look of recognition on his face. The two had reached certainty at the same moment, and Alex felt a kind of shock go through him. It *was* Peter. It really was.

Alex's impulse was to jump up and run to him, but he couldn't make a scene and interrupt the sacrament. He nodded at Peter, smiled, tried to show that he recognized him, and he saw the elation in Peter's face. But he also saw how tattered and weary he looked. He wondered what the boy had been through since he had seen him last. And then the other realization struck Alex: Peter didn't know. He didn't know that Alex and Anna were married, didn't know about his nephew— probably didn't even know his family was alive.

Alex watched Peter take the little glass cup. He shut his eyes and drank, carefully, obviously well aware of what he was doing. Alex wondered how long it had been since Peter had had this chance to renew his covenant.

When everyone had received the water, the priesthood brothers returned the trays, covered them with the linen tablecloth, and walked back to their seats. Alex stood again. "Brothers and Sisters," he said, but he was shaking. He took a long breath and tried to calm himself before he said, "Some of you remember the Stoltzes, who were members of the branch before the war. Heinrich Stoltz was in our branch presidency. What I have just realized is that Peter Stoltz has come in and is sitting in the back of the room."

There was a little stir as the members looked around at Peter. Some knew him, greeted him out loud, and they were still smiling when they turned back to look toward Alex again.

What Alex had in mind was to tell Peter—and the congregation—about the Stoltz family, but his voice cut off, and he stood there silent. President Meis took that chance to stand alongside Alex and say, "Peter, would you like to come forward and greet the members, perhaps bear your testimony?"

Alex could see Peter hesitate, but then he stood and walked forward. Before he turned toward the members, he grasped President Meis, hugged him, and then took hold of Alex. Alex wanted to tell him so many things, but how could he put it all in a simple greeting? So he only said, "Peter, welcome."

Peter turned then, still holding his cap in his hand. "I'm happy I found you," he said. "I've been in Frankfurt for a few days, and I've asked all around where your meetings were held. It was only this morning that I found someone who knew." He hesitated, and Alex watched his shoulders rise as he took a deep breath. "I've been through some hard things since I left Frankfurt with my family. Sometimes I thought God didn't care about me. But I can testify to you that he didn't forget me— even when I had given up on him." He looked toward the floor and breathed deeply. "It's so good to see you again. I know only a few of you, but it's the closest I've felt to home in many years. I've lost touch with my family. I don't know where they are. Maybe someone here knows something. It's what I hope. It's why I came to Frankfurt."

Now Peter had lost his voice. He didn't close his little

speech. He took a first step to return to his seat, but President Meis grabbed his arm and pulled him back. He put his arm around Peter's shoulders and thanked him, told him, "We do know a good deal, Peter." Then he looked at the members. "I want *Bruder* Thomas to take a few minutes, and I want him to tell Peter, and all of you, some wonderful things. This is a great blessing, what has happened here today, and I want all of you to know about it."

Peter turned toward Alex, looking curious. Then he slipped to a front table and sat down. Alex looked down at Peter. He thought he was under control until he tried to speak, but it was all he could do to get the words out. "First," he said, "Peter needs to know that his family is fine. His mother and father and sister are in London, as many of you know, and they are doing very well." He nodded to Peter. "I'll help you contact them."

Tears were running down Peter's cheeks now. He nodded back to Alex.

"But I'm afraid I'm going to shock Peter with what I wish to tell him next. Many of you know—but Peter doesn't—that I'm now his brother-in-law."

Peter's head moved backward, as though he had taken a little push against his chin.

"I married Anna, Peter, and we have a little boy. Your nephew. His name is Eugene."

Peter's eyes widened.

"Peter, I've been searching for you since the war ended. I've been in prisons and displaced-person camps all over Germany. I've written letters, inquired through the Red Cross, done everything I could to locate you. Your father also came to Germany while the war was still going on, and he searched for you, put his life in grave danger trying to find you. When he and your mother and Anna learn that you're here and in good health, they'll be brought back to life. It's what they have prayed for night and day since you were separated from them at the French border a year and a half ago."

Alex looked away from Peter, at the little congregation. "Brothers and Sisters, I know that many of you lost your loved ones. I don't know why some of us were saved and brought back to our families, and others weren't. But I do feel a witness today that God has had a hand in Peter's return. I don't know where he has been, and maybe on another occasion, he will want to talk to us about that." Alex saw Peter look down, and he wondered—maybe that was not a story Peter wanted to tell. "But whether we ever know that story or not, what we do know is that Peter has come back to us with a knowledge that God loves him. I suspect that everyone in this room has felt abandoned at times during the war, but Peter has told us the truth. God was with him even when he thought he was alone. That's the message we must all remember."

Alex felt tears spill onto his cheeks. He wiped them away, stopped. After a moment, he said, "Brothers and Sisters, I too felt very far from God during the war, and I've struggled to get his Spirit back. I haven't done very well, and I don't know how I'll feel tomorrow, but at this moment, I feel God with me, with you, and I feel blessed to be here today."

Brother Fichte, Rudi's father, had been asked to speak. Alex apologized for taking so much of his time, and he introduced him. Brother Fichte was a quiet man, not one who liked to stand before a group, but he was also moved by what had happened. He did his best to build on what Alex had said. But his talk seemed rather long. All Alex could think of were the questions he wanted to ask Peter.

When Brother Fichte finally ended his sermon and sat down, Alex announced the closing hymn and prayer, and when the meeting was finally over, he stepped immediately to Peter, took him in his arms again. "You're my brother, Peter," he said. "Can you believe it?"

"I don't understand," Peter was saying. "When did you marry her? How did you find her?"

"I'll tell you. I'll explain everything. But greet the others for a few minutes. I need to share some rice I brought today. Then we'll talk."

"Where are you staying, Peter?" President Meis was asking by then.

"Nowhere. I tried to sleep in the train station, but they sent me away. I've slept in the streets for three nights."

"You'll stay with us tonight—and for as long as you need to," President Meis told him, and Alex saw the relief in Peter's face as he nodded his acceptance.

Alex walked to the corner of the room, near the kitchen door, and he hefted the bag of rice. He carried it to a table and tore the top open. Members lined up, some with open coat pockets, others with hats or satchels, and they accepted their share of the grain. They thanked Alex. "This will help so much," Sister Walter told him. "We have enough to get by, but this will be something extra, something special. My little ones won't be so hungry."

Alex wished he had been able to bring more. He knew how well he ate, and it pained him every day to think how little the members, Germans in general, had to live on.

When the rice was gone, and the room had mostly cleared, Alex went back to Peter, who was waiting at the table where he had sat during most of the meeting. "I'm trying to think whether this can all be true," he told Alex. "I've wondered so long about my family, but I never thought of this—you and Anna. But it was what she always wanted."

"I was in England, in a hospital, when your parents escaped. Anna wrote to my family in America to find out where I was. I was lying in bed one day, and she came walking in—almost the way you did today. We got married before I had to go back to the war. But tell me about you. Where have you been?"

"It isn't so good, what's happened to me." Peter was holding his cap in both hands. He looked down at it. Alex thought of the innocent face he remembered, the boy he had first known in 1938. Behind several days' growth of beard and the tousled hair, that face was still there, but not much of the innocence. Peter was not just older; he looked tired and haggard. Alex wondered what he had been through. "I fought for Germany. I was in the German army."

"We knew that. Your father learned that much. You registered as Peter Stutz, didn't you?"

"You knew that?"

"Your father almost got himself killed finding out. He walked right into the military records office and pretended he was tracking you as a runaway."

"I did run away—finally. But not until almost the end."

"We thought maybe you had. Where did you fight?"

Peter was still staring at his cap. "I didn't fight Americans. I was on the eastern front."

"We knew that much, too, or thought we did. And we knew you had no choice."

Peter took a long look at Alex, as though he wondered whether Alex could mean what he had said. But he didn't ask. "Tell me about my nephew."

"He's six months old, Peter, but I've never seen him. Anna writes me four or five times a week, and she tells me all the things he does. He crawls now, and pulls himself up in his crib. To hear Anna tell it, he's quite the genius. Here—I've got a picture."

He got out his wallet and let Peter look at the lovely little face, so much like his mother's. Peter's tears started again as he looked at it. "How can I let my family know that I'm alive?" he asked.

"We'll send a telegram. I can do that at my base—if not tonight, first thing in the morning."

"Do they want me back, *Bruder* Thomas?"

"Peter, how can you ask that? Of course they want you

back." But Alex understood. He knew the shame Peter had to feel. The last thing any of the Stoltzes had wanted to do was fight for Hitler. "What I want to know is where you've been since the war ended. I've looked everywhere I could think of."

"A family took me in—the Schallers. The father had been killed in the war, so I worked in a mine to provide for them. I wanted to find my family, but I didn't know how—and this family needed my help."

"What brought you here?"

"Frau Schaller got a job with the British army. Once she had a way to look after her family, she told me I had to go look for mine. So I came here. I thought President Meis—or someone here—would know where they were."

"How did you travel?"

"I walked, mostly—and I caught rides when I could. But no one stopped me. The Americans don't care that you come into their zone. They're not like the Russians."

"Have you eaten anything?"

"Not much. Not for a few days. I had food with me . . . but I met so many on the roads who were hungry."

"You gave your food away?"

"Some of it."

"Oh, Peter, you've always had such a good heart. You haven't changed at all."

But Peter looked hard into Alex's eyes. "No. I have changed," he said. "I . . ." But he stopped, didn't explain.

Alex wanted to see what was inside Peter, but his eyes were like panes of dark glass, like mirrors. Alex knew better than anyone what Peter had seen and done. The two of them didn't have to talk about that. "Do you want to go to England?" Alex asked instead.

"Yes. Maybe. But when will my parents come back to Germany?"

"They're not coming back, Peter. My family is trying to arrange for them to move to Utah. They're going to emigrate when they can. That's where Anna and I and the baby will be. That's where you should go, too."

"Would we be welcome there?"

"Yes. Of course. Our family would make you acquainted with everyone. They would know that you fought the Nazis, and—"

"I didn't fight the Nazis."

"You did, Peter. You only fought for Hitler when you were forced to do it."

Peter looked toward the windows. "I want to be in Germany," he said. "I want to rebuild our country. And there's someone I met—a friend."

"A woman?"

"Just a girl. But . . . I don't know. I would never see her again if I went to America."

"You could come back and get her. You could move her to America with you."

"She's not a Mormon."

"Will she be?"

"I don't know. Alex, this is all so strange for me to think about."

"At least go to England. See your family. They need that."

"How can I get there?"

"Don't worry about that. I'll get you there."

Peter nodded, but he looked troubled.

President Meis had tidied up the place a little, put the chairs back around the tables, swept up a little rice that had fallen on the floor. Now he came to the table where Alex and Peter were sitting. "I need to close up now," he said. "Maybe *Bruder* Thomas can drive us back to my place in his jeep."

"Of course I will," Alex said.

Peter stood, and the three of them walked to the front door. As President Meis was locking up, Peter asked Alex, "I've had a question on my mind for a long time. Do you know what happened to the Rosenbaums?"

"I know more than I wish I did," Alex said. "The parents were put to death in Poland. What I don't know is what happened to little Benjamin."

Peter nodded. "I always hoped they would survive somehow. We tried to help them, but we let them down."

"No," President Meis said. "If you tried to help them, you didn't let them down."

"I want to find Benjamin. I've never stopped thinking about him."

"I'll keep looking. But Peter, he's almost surely dead."

"I know. But I want to look. That's just one more reason for me not to go to America."

"You can decide all that later," Alex said. "But go to England and see your family. That would be the greatest blessing you could give them. Maybe I can get you there for Christmas."

"I do want to do that," Peter said.

"That's good," President Meis said. "But what you need now is some dinner." He laughed. "We're blessed to have some rice. And we do have plenty of blankets. You can sleep warm tonight."

Tears appeared in Peter's eyes. "Thank you," he said.

Alex took hold of him again, grasped him tight. "Peter," he said, "this is the best thing that could have happened. Now your family can begin to heal. You can, too."

8

Wally was sitting between LaRue and Beverly, close to the front of the stake house chapel. They were attending stake conference this morning, December 9, and Mom was on the stand with Dad. Today he would be released as stake president.

President David O. McKay, second counselor in the First Presidency, was sitting next to Mom and Dad. He was presiding and had been sent by President Smith to reorganize the stake. Wally liked President McKay as much as any of the General Authorities. He was a kindly man—pleasant and tranquil. Once, when Wally was thirteen or fourteen, he had sat next to President McKay at the dinner table in their home. The apostle had teased Wally about leaving his green beans uneaten. It was the sort of thing Dad had always turned into one of his speeches about hungry people in bread lines, but President McKay had only joked that he had grown tall from eating his string beans—and Wally had eaten his, not because he took the idea seriously but in response to President McKay's attention.

President McKay *was* a tall man, with white hair and a broad, warm smile. He sat now with his hand resting affectionately on President Thomas's arm. LaRue leaned toward Wally and whispered, "President McKay is the nicest man I know. At Gene's funeral, he was the one who understood what I was feeling."

Wally had heard the story from Mom, how Elder Joseph Fielding Smith had taught the doctrine—powerfully—but President McKay had offered consolation.

After the opening hymn, "High on a Mountain Top"—one of Dad's favorites—and after the opening prayer, President McKay stood and walked to the stand. He smiled, nodded, and said, "There's no doubt in my mind that you know why I'm here."

The members laughed quietly.

"We're going to release your good president today, but before I do that, I want to say a word or two about him." For a few minutes he spoke of President Thomas's leadership, his strength, his vision—all the things Wally would expect someone to say about his father at a time like this. But then he said, "I've also seen another side of this man—a side that I'm not sure all of you know so well. I was here, as many of you were, on the day of Gene Thomas's funeral. I wasn't surprised that President Thomas understood the gospel, accepted the loss, and carried on so well—never really missing a step—but I remember sitting in his office with him that day, and I remember how he wept. He had lost a son, and his theology made a great difference, but he was still in pain. I hope he doesn't mind if I tell you what he said to me that day." He glanced back at President Thomas, who gave a little shake of his head. "He said, 'I have one regret. I'm not one to show my love the way I wish I could. I'm not sure Gene knew how much I loved him. I should have made that more clear to him before he left home.'"

President McKay hesitated for a moment, and then he said, "On the one hand, that's a lesson for us all. We should not only recognize our love, we should express it. But I told President Thomas that day, 'Don't worry, President, Gene knew. You care about your kids—and the people in your stake—and they *all* know it.'"

"That's right," Wally whispered to LaRue.

"He cares a little too much sometimes," she said, but she was smiling, and Wally didn't hear any real resentment in her voice.

President McKay went ahead with the release, and then he offered the name of one of President Thomas's counselors, James Webber, as the new president. That was certainly no surprise, and the members sustained him, with his new counselors.

President McKay asked the new presidency to come forward and take their seats on the stand, and then he said, "President Thomas is a great man. In fact, he's almost as impressive as his wife." The members in the congregation laughed. "I'd like to hear a few words from her today, and then we'll ask President Thomas to speak to us."

He turned then, met Bea on her way to the podium, shook her hand, and then leaned forward and whispered something to her. She laughed, and then she faced the microphone, pulling it down to her level. "President McKay just promised me that he'd try to find something else for my husband to do—so he wouldn't be around the house too much," she said.

Again everyone laughed, but Wally was surprised at how shaky his mom's voice was when she began to speak again. "I remember the day my husband was called to this position," she said. "I was sick at heart. I was glad that he could serve, but I wondered what it would mean for our family. We had six children at home, and I knew that Al would be gone a great deal. The burden of dealing with so many challenges, often by myself, frightened and worried me. What I didn't know, of course, was that a war was coming, and that my worries would change so much. Many times during the war I wished that I could have my children together at home—that I could deal with the simple problems of raising a family. And many times I thanked the Lord that I was married to a man who knew how to turn to God at the hardest times, who stood at the head of

our family as a spiritual light and never once doubted his con-
victions."

She raised a handkerchief to her eyes—a pretty embroi-
dered one, trimmed in lace. Wally had given her a set of three
like that one Christmas when he was in high school. Could this
still be one of those? It seemed as though decades had passed
since then.

"I don't mean to cry. This is a very happy time for us. Wally
has come home, and Alex and Bobbi are going to return before
too much longer. And best of all, I have a wonderful little
grandson I'm going to see one of these days. God has been
good to us, truly. We lost a son, and that will hurt my heart as
long as I live on this earth, but at least I know that that pain
won't last forever. I will see Gene again."

Wally was taken by surprise when his mom suddenly
laughed. "And I'll tell you what else makes me happy. I've been
working on President Thomas, trying to reform him a little. I've
found out that you *can* teach an old president new tricks. He's a
better man than when I started training him."

The congregation laughed hard, but no one harder than
LaRue. She pushed her elbow into Wally's side and said, "I've
taught him a few things, too."

Beverly bent around Wally and said, "LaRue, don't talk so
loud," but that only made LaRue laugh harder.

Wally was watching his mom, who had stopped laughing
as quickly as she had begun. "I shouldn't have said that," she
said, when quiet fell over the chapel. "I always say more than I
should. Here's what I really should have said. Al Thomas is as
good as any man I've ever known. He couldn't do anything dis-
honest or wrong, couldn't cheat someone or hurt anyone to
save his life. His only problem is that he wants the rest of us
to be as good as he is, and sometimes he makes us feel that we
can't live up to his standards. But he doesn't mean it that way.
He doesn't mean to tell us we're down too low; he only wants

to help us up a little higher. That's the honest truth. And it isn't something I've always understood."

Sister Thomas bore her testimony after that, and she sat down, but Wally was lost in thought about what she had said. She did say more than she should, at times, but Wally liked what she had said today. She had hit on something about his father that he had always known and never exactly understood.

When President Thomas stood at the podium, he seemed solemn, as he always did on such occasions, but he said, "I was hoping to leave my calling with a little dignity, but Sister Thomas has ended all chance of that." Then he grinned and the audience chuckled again.

"She was telling the truth when she said that she's tried to improve me. And I've been trying to follow her advice. And I'll tell you why. I want to be worthy to be with Bea for eternity, and I know that I'll always have to stand on my tiptoes to come close to being as big a person as she is. She told you that I've tried to lead my family, but if I've learned a lesson during these challenging years, it's that a man doesn't walk ahead of his family. He walks alongside his wife, and that makes the leadership not double but ten times stronger."

President Thomas talked then about the good years he had experienced as stake president, and he expressed his gratitude to the stake. But he didn't talk long at all, and he didn't give a sermon. Wally was surprised by that. In the end, he said, "I know that I've asked a lot of you. Looking back, some of my talks from this podium may have been a little stronger, a little more demanding, than they should have been. Maybe it's made you feel that I had no understanding for the weaknesses we all share. And maybe I've discouraged some of you instead of giving you hope that you could deal with your weaknesses. I can only say that I've meant well and believed in you, and that I was admonishing myself right along with you. In the last couple of years I've seen my own weaknesses more clearly. I think, as I've done that, I've understood a little better that we all have a long way to go—and an eternity to make the progress we need to make. I'm not sure I would take back anything I've said to you, but I wish I had spoken, at times, in a softer voice and had shown a little more compassion. One thing I've learned is that it's very difficult to change, and every time I think I've made a little headway, I have a way of slipping into old habits. I suppose that's how it is for all of us."

Wally was sitting close enough that he could see the tears glistening in his father's eyes, and he was touched. He felt LaRue grasp his arm, and he knew that she was too. President Thomas thanked the members again, bore his testimony, and sat down.

The new presidency spoke after that, and each of them spoke glowingly of President Thomas, but Wally could tell this was a hard day for his father. He was a man driven to do well, and clearly he was feeling certain regrets about his service as president. Wally didn't think he should be that hard on himself, but he wasn't surprised that he would be.

When the meeting finally ended, a great many people crowded to the front of the chapel and shook hands both with the new presidency and with the Thomases. Wally and his sisters were caught at the front by the people coming forward, and Wally could hear the praise that was being poured out on President Thomas—but he also heard his father's reticence. As Wally tried to work his way up the aisle, he was also greeted by dozens of people who had not had a chance to see him since his return. Most of them wanted to tell him how much they admired him. Wally was as hesitant as his father to accept such unqualified praise—and he was embarrassed.

Somewhere in the middle of all the attention, LaRue told him, "Bev and I are going to ride home with Mom and Dad. They parked where they can get out faster." Wally glanced to see that his parents were going to leave by the funeral door exit. He realized that he should have done that himself, but his car was the other way, in the parking lot out back, so he continued up the aisle.

As he came out the door, a brother—a man whose face he remembered, not his name—grabbed him by the hand. "Wally, welcome home," he said. "I can't tell you how relieved we all were when we found out you had made it through that awful mess over there."

"Thank you," Wally said. "I'm happy to be home." At that moment Wally felt someone tap him on the shoulder. He only wanted to escape, not shake everyone's hand, so he was already stepping away as he turned to see who else wanted his attention.

It was Lorraine.

Wally stopped and took a breath. She was wearing a green dress, and her eyes were picking up the color, her cheeks aglow from her own obvious self-consciousness. "Welcome home, Wally," she said.

He tried to say something, but he was a little too off-balance.

"How are you doing?" she asked.

"Fine. Just fine."

"It's really good to see you."

"It's good to see you, too." But the words sounded perfunctory, as though he were talking to an old school chum.

"Well, I just wanted to say hello." She glanced down, and he could see that she was embarrassed. She was about to walk away.

"I heard that you've moved back to Salt Lake," he said.

"Yes. I quit my job in Seattle. I wanted to be home for a while . . ." She didn't finish, didn't say, "before I get married."

Her voice brought back everything—all the feelings he had never managed to overcome.

"I'm living with my parents again—for right now."

"I am, too. For now." He drew in some breath. "When are you getting married?" He had meant to use her name, but the word carried too much affection for him. At the last moment he had known that he couldn't say it.

"I'm not exactly sure. My fiancé is staying in the navy, and he's still at sea."

"Well . . . that's . . . too bad."

"Yes. It's hard to plan anything."

"But it shouldn't be too long now, I wouldn't think."

"No. Not long."

Wally was still nodding, glancing away, but always coming back to her eyes, her skin, her contours. She was made of perfect lines, always had been—curved but delicate, subtle—and her motions so much a part of her beauty.

"What are you going to do now, Wally?" He was about to answer, but someone else wanted to shake his hand, had hold of him by the arm.

He turned and greeted the couple, thanked them, said something, and then turned back, but she had moved off a little. "Well, I need to go. My parents are waiting." Wally saw that they were standing not far off. They waved to him and smiled.

"I'd love to talk with you just a little. It's been so long."

"Well, sure. That would be nice."

"Could I give you a ride home? I have my car here."

He saw the color in her cheeks rise, saw her hesitate. "Well . . . I suppose so," she said. "Let me tell my parents." She walked away, and Wally watched those lines, saw them flow, her skirt swinging easily, her arms.

Someone else was talking to him now, but he kept glancing at Lorraine. She was talking too long, too seriously, with her parents, and he knew what they were saying, that it wasn't proper for her to ride home with him. As Wally continued to talk to the family in front of him, he watched her return, and he feared the worst, but at least her parents were leaving, and she was standing, waiting.

When he walked to her, she said, "My parents think people are going to see us together and *talk.*"

Wally laughed. It was the first time she had sounded natural, and Wally thought he had picked up on something else. In her voice, her expression, he thought he had caught just a hint of flirtation. Or maybe not. He told himself not to think so.

By the time Wally and Lorraine headed for the parking lot, it was mostly empty. Wally opened the door for her, and he was struck by how familiar that seemed, how many memories it brought back. "Where did you get the car?" she asked.

Wally walked around and got in before he said, "I got some back pay for the years I was gone. I also happen to know a car dealer. He gave me a good price. But the old thing is kind of a wreck."

"So is that where you're working—at the dealership?"

"No. I'm working at the parts plant—where *you* got your career started." He was glad that he was relaxing enough to joke a little, but he still found it easier not to look at her.

"Are you going back to college?"

"I probably will at some point. But Dad needs the help, and I need to get back into the swing of things. So I'll work for a while and then decide what I want to do for sure later. Dad's paying me a lot more than I deserve. It's really too good of a deal to pass up."

"That's great, Wally. I can't believe how good you look. I was expecting you to be skinny as a scarecrow."

"Hey, I was, believe me. I still weigh less than I did when I left here. But all I do is eat." He started the car and drove forward, lined up behind the last of the cars heading out of the driveway from behind the stake house.

"You seem older, Wally."

"Well . . . I am older. About twenty years older, probably."

"Was it really awful?"

Wally glanced at Lorraine, who was sitting all the way

across the seat, close to the door. He remembered teasing her about doing that, long ago. "I think we manly Gary Cooper types are supposed to say something like, 'Ah, shucks, ma'am, it weren't much.'" He laughed. "But sure, it was bad. Worse than I know how to tell you."

"I always thought about you and wondered what was happening. I prayed for you all the time."

"I thought about you, too, Lorraine." He hesitated, glanced at her again, and then drove the car out onto the street and turned north. "I know you're getting married right away, and I don't want to be out of line in what I say, but thinking about you was one of the main things that got me through. I always figured that you were married, so I didn't really think I'd come back and find you here, still single, or anything like that, but I would go over my memories. I'd try to relive them in my mind—just so I could recall what life was like, and that I had something to stay alive for."

"What were your favorite memories?"

He laughed again. "Maybe I shouldn't say."

"No, come on. Because I have a lot of nice memories too. I'm just wondering which ones stuck in your mind."

"My favorite was always that night we were up at Lagoon on the Twenty-Fourth of July. We watched the fireworks, and then we danced . . . out in the parking lot."

"The band was playing, 'I Get Along Without You Very Well.'"

"So you remember that?"

"I've thought about it a thousand times. That was the same night you took me up to the Country Club, and we stole those golf balls out of the pond."

"And I kissed you." But he knew he shouldn't have said that, and so he forced himself to laugh again, and he said, "That's also when you told me that you didn't want me to do that ever again."

"But you did."

"Well . . . yes."

There was a silence for a time, and then Lorraine said, "You were kind of a dangerous guy then. Or at least I thought so."

"You told me that I'd never get my feet on the ground—never make anything of myself."

"I know. That was cruel." She set her hand on the seat, as though she were reaching halfway to him. He glanced down at her long fingers, thought of the times they had walked together, holding hands.

"Hey, you were right. Dead right. I was heading nowhere. Maybe I still am."

"No. You'll do great now. I'm so happy for you, the way things are turning out."

"Well, I hope things go all right. It sounds like everything is working out just right for you."

"I think so. I learned a lot during the war—in different ways from you, of course, but I did some growing up myself."

"How are you different?"

"I gained a lot of confidence. In my job, I had to make decisions. I had to lead people—both men and women—and trust in myself. It was exciting. And satisfying. The best thing that could have happened to me. But now I'm ready for a quieter life."

Wally was turning, heading up to Thirteenth East, where Lorraine lived. He wanted to take a longer drive, but he didn't know what she would think if he took her any way but straight home. "Are you sure you won't miss all the excitement?"

"I don't think so. I'm starting to feel like an old woman. I want to get a family started before I get any older."

"You're just as beautiful as you always were, Lorraine. Even more."

Wally knew that he had gone a little too far. The words were not exactly inappropriate, but he heard the fondness in his voice, and clearly, so did she. "Thank you," she said, softly, formally, and then not another word.

When Wally stopped the car in front of Lorraine's house, he didn't turn the engine off. He tried to lighten his voice when he said, "It's been great to see you. I hope you get your wish—and have those babies right away. I'd like to meet your fiancé one of these days."

"He wants to meet you, too. He told me that."

"Well . . . good." But then he couldn't resist telling her what he was thinking. "This reminds me of the last time I saw you—that day I told you I was going into the Air Corps." He laughed. "I wanted you to beg me not to go—and you wouldn't do it."

Her hand was on the handle, but she didn't open the door. "Wally, I know I hurt you that day. But it was hard for me, too. I went to my bedroom and cried until I thought my heart was going to break. But I really did think I was doing the right thing."

"Lorraine, there's no question about it. It was the right thing."

She had been looking down at the seat, but her eyes came up now, engaged his. "Is that really how you feel?" she asked.

He didn't know what she was asking, but his chest suddenly stiffened. What did he dare say? "Well . . . I'm just saying that you were right about me. It was the right decision, at the time."

She was still looking at him, not speaking, but he couldn't tell what she was thinking.

"You stood on the porch that day, and the sun was setting, so everything was sort of yellow and hazy. You said, 'I love you too, Wally, but it would never work.' "

She nodded.

"Then you walked into the house, and the screen door sort of stuck when you tried to pull it open the first time. Then, inside, I could see you through the screen, walking down the hallway. You were wearing a blue dress, with white polka-dots. That's what I remembered all the years I've been gone—you in that golden light, saying you loved me, then walking away. I've seen the whole thing in my mind so many times it's still like it happened yesterday."

"Wally, I don't want you to take this wrong. I shouldn't even say anything like this. But I just want you to know that I've thought about that day over and over, too—all these years. It still hurts me, too, even now. But I guess, in life, we all have memories like that. It hurt me when I sent John, my fiancé, back to sea this last time, too. Maybe bittersweet memories like that make life more meaningful, and hard choices make us grow. Do you know what I mean?"

Wally couldn't think of it that way, not now, but he said he did, and then he added, "We had that time together, those years we were such good friends. We'll never lose that. We just have to see what's coming next—what other good things life has for us."

"You're going to find someone wonderful, Wally. I know that. She'll be a lucky girl."

Wally tried to laugh, but he was struggling now. "I hope so. Right now, I'm still afraid to ask a girl out on a date. That's one step I haven't taken yet."

"You will, Wally. Don't worry, the girls are going to be after you—by the dozens. You're a catch now. You've got everything going for you."

"I'll take your word for it." He grinned.

She opened the door and got out. Then she bent back down to say, "Thanks, Wally. It really was great to see you."

But Wally was crushed by how much this felt like the last time they had said good-bye, and he hated the idea that he had to go through this again. So he said the only thing that seemed to leave a door open. "Will I see you again?"

"Well, who knows? Maybe somewhere." And then she made herself clear. "I'm getting married here in Salt Lake. I'll send you an invitation. But after that, it's hard to say where we'll live. Probably lots of different places."

"Yeah, I'm sure that's right. Well . . . good luck, Lorraine. God bless you."

"You too, Wally. Good-bye." She shut the door.

Wally drove home, numb. He had wanted to see her and yet feared it, had sensed that he might feel this way, and now he had left himself wide open for another round of torment. He told himself what he had been saying for five years: that he would find someone else he could love as much. His only problem was, he couldn't imagine that actually happening, at least not at the moment.

When he parked the car at home and walked inside, Dad was in the living room, sitting in his chair. "Did it take you that long to get out of there?" he asked.

"Sort of. I ran into Lorraine Gardner. We talked for a few minutes, and then I gave her a lift home."

"So what's going on with her?"

Wally tried to sound off-handed as he told his dad about the impending wedding, but his mother heard him from the kitchen and stepped out. "You gave her a ride home?" she asked.

"Sure. I didn't want to hold her parents up, and it was kind of fun to talk to her for a few minutes."

"She's as pretty as ever, isn't she?"

"She's beautiful."

But Wally hadn't handled the word as well as he wanted, and his parents seemed to hear that. "This is hard for you, isn't it, son?" Dad said.

"Well . . . yes. A little harder than I expected. But I've been through some harder things. I'll manage this one all right."

"You'll meet someone, Wally," Mom said. "You have to start asking some girls out—right away. If you don't, I'll start arranging dates for you."

"I might have to let you do that. I'm scared to death to try it myself."

"These days, the girls just might ask you," Dad said.

"They're getting bolder all the time, and you fellows are in short supply."

Wally nodded and tried to smile. He took a step toward the stairs and then stopped. "Say, Dad, I wanted to tell you, I don't think you need to regret anything about your time as stake president. You really shouldn't."

"Now that's funny. I seem to remember you saying something about the length of the talks I used to give."

Wally reached under his suit coat and stuck his hands into his trouser pockets. He shook his head and laughed. "Well, some of them were a little long," he said. But then he added, seriously, "I hate to hear you questioning yourself about asking too much of people or being too hard. There's nothing hard about you. I was just too young to understand that back then."

Dad nodded. "Thanks," he said quietly. "Your saying that means more to me than you probably realize."

Wally thought about walking over to his dad and embracing him, but he had already done that a few times since he had come home, and it usually ended up embarrassing both of them. So Wally hugged his mother instead, and he said, "In the camps, you could tell the guys who had good families. They had more to live for. More of them made it through. And I had the best."

Mom said, "And now it's time for you to have a family of your own. That would be the best thing in the world for you."

"Maybe you'd better fix me up with a date, then," he said, and he laughed. "I can't marry a girl unless I take her out a time or two. At least I think that's how it works."

"Don't worry; I have girls in mind already."

"Good."

"Do you want a date this week?"

"No. Not quite yet."

"When?"

"Soon. I'll tell you when."

"Will you really?"

"Yes. I promise."

Wally went upstairs to his old room, the one that he and Gene had once shared. He sat down on his bed. He really did need to start dating right away. That would be the best thing for him. But what he found was that a new image was in his head, a replacement of an old one: the car door shutting—firmly, solidly—and then Lorraine retreating up the same sidewalk and into the same house where she had disappeared from his life the last time. This time her dress was green, but her walk was the same, that lovely way she moved.

Anna went shopping for groceries on Monday morning while Gene napped. When she got back, she stepped into the kitchen where her mother and father were sitting at the table across from each other. Anna saw immediately that something had happened. Frieda Stoltz had been crying, her eyelids rubbed red, but she looked bright, enlivened. Heinrich Stoltz was sitting up straight, his eyes keen. And then Anna knew what it had to be. "Have you heard from Peter?"

"Yes. Yes," her mother said. She stood up and grabbed Anna in her arms. "We got a telegram from Alex. Peter showed up in Frankfurt. He's fine. He's healthy and well."

Anna had to put her net full of groceries down. She felt a little dizzy. For the past few weeks she had resigned herself to Peter's loss—and now he was alive again. "Oh, Mama," she said. Her father was coming to her now, and she turned and clasped him tight.

Her mother leaned her head against Anna's shoulder at the same time, and Anna felt her tremble with new tears, heard her father whisper, "It's so good. It's such a relief."

"Where has he been all this time?" Anna asked.

"We don't know," Brother Stoltz said. "Alex only told us

that Peter had found him at church, in Frankfurt. He says that a letter is also on its way. I'm sure he'll tell us more in that."

"But Peter is healthy? Is that the word he used?"

Sister Stoltz stepped away and pulled the telegram from her apron pocket. "Yes. Healthy."

Anna took the telegram and read it. She was almost frightened that somehow her parents had misread the words, that it wasn't really true. But there it was: "He's healthy and doing fine. I will arrange to have him travel to London."

It was all so wonderful and yet baffling. Where had he been? Why hadn't he made his way to Frankfurt sooner? "I wonder—how soon will he come?" Anna asked.

"It shouldn't take long," Brother Stoltz said. "I would think he could be here for Christmas."

"Oh, Papa, what a gift. I can't believe it yet."

She took him into her arms again, and for the first time, he began to cry. "It's more than I deserve," he said. "I was afraid that my mistakes had killed him, and I would have to live out my life knowing that."

"You made no mistakes, Papa. It all worked out all right. And we'll be back together again. Just think what it will be like to have him here for Christmas."

"We have no Christmas gift for him," Sister Stoltz said. "We need to go shopping so we'll have something under the . . ." She stopped and laughed. "We have no tree either."

"Still, we need a gift for him," Anna said.

"Let's go now," Brother Stoltz said. "It will be a little outing for us. We need to celebrate."

"You two go," Mother said. "Gene is still sleeping. I'll stay with him. And when you get back, I'll have a nice meal ready. Like Sunday dinner."

"No, no, Mama," Anna said. "Gene will be awake before long. We'll wrap him up and take him with us. He'll like the air."

Sister Stoltz laughed. "Peter will love Gene so much," she said. "Can you think how he will pamper him?"

What came to Anna's mind was a picture of Peter—young Peter—kneeling on the floor with little Benjamin Rosenbaum. Peter had been such a kindly boy. But she had to wonder, what would he be now? What had the war done to him? And what had Alex meant by "healthy"? Was Peter really all right?

In the next few minutes everyone got ready, and Anna picked up Gene, who was beginning to stir anyway. He woke up for a moment but then settled in and slept in her arms as she and her parents walked to the Baker Street Station and then rode the Underground train to Oxford Street. They ended up in Selfridge's department store, wandering about, looking at clothing and "Men's furnishings," hardly knowing what might be appropriate. "I have no idea what size shirt he would wear, or coat. He probably needs everything," Sister Stoltz said. "But we'll have to wait until he gets here to know what to get."

They considered warm mufflers, stockings, underwear, but all of it seemed so ordinary and uninteresting. Finally Brother Stoltz said, "When I was in Germany, and alone, what I wanted most was a Book of Mormon. The branch president in Karlsruhe lent me one, and that was the nicest gift I could have received."

"But he doesn't know much English, Heinrich," Sister Stoltz said. "Where could we find German scriptures?"

Brother Stoltz had stopped by a display of suitcases, all leather and very expensive. Anna had looked at the prices and realized they were more than the family could think about spending. But she liked the idea of the scriptures. "We should buy them in English for him," she said. "He needs to learn. We can read with him and help him translate. It's a good way to help him."

"Yes," Brother Stoltz said. "I think this is so. I'll give him English lessons—and help him study other books, but we could all read the scriptures together."

"They won't have a Book of Mormon here."

"No. We can get that at the church. But we could buy him a nice Bible, leather bound."

"Can we afford it, Heinrich?"

"Yes. We can do that much. Let's walk down the street. I know where there's a bookstore."

And so they went back out into the cold. Little Gene was awake and looking about by then, and Oxford Street was charming. Christmas decorations, for the first time in many years, had returned to store fronts and light poles. And all the lights were on again, everywhere. Gene seemed to wonder at it all. He gazed about, turning his head this way and that, and Anna kept telling him, "See the pretty bells. See the Christmas tree." She wished so much that Alex could be here to share all this, to be with Gene on his first Christmas.

At the bookstore, the Stoltzes found a host of Bibles and chose one that was especially well bound. "This one will last him for a lifetime," Brother Stoltz told Anna and his wife. "It could be his family Bible."

Sister Stoltz took hold of his arm. "Oh, Heinrich," she said. "I just keep thinking, we have everything back. Peter can marry and have grandchildren for us. He can be with us as we grow old. We won't have to spend the rest of our lives missing him."

"It's what I've been thinking too," Brother Stoltz said. "I had given up on all those things—without even knowing I had done it."

The three were crying now, there in the bookstore. Anna held Gene close, and Brother Stoltz took his wife into his arms. "It's over," she whispered. "It's finally over."

And Anna, of course, knew what her mother meant. The family had first gone on the run in 1941. Four and a half years had passed, and every day had been full of worry. Now, for the first time, the Stoltzes had much to be thankful for and little to fear. Anna certainly wondered whether Peter was really all right. She worried about Alex at times, and wondered about the future, but all that was nothing compared to the terror they had known—hiding in Berlin and then making their escape from Germany—or the constant anxiety since the day that Peter had been separated from them at the French border. All of that was finally over, and life could go on. The idea was hard to accept, the change too sudden.

What also struck Anna was that her family could now take the Thomases up on their offer. President Thomas had written to the Stoltzes about emigrating. He had said that not only could he sponsor them, so they could gain permission, but he could also offer work to Anna's father. Brother Stoltz hadn't wanted to go until he was sure about Peter, but now the family would be free to move ahead with the plan. And maybe, before too much longer, Alex would be discharged from the army, and the *whole* family could be together in Salt Lake City. Anna tried to think what it would be like to be in Utah, where so many people believed in the Church, and where Gene could have two sets of grandparents, uncles and aunts, and in time, cousins to play with. Alex's brother Wally was home now, and Bobbi would be released before long. It was all what she had dreamed of for so long, and now it really could happen.

For the next few days the Stoltzes spoke of little else but their new joy. They waited for Alex's letter, and when it came, they read it together:

Dear Family:

I hope you got my telegram and know by now that Peter is here in Frankfurt, not just alive but looking very well. He thought his best chance to find you was to locate the Frankfurt branch and see whether President Meis or other members knew where you were. So he made his way to Frankfurt, asked around until he found someone who knew where the branch met, and finally located the building. We were holding sacrament meeting when he walked in, and at first I didn't know him. He's grown into a man— a handsome young man—and even though he looked rather ragged in his old clothes, he still looked strong.

You need to know that Peter has been through a lot. Just as Heinrich suspected, he fought the Russians in the east, and he barely survived. He was very sick at one point, and I guess he almost died. There were times when he had more or less given up on God, religion, and everything else, but he does believe that God preserved his life. He suffered beyond anything you can imagine from the cold and hunger, and from the constant exhaustion. His entire regiment was killed off, a few at a time, and he thinks he may actually be the only survivor. Eventually, when everything was turning into chaos, he ran from the army—which he never wanted to be part of in the first place—and a farm family took him in. The husband in the family had been killed in the east himself, and when the war ended, Peter didn't feel that he could walk out on the woman and her children. He worked the farm for them until the family fled the Russian zone, and then he worked in a coal mine to provide for them. He wanted to search for you sooner, but he waited until the family was managing on its own.

There's something else you need to be careful about. He's convinced that what he did was wrong. He went into the army to save his life. He thought he could hide in the military and somehow avoid the killing. But there was no way out, once he was in, and he ended up fighting the "enemy," even though he thought he was on the wrong side of the war. He now tells me that he should have gone to prison or accepted a death penalty rather than kill for Hitler. I've talked to him about that, and so has President Meis, and we'll keep talking, but when he arrives in London, you may find that he's still ashamed. He told me that he has feared for a long time that you would all be disappointed in him, perhaps not even want him back. I've told him that isn't the case, but he's having a hard time justifying his actions to himself. He'll need a lot of love and support from you.

I'm working today to find transportation for him. I'd like to see him get to London for Christmas, but travel is not easy in Germany right now. He may not be able to make it quite that soon. Without my help, he probably wouldn't be allowed to leave the country, but I can cut through a lot of red tape—or at least I think I can. It's possible that he could be held up for a time getting the proper papers. But I'll do all I can. Don't be too disappointed if he doesn't make it for Christmas. Just know that he'll be there soon.

I told you before that Kellerman has been arrested. I heard this week that he will go on trial some time this winter. For now, he's in prison. Gestapo agents are not always punished harshly. Most of them claim that they were only doing what was expected of them, and they aren't responsible for their actions. By now, you've been hearing that from all those Nazi thugs being tried in Nuremberg. I think, in Kellerman's case, that his actions were so heinous that he will be held accountable. I'll be certain to be included as a witness when the trial comes. I have no idea what's in the man's heart, if anything, and I don't want to be his judge, but I do want the court to know the effect his actions have had on all of you.

My status with the army hasn't changed. I've stopped bringing it up with my CO. It only makes him angry. But still, I'm hoping that before long someone will recognize that the army has asked enough of me. I've always thought that within a year from the end of the war in Europe I would get my release. So let's hope that at least by May I'm with all of you, maybe in Utah.

I hardly know how to tell you what it was like when Peter walked into our meeting. I didn't recognize him until I saw that he had recognized me, and at that moment the sacrament was being passed, so we merely sat and stared at each other, both of us about to burst with emotion. But he still didn't know I was his brother-in-law. He was almost floored when I told him, and he was excited to know you were all well and that he has a nephew. I think he will be all right, in time, but he's suffering from the usual difficulties soldiers face, and in his case, much more. Be patient with him, and more than anything, reassure him. He needs to know that you love him.

Merry Christmas, everyone. Give Gene kisses for me. I'm proud of his every achievement. He's certainly a prodigy. With your German blood in his veins, he'll probably start writing symphonies any day now. I thought for sure I would see him by now, and it's not easy to send Peter off and not be able to come home for Christmas myself, but let's take heart in the thought that this is surely my last Christmas away, and now we can trust that everyone will be together next year.

Love,
Alex

The Stoltzes were together in their little living room, Heinrich and Frieda on the couch, Anna in the chair across from them. They each took a turn at reading the letter a second time. "I'm tempted to write to Peter right now," Brother Stoltz said, "but I think it might be better if I wait and talk to him. The boy needs to know that he has nothing to be ashamed of."

"But neither do you," Anna said. "Both of you have to leave the war behind now."

"I know. I know." But Anna could hear in his voice that there were still plenty of doubts left. And for Peter, things had to be worse.

Gene crawled to Anna and grasped her leg. She picked him up and held him close. She knew for certain now what she had only suspected for the past few days: the ordeal wasn't over, not entirely. Peter had more to deal with, more to overcome. What she found herself thinking was that she didn't want the aftermath of all this pain, of everything her family had been through and all that Alex had suffered, to be passed along to Gene somehow.

* * *

Peter was worried about the things he would have to tell his family, but still, he wanted to see them, wanted to go "home." Before he left Germany, however, there was something he needed to do. He needed to visit the Schallers one last time. He could write, but he wanted to see them, tell them goodbye. He didn't know when he would return to Germany.

Alex seemed to understand. He arranged for a ride in an army truck that took Peter to the border of the American zone. From there Peter was able to catch a train to Hannover, and then he hitched a ride with a British military truck. He ended up walking the last few miles to the farm, outside Hildesheim, just as he had done when he had departed a couple of weeks before, but he didn't mind that. The day was cold but bright, and he was happy to be getting back to where he still felt most welcome.

By the time he had arrived, the sun, setting very early this time of year, was almost gone, and the cold was deepening. At

Frau Heiner's house, Peter had always come and gone without knocking, but he didn't feel comfortable doing that now. He didn't want to frighten anyone. So he knocked on the front door. It was Thomas who opened it, and then who shouted, "Katrina, you can stop crying. Peter is back."

Peter stepped inside and then walked toward the kitchen. By then Katrina was rushing out the kitchen door. She almost ran into him. "Peter!" she gasped, and she reached for him.

But he didn't take her into his arms. He knew he shouldn't do that. He patted her on the shoulder, reaching over her extended arms. "How are you?" he asked.

She let her hands fall to her sides. "Are you staying? Will you live here again?"

He didn't want to be abrupt about all that. He wanted to tell her gently. So he only said, "I located my family. They're in London. It's quite a story how I found out where they are."

Clearly she knew what that meant. He saw her draw in a quick little breath and then fight hard not to show her disappointment. "It's good you found them," she said.

"It was a big relief, to know they are all right."

She stood still, her arms still limp at her sides, her bedraggled sweater showing how thin she was, how little flesh covered her ribs. "You have new clothes," she said, maybe aware of her own.

"Alex got some for me. This is an army coat. And trousers." She nodded.

"Is your mother here? And Frau Heiner?"

"They're in the kitchen."

"I'll tell you what happened—all of you."

She nodded again and stepped aside, letting him lead the way. Frau Schaller and Frau Heiner were sitting at the kitchen table, but they hadn't started to fix dinner. Peter knew that Frau Schaller would have returned from work only a short time before. She stood up when she saw Peter, walked to him and hugged him, kissed him on the cheek. "What a joy to see you back," she said.

"I found my family."

"You did? You've seen them?"

"No. They're in London. And my sister is married to a missionary I knew. She has a little boy. I need to tell you the whole story." Frau Schaller smiled, but she glanced toward Katrina, and Peter could see her concern.

Peter shook hands with Frau Heiner and then sat down at the table across from her. Katrina sat down next to him, and Frau Schaller walked around the table and sat next to Frau Heiner. Thomas and Rolf had come in too, but they remained near the door, as though they weren't sure how long they wanted to stay. Peter told the story without much detail—how he had found the meeting place and then seen his old friend *Bruder* Thomas.

"He was the missionary who taught you about the Mormons, wasn't he?" Katrina said. Over the past few months Katrina had asked Peter everything about his life, and Peter, somewhat reluctantly, had filled in more and more details. For one thing, Katrina knew a great deal about Mormon beliefs now, and she seemed to accept them. Or at least she accepted Peter—with his beliefs.

Peter told them all about his stay in Frankfurt and the telegram that Alex had sent.

"Have you heard from your family yet?" Frau Schaller asked.

"No. There hasn't been enough time for a letter to get here." Peter looked down at the threadbare tablecloth, and he was surprised at what it made him feel. It seemed as though he was abandoning these people—his family of sorts. Everything here—the coal-dust smell he had carried into the house, the bare light bulb that hung over the table, the worn floor—was part of him now, and good.

"So what will you do now, Peter?" Frau Heiner asked.

Peter didn't look at Katrina, not even at Frau Schaller. "I'm going to go to London just as soon as I can," he said. "I want to get there by Christmas, if it's possible."

"And then what? Will your family return to Germany?"

"No. They plan to emigrate. Alex's family is trying to clear the way so that they can go to Salt Lake City, in the western part of the United States."

"Where the Indians live," Thomas said.

"Alex said there *are* some Indians, but they're not like the ones you see in the movies. They don't wear feathers."

"Rolf and Thomas know nothing of movies," Frau Heiner said. "They only know how boys play."

Peter sneaked a peek at Katrina. She was staring ahead, her thoughts obviously far away.

"That's the Mormon city, isn't it, Salt Lake City?" Frau Schaller said.

"Yes. It's where Alex lives."

"Do you want to live there? Or do you want to come back to Germany?"

"I don't know. I would rather live here, I think, but I've been away from my family for a long time. I want to be with them again."

"Yes. Of course. But in time, you might want to return, don't you think?"

Peter knew he needed to talk to Katrina alone and discuss some of these matters. He could feel what he was doing to her, announcing all of this so dispassionately. "It's possible. I can't say for sure. I just don't know what I'll do."

Frau Schaller was nodding. Katrina was still staring. "All the same, this is good," Frau Schaller said. "We must make you some dinner. How long will you stay?"

"Just tonight, and then I have to go back to Frankfurt."

"I understand. And I want you to know, my job is going very well. You helped us through the worst, and now we'll do fine. We'll never forget you. We'll think of you as a savior to us, always."

"Thank you. But if I helped you a little, it's not nearly so much as you helped me. I was almost finished when you took me in."

"No, no. You would have found a way."

"I might have found food somewhere else. I don't know. But I was broken down, inside, and you helped me get better."

"Peter, all we did was love you. And no one could help but love a boy like you."

But that was more than Peter could imagine. He didn't want to cry, not with Thomas and Rolf already prepared to laugh at all this talk, but it was difficult to think that he could leave these people and never see them again. He looked at Katrina, more openly this time. Tears were running down her cheeks. She didn't bother to wipe them away.

"Listen, while we fix a little something, why don't you and Katrina go out to the living room where you can talk a little."

"All they want to do is *kiss*," Rolf said, and he and Thomas began to laugh.

"Rolf! Don't say such a thing," Frau Schaller told him. But then she said, "The living room isn't very warm, but go out there. And Rolf, Thomas, go and get some air. You've spent too much time in the house today."

The boys were laughing again, but at least they didn't say anything. They grabbed their coats from the pegs by the door, and they headed out the back way. Peter was embarrassed by all of this. He had tried so hard to avoid the idea that he was Katrina's boyfriend, and yet everyone in the family thought of him in that way.

Peter followed Katrina to the living room, still wearing his army jacket, and they sat next to each other on the couch. Katrina switched on a floor lamp, but the room was still mostly dark. Long ago Frau Heiner had sold off most of her furniture, and this old couch and lamp were almost the only pieces she had left. They sat alone, like a little oasis, on a bare wood floor.

"I'm happy for you," Katrina said. "It will be so good for you to see your family."

"Then why are you crying?"

"I'm not crying."

"Then why are tears running down your face?"

She wiped the tears away with the palms of her hands. "They're not," she said. But then she asked, "Will you ever come back?"

"I don't know."

"You won't."

Peter looked away from her. "I don't know whether we'll really go to America. And if we do, I don't know whether I'll like it. I might want to come back."

"American girls are beautiful."

Peter didn't want this. "Katrina, you'll have a hundred boyfriends between now and the time you get married. You'll laugh at the thought that you ever . . . thought of me this way."

"You know that isn't true."

"No, I don't know it." Peter rubbed his hands down his pant legs, felt the stiffness in his thighs. It had been a long day.

"Do you like me, Peter?"

"You know I do."

"For a friend. That's what you always say."

"That's right. And that's how it is. You're very young and, as you always tell me, so am I."

"I'll always love you."

"Katrina, don't say that." He looked away from her. The room was all shadows, and they were sitting in this bit of light as though they were separated from everything.

"That's what Mama says—that I shouldn't tell you how I feel. She says I should not pay so much attention to you, and then you will like me more. But I can't do that. I can never hide the things I really feel."

"You're sixteen. Feelings change."

"I'm seventeen."

"Just barely."

"That's still how old I am. And Mama says I'll be pretty someday—that I won't always be skinny and flat chested. Then you'll like me better."

"Katrina! I'm not like that. I don't like a girl just because of her shape."

"Then what do you like them for?"

Peter was in a trap. The truth was, he had never known other girls, never had the chance, and he had certainly never liked anyone as much as he liked Katrina. "I don't know. I like a girl for . . . everything. The kind of person she is. "

"How *is* my everything?"

When he looked at her, she was smiling, wide and child-like. "I like you, Katrina. You're funny. I like how honest you are." He hesitated, and then he added, "And you have the prettiest eyes I've ever seen."

"Really? Do you mean that?"

"Yes." He was looking into her eyes now, and he was sure he was telling the truth.

"Peter, please come back. At least come back and see me once, when I'm older. See if I'm pretty. See if you like me."

"I've seen you, Katrina. I know you. I'm not worried about that. But I don't know what will happen. I might end up staying in America the rest of my life. I don't know whether I could ever afford to come over here."

"You said you might not like America."

"But I might. I just don't know."

"I could live either place, Peter. I would like America."

"I don't want to talk about this. We can't make plans. Too many things are uncertain."

"Just tell me that we'll see each other one more time before you marry someone."

"I can't promise that, Katrina."

But he was still looking into those brown eyes, with all the golden flecks, and she was leaning toward him. And then he kissed her, even though he hadn't meant to, and after, he told her, "I'll try. All right? That's all I can promise."

He had told himself not to say anything like that, but now she had wrapped her arms around his neck, and she was pulling him close again, kissing him again, and at the same time laughing. And when she let him go, she grinned into his face and said, "I knew it. I even told Mama. You love me. I know you do."

That was something he wouldn't say. But it did seem possible.

10

Hardly a day passed without Bea Thomas asking Wally whether he wanted to be lined up for a date. Wally kept telling her that he wasn't quite ready for that, but then one morning, while Wally was eating his breakfast, she asked him, "Are you going to the stake Christmas dance?"

"I might," he said. "I talked to Chuck about going. We were thinking we'd just go stag and see whether we still know how to dance before we try out our dating skills, full-fledged."

"Okay. But listen. I talked to Sister Iverson, and her daughter just happens to think you're about the best-looking guy around."

"Are you kidding?"

Mom came to the table and sat down across from Wally. "No. Not at all. And this Iverson girl—Patty—she's cute as a bug's ear."

"I'm not sure that's the best recommendation I can think of." Wally was going after his third egg, and he had already eaten several strips of bacon. He was eating a little more carefully these days, but he still relished every fresh egg he ate.

"Trust me. She's really pretty. I told Sister Iverson you probably wouldn't ask anyone to the dance, so she said she'd make sure Patty went without a date. I'm supposed to make sure you at least ask her to dance a few times. Will you do that?"

"I guess so. I have to dance with someone. It might as well be someone who looks like a bug's ear."

Mom ignored that one. "You might think she's a little young for you. But she started up to the U this year, so she's probably nineteen by now, or close to it anyway. And she's smart as a whip."

"Cute as a bug's ear *and* smart as a whip. How does she dance—light as a feather?"

"Well . . . that I can't promise. But Wally, I'm serious. She's pretty and really nice, and she's already interested in you. Give her a chance. All right?"

"I'll give her a *dance* for right now." Wally slid his chair back and stood up. He needed to get to work.

"Not just one. Get to know her."

But Wally promised nothing more, and the truth was, he worried about the situation all week. On Friday night, which was only four days before Christmas, he spent more time getting ready for the dance than he had for anything he had done since high school. He had three new suits that he had bought for work, and he put on the one he liked best: dark blue, double-breasted, with a thin pinstripe. By the time he had wet his hair down and combed it back, he found himself thinking that he didn't look bad at all. But every time he imagined himself asking a girl to dance he felt his stomach take a little jump.

Still, he wasn't half so nervous as Chuck. Chuck had come home a couple of weeks after Wally that fall, and he and Wally had spent a fair amount of time together, but Chuck was having a harder time adjusting to life at home. When Wally stopped by Chuck's place to pick him up, he had gone back to the bathroom to change his tie. "He's already tried four or five different ones," his mother told Wally. "Help him, all right? I never thought I'd see him like this. He hasn't found a job yet, but that's mostly because he's afraid to look. He hardly leaves the house, except when he goes somewhere with you. I keep telling him he's got to get back into the swing of things, just a little at a time, but he's scared to try anything."

"He was the one who talked to me about going to the dance, Sister Adair."

"I know that. But that's only after I practically talked his leg off. If you had told him you weren't going, he wouldn't have gone by himself."

"Well, I'm pretty nervous myself. I guess we'll have to help each other out."

When Chuck came striding into the living room, he looked out of breath, but Wally could see one big change immediately. Since Wally had seen him the week before, he had had his remaining teeth pulled, and he now had false teeth. They looked a little too straight, too white, too big for his mouth—but still, he did look better than when he had come home.

When Wally and Chuck got into Wally's car, however, the first thing Chuck said was, "I feel like a real mug with these new teeth. They don't look natural."

"You'll get used to them. They look fine."

"I look like some old coot, sixty years old. The darn things click when I talk."

The fact was, Wally had picked up a hint of that, and maybe even a bit of a whistle. "Chuck, a lot of people have false teeth. Don't worry about it."

"You know what, Wally? This isn't as good as I thought it would be—being home."

"We probably built it up a little too much."

"Do you ever tell anyone that?"

"No."

"I don't either. My parents think I'm losing my mind, but they don't have any idea what's going on inside my head all the time. I'm not sure I know myself."

"Chuck, we're going to be all right. We have to do it like

we did in the camps. We just take it a day at a time, do what we have to do."

"I thought I was through with that."

Wally knew what he meant. And yet, he could feel that Chuck was struggling more than he was. "We've got to stop doing things, just the two of us. We need to get dates, go to the movies, things like that. I don't know about you, but I want to find someone to date, you know, regular, and start thinking about getting married."

"I need to think that way, too, I guess, but so far I can't imagine what kind of husband I would make. At the very least, I've got to find a job."

"You will. Do you know what kind of work you want to do?"

"No. I don't have the first idea."

Wally made up his mind to check with his dad about work for Chuck, but he decided not to push the matter any further tonight.

At the dance, Wally and Chuck soon found that they had arrived on time—or in other words, way too early. A couple of girls were still putting the final touches on some table decorations around the punch bowl. On one wall, in red and green letters, was a sign that read "Winter Wonderland," and all around it were lacy white paper cut-outs of snowflakes. Smaller snowflakes were hanging on strings from the ceiling. It all looked nice enough, but the band was just settling in, getting ready to play, and Chuck and Wally were two of the first to have shown up. "Should we go somewhere for a while and come back later?" Chuck asked.

"Nah. Let's stick around. People will get here before long."

But the flow of stake members was slow for a time, and most who did arrive seemed to be older people, in couples. Wally was starting to wonder whether he and Chuck would be the only ones there without dates. The two of them stood out of the way, near a corner, talking, watching, and waiting, until the hall gradually did fill up. By then they could see that there were some young women standing together in groups, but most of them looked like high school kids. "Criminy, Wally," Chuck finally said. "I'm not going to rob the cradle. There's no one around who's our age. Let's just go."

"Hey, most of the girls our age are married," Wally told him. "We might have to get to know some of these younger ones."

"Well, then, you go first. Grab one and show me what you can do. You used to really cut a rug."

"I'll go when you go with me."

But neither made a move, and they might have stood around all night if it hadn't been for LaRue. Wally had seen her come in with some girlfriends a little earlier. Someone had asked her to dance almost immediately, and she had hardly missed a dance since. All the same, she dragged a young man with her and walked toward Wally and Chuck. "Hey, I'd begun to think you two weren't even here," she said, as she approached. "Why are you hiding out over here?"

"There's no one for us to dance with," Wally said. "We're too old for the girls who came stag."

"Hogwash," LaRue said. "Mom told me I have to make sure you dance with Patty Iverson. Do you even know which one she is?"

"I thought I'd recognize her—from a picture Mom showed me—but I haven't seen her yet."

"Yes, you have. Look, she's dancing with that guy in the brown suit, right there by the bandstand."

Wally looked through the crowd. The band was playing "Dancing in the Dark," and people were swaying and spinning. He could see a dark-haired girl in a brilliant red dress. In fact, he had noticed her before. She was about as flashy as anyone out there, and as best he could tell, very pretty. "That girl's got a date," he said. "She's been dancing with that same fellow the whole night."

"Wally, that guy just glommed onto her, and he's keeping her for himself. But you can cut in any time you want."

Chuck laughed. "Go ahead and do it," he said.

But Wally hated the idea of walking out and tapping some guy's shoulder. If he did dance, he wanted to ask someone, quietly, and then stay along the edges of the hall while he tried out his unpracticed dancing skills.

"Wally, Mom always says you were the best dancer at East High. It'll all come back to you in a couple of minutes. Listen to the music. You know what to do."

Actually, Wally had found himself tapping his toe, feeling that he did want to get out there.

"Look at Patty. She's the prettiest girl here." LaRue glanced at the tall kid who was holding her hand, and he gave his head a little shake.

"That's what worries me," Wally said.

"Do it, Wally," Chuck said. "Go ask her now, before this number ends."

Wally was thinking. She was too far away. He wasn't going to make that long walk all the way across the hall. But he didn't say that. "Just a minute," he said. "I will . . . at some point."

LaRue laughed at him. "Well, I'm going to go dance. But you'd better get out there pretty soon. Mom's going to hold *me* responsible if you chicken out." She walked off with the boy, still holding his hand.

The song ended, and the guy in the brown suit wasn't walking off the floor with Patty. The two stood on the floor and talked with another couple. "Why don't you cut in on that other girl?" Wally asked Chuck. "The one she's talking to."

"Maybe I will. But not just yet. You get us started."

Wally nodded. He knew better than to wait for Chuck. But he waited until the next number began: "Harbor Lights." That was nice and easy. Wally figured he could handle it. And Mr. Brown Suit had just made a major mistake. He was moving Patty closer, working his way around the outside of the hall.

"This is it," Chuck said. "This is your chance."

Suddenly Wally was stepping onto the floor. As the guy swung Patty around, she spotted Wally coming toward her, and she gave him a big smile. She *was* pretty. She was wearing lipstick as bright as her dress, and her teeth were as white as the snowflakes. And she had dimples! Wally loved dimples. He reached out and tapped the shoulder of that brown suit. The man—a much younger guy than Wally had realized—seemed just a little upset. But that might be all right. Maybe that meant he would be back after a dance or two. Wally could dance a couple of times and be out of this situation before he had to think of something to talk about for very long.

"Hi," he said, as he took hold of Patty, touching her waist, her surprisingly little hand. "My name's Wally Thomas."

"Oh, come on. Do you really think I don't know that?"

"Well, I wasn't sure."

"Every girl in Sugar House knows who you are. You're the handsome war hero."

"Not really."

"I even remember you from before the war. I was kind of young, but you were that good-looking high school boy, President Thomas's son." She smiled, and her dimples sank deep. She had eyes as dark as her hair, and pretty skin. But Wally couldn't help thinking that she looked like a little girl. Mom said she was eighteen, but she seemed even younger than that.

Wally had fallen into a foxtrot step quite easily, and since he couldn't think of anything to say, he brought Patty in a little closer and concentrated for a time on his dancing. He began to make some turns, to feel the music. He liked that, felt as though he hadn't really forgotten much. Patty wasn't a bad dancer either, but she was a little too short, and maybe just a little stiff.

When the music stopped, Wally didn't know what to do. He half expected Patty to walk to the side and thank him. But she turned toward him, kept hold of his arm. "Wally, you're a *wonderful* dancer. You must have been practicing."

"That was the first time I've danced since I got home."

"Really? Oh, my. You're a natural."

Something in her tone of voice seemed too enthusiastic, maybe just a little forced, as though she were nervous herself—and at the same time, aware of the effect her smile, her dimples, could have on a guy. He tried to think of something he could say to her.

"What are you doing now, Wally?"

"I'm working for my dad. I might start taking some college classes before long, but right now, I'm just trying to figure out my job."

"You're too modest. My mom told me you're the manager of the whole plant."

"Not exactly. Not yet. If anyone is the boss, it's my mom." Wally wondered if Patty's remark wasn't a little too transparent. He could almost hear Sister Iverson saying, "That Wally Thomas is going to take over the Thomas businesses someday. He's going to be *rich*."

"I'll bet your mother is anxious to quit working, now that the war is over."

"I'm not so sure about that. I think she likes it."

"Really? I wouldn't want to be boss over a bunch of people—especially men." She put her hands on her hips and tried to make a gruff face. "Get to work, Buddy!" she said, and then she laughed. "Do you think some big guy would listen to me?"

"I've got a feeling that you could smile at a fellow, and he'd do just about anything you wanted."

Wally knew he was flirting, knew that he had returned to an old game he had almost forgotten, but it came as naturally as the dancing, and he saw the words take effect. Patty turned her head a little, gave him a gleaming sidelong smile, and then leaned close and whispered, "All right then. I *command* you to dance with me again."

The band had just begun to play "Mexicali Rose." Wally was relieved to stop talking and dance again, but as he took hold of her, he said, "Your wish is my command, Miss Iverson," with a certain sort of dreaminess in his voice.

She moved in close to him, looked up and winked. "Be careful," she said. "You have no idea what I might be wishing."

Wally let that one go. He was almost too good at this—or *she* was. As he twirled her around, he looked for the fellow in the brown suit, but he was suddenly afraid that the guy might come back too soon. This girl was dazzling, and he did like being close to her, smelling her perfume, touching her back, feeling her hair brush against his face—no matter how much she scared him.

When the number ended, Wally talked with her again—talked about the U, her uncertainty about a major, her sorority—and then they danced to "I Don't Want to Set the World on Fire." The band gave the number an upbeat tempo, and Wally got up his nerve to try some swing steps. Patty did all right, too, and by the time the song ended, she was looking wonderfully flushed and was telling him, "Wally, you're the best dancer I've ever danced with. I can't believe you haven't been practicing."

Wally was looking about, trying to spot Chuck, but the guy had disappeared. Wally hoped that he had found a partner and was dancing too.

"Wally, I've heard that POWs had to put up with terrible, terrible things from the Japs. Was it really so awful as everyone says?"

"It was pretty bad."

"I'll bet it made you strong, didn't it? My mother said she heard that you have a testimony that's just really *burning*."

"Well . . . I wasn't a very religious young man. Something like that does change how you feel about your beliefs."

"That's so neat." She was trying to look serious, but that glowing smile kept sneaking through.

"Neat?"

"I mean, it's just so swell that you have a burning testimony and everything, and you're such a good dancer, too."

Wally was stopped. He couldn't think of a word to say.

"I don't think the younger boys, the ones who didn't go to war, will ever be as strong and mature as you war veterans are."

"Well . . . some guys . . ." But Wally couldn't bring himself to tell her how the war had actually ruined plenty of men. "I just appreciate the way everyone back home supported us guys who were out there," he said, and then he took her hand and began to dance again. The band was playing "I Love You for Sentimental Reasons." What Wally was looking for now was an excuse. At the end of this song maybe he would tell Patty that he couldn't leave Chuck on his own all evening.

But then he spotted Chuck—dancing. He was not far off, and he was looking over a girl's shoulder, grinning. Wally was happy for him and pleased that he seemed to be dancing just fine, even enjoying himself, but then the two turned and Wally realized that Chuck was dancing with Lorraine Gardner. Wally felt a little thrill at seeing her, but only for a moment, and then he realized that he didn't want her there. The comparison had already been in his head, even without seeing her.

Chuck was dancing in a straight line, his feet pounding a little too emphatically with the beat, and he was working his way straight to Wally. As he got close enough, he said, "Hey, Wally, look who I found."

Wally stopped dancing, turned, but kept hold of Patty. He planned to say, "Nice to see you, Lorraine," and then dance away.

"How about we change partners for a dance?" Chuck said.

Wally felt himself clench. He couldn't do that. He gave his head a little shake, but by then Lorraine was turning, smiling at him, and he felt himself deflate. Her serenity, her maturity—

it was all such a contrast to Patty that he suddenly felt he was clinging to a cartoon character, an animated little girl, cute but embarrassing. "Hi, Wally," Lorraine said.

And Wally did what he had to do. He introduced the girls and listened to Patty say, "Lorraine, I know you. I've looked up to you all my life. You're about the prettiest woman I know."

Lorraine let that pass and looked at Wally with a warmth that seemed inappropriate. Was she doing this on purpose just to make him feel silly?

Chuck still looked as jittery as ever, but he said to Patty, "I'm Chuck Adair. May I have this dance?"

Patty tossed a pitiful glance at Wally as if to say "Help!" But he didn't know what to do, and Chuck was soon doing his pounding foxtrot, taking Patty away on another straight line. Lorraine was standing in front of Wally. She reached up, brushed her pretty hair to the side, and said, "It's just like old times."

"Not exactly," Wally said, in defense, and he was rather angry. Chuck had apparently cooked up this plan for some reason, but he couldn't think why Lorraine would go along with it. Still, he took hold of her, began to dance, and he felt her move with him, perfectly, from the first step. She was taller than Patty, smoother, more relaxed, and with each step she moved closer to him, until they were almost touching. But it hurt to be close to her, and Wally wanted out of the situation as soon as he could be.

After a minute or so, Lorraine let go of his hand, reached up and brushed her hair away again, and as she did, she smiled, and there was something clever, mischievous in her manner, as though she were having fun, trying to tantalize him. It wasn't like her to act that way. Maybe time had changed her in ways he hadn't realized.

When the music ended, he said, "Lorraine, I can't do this. I don't think we should dance together."

"Why not?" she asked, and again she smoothed her hair

back. It wasn't a mannerism he remembered, and it seemed awkward, somehow purposeful.

"I just don't think we should. It bothers me."

"What do you mean?"

"Come on, Lorraine. This isn't like you. You know what I'm feeling."

"No, I don't. Tell me." Again, there was a style in this that Wally couldn't identify, a playfulness that seemed almost cruel.

"Don't do this, Lorraine." He took hold of her arm, by the elbow. He was going to walk her off the floor, and then he was going to leave. Right now, he felt he could leave Chuck to walk home on his own.

"Wally, let's just dance one more," Lorraine said. She brushed her hair aside once again, and this time she left her hand against her cheek.

"No, really, Lorraine. I—"

"Wally, look at my hand."

For a moment her meaning wasn't clear to him. And then he saw—even realized—but he couldn't change his thinking so suddenly. It was too much to believe. And yet, there it was: her bare hand, no ring on her finger. "What . . ." But he couldn't think what he wanted to ask.

"Wally, I sent the ring back to John. I'm not going to marry him."

The band began to play again—"Moonlight Becomes You." Wally felt the dancers begin to move, sensed the motion, but it seemed at the moment that the world had evaporated around them. He took hold of her hand and looked at it again, then looked into her eyes, trying to see what she might be saying to him. He couldn't think right, and he needed to. He couldn't presume too much—and then be devastated again.

"Let's dance," she said.

This time she came close enough to touch, her hair against his cheek, her softness against his chest, and he was suddenly afraid that he would cry. Nothing this good could happen to him. It wasn't possible.

The band's singer, a woman with a pretty, deep voice, was singing, "I'm all dressed up to go dreaming."

"Wally, I never felt sure about John. I kept telling myself that he was a good choice, but I never really felt sure about it. Finally, I just decided I couldn't marry someone unless I knew *for sure* that it was right."

What did that mean? Maybe it was her way of telling him that she would have to see whether she could ever be sure about Wally. *Don't jump to conclusions,* he kept telling himself.

And then she leaned back a little. "Wally, when you left me at home after conference, and you drove away, I felt the way I did clear back when you went into the army. I went into the house and cried and cried. And that's when I made up my mind. I had to send the ring back."

Wally was out of breath now. "Is it all right if we leave?" he asked, in a kind of gasp.

"Yes," she said, and she laughed. "I'm sorry, Wally. I shouldn't have surprised you this way. I didn't know when I could talk to you. I wanted to call, but I wasn't sure what to say."

Wally was nodding, and then he was moving her off the dance floor. He did think of Chuck, sort of vaguely, but not enough to slow him down. He escorted her out the door, stopped to get her coat, only waved toward those who greeted him, and kept going to his car in the parking lot. Once he had opened her door, had walked around and sat down behind the steering wheel, he started the car and turned on the heater, but it was blowing cold air, so he turned it back off, and before he thought where he was going to go, he tried to think of the right question.

"Lorraine, what would it take to be sure of someone—so you *knew* you wanted to marry him?"

She took hold of his hand, waited until he looked at her.

There was no moonlight, but there was a light pole not far from the car, and something like moonlight was across her face. "I'd have to know, absolutely, that I was in love with him, and that he loved me. And I'd have to know that he was a truly good man and would always be good to me. And he would have to be strong and worthy, someone I knew I could be with for eternity."

Wally tried to think of the next question.

"Wally, he would have to be you."

Wally drew in some air. How could this be true? How could he have gone from nothing to everything in only a few months, only a few minutes?

"I love you, Wally. I've never stopped loving you."

Wally turned and took hold of her shoulders. "Lorraine, you've been absolutely everything to me for as long as I can remember."

He finally took her into his arms, held her for a time, and then moved back enough to kiss her. The soft roundness of her lips was familiar and new at the same time, and the touch sent a numbness through him. He leaned back and looked at her. "Lorraine—"

"Don't ask me here. Not in this cold, old car. We're always going to remember this, and it ought to be romantic."

Wally let his mind run ahead, tried to think when, where, how. What would be romantic? He didn't want to put this off. His mind ran back the other direction, searching for the things that mattered to them. Then he knew. "Just a minute," he said. "I'll be right back," and he jumped out of the car.

Wally ran to the church and hurried into the recreation hall. He worked his way through the crowd, ignoring a couple of people who tried to talk to him. As he approached the bandstand, he reached for his wallet and pulled out a couple of dollar bills. He found the band leader, who was playing the clarinet at the moment. Wally waited for maybe thirty seconds but couldn't stand it, and so he interrupted, pushed the bills into the man's hand, and said, "You *must* play, 'I Get Along Without You Very Well.' Will you? Next song?"

"Sure," the man said, a big fellow who was smiling, probably at Wally's urgency.

But Wally didn't care. He trotted to a side door, pushed the handle, and swung the door wide open to the cold. He grabbed a young man who was standing nearby. "Listen, I need your help," he said. He reached into his pocket, found a quarter, and handed it to the boy. "Keep this door open until this next song is over, no matter what. If people ask you what you're doing, tell them the building was too hot—or something—but stall them until the song is over. It'll be 'I Get Along Without You Very Well.'"

The boy was nodding, so Wally took off. He ran halfway to the car before he realized that he had time, that the new song wouldn't begin for a time. He slowed, tried to catch his breath, tried to think exactly how to handle this. As he approached the car, the previous song ended, and he knew the timing was right. He opened the door on Lorraine's side and said, "Excuse me. Could I have the next dance? The parking lot is available."

She smiled when she realized what he was doing, and she said, "And a lovely parking lot it is, sir." She slid across the seat and then stepped out, reaching for his hand as she did. But the song hadn't started, and Wally felt as though he would burst during the silence. She seemed entirely agreeable to dancing in the quiet, however, and she put her arm around him. He took her hand and began to dance, setting the rhythm himself.

Then the song began. It came softly from the building, only just audible, but clear enough, and when she heard it, she said, "Oh, Wally, of course. I should have known."

He kissed her, and then they danced among the cars, in the cold air. She was wrapped up in her coat, but she still felt wonderful next to him. She began to sing, softly, with the band.

How many times had Wally let the words run through his head? How long had he been dreaming that this could happen?

He stopped dancing when he knew that the number couldn't last much longer. He kept her hand in his, and he knelt on the blacktop, on one knee. "Lorraine," he said, "will you marry me?"

"Yes, Wally, I will." She hesitated and then added, "but only on one condition."

"Which is?"

"That we not wait until spring. Let's get married right away, okay?"

"Oh, yes," he said, too aghast to be clever. He stood, and he kissed her again, but he had begun to cry, and so he ended the kiss quickly, and he held her in the silence, after the song had ended. "Father in Heaven, I thank thee for this," he whispered.

Lorraine was crying by then too, and she told him, "Wally, this was supposed to happen. This is the right thing for both of us."

Wally was thinking it was the right thing for all his forebears, for all his posterity. It was God being in his life, just when he needed him most.

Wally and Lorraine didn't forget about Chuck. But they didn't want to tell him first. So Wally went back and made sure Chuck could get a ride home. And Wally admitted that he had never been so happy in his life—which told Chuck all he needed to know. "How are things going with Patty?" Wally asked.

"She put me on the bench," Chuck said, grinning. "But I got back in the game. I've danced with four other girls."

"Good! Nice going, Chuck. It wasn't so bad, was it?"

"It was terrible. But I feel—you know—like I've made a little headway tonight."

"That's great. I'll talk to you tomorrow."

And then Wally hurried back to Lorraine. They drove to

the Gardner's house, where Lorraine's parents admitted that they weren't surprised, that they had seen this coming for a few days. They even seemed not to mind. Maybe Lorraine had convinced them that Wally really had changed.

Afterward, Lorraine and Wally drove to his house. "Stay on the porch for just a minute," he told Lorraine. And then he stepped quietly in through the front door. He found his parents sitting in the living room together, both reading.

"Well, you're home early," Mom said.

"Yeah. I did about all the dancing I wanted to do."

"Did you dance with Patty?"

"Yes, I did. She's pretty, just like you said."

"Do you want to take her out on a date?"

"Actually . . . I don't think so. See . . . well . . . something a little surprising happened tonight."

"What's that?"

"I got engaged."

Dad, who hadn't been paying much attention, looked up from his book. He and Mom both looked amused, as though they were waiting for Wally to tell the rest of the joke.

"Really, I did. I'm getting married right away. That way I won't have to worry about a lot of dating."

"Oh, I see," Mom said. "It's a wonderful plan. And who is this young lady you've chosen to marry? Not Patty?"

"No. Someone else. Do you want to meet her?"

"That might be nice."

"All right. Just a minute. She's outside."

Wally stepped outside, took Lorraine's hand, and led her through the door, then on through the front entryway and into the living room. As she came out of the darkened area and into the light, Wally saw his mother's hand leap to her face. "Oh, Lorraine," she said. "Lorraine. Is this really happening? Are you two serious?"

"We are," Lorraine said.

Mom was up by then, crying hard, instantly. "This is too wonderful. Too wonderful. It's what we always wanted."

Dad was out of his seat by then. He came to Lorraine and took her into his arms. Wally stood and watched, tried to believe it, but he was still trying to convince himself that all this had really happened.

11

It was Christmas morning, early. Beverly, in a nightgown and robe, was mixing up dough for hot rolls while Mom was stuffing the turkey. Wally had already driven to Lorraine's house and brought her back. Over the weekend Wally had bought a ring, and he and Lorraine had made the engagement official. They had spent part of Christmas Eve with Lorraine's parents and part with the Thomases, and now, before LaRue was even out of bed, here they were in the kitchen.

"Hey, when do we get started?" Wally wanted to know. "I think Santa's been here."

"It used to be I couldn't make you kids stay in bed on Christmas morning," Mom told Wally. "Now, the girls don't want to get up."

"What are you talking about? I'm up," Beverly said. "And LaRue told me she'd be down in a minute."

"I'll bet she rolled over and went right back to sleep," Mom said, and she laughed. She had put on a dress already and was wearing a pretty white apron, but her hair was still pinned up and wrapped with a scarf.

Beverly didn't admit it, but she knew her mother was probably right. It would be just like LaRue to stay in bed as long as she could.

"Is Dad still in bed?" Wally asked.

"Are you kidding? He's in his office. I don't know what he does in there, now that he's released, but it's still his little sanctuary."

"I'll go wake LaRue up," Wally said. "I've been looking forward to this too long. I want it to be as much like the old days as possible."

"Well, it would be a lot better if Bobbi and Alex could come home. I'm feeling a little blue about that this morning. I want to see the baby so bad I can hardly stand it." She looked up from the turkey for a moment. "We did get some new snapshots of him. They're over there on the cabinet."

Beverly got the pictures and showed them to Lorraine, who looked at each shot carefully before she passed them on to Wally. "He's *beautiful*," Lorraine said. "Too pretty to be a boy."

"What are you talking about?" Wally said. "Us Thomas boys are all beautiful." He reached out and caught Beverly in a headlock. "And the girls are *almost* as pretty."

"Don't mess up my hair," Beverly said, but he let go more quickly than she expected—or wanted—so she clung to him, with her arms around his waist. She still liked to be close to him. She had thought so many times that he ought to be home on Christmas, and now, finally, she had him there. But she also felt the way Mom did. She wanted Bobbi home. And she wanted Alex and Anna, and little Gene. She wanted to hug Gene, and she wanted to play with him on the floor, give him lots of Christmas gifts.

Next year. That could happen next year, everyone said, but that still seemed much too long. She was going to miss knowing him during all these precious months when he was little.

"Richard is coming over this afternoon," Mom said. "He's prettier than any of you Thomas boys."

"That's right," Beverly said. "And he's going to give up on Bobbi one of these days and marry *me*."

"That's what Bev would like, anyway," Mom said. "She's got such a crush on that man."

"Oh, I do not," Beverly said. "He's *very* old. Even older than Wally." She squeezed Wally harder around the middle.

"Come on," Wally said. "Let's go roll LaRue out of bed."

So Beverly followed him up the stairs, and Wally pounced on LaRue, rubbed her face with his whiskers, tickled her, and then, finally, pulled her out of bed by the arm. She ended up on the floor, looking frazzled but not upset. Wally could always get away with things she would have thrown a fit about, had anyone else tried.

"Leave me alone," she said. "I'll get ready. I'll be down in a minute."

"No, you won't. You'll take an hour," Wally said. "And it's *Christmas*. I don't want to wait to open my presents."

"I won't take a bath now. I won't wash my hair. I'll jut run a brush through it and put on my robe."

"Okay. It's a deal. I'll give you thirty seconds—no, one full minute—to get downstairs."

"Hey, give me time to go to the bathroom, for crying out loud."

"I did. That's why I added thirty seconds." Then he turned around and looked at Beverly, who had stayed close to the door. "Come on, Bev," he said. "Let's go open LaRue's presents for her."

LaRue was up now, heading toward her closet. "You'd better not," she muttered, but Wally was already flying downstairs. "Hey, Dad," he was yelling. "Come on out. LaRue's going to be here in *one* minute, and the festivities will begin."

In a moment Dad's door came open, and he stepped out, smiling. He had already shaved and dressed, but he had taken to a little more casualness lately. He didn't have a white shirt on, or a tie. He had on a blue sports shirt, and his top button was unbuttoned. "What's all the racket around here?" he said, but he was laughing. "Where's Lorraine? Did you go get her?"

One thing Beverly knew was that Dad was crazy about Lorraine. And she seemed to know it, too. She appeared at the kitchen door just then, walked over, and gave him a kiss on the cheek. "Merry Christmas," she said.

"You haven't changed your mind, have you?" he asked. "Do you still want to marry this boy of mine?"

"I still do. After all these hours."

"Well, that's good. I hope you can train him to behave. You might have to spank him with a newspaper once in a while."

"Don't give her ideas," Wally said. "I already follow her around like a little puppy."

"Is that why your tongue is hanging out?"

Bev loved all this. She liked Lorraine so much, and she liked the happiness in her dad's voice. He had been a little at loose ends lately, home more than ever before, and often silent.

"Dad," Wally said, "that paperwork still hasn't come through from Bendix. I called back there last week and the lady said she sent it, but it ought to be here by now."

"Well, the post office is probably really slow right now. People are sending a lot more cards than they did during the war."

Mom stepped through the door. She had taken off her apron. "None of that," she said. "I won't hear any shop talk today." She turned and called, "LaRue, you now have ten seconds, and then we're starting." But then, as she walked into the living room, she asked Wally, "Who did you talk to at Bendix?"

"I can't remember for sure. They gave me the runaround and finally put me on the phone with a woman named Dixie, or something like that."

"Okay. That's your mistake. Always talk to Mary Ann. And don't let them give you that business about the paperwork being in the mail. They always say that."

"Now who's talking business?" Dad said.

Beverly heard LaRue's steps on the stairs, and then she heard her shout, "Don't look up and hurt your eyes. The sun has just appeared. Ta-da!" She entered the living room in her old flannel robe, strutting like a model. She actually looked great—even dressed that way, and even with her stringy hair. Bev would have given anything to look that good so early in the morning.

Mom hadn't set out presents by the tree this year, the way she had when the kids were young. Some of the presents were from Santa Claus, and some from Mom and Dad or others in the family, but everything was wrapped. So the pile was very high. Alex had sent things from Germany, Bobbi from Hawaii, and even the Stoltzes had sent a little box from London. Wally sat on the floor and handed out the gifts, and he made sure the old rule applied: no one could open a package until the last person had finished opening his or hers and had shown the gift to everyone. Bev was amazed, and pleased, at how long it took. And she was excited about all presents she got: sweaters and skirts and blouses, new shoes, a watch from Germany, a teak jewelry box from Hawaii, a beautiful red robe from Wally, and a doll from LaRue to remind her, as LaRue said, that she was still the baby of the family. But it was a beautiful doll with a china face, carefully chosen, and Beverly loved it.

LaRue had most of the same things, including a robe like Beverly's, which she changed into immediately. Mom and Dad and Wally received lots of nice gifts too. The best moment came when Wally opened a box and found the tie that he had helped LaRue and Beverly buy for Dad, all the way back in 1939. It was a wide maroon thing with a flock of ducks hand-painted across it. "I thought you deserved that, Wally," Dad said. "It's been close to my heart, so to speak, all these years, but since you liked it enough to choose it for me, I wanted you to have it."

"Hey, it's great," Wally said. "I'll wear it to church this Sunday."

"You do that."

"In fact, I'll wear it every Sunday . . . as long as Lorraine doesn't mind."

"Go right ahead," Lorraine said. She rolled her eyes and laughed.

Beverly loved to watch Lorraine and Wally touch each other, glance at one another and smile, lean together as though magnetized. She wanted so much to have someone that close to her someday.

The Stoltzes had sent the family a porcelain figurine of a lovely white swan. "Oh, my goodness, that must have cost them so much, and they have so little," Mom said. She carried it to her little knickknack shelf in the corner and placed it alongside the cats. "I'll have to think what we're going to do with it after we get our new furniture."

Bev had heard her parents talking all week about the furniture they had been picking out and ordering at Southeast Furniture in Sugar House. Mom said they had given Wally time enough to see the old house the way it had been, but now she really wanted to get some new things.

When all the presents were finally open, Mom told everyone that she wanted them to eat something decent for breakfast before they ate a lot of Christmas candy. "I love hearing you say that, Mom," Wally said. "On Christmas, all these years I've been gone, I would try to have my own Christmas day—you know, in my mind. I'd think all day about what you were doing back here. I'd say to myself, 'The presents are open by now, and Mom is saying, "Let's all eat a good breakfast before we start in on a lot of sweets."'" He turned to his dad and said, "And it's time for you to say, 'Don't anyone run off. I want to have a little meeting right after breakfast.'"

"That's exactly what I *am* going to say. So don't run off."

"We do need to run over to the Gardners before too much longer, but I'll tell you, I wouldn't miss your meeting for anything in the world. I want to hear your speech—every word of it. I've been looking forward to it for five years."

Bev laughed, and so did everyone else. They all knew how much Wally had fussed about the meetings—before LaRue had taken over the job.

Mom was serious about the breakfast. She scrambled eggs, and Lorraine made toast. Wally poured glasses of milk while he teased the girls, and then everyone ate together at the table. When they returned to the living room and took their seats around the tree again, Dad said, "I want to do something a little different this year. But let's start with a song and a prayer."

He called on Mom to pray. After the family sang "Silent Night," she thanked the Lord for the glorious day it was. By then, the mood was changing, everyone seeming to sense what an important time this was, finally to have Wally there again, and now, Lorraine. Dad still sounded almost jovial, however, when he said, "I'm not going to give a speech this year. I wouldn't dare, with Wally back. I'll say something at the end— but only for two minutes. And you can time me with all those new watches Alex sent you. What I want is for all of you to take about the same amount of time—two minutes or less— and just say what you're thankful for this Christmas. I'll ask Bev to start."

Beverly was taken by surprise. She hardly knew what to say. There were lots of things to be thankful for—but all of them were so obvious. "Well . . . okay," she said.

"Come on, speak up," Dad said, "or no one will hear you."

"All right." And she did try to raise her voice. "I'm thankful that Wally's home, of course. But I wish he wouldn't leave us quite so soon." She tried to laugh, but the truth was, she had had a hard weekend, just thinking that Wally would be leaving home all over again. "I *am* thankful that he's marrying Lorraine. I always prayed that she would wait for Wally, and we could have her in our family. Now I wish she would come to live with us—instead of taking Wally away."

Beverly hadn't been able to keep the emotion out of her voice, and she was a little embarrassed. But she was sitting next to Wally on the big couch, and he turned and kissed her on the top of the head. Lorraine reached across Wally and took hold of Beverly's hand. "Thank you, Bev," she said. "I'm sorry to steal him."

"Don't worry," LaRue said. "In another month or two, we would have gotten tired of him."

Everyone laughed, but Mom said, "I hate to admit it, because it sounds so selfish, but I was praying for the same thing. I wanted Lorraine for myself."

"I did, too," Dad said.

Lorraine gripped Beverly's hand tighter, and said, "I prayed for almost the same thing. I kept asking that I'd know the right thing to do, but I could never feel sure of John. I just kept thinking about Wally."

Wally said, "I guess I'm the only one who didn't pray for this marriage to happen." He laughed softly. "I didn't dare. I thought it was too much to ask for. It's lucky the rest of you had more faith than I did."

Everyone sat quietly for a time. Wally pulled Lorraine close to him. Dad finally said, "Well, we're off to a rough start here. At this rate, you'll all be bawling too much to talk." But there was emotion in his voice. "Lorraine, I guess we've heard what you're thankful for. Is there anything you want to add to that?"

"I'm thankful for all of you. Even when Wally wasn't much to brag about, I loved him. I always wanted to be in your family."

LaRue was sitting on the floor, close to Wally. She slapped his knee and said, "See, Wally. Without us, you never would have had a chance with her."

"Hey, I'm starting to think that's right," Wally said.

"I don't think I'd better joke about that," Lorraine said. "I love Wally so much. And I have for a long time. I tried to let him go, but I just couldn't." She took hold of his hand again. "And now we have an announcement. It's something else I'm thankful about."

"We know you're engaged," Bev said.

"Yes. But we've set a date. And it's going to make life a little crazy for a month, but we don't want to wait a long time. We're getting married on the twenty-fifth of January."

President Thomas grinned. "That one is not news to Bea and me. We talked to the kids about it last night. But we're really pleased. There's not one reason to wait a long time at this point."

This was even worse than Beverly had thought. Wally would be gone so soon. "Congratulations," she whispered to Lorraine, but it was hard for her not to show what she was really feeling.

"So tell us what you're thankful for, Wally," Dad said. "As if we didn't know."

"I can't even start to tell you how wonderful everything seems to me right now," he said. He pulled Lorraine in close to him again. "Sometimes I thought I would never see all of you again, never have another Christmas at home. And I didn't even dare imagine that Lorraine would still be single." He looked down at Lorraine's hand in his, the pretty ring. "But I could give you a list of things I'm thankful for that would take me all day to name off. I'm thankful for hot water and soap, for toothpaste, toothbrushes, a bed to sleep in, sheets, and pillows. I'm thankful for my razor, for good shoes, for decent clothes, for a warm house, just the smell of that turkey Mom's cooking. I was thinking this week how wonderful a thing a set of fingernail clippers is. I could say a prayer at night, just giving thanks that I own a pair."

"We forget about all those things," Dad said.

"I'll tell you something else. I'm thankful for my country. When I saw the Golden Gate Bridge, I cried like a little kid. I don't think anyone in the world is as blessed as we are— especially right now. I'm proud we fought for the right things, but I'm also thankful we didn't have to fight in our own land, the way so many countries did."

"I agree with that," Dad said. "In fact, I'll only need about a minute and a half now, because that was something I was going to say."

"Before you move on," Wally said, "let me add one more thing. The Lord did something for me right after the war ended. I haven't said much about it because it's hard for me to explain. But one day, just when I could have been full of anger, I felt the Lord reach inside me and pull out all the hatred and resentment. I don't know why I received that gift because a lot of the men will never get over those feelings. But I don't feel any hatred toward anyone, and that's what I'm most thankful for today. Of course, part of why I feel that way is that I know Lorraine never would have wanted me if I'd come home full of bitterness."

Dad nodded and then seemed to consider for a time before he said, "Wally, I think you received that gift because you were ready for it. When it came, you didn't fight it off; you recognized what a treasure it was."

"Maybe. But I was angry, and then I wasn't. And I didn't do one thing to try to change."

Beverly didn't believe that. She knew Wally. She had always known how kind he really was. She remembered how sweet he had been to her. Even his teasing had always been fun, not hurtful.

Dad looked down at LaRue. "What about you, LaRue? What are you thankful for?"

"I've been thinking about the things Wally said—about having shoes and clothes and soap and everything. It bothers me that we have so much stuff while almost everyone in the world is suffering right now. It doesn't seem right. We shouldn't just be thankful, we should be doing something for those people. And maybe we shouldn't be getting so much."

Beverly saw everyone look at LaRue as though they were not quite certain she was serious. Finally, Wally said, "Excuse me. But when did Bobbi get home? I thought that was LaRue sitting over there."

"Be quiet," LaRue said, and she stuck out her tongue at Wally. "I really mean it."

"Are you saying we're too materialistic—that we commercialize Christmas too much? Because I seem to remember hearing that somewhere before."

"Now I have *nothing* left to say," Dad said, and everyone laughed.

"Okay, okay," LaRue said. "I know how I've always been. But I still think what I just said is true."

"Today, you feel that way," Mom said. "What about when the after-Christmas sales begin tomorrow?"

"I don't want to go this year," LaRue said seriously, even defensively, and Beverly could tell that LaRue meant it.

Dad also seemed to trust in LaRue's sincerity. "LaRue, I agree with you," he said. "One of the things I wanted to tell all of you today was that your mom and I made a sizeable donation to the Church a few days ago. The Brethren are getting ready to ship food and clothing and supplies to Europe and Asia, and they're trying to get permission to do it. When it happens, I want you to know that our family will be involved."

Mom added, "We've had lots of letters from Alex, and he's told us how much hunger there is all across Europe. And Bobbi tells us the same thing about Japan. We want to help, and not just on a one-time basis. We'll keep doing as much as we can. Evil men may have started this war, but the starving children don't deserve the punishment for it."

Dad nodded, and then he said, "Go ahead, Bea. Tell us what you're thankful for."

"Oh, I think everyone has said it all. I could just sit here and look at Wally and Lorraine together and never ask for another blessing in my life." She laughed. "I just hope they get busy and have some grandchildren for me, really fast. That's where I'm still greedy."

"I'll do the best I can, Mom," Wally said, and he grinned.

Beverly could hardly believe he would say such a thing—or that Mom would laugh about it. And LaRue only made things worse by saying, "Anything for Mom. Right, Wally?"

Beverly was sitting next to Dad's chair, on the floor, where everyone could look at her. She stared straight at her own knees. She hoped no one would start teasing her about blushing, but she could feel her cheeks, her ears, catching fire. She was relieved when Dad ignored the talk and said, "Well, you have taken all the things I was going to say. I wanted to tell you about the donation we made to the Church, for this relief fund, but I've said that now. Why don't we just kneel down for a family prayer, and I'll say that."

So everyone knelt, and Dad, in that strong voice of his, pronounced the words slowly and distinctly, "Our Father in Heaven, we have gathered here today as a family to celebrate the birth of thy Son, and to share our joy in having *our* own son back with us."

Then the formality left his voice as he said, "Oh, Lord, how can we thank thee enough? When we lost Gene, we feared that we would never be happy again, but now we know the joy of meeting after a long absence, and we realize the day will come when we'll experience an equal joy, or greater, as each of us, in turn, crosses the veil and finally gathers with thee, and with Gene. We thank thee that Wally and Lorraine will soon be joined for eternity, sealed forever to each other, and to us. Bea and I have little more to ask of thee, Father, except that we'll have the strength to weather all the further tests that come to us in this life."

He prayed then for Bobbi and Alex and Anna and little Gene, and for the Stoltz family, and asked that the *entire* family might gather on the following Christmas. When he was finished, everyone was silent, as though they were moved too deeply to break the mood they felt. Beverly saw LaRue look across the room at Wally. He nodded to her, and LaRue

nodded back. Beverly didn't know exactly what they were saying to one another, but she knew that LaRue was struggling
with some things and that Wally had spent a lot of time with
her lately, just talking. And now LaRue seemed pleased by
something and willing to let Wally know that.

* * *

The Stoltzes were sitting in their little living room. It was
Christmas afternoon, and Peter hadn't arrived. What was worse
was that they hadn't heard from him for over a week. Anna
thought it would be easier if she and her parents had known
for sure that Peter was on his way, or that he would be coming
sometime soon. What she feared was that the American military officials had decided not to let him leave the country.
Because he'd fought in the war under an assumed name, there
might be complications in establishing an identity, in receiving
permission to travel. He might even be suspected as a Nazi.
What Anna and her parents all kept clinging to was Alex's
promise that he had the right connections, that he could get
something done.

The Stoltzes had actually received an abundance of gifts,
almost all of them from Alex's family in Salt Lake City. Three
large boxes had arrived a few days before Christmas. The
largest one had been mailed to Master Eugene Thomas. And
the box had been a treasure trove of things he needed. There
were clothes to last a year, in increasing sizes, and a dozen
heavy cotton diapers. But with it were also American powders
and lotions, wonderful baby foods and bibs and spoons. There
were also toys. What Gene loved most was a little wheeled toy
with a bell on it that rang when he pushed it across the floor.
He would roll it and laugh and then crawl after it. The Stoltzes
watched him play with that and a soft toy tiger, and this provided most of the joy in their day.

There were two lovely dresses for Anna, a soft blue one she
could wear to church and another for everyday. There were
also some wonderful fabrics. Sister Thomas had sent a note that

said, "I don't know your size, Frieda, but I've heard that it's hard to get material in England. Maybe you can sew something from these. I hope you have access to a sewing machine." What she had sent was a pretty cotton print, some cream-colored nylon for a blouse, and a lovely rose crepe for a dress. She had even sent thread and buttons. Sister Stoltz was thrilled by all of it. A woman in the building had a treadle sewing machine that she had offered to lend to Frieda, and so she knew she could make the most of the fabric. "I won't look quite so threadbare," she told Anna, but not in front of her husband, and Anna knew why. She didn't like to make him feel bad about the sparseness in their lives.

Brother Stoltz was also thrilled with his gift. President Thomas had sent him a copy of *Jesus the Christ,* by James Talmage, and *A Marvelous Work and a Wonder,* by LeGrand Richards. Brother Stoltz knew of these books, had known members in the London branch who owned them, but to possess them himself was obviously thrilling to him. And then he opened a letter inside one of the books. President Thomas had written a note: "Dear Brother Stoltz, we know that you have lost much of your livelihood by taking your stand against Hitler. We honor you for that, and we want to help. You are such a blessing to our grandchild, and we can do so little. Let us help you a little for now with this small token of our appreciation. I will send more later and continue to help, if you don't mind." Inside the letter was a folded money order for $500. It was more money than the Stoltzes had seen at one time since they had gone on the run in Germany. It would go a very long way when converted into pounds, and it would make life much easier for them for quite some time.

Anna knew that the money was not easy for her father to accept, but she told him, "They want their grandson to be all right. It's only right that they want to share in taking care of him."

"That's right," Sister Stoltz said. "It's not a handout. It's a fine thing for them to do for us."

Heinrich seemed to accept that, and Anna thought she saw some relief in his face. He sat and read the first chapter of *Jesus the Christ*, struggling a little with the English at times and looking up quite a few words, but obviously delighted with the project.

The Thomases had sent nothing for Peter, having sent the box before anyone had known that he had been located, and Anna wished that they had something more for him, with all these other presents. But in Germany, before the war, they had never given lots of gifts, and the Bible and Book of Mormon the family had bought should surely please him—if he got there someday.

By evening, Anna was actually glad to have the day almost over. It was one more Christmas without Alex, and one more without Peter, ended. She hoped that she would never experience another year of the same kind. And maybe tomorrow they would receive mail, some word about what was happening to Peter.

It was well after dark when someone knocked at the door. "Who can that be?" Sister Stoltz said, but it was hard for Anna not to hope. Both got up at the same time, and then Anna nodded and let her mother be the one to go to the door. But she stood and waited, watched the door from across the kitchen.

When the door opened, Anna saw a young man. A full second, maybe two, passed before her senses could accept what she was seeing. There was Peter, a man—not the boy she had held in her consciousness all these years. He was tall, taller than his father, but slender. He hadn't shaved for a few days, and a rather fleecy beard covered his chin. But she knew his eyes, her father's eyes, deep and good and unchanged.

"Peter!" Mother gasped.

Anna hardly knew what happened after that. Everyone ended up inside, in the kitchen, all wrapped around each other, all crying. No one could think of much of anything to say. Mother kept repeating, "Peter, you're home. Home at last," and Anna heard her father say, "Oh, Peter, I'm sorry for what I put you through."

But Peter still hadn't spoken his first word.

After a time, Anna thought of the baby and went to her room. She brought back Gene, still asleep, but with his eyes rolling open at times, and she put him in Peter's arms. Peter held him close and sobbed. Finally he said, "I thought I would never see you again. Any of you."

It was a long time before everyone could sit down at the kitchen table. Anna took Gene back, rocked him a little, and put him in his crib. When she returned to the kitchen, her father was saying, "I've always wondered what happened that day—there at the border."

"I saw the guard coming, with a dog, and I had to go back. Then I heard the shooting, and I didn't know whether any of you had been shot. I went back to Bure, the way Crow told us to, but he didn't come, and then a policeman tried to arrest me, so I ran. I went back to Basel, but the Gestapo was waiting for me there, at the British consulate."

"They arrested you, didn't they? I found that out."

"Yes. They took me into Germany. But the train I was on was bombed, and I escaped."

"That was a miracle, Peter."

Peter looked down at the table. "Maybe. I don't know. But it put me in a bad position. There was nowhere to go. Everywhere I turned, I knew I would be arrested again, and I had no food, no money."

"That's why you joined the army, isn't it?"

"Yes. But I didn't have to join. I could have gone to jail."

"They would have killed you."

"Probably."

"You did the right thing."

Peter looked at his father, and Anna saw the shame, the worry. "I don't know. But I don't want to talk about it now."

"You did the right thing. There are things I did, Peter—things I wish I had done other ways. We all have those regrets. But you did the only thing you *could* do, and you survived a nightmare."

But Peter didn't seem to accept that. Anna could see that he was troubled—seriously troubled—and she wondered what it would take for him to heal. "It's Christmas, Papa," she said. "Let's think about that—and not all these other matters."

Peter nodded. "There's something I want to tell you," he said. He looked at his father. "Papa, one time, when I thought I was lost, and God didn't care about me, I heard your voice. I heard you speak to me and tell me you still loved me. I heard it in my head, and it kept me going."

Brother Stoltz bent forward and held the sides of his head in his hands. "I spoke to you so often," he said. "I always believed that somehow you would hear me."

His tears were dripping onto the table.

1 2

Bobbi Thomas was on a train, on her way home. She had hoped to get out of the navy before Christmas, had even received promises that she would, but her papers hadn't been processed until January. She was still irritated about that, but at least she was going to be home in time for Wally's wedding. Now, however, as she crossed the Sierra Nevada, she wondered whether she shouldn't have stayed in Hawaii until spring. She had longed to see winter again, to know four seasons, but the snow was piled so high in some of the passes that the train was delayed several times. She was reminded of just how cold and inconvenient winter could be.

By the time the train approached the Wasatch Front, however, and she could see "her" mountains in the distance, she was moved by her sense of the familiar. This was, after all, home, and nowhere else ever could be. Before long she would be seeing her family. She walked to a little rest room on the train and washed her face, tidied her hair, and put on a little lipstick. She hadn't been able to get a berth in a Pullman car, so she had sat up all night, and she was afraid she looked pretty dragged out. She found herself quivering a little, partly from the excitement, perhaps, but also because she hadn't slept much. Maybe, too, she had spent too much time during the night wondering about

Richard. He had written regularly lately, and he was saying all the right things. His hands continued to improve as he exercised them every day, and he was eager to have her home. But none of this seemed to fit with the confusion and reticence she had seen in him before he had left Hawaii. She wondered whether he was only saying what he thought she wanted to hear.

Bobbi had her answer. She was going to marry Richard. What she didn't feel was any peace with the decision. There were times when she wanted to say, "Lord, I know I asked, and so you answered, but couldn't you have ignored me? You've done it plenty of times before. If he's the right one, how come I have so many questions in my mind?"

The train stopped in Ogden for much longer than Bobbi liked, but she didn't get off. She sat and watched the sun rise higher above the mountains. In her car she had heard eastern people and southern people, talking in odd accents, but now some of the people boarding spoke with a certain absence of music that she associated with her own speech. She couldn't have said what it was in the voices that she recognized, but it sounded like home. One man sat down and began to read an *Ogden Standard-Examiner.* When he opened it, she saw the back page, with a huge ad for new Fords, now back on the market, but when he turned the paper around, the headline read: "VIO- LENCE FLARES IN CHICAGO, LA STRIKES." So much was changing in the country now. People wanted to put the war behind them, but they had lost their common goal, and with that was coming renewed discord, and maybe even some greed. Bobbi understood that, but she wondered whether people at home had learned the right lessons from the war. She had seen Tokyo, knew what war meant. She had read recently that Emperor Hirohito had been forced to announce to his people that he was not to be considered divine, and she knew how humiliating that would be to all the Japanese. She almost hated to see Americans getting so much so fast.

The train finally pulled from the Union Pacific station and

pushed south toward Salt Lake City, past Kaysville,
Farmington, Bountiful. She had driven through those towns, on
Highway 89, and she knew the sort of people who lived in the
houses. They were good and solid—her people. She liked
the look of the planted trees, the straight streets laid out on a
grid, but she also knew that most of these people hadn't seen
as much of the world as she had. She didn't want to return
home smug about her experiences, but she couldn't escape the
idea that her vision of life had been broadened beyond that of
those who had stayed at home. She had known and even been
friends with people who would have created suspicion here.
Mormons had a way of talking about "us" and "them" and feeling a little superior, morally, to all of "them." "That's what *we*
believe," people would say, "but out in the world . . ." And the
contrast always made everyone else seem corrupt and godless.

How would she like living here again? She wasn't the same
person. In some ways she wanted everything back—the way
she remembered life at home—but she knew there was no way
to slide back into her old ways and cast aside her understanding of people, or the way she perceived her world now.

During the last few miles—as the train approached the Rio
Grande station in Salt Lake City—Bobbi stopped asking such
questions. She pictured her parents at the train, and probably
LaRue and Beverly. She wondered whether Wally would be
there too, or whether she would have to wait to see him. And,
of course, she wondered whether Richard would come with her
family. She thought she knew him well enough to guess that
he would not want to be part of a crowd. That would make
him feel too much of a spectacle. And, actually, Bobbi was
relieved to think that he might not be there. She could "come
home" first and then answer her questions about Richard later.

As the train rattled into the station, she leaned close to the
window and looked out to the platform, but she couldn't see her
family or anyone else she knew. She hoped her parents had gotten her telegram from San Francisco. She had given them the

arrival time. The train was more than an hour late, but she didn't think Mom and Dad would turn around and go back home.

She got her two suitcases down and put on her navy coat. In San Francisco she had changed into civilian clothes—a cotton dress that was hardly suited to the weather—but her only coat was a navy raincoat that she hoped she would be wearing for the last time. She followed a big fellow who was working his way to the door of the car. As she stretched to reach the wooden step that a porter had set by the train door, she tried to take a quick look around at the same time, but still she saw no one she knew. And then she heard footsteps coming, and she glanced to her right. "Bobbi," she heard, and she saw Richard. He was wearing a dark blue overcoat, a white shirt with a tie showing at the neck, and a gray felt hat. No wonder she hadn't noticed him; she had never seen him dressed like that. His tan had faded, too. He hardly seemed the man she had known in Hawaii.

And now he was taking her into his arms as though he owned her. "Oh, Bobbi, I'm so glad you're finally here," he said. She liked the warmth of his voice, the enthusiasm she had sometimes accused him of lacking—liked it more than she had expected. She hugged him back, her face pressed to his chest, but she didn't kiss him.

"Where is everyone?" Bobbi asked.

"I talked them into letting me pick you up. I wanted to see you first and have a chance to talk things over just a little."

"Oh. Are they all at home, or—"

"Yeah. Wally wanted to come too. I hope you don't mind my delaying you seeing him just a little. He said he'd be at your house when we got there."

"No. That's fine. I don't mind." But Bobbi did mind. She wasn't ready to "talk things over."

But now Richard was picking up her luggage and striding off toward the station. She followed him out to his car—a surprisingly nice car, she thought, without exactly deciding what kind it was. He opened the door for her and then put her baggage in the trunk. When he got in on his side, he threw his hat onto the backseat and turned toward her. "I've done the wrong thing again, haven't I?" he said.

There was something childlike in his voice. She had hurt him already with her stiffness, and he had read her exactly right. But she was also looking into his good face, those wonderful silver-blue eyes. "No. I'm sorry," she said. "I'm glad you're here. It just took me by surprise."

"I need to talk to you, so I'm going to drive just a little, without delaying you very much. Is that all right?"

"Sure."

Maybe he knew her better than she thought. He started the car, backed from the parking place, and then drove up Broadway. At State Street he didn't turn south, as she thought he might, but kept going east. "Bobbi," he said, "I wish, in a way, I had never been sent to Hawaii so soon after everything happened to me. I don't think I was ready to see you. I had too many things going on in my head, and I couldn't be the kind of guy you needed."

"Richard, I don't want you to behave some certain way just because you think that's what I like. I just want you to be yourself."

"I know. But I couldn't do that. You have no idea what kinds of things I was thinking about. I'm amazed now that I could even carry on a conversation."

"But that's just it, Richard. You wouldn't tell me anything."

Richard didn't respond to that. He kept driving for a couple more blocks, up the hill toward the university, and then, at Thirteenth East, he finally turned south. This was another way home, and that relieved Bobbi. "I wouldn't have known what to say then, Bobbi. I was too confused about the things that kept going through my head. But a guy coming out of something like that probably has to get it behind him a little. Some men talk about those kinds of things, and others don't. I just don't know what there is to gain by going over it. Mostly, it's a matter of moving ahead."

Bobbi thought of what Sister Nuanunu had told her. There were times, she had said, when a person had to look ahead, not back, and accept the good things life offered without questioning everything. Now Richard was saying the same thing, and maybe that was right. But why couldn't she *feel* the rightness? "Richard," she said, "memories don't go away just because you don't talk about them."

"No. But they calm down a lot. See, that's what I want to talk to you about. But I'm getting ahead of myself." He slowed at Fifteenth South and turned east again. "There's a place I want you to see. Just hang on a minute." He glanced at her and released his best weapon—that innocent smile she loved so much. The effect was surprising, too. Some of her resistance did melt away. But still, she wondered where he was taking her, what he had in mind.

He was driving now, not talking. When the pavement stopped, he turned onto a muddy little dirt road through sagebrush and matted cheatgrass. It all seemed little more than wasteland, with patches of snow here and there in the shadows of the brush. It wasn't exactly Bobbi's idea of a romantic spot— not compared to the places where the two of them had talked in Hawaii.

Richard stopped the car and then came around and opened the door for her. "It's kind of cold out here, but I want you to get out and take a look."

Bobbi nodded, and she did get out. But it was more than "kind of" cold. A brisk wind was blowing, and it cut through her summer clothing. She also wasn't sure what she was supposed to be seeing. She looked down into the valley, where gray-brown smoke was hanging over the city, and beyond that was only the dim blue of the Great Salt Lake. There was nothing inspiring in any of that.

Richard stepped up next to her and put his arm around her

shoulders. "Bobbi, I'm afraid, the way I acted in Hawaii, I might have ruined things between us. I hope not, because that would be the worst thing that could ever happen to me. I've straightened everything out in my head now. I'm doing just fine. Working for your dad has worked out better than I ever could have hoped. I can provide for a family right now, without going back to college—the way I used to talk about."

"Richard, you told me that in your letters, too. But I don't understand. I thought you wanted to read all the books you could. Learn everything. Teach. You said you didn't want to work for a business."

"I know. But that was part of all that confusion I had going on in my mind. Now, I don't feel that way. I want to make something of myself, provide a good life for my family. Like I said before, I want to move ahead."

"Wouldn't it be good to take some time and—"

"Bobbi, we've both lost a lot of years already. I don't want to wait anymore. I love you, and I want to marry you right away."

Bobbi was silent. She liked this in a way—liked that he wanted her, was willing to say so with some force—but she didn't want to start setting dates. What she wanted was for her heart to change.

"Your dad bought all this land up here, and he's going to develop it. It's the part of Salt Lake that is going to grow like crazy in the next few years. It'll all be new, but it's not very far from where you grew up. Wally told me that you and your brothers played up here in these hills when you were kids."

"We did."

"Well, I thought it was the perfect place for us, so I bought this lot right here." He waved his hand to indicate the land in front of them. "I bought a double lot so we could have a big yard, and no one could build right behind us. We'll always have this view of the valley. It's going to be a wonderful place to raise our family. A great neighborhood." He stepped around in front of her, took hold of her shoulders, and looked her in the eyes. "Bobbi, I want to start all over. I want to propose again. Will you marry me? I promise I'll be the kind of husband you need."

"We're still engaged, Richard. I never said we weren't."

"I know. But let's recommit."

What did it mean exactly? How soon did he want to get married? Bobbi took a breath, didn't respond, but she saw what she was doing to him.

His eyes angled away from hers; his chin dropped. "Bobbi, did I do this wrong? I just wanted to show you that I'm all right now—not like I was in Hawaii, or on the phone that day. I couldn't even make it clear to you then how much I love you."

"Richard, this doesn't seem like you. I hardly know you today."

He nodded, smiled rather sadly, and then turned away. "I know. It's not how I usually do things. But it's more the way I want to be from now on. I'm also going to talk about things I feel, the way you said David Stinson always did."

The comparison, in a sense, was the worst one Richard could have called to Bobbi's mind. David would have done something like this with so much charm and exuberance. But still, what Richard was doing was what she had always said she wanted from him: he was even trying to change himself to fit his idea of what she wanted. And he was talking about looking ahead. Bobbi had told herself hundreds of times that she couldn't spend her life imagining that David was the only man who could have made her happy. She had to look to the future.

And now Richard was staring off into the valley, looking crushed, and she couldn't stand that. "Richard, you don't have to change for me. I want us to talk to each other, openly, but you don't have to be someone you're not."

He shrugged, and she sensed that he was feeling foolish, found out.

"We're engaged, Richard," Bobbi said. "That hasn't changed." She wanted to stop at that and commit to nothing more, but he was still looking away, seeming destroyed. He needed more from her, so she said it. "This is a beautiful spot for a house, Richard. And I do want to marry you."

"Bobbi, you don't need to . . . say that."

This time she moved in front of him, and she wrapped her arms around his body, leaned her head against his shoulder. "Richard, I'm sorry. I'm the one who's been confused lately. But I feel better about this now. We'll talk some more about everything. But I do want you to know that I love you."

His silence told her that he still didn't trust this, that he was probably still embarrassed by her earlier hesitancy.

"Richard, I've prayed and prayed about this. And I got my answer—even before I knew that David had died. You're the right one for me. That's what the Lord told me."

Bobbi felt Richard's chest swell, and then felt the wisp of air on her hair as he let his breath blow out. "I'm glad for that, Bobbi. But I can just hear you: 'Are you sure about that, Lord? Because I'm not.'"

Bobbi laughed. He did know her. And without warning, it suddenly felt comfortable for her to say, "I want to marry you, Richard. It is time to move ahead."

"All right."

"Let's go home now. I want to see my family and get settled down for a day. And then we'll start to plan. Okay?"

"Okay." He took her hand and walked her back to the car. Now that he was more subdued, he seemed himself. She thought of their times together on Sunset Beach, the warmth between them. She stopped, wrapped her arms around his neck, and kissed him.

He kissed her gently, almost carefully, but then he held her in his arms for a long time, and Bobbi felt everything coming back. She did love this man. She didn't want him to worry about that, to try to adjust his life for her. She wanted to make him happy. "Richard, I'm sorry," she said. "I'm the one who did this wrong. I do love you."

"I got really scared when I thought I was losing you," he said, and that seemed to be his explanation for how he had handled things today.

"I shouldn't have put you in that position. I shouldn't have made you worry," she told him, and then she shivered. "I'm freezing. Let's go."

In the car, Bobbi sat close to Richard, put her arm through his, as he drove down the hill. And now she wished she had a little more time with him before everything got crazy. But when Richard parked the car in front of her house, she felt the excitement again. She looked at the porch and saw that a man was sitting there in the old love seat. He was wrapped up in a big coat and hat. And then she realized that it was Wally. "Wally!" she screeched, and she jumped from the car before Richard could come around. She raced toward the front steps, and by then Wally had jumped off the porch. They met in front of the house, on the sidewalk, and Bobbi leaped into his arms. Wally grasped her tight, and Bobbi felt more "home" than she had in many years.

When Wally put her down, Bobbi stepped back to have a good look at him. He was flushed from the cold, and his face was changed—older, of course, but also more satisfied, more at peace. "Are you as happy as you look?" she said.

"Happier," he said, and he laughed. "I've been waiting out here because I wanted to see you first, before the whole gang got hold of you."

"Oh, Wally, this is too good to be true. A big chunk of my heart has been missing all these years, and you've just put it back."

"I still think I'm dreaming. I didn't know life could be this good."

By then Richard had come up to them. He was carrying Bobbi's luggage. "What did she say?" Wally asked. "Is she ready to get married?"

Bobbi took a breath. Had Richard told the whole family what his plans had been?

"She is," Richard said, and he ducked his head a little. "Bobbi, I only told Wally about this. Not the others. I needed his advice."

He does *understand me,* Bobbi told herself again, and her satisfaction took another leap. "We don't know when yet," Bobbi said. "But he showed me where we're going to live. That's pretty exciting."

"Lorraine and I will be up there, too. Not too far from you two. Richard and I want to start both houses as soon as spring breaks."

"It sounds like you and Richard are getting to know each other pretty well."

"Hey, we work together every day."

"Wally thinks straight," Richard said. "And he's been through some things. He's been a big help to me." Bobbi liked that. "Listen, I'm going to walk inside and let you two talk for a minute—and freeze yourselves. I'll tell your family to give you a few minutes."

"Thanks," Bobbi said. And then she looked at Wally again.

"Are you really okay, Wally? Don't you have any illnesses, or aren't you having trouble adjusting to everything?"

"Well, yeah. I have trouble looking at Lorraine. I want to cry every time—because she's so beautiful and she's mine. But I guess I can deal with that."

"Be honest with me, Wally. Didn't all this change you?"

"Sure. It changed me." He nodded, dropped his glance. "Mostly for the better, I hope."

"It didn't take the fun out of you, did it?"

"Well . . . it did while I was over there—most of the time. But those things come back."

"Our ship loaded up with POWs in Japan. We brought them back to the States, so I spent quite a bit of time with them. Some of them were a real mess, Wally. I saw guys who would sit and stare all day. Some of them were scared to death to go home. They felt like they weren't human anymore. They kept telling me that they wouldn't know how to live around regular people."

"I know. We all felt some of that at first."

"Wally, I don't think any of those men are going to be as normal as you seem to be. At least not this fast."

"I understand what you're saying, Bobbi, but I think my little group did better than most. We had our own church meetings, and we tried to keep straight about the things we believed. God helped me, too."

"Do you get nervous at all?"

"I do, sometimes. Sure." A little puff of steam drifted from his mouth. Bobbi was so pleased to see how full his cheeks were, how healthy he looked.

"What makes you nervous?"

"Life is a little too busy now, too complicated, but I'm getting used to it. And I have a feeling that sleeping in a bed with Lorraine is going to be a whole lot better than sleeping on a mat on a cold floor—with a room full of stinking men."

"Maybe. But you won't know for sure until you try it." Bobbi felt herself blush—not sure what he would think she meant. But the thought crossed her mind that sleeping with Richard might be rather nice, too.

"Bobbi, I really came out here to tell you something."

"Okay."

"Richard is trying to do all the right things, and he's a great guy. I think you've made a great choice. But he's struggling more than he wants to admit. You need to let him handle things his own way, and you need to give him a lot of love and support. I really think he'll be fine. But don't force things. He told me that you want him to talk about his experiences, but for a lot of guys, that's the last thing they want to do."

"Wouldn't it help them?"

"Some guys need that. Other guys just want to put it all behind them."

"But can they?"

Wally stepped back just a little more. He tucked his hands into his coat pockets. "I don't know for sure. But I don't think it helps to keep asking him."

"Did he tell you what happened to him?"

"No. But he's trying hard to put it all behind him, and I'll tell you, he loves you so much he'd do anything for you."

"Really? Is that how he seems to you?"

"Definitely. You know me. I never did like your old friend Phil. And I worried about that professor you liked. But I like Richard. He's a real guy. And he'll knock himself out to give you a good life."

Bobbi did feel sure about that. "But Wally, is he cut out to be a businessman? I'm afraid he's trying to do that just for me."

"I'm not sure, Bobbi. He's sure working hard at it. But I wouldn't say he likes it as much as I do."

"Is it what he ought to do all his life?"

"I don't know. He does everything just fine, but I don't get the feeling that it means very much to him. I could be wrong."

About then the front door flew open, and there was Beverly, sweet little Beverly turned into a tall teenager, flying toward Bobbi, jumping off the porch. "You're so lucky," she whispered into Bobbi's ear. "I wanted to marry Richard, but you got him."

"I'm just lucky that I saw him first." She set Beverly down and looked at her again. Her face was still childlike, simple, but almost shockingly a mirror of her own: the same pale eyes and even freckles across her nose.

"Bobbi!"

Bobbi turned to see LaRue bursting out the door. The girl was stunning, so mature. She didn't leap, not like Beverly, but she hurried down the stairs and grabbed Bobbi. And now Bobbi could see Mom and Dad over LaRue's shoulder, at the door. "I love you, LaRue," Bobbi said. "It's so good to see you."

"Come in," Mom was calling. "You don't have to stand out there."

So Bobbi rushed up the porch steps and into the front entry, where Mom embraced her first. "You're going gray, Mom," she said. "I can't believe it."

"You should. You and the other kids gave me all those gray hairs."

"Not me. I'm a good girl."

"Yes. Out there wandering around the ocean, worrying me to death all the time."

Bobbi laughed, and then she turned to her father. "Welcome home, Barbara," he said. Bobbi smiled. He was the only person in the world who called her that, but from him, the name sounded like love.

Lorraine was there too, looking radiant, still so trim and perfect. Bobbi grabbed her hands and said, "You're going to be my sister now. It's what I always hoped would happen."

The two hugged one another, and Richard waited close by. When Bobbi stepped back, he took her under his arm, held her close. Everyone was collected around them now, still in the entrance, and Bobbi loved the feel of the house, still unchanged, still so solid, still who she was and always would be.

"Barbara, Richard just told us that you two sort of sealed the deal. Congratulations."

Sealed the deal? Good ol' Dad—always a way with words. But Bobbi only said, "Thanks, Dad." She was still taking deep breaths, letting the home air into herself, savoring the smells. "It's over," she said. "It's finally over."

She meant the war, of course, but much more. Wally was home, and he seemed better than ever. What struck her was that she didn't feel afraid of *anything*—not even her future—and she couldn't remember the last time she had felt that way.

13

LaRue and Beverly couldn't attend Wally and Lorraine's marriage ceremony in the temple on Friday morning, but they had a good time at the reception that evening. Lots of people from both Wally's and Lorraine's wards came, and many others from around the stake. The Gardners had arranged for a band to play, and everyone danced, from old folks to children. People brought lots of food and enjoyed it, and the floor of the recreation hall was crowded for every dance. Late in the evening some of the girls, LaRue and Beverly among them, decorated Lorraine with ribbons from her presents, and then Lorraine's brother Glen asked her to get on board a little red wagon. Lorraine had to drape her long train over her arm and hoist up her dress, but she laughed about all that and seated herself in the wagon. Glen and one of his friends pulled her all the way around the hall as everyone applauded and laughed. All the while, Wally stood by watching, looking proud.

Then everyone cleared the floor, and Wally and Lorraine danced alone while the band played "I'll Get By as Long as I Have You." Wally's dancing skills had certainly come back to him, and LaRue thought he looked wonderfully handsome in his tuxedo. Lorraine was elegant in her satin wedding dress, with a pretty tiara pinned into her hair, the attached veil falling down around her shoulders. LaRue couldn't help but think of Fred Astaire and Ginger Rogers.

After the two danced, Lorraine's mother called for all the unmarried girls to line up, and Lorraine stood with her back to them and tossed her wedding bouquet over her shoulder. Beverly seemed to be in the right position to catch it, but a tall girl from the Thomas's ward, Eva Winston, reached over her and snatched it with one hand. That brought lots of laughter, and LaRue heard a man say, "These older girls, they start to worry. They're not afraid to go after that bouquet." It was true that Eva was over twenty, but LaRue didn't know why anyone would think she was getting desperate. LaRue didn't want to marry until she was much older than Eve.

It was after midnight by then, so the band played one last number, "The Last Waltz," and then the crowd began to leave. LaRue knew that all the presents had to be carried out to cars and the decorations around the gymnasium had to be taken down, but she was tired and wished that Mom would let them do all that on Saturday morning. "I don't know why we have to do everything tonight," she told Beverly.

But Beverly was still flushed with excitement. "I'd rather do it now and get it over with," she said. And then, as though the idea was connected, she added, "I danced almost every dance."

"You mean you got your feet stomped on by all the old men in the ward," LaRue told her.

"Not really. The old ones are the best dancers." She giggled, and then she leaned close to LaRue. "I also danced with Keith Pedersen. Did you see that?"

"Is he the one with the pimples?"

"LaRue!"

"Well, he is."

"He may have a few pimples, but he's *cute.*"

LaRue was folding up a nice tablecloth that was stained with drops of red punch. She hoped the spots would come out. The cloth was a family heirloom that had been handed down from one of Mom's great-grandmothers. LaRue couldn't remember the story exactly, but someone had carried it across the plains—or something of that sort. It was Belgian lace, Mom always said.

"Wally and Lorraine didn't leave yet, did they?" Beverly asked.

"No. Lorraine's in changing into her travel dress."

"Where are they going?"

"No one will say. Mom acts like it's some kind of huge secret. I hope Wally doesn't try to drive too far in that old Nash of his."

"I hope he washes it before they leave."

Earlier in the evening LaRue and Beverly had been in on decorating Wally's car. Glen and some of Lorraine's cousins had helped, and they had used white shoe polish to write "just married" across the back window and across the doors on both sides. They had run streamers from the hood ornament over the top, filled the hubcaps with pebbles, and tied a rope onto the back, with cans to rattle on the street. LaRue had always loved to do things like that, but tonight she had almost wished that everyone would leave the car alone. She wanted Wally and Lorraine to have a wonderful time, a really perfect time, and cleaning up the car was bound to be extra trouble for them. There had even been some talk of shivaree—of grabbing them and driving them off in two separate cars, keeping them apart for half the night. LaRue was glad that Dad had walked outside and told the kids, "I don't mind if you fix up their car a little, but I won't stand for any silliness tonight. Leave those kids alone when they come out of the building."

"We'll just throw rice at them, President Thomas," Lorraine's brother had said, and LaRue was certain that nothing more than that would happen.

Chuck Adair was helping to carry presents out to his car. As he passed LaRue, he said, "Bobbi's next, and then it's your turn."

"Not me," LaRue said. "I'm just a child. You're the one who needs to get married."

Chuck stopped. He was holding a big box decorated with white wrapping paper. "I did go out on a date last week," he said, and he grinned.

He still looked strange to LaRue, with those new false teeth of his, but he wasn't a bad-looking guy. She still remembered when she was a kid, and he had been the biggest sports star at East High. "You mean that's the first time?"

"Afraid so. Lorraine finally fixed me up. I figured the girl would be as ugly as a mud fence, but she wasn't. I kind of liked her."

LaRue was ready to say, "That's why I won't get married soon—there are too many pretty girls in this world," but she stopped herself. That was the old LaRue—the one who would have batted her eyes and smiled just to hear Chuck tell her how beautiful she was. Instead, she said, "Chuck, that's good. I'm glad to hear it. If you get married, you and Wally and your wives could have a lot of fun together."

"Hey, it was just one date. Besides, I'm a poor man. I can't get married for a while yet."

"Have you found a job?"

"Sort of. Something for right now. But it doesn't pay much. I'd be a sorry choice for a husband." He laughed, and then he walked away.

By then Beverly had hold of LaRue's arm. "Look at Lorraine," she said.

LaRue turned around. Across the hall, Lorraine was standing with her mother. She was wearing a turquoise dress with a short bolero jacket. Her hair was down now, but she had on a little pillbox hat that matched her dress. Wally walked over to her and said something, and Lorraine laughed, but LaRue thought Wally seemed self-conscious. All evening he had looked overwhelmed, almost confused. He had danced with

LaRue earlier, and he had told her, "I didn't expect so many people. So much . . . of everything."

"I'm not surprised," LaRue had told him. "Everyone in Sugar House knows both of our families."

"I know. But I'm still not used to . . . all this." And that's what LaRue kept seeing in Wally, that he was still astounded that life could offer such pleasures. He kept staring at Lorraine as though he were worried that any minute she would fly off to heaven. He leaned toward her now, whispered something, and LaRue knew that he was telling her how beautiful she was. LaRue could only wonder whether anyone would ever adore her that much. But LaRue was more complicated than Lorraine and, she suspected, much harder to love.

"Hey, thanks, everyone," Wally called out. "This has been great."

"They're getting ready to leave," Beverly whispered. "We'd better go outside."

She and LaRue hurried to the back door, where the Nash was parked. Outside, two of Lorraine's cousins, Judy and Donna Lowry, were already waiting with a bag of rice. They were pouring out handfuls to everyone who came out.

When Wally and Lorraine finally appeared at the door, they stopped and hugged both sets of parents and talked for a few minutes. LaRue saw her father slide some extra money into Wally's coat pocket. Wally thanked him, hugged him again, and then hugged Mom one more time.

Then he faced the crowd and grinned. "Hey, who's been messing with my car?" he asked, but he certainly didn't look surprised. He took Lorraine by the arm, and they walked down the steps. Then he stopped, seeming to realize what they were going to do. "Hey, don't throw rice," he said.

LaRue could tell that Wally was serious, but she couldn't think why he would care. She saw that everyone else was as confused as she was.

"That stuff kept me alive for three and a half years. It's the only thing I had. If you throw it on the ground, I might stop and pick it all up—one grain at a time. I did that, you know—lots of times."

He was smiling. But LaRue knew this was not a joke to him, and she let her fists, full of the rice, drop to her sides. Wally and Lorraine passed through the group, and everyone stood silent.

Wally seemed to feel the awkwardness. He turned back and said, "Hey, I'm sorry. I didn't mean to ruin your fun."

"That's all right," someone said.

"Anyway, thanks. It's been a great night." He reached into his pocket and pulled out a set of keys. But then he took hold of Lorraine's arm, and the two of them bolted across the parking lot. LaRue knew immediately what was happening. Wally had Dad's keys, and he was heading to the Hudson. But no one chased them. They merely stood and watched, still quiet. Wally helped Lorraine in on her side and then trotted around to his door. He waved and called out, "I'm afraid you decorated the wrong car."

He got in, started the engine, and drove from the parking lot. But already people were lining up with their rice. They dropped it all back into the bag where they had gotten it.

* * *

Bobbi had hugged Wally and Lorraine, told them good-bye, but she hadn't walked out to watch them make their escape. She was sitting on one of the wooden folding chairs that lined the gym. Richard was helping to carry out the gifts, and Bobbi had stayed behind to help clean up, but her feet, after an entire evening in heels, were killing her, so she was taking a moment to sit down.

She was rubbing her foot when she saw Grandma Thomas walking her way. "How about rubbing mine next?" Grandma asked.

"Do your feet hurt?"

"Are you kidding? I've got corns on my feet that are older

than you are. It's only vanity that makes me put these horrid high heels on."

"Hey, you were dancing up a storm. You and Grandpa looked great out there."

"No, no. That man can't dance a lick. You should have seen me when I used to dance with Teddy Horne. I was in my prime then, and Teddy was a professional dancer. We used to put on quite a show."

"I thought you told me you got married when you were still a kid."

"I did. This was after I was married. Teddy and I, we used to put on floor shows. I took lessons for years. He was my teacher." She sat down next to Bobbi, stretched her legs out, pressed her heels against the floor, and pried both shoes off. Then she let out a long, loud sigh.

"Grandma, if I talked to you a hundred years, I'd never find out everything about you. I didn't know you did *floor shows.* You're always surprising me with something like that. "

"That's because I make most of it up. Old people can lie and no one knows any better. Everyone who could call me a liar is already dead."

Bobbi laughed. She put her foot down, hoisted the other onto her knee, and began to rub it. "I'll bet you really were some kind of dancer," she said. "I can picture that."

"That part wasn't a lie. Not even the floor shows. Where was your Grandma Snow tonight?"

"She and Grandpa were tired this morning after the temple ceremony and the wedding breakfast. They said they would come over if they could, but I'm not surprised they didn't."

"Well, you'd better get married right away—while they're still able to be there."

"Yes, I guess that's right."

But Bobbi heard the hint of hesitancy in her own voice, and she could tell that Grandma had picked up on it too. "Have you set a date yet, Bobbi?"

"Not an *exact* date. But I'm sure it'll be fairly soon."

"What's going on?"

Bobbi really didn't want to talk to Grandma about this. "Nothing. We just haven't settled on a date."

"Why not?"

"I just got home, and . . . you know . . . it takes a while to get everything organized. Besides, Mom had Wally's wedding to think about first."

"You need to take lessons from me, Bobbi. You're the worst liar I know."

"Liar?" Bobbi laughed.

"Tell me what's troubling you about Richard. If you don't want him, I'll divorce that old guy of mine and run off with him."

"He'd probably go for you, too."

"Bobbi, come clean with me. I want to know what's going on." Grandma was dressed in a purple dress, elegant but bright, and decked out with a huge jeweled broach. But it was especially the long silk gloves that made her seem overdressed for the occasion—as she almost always was.

Bobbi planted both her feet on the floor and sat up straight. "Nothing is going on. We're getting married. I just want a little time to get back to normal life and everything."

Men were walking across the hall, their arms full of boxes, and the last of the band members—the drummer—was carrying out his equipment. Grandma watched, not saying anything for a time, but finally she announced her diagnosis. "It's that professor who got killed in Okinawa. That's who you're thinking about."

"No, Grandma. I decided I would marry Richard before I knew that David had died."

"Maybe so. But Richard was the *practical* choice, not the one your heart had chosen."

Bobbi tried to think about that. "No. That's not true," she finally said. "I prayed and prayed, and I got my answer."

"Oh, Bobbi, what a pile of manure."

"Grandma!"

"Just be glad I chose *that* word. I had a better one in mind."

"Why?"

"Bobbi, don't start blaming God. You can't go through life half committed to Richard and always saying, 'Well, I guess that's what the Lord thought I should do—whether I wanted to or not.'"

"I know. I've thought about that. Maybe that's why I haven't set a date yet. I want to *feel* right about this first."

"Well, at least you're telling me the truth now."

Bobbi slumped down in her seat, leaned her head against her grandma's shoulder. "That first day, when I got home, Richard tried so hard. He said all the right things. I think he really wants to open up with me. But he won't do it—or can't. He holds so much back all the time."

"Oh, Bobbi, you're making way too much out of this 'he doesn't talk to me' business. Once you're married, you won't have time to talk. He'll be working and you'll be washing diapers. You'll just be lucky if you can get the man's nose out of the newspaper when he finally gets home at night."

"But I don't want that kind of marriage. That's how Mom and Dad have always been."

"Your parents don't have a bad marriage."

"It could be better, Grandma."

"Bobbi, how old are you now? Twenty-five?"

"Twenty-six."

"Twenty-*six*, and you don't know the first thing about life. I've always loved you more than any of my other grandkids— don't quote me on that—but you've never had one bit of sense in you. You imagine life, how it ought to be, and then you get all upset if it doesn't magically turn out exactly the way you picture it."

Bobbi knew there was something to that, but she didn't admit it.

"Bobbi, that Richard is about the prettiest thing I've ever seen. He's got those silver eyes that make my knees go weak. Either that, or my garters are pulling too hard."

Grandma suddenly burst into that deep, rough laugh of hers, and Bobbi couldn't help but laugh with her. Still, she said, "Looks aren't everything, Grandma. You know that."

"Maybe not. But they're plenty important. When you finally get your babies to sleep at night, and you think you're about to fall asleep yourself—that man could get your motor restarted."

"Grandma, you're terrible!"

"I am not. No one tells girls the truth about anything. Sex is not the most important thing in a marriage. Not by a long shot. But it surely can make everything else a lot nicer. And if you can't get excited about cuddling with that fellow, you've got something wrong with you."

"I do like the way he looks. And I like kissing him. But I just keep thinking that—"

"That's right. You just keep thinking."

"I have to. That's how I am."

"No, Bobbi. I've watched Richard when he's with you. He's like a man with his favorite horse. He—"

"What?"

"Don't you know what I mean? Haven't you watched the way a man will pat his horse, rub its shoulders, scratch its ears. There's no greater love than that."

Bobbi was laughing again.

"Bobbi, he's so kind and sweet with you. That's all you need to know about what he *thinks*. He's not some slick young fellow who knows how to spread on the sweet talk. He's honest. He's good. He's willing to work hard for you, and he has a good future. You two will talk plenty, but he's always a man who will say more with his actions than he will with words." She waved a finger at Bobbi—a finger in purple silk. "Bobbi, you hang on to him. You get him to that altar before he gets tired of your silliness. If you lose that boy, it will break my heart. I want to live a few more years just so I can come over to your folks' place on Sundays and stare at him over the dinner table."

"Grandma, I had no idea you were so superficial." Bobbi sat up again. "I'm quite disappointed in you."

"I'm not superficial. I'm just the only honest person left on this planet. No one knows how to listen to the truth. It scares them."

"You told me you were a liar."

"Well . . . I was lying about that."

Bobbi gripped her grandmother's arm. "You know what?" she said. "I think you're right."

"About what?"

"About Richard. I think we need to set a date—and not too far off. But I think I'm right too. I won't settle for that old-fashioned kind of marriage where the man goes off to work and then comes home, reads the paper, and falls asleep in his chair. I want *all* of Richard, Grandma. I'm happy to look at him, but I also want to *know* him. And I want him to know me."

"Bobbi, that's fine. Try for that kind of closeness. Maybe it's possible. But we all have some things inside us that we don't reveal to *anyone*. You have to leave that part of Richard alone. You'll make him *and* yourself miserable if you keep pushing on bruises that are better not touched."

"I don't want to believe that. I want him to know the very worst things about me—and still love me."

"Oh, Bobbi, you are so dreadfully stupid. Half of marriage is what you don't know. It's all about the mystery. Two people can live together for a whole lifetime and only know a little about each other. But that's okay. It's part of the romance, part of the fun."

"I don't know, Grandma. It just seems like it's giving up to live that way."

"Sure, you could call it that. Or maybe you could just say

that it's being human together, sticking it out, doing your best even on the bad days."

Bobbi thought she understood that much. She knew that no marriage could be as perfect as she wanted hers to be. But she also knew that Richard was suffering, and that he was pretending not to suffer. That had become very clear to her the past couple of weeks since she had come home. She did love him; she did want to marry him. But he had to let her help him. What kind of marriage would she have if she couldn't even help her husband with his pain?

When everything in the recreation hall had been put away, the floor swept, and the dishes washed, it was almost two in the morning. LaRue had lain down on some chairs by then and had fallen asleep. But Beverly had dried dishes and utensils and the whole time talked with her mom about how beautiful everything had been. And she had asked all about the temple ceremony, wanting to know every detail that Mom would tell her.

Beverly waited until the last second to wake up LaRue, who managed to wander outside, still half asleep.

"Now the fun part comes," Dad said, when they stepped outside into the cold. "We have to drive home in Wally's car."

Beverly, of course, was well aware of that. "Dad, take off those cans," she said. "Everyone's going to be looking at us."

"Who's *everyone?* No one else is even up this late."

"Some people will be. I'm going to slide down in the back seat and hide."

Dad pulled a pocketknife from his pocket and cut the cans off the back, then opened the trunk and threw them in. "I'm glad we don't have very far to drive," he said.

But Mom seemed to think the whole thing was funny. "We look like newlyweds, if you ask me," she said. "We don't have to claim the girls. We can say they were just a couple of hitch-hikers we picked up."

Beverly rolled her eyes. Mom loved to say things like that.

But joking was one thing, and sliding across the seat so she was sitting almost on top of Dad was another. Beverly groaned, and then she did slip down, far enough so she could peek out and then duck if anyone was on the street. But Dad took his time driving home, especially with all those rocks rolling around in the hubcaps, and Mom kept singing "The Last Waltz." Beverly was just glad that she didn't see anyone she knew.

* * *

Earlier that night, Wally had been overjoyed by his safe escape. He told Lorraine, "I'm glad Dad let me take his car. I didn't want to drive all the way down State Street in that Nash, with all that stuff written on it."

"I'm just glad we don't have to stop somewhere to clean it up." Lorraine was sitting close to Wally on the front seat. She took his arm. "Everything was nice, wasn't it?" she said. "It's been such a nice day."

But the words had a strange effect on Wally. He hadn't realized until that moment how nervous he was. "Yeah, it has been. Just about everybody came."

"I couldn't believe that some of my relatives drove clear down from Idaho. We were lucky the weather's been so nice."

"That's for sure."

But then she said nothing, and Wally couldn't think of anything either. He was starting to realize that the Hotel Utah wasn't all that far away.

"Charles Gardner—you know, my cousin—he and his wife Bonnie didn't come. I wonder where they were."

"Something must have come up, I guess."

And then again, silence.

Wally stopped at a stoplight and shifted, waited. Half a minute went by.

"Mel wasn't there. But he told me ahead of time that he couldn't make it."

"You mentioned that."

The light changed. Wally drove on, a block, two blocks, and neither spoke. "Are you okay?" Wally finally asked.

"Sure."

"I want to be a good husband, *Mrs. Thomas*."

"You will be, *hubby*."

But now Wally was pulling into the parking lot by the hotel. He and Lorraine had put their suitcases in the trunk of the old Nash earlier, and Wally had made sure his sisters had seen him do it. Later, they had secretly moved the baggage to the Hudson. When Wally parked, he got out, walked around, and opened the door for Lorraine, and then he opened the trunk and got out the two suitcases. Lorraine walked next to him, grasping the sleeve of his suit coat, until they reached the side entrance of the hotel, where a doorman took the bags. Wally wasn't used to such things, not having stayed in a lot of hotels in his life, and he wondered how much he should tip the man. He gave Lorraine his arm and followed the doorman to the front desk in the lobby. What he felt, however, was that the doorman knew—that everyone who looked at them knew—that he and Lorraine were newlyweds.

"Mr. and Mrs. Thomas," Wally said to the night clerk at the desk. "We have a reservation."

"I'm afraid it's too late, sir. We're all filled up."

Wally was stunned. "But I made a reservation. I told the girl I'd be getting in late."

By then the desk clerk was smiling. "Just teasing you, sir. We have your room. I believe you rented one of our nicest suites."

At least he didn't say "the bridal suite." "Yes, that would be right," Wally said, and he tried to smile, but he wasn't feeling as playful as the desk clerk seemed to be. He filled out the registration book quickly, and then the clerk rang a bell on the desk and a bellboy appeared. "Let's see, you're another guy," Wally said. "I guess I owe something to that fellow on the door."

"If you like, sir, you can give it to me and I'll take care of him."

Wally wondered whether that's how things were normally done, but he certainly wasn't heading back to the door to tip the other man. He took hold of Lorraine's arm and followed the bellboy to the elevators.

"Have you and your wife stayed with us before, sir?" the young man asked. He was in his early twenties, probably a soldier just home from the war.

The question was appropriate enough, but Wally heard the tone, saw the little smile, and he wanted to tell the guy to lay off. "No. We haven't."

The bellboy gave a rundown on the accommodations, the dining room on the twelfth floor, the Empire Room with dancing and dining on the main floor, and the coffee shop at the lower level. When the elevator stopped on the tenth floor, he led them, a suitcase in each hand—held loosely in his white gloves—to a room down the hallway. He used the brass key the desk clerk had handed him to open the door, and then he reached in and turned on the lights. Then he made rather a long and grandiose show of explaining the details of the room—the radiators, the windows, the room service and maid service they might expect. Wally kept nodding and saying, "Good. That's fine." And he noticed that Lorraine was standing more or less behind him, where the bellboy couldn't look at her directly.

Finally the boy approached Wally and handed him the key, but then he had the nerve to say, "Have a *wonderful* stay with us, sir," with a glint in his eye that was clearly suggestive.

Wally got a dollar out of his pocket and handed it to the guy. He knew it was more than he should have given, but he had no quarters in his pocket, and he didn't want to ask for change. He just wanted the guy out of the room.

When the door finally shut, Wally turned and looked at

Lorraine. Her face was flushed. "I wish you hadn't even tipped him," she said.

"Don't pay any attention to all that. It doesn't matter to us."

But now they were facing each other, alone in the room. Lorraine looked away, gazed about the room. "It's so beautiful, Wally. You shouldn't have spent so much."

"It's okay." Wally wasn't worried much about the money. The room had cost over ten dollars, with tax, but it was just one night. He wouldn't be so extravagant on the rest of the trip. They would be driving to Palm Springs, California, the next day. Wally had arranged for a nice motel there, but not one that was so expensive.

"Lorraine, I just want to tell you one more time how much I love you."

But the words seemed awkward, and Lorraine sounded distant when she said, "I love you too, Wally."

"Are you glad you married me?"

"Of course."

They finally looked into one another's eyes. It struck Wally that he had been with her all evening, but he had never really seen Lorraine—only a bride, only a beautiful woman in a lovely dress. Now he had her eyes, and the tension, rather suddenly, passed away. He took hold of her shoulders. "Lorraine, I can hardly believe this is real."

She nodded. "I know."

"I used to imagine you. There was a little daydream I would allow myself sometimes. I would picture myself coming home and finding out you were still single. I would ask you to marry me, and you would say yes. But no matter how many times I imagined it, I never believed it."

"I would think about it too, Wally—even when I knew I shouldn't."

He pulled her to him. "Sometimes, when I first wake up in the morning, for a second or two I have this horrible idea in my head. I think that I'm still in Japan and I've only dreamed all these things. And then, when I convince myself that everything is real, I have to pray—just to tell God one more time how thankful I am. I'm going to do everything I can to make you happy, Lorraine. I promise you that."

"It's going to take all my effort just to be good enough to be worthy of you, Wally."

"Oh, no. Don't say that. That's just not true."

"You're the best man in the world, as far as I'm concerned. And I mean that. It's not just something to say."

He pulled back enough to look at her for a moment, and then he kissed her, loving the delicate touch of her lips. She held him, kissing him in return. And then she whispered, "I'm going to go get my nightgown on."

Wally took a deep breath and nodded to her, but he wasn't nervous now. Everything seemed exactly right.

14

Alex Thomas drove his jeep to the little village of Langen, outside Frankfurt. A group of Mormon refugees from Poland had settled there and were in great need. President Meis had met with them a time or two and knew that they were getting by on very little. He had provided what he could for them, but the resources of the members in Frankfurt had been limited. Now, however, food was supposed to be coming soon, along with blankets, clothing, and coats. Word was reaching German leaders—and had come directly to Alex from his father—that President George Albert Smith had met with President Truman to tell him that the Church had relief supplies ready to ship. President Smith had promised to help fellow Mormons but also to provide supplies for members of other churches. President Truman had apparently been impressed with the plan, but the shipments had sat waiting as red tape had needed to be overcome before all the governments involved would let the Church send the supplies and a representative to distribute them.

Now, at last, Apostle Ezra Taft Benson was in Europe. He was traveling throughout the continent, reestablishing missions, visiting branches and districts, distributing the food and supplies, and trying to help the members get the Church organization back in full operation. At some point he would be coming to Frankfurt, or to some nearby city, and the members would be called together for a conference, but word on the date for that meeting had not yet come. Everyone understood that travel in Europe, and especially in Germany, was still difficult; many railroad lines were repaired, but operations were spotty and unpredictable.

Alex found the Saints in Langen living in a barracks built of rough, unpainted lumber. When he knocked, the woman who opened the door was skeletal, colorless. She wore a ragged dress made of coarse, thick wool, and instead of shoes she had burlap bags wrapped around her feet and ankles, tied with heavy string. Even the burlap was worn and dirty. She looked at Alex blankly, except perhaps with a hint of suspicion.

"My name is Brother Thomas," Alex said in German. "I'm in the branch presidency of the Church in Frankfurt. The president sent me to see how you're doing."

"Come in," she said. "Can you help us?"

"I have a little food in my jeep, and some blankets. More things will be coming before too much longer—much more."

"Bless you," she said, and now he saw a softness appear in her face.

The little building was divided into sections, and in this first room were a surprising number of people—fifteen or so, counting all the children. Most of them were lying on bunks or sitting on the floor. But there was almost no motion in the room—the children were not even playing—and the only light was from a bare bulb hanging over a little table. Alex couldn't see very well, but everyone looked as empty and worn as the sister who had come to the door.

"Are you Sister Diederich?" Alex asked.

"Yes."

"You spoke to President Meis before?"

"Yes."

"He told me that you walked all the way here, pulling a wagon."

"That is true."

"How far was it?"

"I don't know. It was very cold, very bad. Very long. Hundreds of kilometers. Can you bring the food in now? And the blankets?"

"Yes. Surely."

So Alex walked back to his jeep, and he made three trips carrying boxes. He feared that the people might grab for the food, but only one younger couple got off their bunks to come and look. They thanked Alex. What he had brought was rice, potatoes, cans of vegetables, and some canned meats. Alex heard the man whisper to his wife, "This might save our Dieter."

Alex shook hands with the man and told him his name. "We're the Hahns," the young man said.

"Is Dieter your son?" Alex asked.

"Yes. He's worn out, and very sick."

"How old is he?"

Brother Hahn wore a threadbare black coat that had lost all but one of its buttons, and trousers that were frayed at the cuffs and caked with mud. "Seven," he said. "Soon eight. He wants so much to be baptized. But he's walked all this way with us, and there's not much left of him. He might not live."

Alex knew what had happened to these people. Many millions of ethnic Germans had lived in Poland and eastern European countries before the war. They were citizens of these lands, but when the war ended they had been forced to "return" to a country where most of them had never lived. They were leaving a trail of blood across Europe, millions of them dying from starvation, illness, and exposure, but a world weary with war and trouble was paying little attention. "Did the Russians hurt any of you?" Alex asked.

"No. We left when they told us to. Some of us in the

Church tried to help each other. We walked together and shared what little food we had. We made it to Berlin and thought our journey might be over, but there was no food in Berlin. Then we heard there was a place where we could stay. The Moderegger family, here, was helping Mormon refugees. But we had to walk again, and some of our people died along the way." He looked at Sister Diederich.

"My children died," she said. "A baby girl and a little son. My husband was killed before, in the war."

"I'm so sorry." Alex looked at the floor. He couldn't believe the heartache this woman must feel.

"Please, sit down," Sister Hahn said. "We don't mean to be impolite."

Alex sat down at the little table in the center of the room. Sister Diederich sat across from him on the only other chair. "Could I open one of these cans?" Brother Hahn asked quietly. I know it isn't time for a meal yet. But my son needs something."

"Yes, of course," Alex said. "You don't have to make this food last very long. Go ahead and eat it, and I'll get more to you as soon as I can—this week." Most of the food was from the army, and Alex had hesitated to take more from the base, but seeing these people, he knew that he would do it again.

"Oh, thank you," Sister Hahn said. Her husband reached into a box and took out a silver can marked "Applesauce."

"There's an opener in one of the boxes," Alex said. "I didn't know whether you would have one."

Brother Hahn searched in the boxes and found the opener, and then he walked to the far end of the barracks. His wife said, softly, "Dieter will like it. He loves applesauce." But then, as she walked away, she added, "I hope he can hold it down."

"Are you going to be all right, Sister Diederich?" Alex asked. He could see her a little better now that his eyes had adjusted to the dim light. She was younger than he first thought, perhaps thirty or so.

"I didn't think so for a time, but yes, I will manage."

"I don't know how you kept going after what you've been through."

"When my baby died, and we had to dig into the frozen ground to bury her, I only wanted to lie down and die too. Still, I told myself that I had to live for my son, to help him through. I tried so hard to keep him going, but he would cry as he walked, and I was too weak to carry him very long. Some of the men tried to help, but they had children too, and everyone was so tired and hungry and cold. My little Manfred walked all one day, and then he went to sleep, out in the snow and cold. He didn't wake up the next morning."

Alex thought that Sister Diederich would cry now, but she only stared past Alex, as though she could see the scene in her mind.

"I couldn't leave him out there like that, but we had no shovel, and the ground was frozen harder by then—hard as stone. I had a spoon and nothing else to dig with, so I broke the ground that way, and some of the others helped me. We dug deep enough to put him in. And we prayed over his grave."

Alex reached across the table and put his hand on her arm. "My little brother died in the war. I was in a hospital, wounded, when I got the word. I had to lie there and think about it—and I couldn't go home to my family. It's not the same, I know. But at least maybe I have some idea how you feel."

"So many have died."

The simple understatement struck Alex hard, summarized far too much of what he felt. He gripped Sister Diederich's arm a little tighter.

"That night, after I had buried my son and then walked all day, I almost gave up. What I wanted was to take my own life—just go with my family, where they all are. But a voice in my head told me, 'Pray. Ask the Lord for help.' So I did. I knelt in the snow and prayed, and the Lord filled me up, made me warm. I knew he was still with me. Then I thought, 'I've lost everything—my husband, my children—but not my Father in Heaven.' So I was all right. I could continue."

"It must be very difficult, still."

"No. Not so difficult. I know what most people don't know. God loves me. He'll help me through this life. And then I'll be with my family again."

Alex nodded. "That's right. That's what we have to remember."

"This food is a great blessing, Brother Thomas. All of us here know that the Church hasn't forgotten us. Most people don't have such people looking out for them. We're fortunate in spite of everything we've gone through."

Alex tried to remember those words as he returned to Frankfurt. He told himself that he still had Anna and his little son Gene—even if he had never seen him. He knew that was something he had to remember. What he hoped was that little Dieter would live, that the dying would end now, at least for one little group.

A few days later Elder Benson came to Frankfurt. When he met with the LDS Servicemen's group, he told of the miracles that had occurred to open the way for him and his companions to travel throughout Europe. What he had sought, in coming to Frankfurt, was permission from General Joseph McNarney to travel not only through the American zone but through the other three zones in Germany and Austria, as well as through areas in Czechoslovakia. But General McNarney's aide, a major, had told Elder Benson that he couldn't meet with the general for a few days—and was very firm about it. Elder Benson and his traveling companions had left the office and then found a place to pray together. After the prayer, Elder Benson had felt prompted to return, so he had gone back to the general's office, where he had met another aide. This officer had been willing to arrange a brief visit with General McNarney. But the meeting had turned into a long discussion, and the general was greatly impressed that the Church had whole warehouses of food and supplies ready to ship. The general had told Elder Benson at first that travel through the occupied zones was impossible, but the more he listened to the Church plan, the more impressed he became. He agreed to do the paperwork and write the letters of introduction that would be needed. The only proviso was that Elder Benson and his assistants travel at their own risk. Elder Benson had accepted that risk, and he told the servicemen that he wasn't worried; he knew he was on the Lord's mission.

Alex felt the power and faith of this good man. Elder Benson had a big voice, but he spoke softly and humbly, at the end, when he bore testimony. He told the servicemen that he wasn't surprised by what had happened here in Frankfurt. Miracles had been happening since before he had begun his trip. At every step he had dealt with impossible obstacles, and each one had been overcome. He had found passage on airplanes that were booked solid, on ships and trains that no one could get on. He had been able to buy a truck and cars in Paris, where none were supposed to be for sale, and amazingly he had been able to obtain gasoline, which was not normally available to civilians. As he closed, he challenged the men to use their leadership abilities and resources to help the local Saints. He told them the Lord would open the way for their own miracles to happen.

When the meeting ended, Elder Benson began to shake hands with the servicemen. As Alex did so, he said, "Elder Benson, I'm—"

"I know who you are. You're Al Thomas's son. I've had dinner with you and your family more than once."

"That's right. I didn't know whether you would remember me."

"I talked to your father not long before I left Salt Lake. He told me you were still over here. How long is the army going to keep you?"

"I don't know. My commanding officer likes the fact that I

speak German. I might be here a couple of months yet—
maybe even longer."

"Your dad told me that you have a wife and little son in
England."

Alex was impressed with Elder Benson's memory. "Yes, I do.
They're planning to go to Salt Lake before long now. They'll
get there before me, the way things look right now."

"Can you wait just a minute? I want to talk to you, but I
want to shake hands with these other men first. Is that all
right?"

"Sure."

Elder Benson worked his way through the line of men who
were waiting to greet him. He was a big man, imposing, but he
laughed and slapped men on the shoulder, and he made no dis-
tinction between officers and enlisted men. When he had finished, he spoke for a moment to Max Zimmer, the new
German mission president who was traveling with Elder
Benson and translating for him, and with Frederick Babbel, a
young German-American who was accompanying Elder
Benson as his secretary. With them was Howard Badger, an
LDS army chaplain, whose officer status helped with some of
the group's military contacts.

When Elder Benson stepped back to Alex, he said, "I
understand you're working with the German branch here. Is
that right?"

"Yes. They've called me into the branch presidency."

"That's good. These servicemen are doing fine. It's the local
Saints who need the help, and you have the background to
provide some strength."

"I'm doing what I can. I've been able to get a little food and
some blankets from the army—whether I'm supposed to or not.
As soon as your supplies get here we can help people a lot
more."

Elder Benson nodded. His eyes narrowed behind his
wire-rim glasses, making him look more serious. "Your

father told me that you've gone through some hard times personally."

"Well . . . yes. Every soldier does, I'm sure."

"It's not easy to take up a rifle and shoot at a man, is it?"

"No."

"It shouldn't be. Never will be."

Alex nodded.

"But we were fighting for the right things, and most of our German brothers and sisters know that now. You believe that, don't you?"

"Of course I do."

"What's been bothering you the most?" The tone of his voice said, "I don't have a lot of time, and I want to help, but we've got to get to the heart of the matter."

Alex hardly knew where to begin, what to say. He didn't want to give Elder Benson the impression that he was indulging himself in self-pity. "I've had trouble sleeping at night. And during the day, memories—flashes of things I've seen—keep coming back to me."

"Your dad said you were right in the middle of the action for a long time."

"That's true. And at the end, I got sent behind the lines. There were some things that happened there that haven't been easy for me to put out of my head."

"So what are you going to do about it?"

Elder Benson was standing tall in front of Alex, his legs set firm and rather wide apart, his hands on the lapels of his dark gray suit coat. He was a bold man, with strong features and intense eyes. There was something of Alex's dad in his manner. "I'm just trying to do the best I can. Actually, I'm already feeling a lot better."

"I'm going to give you some advice, Brother Thomas. Is that all right?"

"I would appreciate it."

"First of all, be thankful that your spirit is refined enough that it was repulsed by what you saw. You're a noble young man, and there is nothing noble or good about war. It's one of the curses of this earth, and the Lord is deeply disappointed in his children that they resort to such behavior."

"But people make it sound like a wonderful thing, like—"

"I know. Some of that is just because we want to honor those who made great sacrifices, the way you did. And then, back home, people don't have to see what it's really like. But all that doesn't matter. Here's what does matter." He put his big hand on Alex's shoulder. "You're an elder. You're a returned missionary. It will be young men like you who will lead this world away from the hellishness of war and back to the Lord. You may feel like sitting down, looking back with regret—and maybe there's nothing exactly wrong with that—but the problem is, there's no time. We need you too much. And we need you right now."

Alex nodded. It's what he knew, what he had tried to tell himself.

"The German Saints need you. And when you come home, the wards and stakes of Zion will need you too. We're fighting a battle with worldliness back in Utah. You can't mope around. You've done what you had to do—just as millions of others have done—and now it's time to help rebuild the spirit of the people. Can you do that?"

Alex hadn't expected such a challenge. "I'll do my best," he said quietly.

"That's good. But what I'm asking you to do is to let all this go and get on with the work you need to do."

Alex nodded.

"You're a husband now, and you're a father. Your wife and son need your strength."

"I know. I tell myself that every day. But these dreams come whether I—"

"I understand. You can't stop that. But don't think so much about them in the daytime and they'll gradually go away."

Suddenly he was smiling. "I know how I sound—like I don't have an ounce of sympathy in me. But I was raised as a farm boy, and I was taught that when the sun came up, the cows had to be milked. It didn't matter whether I felt like milking or not; I had to get myself up and going. That's what I'm asking you to do."

Alex was surprised at how simple that seemed, how right—and yet, how hard to do.

"You know what the answer is. It's always been the same. Forget yourself. The more you look inside, the worse things seem. Concentrate on your suffering brothers and sisters, do all you can to help them, and you won't have time to think about yourself. You do that and God will heal you. It might not happen overnight, but it will happen. That's a promise I can make you as a servant of the Lord."

"Thank you, Elder Benson. That does help."

"What are you planning to do with your life, Brother Thomas? Do you know what kind of work you want to do?"

"Not exactly. I can go to work for my dad if I want to, but I'd like to get some more education. I used to think I'd like to be a teacher, maybe at a college, but it's hard to know for sure what's best now."

"Well . . . I wouldn't plan too far into the future."

Alex thought he had heard wrong for a moment. "You wouldn't?"

"No, and I'll tell you why. There's no way you can know all the things the Lord might have in store for you. Go home and finish your education. Prepare yourself the best way you know how. And then, when you take a job, work hard at it. Be the best you can be; give your employer all you have. If you do something well, someone will come along and give you another opportunity. That's what always happens. And when that opportunity comes, pray about it. Ask the Lord if that's what you're supposed to do. If it is, go after it. Work at it like that's your life's ambition; don't just put in your time. If you do that, another opportunity will come along—and more and more will follow. That's how my life has always gone. When I was your age, I never could have imagined the things that have happened to me."

Alex nodded. But he had never really thought that way. He had been trying to see much further into the future than Elder Benson was suggesting.

"Well, I've got to be going. But I'll see you back in Salt Lake someday, and I want to see a big man. I expect great things from you."

He shook Alex's hand again, and he walked back to his traveling companions. Alex was left almost out of breath. He just hoped he could hold onto the resolve he felt at the moment. He knew the bad dreams couldn't be willed away, but maybe he could pay less attention to them and fight off the malaise that often filled his head during the day. He wanted to be strong, to be the kind of man Elder Benson expected of him, and above all, he wanted to be the husband and father Anna and Gene needed.

On Sunday Elder Benson spoke to the German Saints. They gathered in the basement of a school that had been damaged during the war. The glass in the windows was mostly blown out and had been filled in with cardboard. There was also no electricity, so the room was cold and dark, the only light coming from windows left open. But leaders from throughout the district had found ways to travel to this makeshift gathering place, and the joy of being together—in the presence of an apostle—seemed to make up for having to wrap themselves in blankets and shiver through the services.

Elder Benson spoke as Brother Zimmer translated, and he greeted the members with his usual force. "During the long time of the war we have often thought of you," he said. "We knew of your difficulties, sufferings, and deprivations, and often, when we were engaged in prayer in the temple of the Lord in Salt Lake City, our prayers for you rose to the Almighty. We knew that you would be capable of withstanding all difficulties. Our greatest worry was only whether you would remain true to the Church, come what may. You are an example for the Church, and how I wish that it were within my power to free you from all worries, difficulties, and cares. I would give everything material to accomplish that, and the same goes for the other leaders of the Church."

He also addressed the difficult topic that worried every German: "The Church will always be opposed to war. When people forget God's word, the seeds of war are sown. And now war has been poured out on every nation. But we have also been taught to be loyal to those who have power over us. You have been loyal to your nation even while abhorring the principles of a government that was out of harmony with the gospel. You have suffered beyond belief, but you have remained true to the Church, and now the kingdom can be rebuilt in this part of the world."

He promised that help was coming, and Alex could feel the relief in the members around him as Elder Benson described the actions of the Church. At every step along the way, he had been told that he couldn't come to Europe, that he couldn't get across the borders, that food and supplies couldn't be distributed. But every barrier had been broken down, one by one, and now he was sure that the supplies would be arriving soon. He described the methods that would be used to get those supplies to the people, both Latter-day Saints and others.

In the end he told them, "I bring you the most affectionate greetings and blessings of the Saints in Zion. They feel that they are one with you. There is no feeling of bitterness to be found against the German Latter-day Saints. They love you as much as those who live in the shadow of the temple." And then he said, "Be united. Be prayerful. Love one another. Husbands, love your wives. Children, love your parents. Remember God in all your activities and seek his counsel and guidance in all your undertakings."

Alex thought he saw the congregation, member by

15

The Stoltzes were on a train, crossing America. Peter was sitting next to Anna, holding Gene on his lap. To everyone's relief, Gene had fallen asleep. He was nine months old now, and quite a handful. At first, as the train had pulled away from New York City, the ride had been a delight for everyone. But half an hour into the trip, Gene had become restless and eager to crawl about. Brother and Sister Stoltz, who were sitting in the seat just in front of Anna and Peter, had taken their turns playing with him, and he had eaten his way through half a box of soda crackers, but it was a long time before he had wound down enough to take a nap.

"I think we're still in Pennsylvania," Anna whispered to Peter. "I knew America was a big country, but I don't think I realized *how* big." The trip would take almost three days, and President Thomas had been good enough to buy Pullman berths for the family so they could sleep in beds at night, but watching the map and seeing how slowly the landmarks moved by was giving Anna a sense of the vastness of the land.

"This part looks a lot like Germany," Peter said in German. He had been working hard on his English and now had a decent reading knowledge, but he wouldn't speak the language with his family. He also preferred to let his family do the talking when it came to dealing with waiters and porters and fellow passengers. That worried Anna. She felt that Peter was holding back, not really committing to a life in America, and the last thing she wanted was for her family to be split apart again. Now that Peter was with them, she wanted him to stay. She wanted him to like this new land, like Salt Lake City, marry a Mormon girl, and stay close by. What worried her was that he had mentioned the daughter in the Schaller home, where he had stayed in northern Germany. He seemed reticent to say much about her, but Anna sensed that his interest was more than passing. Anna hoped he hadn't tied his heart to Germany—and to the girl—so much that he would never be happy in the United States.

A waiter in a white coat walked through the car. He smiled at Peter and whispered, "Bet you're glad to have that boy calm down for a minute." Earlier, at dinner, he had waited on their table, and he had laughed at Gene, who couldn't sit still long enough to eat.

"I wish he could sleep all the way," Anna said, and she laughed.

"How far you going, ma'am?"

"To Utah."

"Oh my. That's a long trip. You let me know if I can help you any."

"Thank you."

The waiter walked on through the car. Peter glanced over at Anna. "Why do the Negroes in America serve all the food?"

"I don't think they always do," Anna said.

"It was that way in the army, too. When Alex took me out to the American army base, all the men who served us dinner in the officers' dining room were Negroes. And that's who was cleaning up around the barracks we passed by."

"Alex told me that Negroes aren't treated very well by some of the soldiers, but I don't know why. I think that's something you have to grow up with to understand."

"Maybe it's something I don't want to understand. Every time we go through a city, I see all the Negroes living together—all in rundown houses. It reminds me of the way I saw Jews living in Warsaw. I don't think it's right."

Anna had thought the same thing, but she feared that Peter was looking for things not to like, and so she merely said, "Things are getting better. Alex says that the war made people change their minds a little." She waited, and when Peter didn't reply, she added, "What I like is how friendly people are in this country. Everyone's been nice to us. Germans aren't usually so friendly to people they don't know."

Peter nodded, apparently accepting Anna's assessment, but he didn't offer his own impressions.

The day was long, and Gene was cranky long before bedtime, but he slept with Anna, in her berth, and slept quite well. On the following morning, after breakfast, Anna was playing with Gene when he dropped a little toy truck. The man across the aisle picked it up and handed it to her. "Thank you," she said.

"You're welcome," he replied. The man was heavy and dark haired. Anna had heard his accent when he had chatted with the man sitting next to him. He sounded like the people she had heard in New York City. "So, are you people Germans?" he asked.

"Yes, sir."

"What brings you to our country?"

He sounded friendly enough, and yet there was something a little brash in his tone. Germans didn't usually ask personal questions so abruptly, so directly. "We're immigrating," she said. "We're moving to Salt Lake City."

"You must have married a GI," he said.

But this sounded like an accusation. She wondered whether there was some resentment in America for German girls who married their victors. Maybe they saw it as gold-digging, or maybe they saw it as a threat to their own girls back home, many of whom would struggle now to find a husband after so many young men had died.

"I *am* married to an American. But we met before the war," she said, and she wanted that to answer any objection, but she didn't know exactly why it should, or why she should feel defensive.

"So your whole family decided to come along—and leave Germany?"

And now the accusative tone was more pronounced. What was he trying to say? "We left Germany during the war," Anna said. "We were living in England."

"You're not Jewish, are you?"

"No." Anna couldn't believe such rudeness. What gave this man the right to ask so many questions? Still, she found herself wanting to justify. "We were opposed to the Nazis. We were in danger. We had to leave."

That seemed the right thing to say. The man nodded, glanced over to the man next to him, who had been listening to all this. "Well, that's good to know. I'm glad some of you Germans didn't buy into all this Hitler master race stuff."

Anna nodded, but she hardly liked his idea of a compliment. The very word *Germans*, the way he had said it, sounded like a dirty name. Anna turned back to Gene, talked to him in English, and the man didn't ask any more questions. But after a time Peter said quietly, in German, "What if you had told that man that I fought for Hitler, that I was in the German army? Then what would he have said?"

"Don't say that, Peter. You were just as opposed to Hitler as the rest of us."

"Try to explain that to *him*."

"Peter, it doesn't matter what other people think."

"Doesn't it? People are going to ask me what I did during the war. What am I supposed to say?"

"Don't tell them."

"So it *is* something to be ashamed of?"

"I don't mean that. But you *were* opposed to Hitler. People understand that men have to fight for their own country. Alex didn't hate the German soldiers, only the Nazi leaders."

"Not everyone is like Alex."

Anna didn't know. But she didn't think Americans would hold Peter's past against him. Maybe a few would, but most people would accept him for who he was. Especially people in the Church would. What worried her was that Peter was so defensive, so ashamed. She feared that he would make things difficult for himself.

By the time the Stoltzes finally reached Salt Lake City, they were very tired. Gene had only gotten more restless, more cross, as the trip had progressed, and that had been wearing on everyone. When the train finally crept to a halt at the Rio Grande station, Anna was relieved, but in those final hours she had become increasingly nervous about meeting the Thomases. She knew they were wonderful people, and she loved the letters she had received from Bea—even one from President Thomas—but still, they were such important people, and she felt so bedraggled after traveling so long. Gene was dirty after crawling about so much in the train, and Anna had used up the last of his diapers. At the moment, he needed a new one. She hoped he wasn't too smelly, too scruffy looking to satisfy his grandparents.

The Stoltzes gathered up all their suitcases. Peter and Brother Stoltz carried most of them, and Anna carried the baby. She stepped down from the train ahead of the others, and then she led the way from the platform into the main hall of the station. When she passed through the gate, she saw the Thomases, knew them from their pictures and their eager faces. Sister Thomas hurried to Anna, President Thomas right behind. One of the daughters was with them, but Anna couldn't think which one she was.

"Oh, Anna," Sister Thomas said. She pronounced it correctly—Ahna—not the way most Americans did, and she had a wonderful face, such a loving, dimpled smile. She wrapped her arms around both Anna and Gene, grasped them tight, as if she had known them all her life. Then she stepped back and said, "Oh, little Gene, let me look at you."

She took the baby from Anna, but he let out a little screech and reached back for his mother.

"Oh, it's all right. I'm grandma," Bea said. But Gene was stretching away from her still, and now he had begun to cry.

Bea let him go back to his mother, and she laughed. "You'll get to know me," she said. "Don't worry. You won't be afraid of me for long. I'll make cookies for you. We'll play together."

Gene clung to his mother, however, and turned his head away. "It's just as well for now," Anna said. "He's awfully wet, and I'm out of diapers."

But now President Thomas was reaching his arms out to Anna. "We know all about wet diapers at our house," he said. "We've seen plenty in our time." President Thomas was so much like Alex. He was heavier, his face more jowly, and his voice deeper, but he had that same jaw line, the same dark eyes. He gave Anna a squeeze, more tentative than his wife's, and then he stepped to Brother Stoltz, who had come up alongside Anna. By now Bea was hugging Frieda, and Anna wondered whether her mother would be comfortable with that, but she was smiling and laughing.

"We're excited to have you here. We can't wait to get better acquainted," Bea was saying.

During all this, Peter was hanging back, and so was the daughter.

"Are you LaRue?" Anna finally asked.

"Beverly. LaRue couldn't come."

"Oh. You're more grown up than in the last picture I saw," Anna said. "It's so nice to meet you at last. And this is Gene."

She turned him, and he looked at Beverly but still clung to his mother. "Hi, Gene," Beverly said. "I love you. I'm your aunt."

Gene seemed to respond. He didn't laugh, didn't let go of

his mother, but he looked at Beverly curiously, as though he were thinking that he might like her, in time.

"I want you to meet my brother," Anna said. "Come here, Peter." He stepped forward now, and in his German manner bowed his head a little.

"Hello," Beverly said.

"Very nice to meet you," he said in English, and he shook her hand.

Then he shook President Thomas's hand, and Sister Thomas's. But they seemed to know that they shouldn't try to embrace him. "Peter," Bea said, "we worried about you for such a long time. And we prayed for you all the time. When we got the letter from Anna and found out you were safe and well, I can't tell you how happy we were. Our own son was a prisoner of war for such a long time—maybe you know that—so we knew how worried your parents were about you."

Anna wasn't sure that Peter had picked up all the words, but she saw him melt a little under the influence of the sentiment. Peter was such a tender boy and yet so wary right now. Anna was pleased that the Thomases would make him feel so welcome.

"Thank you," he said, and then he smiled. "My English is not good. Not yet."

"It sounds wonderful to me," President Thomas said. "I wish I spoke a little German, but I can't say anything but *auf Wiedersehen*, and I think it's the wrong time to say that."

Peter laughed. So did Brother and Sister Stoltz. And all of Anna's nervousness was gone. These people were as good as Alex.

"We brought two cars over, since we knew you'd have a lot of luggage. We thought you might like to come over to our place first and get a chance to rest for a minute. But I might as well tell you, I bought a little house awhile back, one I thought I'd end up renting out, but it's open right now. We furnished it to some degree, although it still needs a few things. But anyway, you can live there for now. And Heinrich, as I told you in my letter, I can put you to work as soon as you like. It may not be the kind of work you want, in the long run, but it will get you started."

"Yes, of course. I'm happy to have any employment."

President Thomas looked at Peter. "You can work in my plant too, Peter. That offer is still open. We need to talk about all that, but I just want all of you to know that you have a place to live, and you have work if you want it. You don't need to worry about any of those things."

Anna looked at her father, who seemed perplexed. "Have you understood all this?" Anna asked in German. Some of the words she hadn't recognized.

"Yes. Certainly."

"What is *furnished*?"

"It must mean *furniture*. It's a house for us, with furniture. How can this be?"

"Alex told me that his father would do this."

But now Brother Stoltz was looking at President Thomas. "It's too much," he said. "If you give me a job, I will pay rent. I can't take everything from you."

"I understand, Heinrich. We'll work all that out. But for now, I want to get you off to a good start, and then I'm sure you'll do fine. You're a smarter man than I am, from what I understand, so I know you don't need me to keep you going too long."

"No, no. This is not so. I am willing to do any kind of work. And Peter will too. We're not proud people."

"Well, fine. But we'll give you a day or two to settle in before we put you on the job."

"Thank you so much, sir. You must know, however, that this is only temporary. We can find our way."

"Oh, sure. I know that. But if you call me 'sir' again, I might wonder who you're talking to. Just call me Al."

"But you're *President* Thomas."

"Not anymore. And that doesn't matter. Friends in this country call each other by their first names. And we're more than friends—we're relatives." President Thomas laughed, and then he looked at Gene. "How about coming to me, little one," he said. But Gene turned and grabbed his mother again, and everyone laughed. Then they all picked up the baggage and walked outside into the April air. Anna had watched the mountains from the train window, but now she stopped and looked up. "See the mountains," she told Gene, who seemed less than interested, but her parents were in awe. They stopped and gazed over the city.

Brother and Sister Stoltz had been less than impressed by some of the open, sagebrush-covered land of the West, but the mighty Rocky Mountains appealed to them. Anna liked the feel of the air, the lovely breeze. Alex had told her how hot it could be in the summer, but it was a perfect day today, with the sky deep blue above the mountains, which were still covered with snow.

The Thomases had two beautiful cars parked outside the station, big ones with large trunks. President Thomas drove one, and Sister Thomas the other. Sister Stoltz was impressed by that—told Anna so. They drove through the wide streets of Salt Lake City, and Anna was amazed by how clean everything looked, more like pre-war Germany than the other cities they had seen in America. And then, when the Thomases parked in the driveway of their house, Anna was impressed at how large it was. And the neighborhood was so pretty, with spacious lawns in all the front yards. Alex had spoken of all this, tried to give her some idea of it, but to Anna, seeing it for herself the first time, it seemed a kind of paradise.

Inside, the house was beautiful, with large rooms and stained glass in the front windows, even a fireplace. Anna knew it was an old house, but it was elegant, with hardwood floors, beautiful rugs, and a fancy stairway leading upstairs.

They had only just stepped inside, however, when an older

woman wearing a bright yellow dress strode toward Anna, taking steps like a man. She was holding her arms wide apart. "Oh, my little Gene," she said. "Let me see you."

Gene cried out, but the woman only laughed, and she pulled the baby from Anna's arms. "I'm your Great-Grandma Thomas," she said, "and we won't have any crying. I love you way too much for that." She walked off with Gene, as he continued to wail, but when she dropped onto the couch and started jabbering to him, he seemed rather interested, and in only half a minute or so, he had stopped his crying.

"Babies love me," Grandma Thomas called to Anna. "It's not because I'm sweet. I'm kind of a mean old bat. But these kids have a way of knowing who's going to buy them lots of toys. They're not stupid."

Anna wasn't sure she understood all that. She didn't know what a bat meant, not a mean one anyway. But she got the part about the presents, and she laughed. She walked to the elderly man, who was standing back, quiet. He was not as large as President Thomas, but he was even more like Alex in some ways. "You must be Alex's grandfather," she said.

He laughed. "I am," he said. And he took her gently into his arms. "My goodness, you're going to add some good traits to our family line. You're so pretty."

But someone had come through the front door, and Anna heard a voice shout, "Not prettier than me, Grandpa." Anna turned back to see a dark-haired young woman, and she knew that this was certainly LaRue.

LaRue hurried to Anna and seemed ready to reach out to her, and then she stopped. "Oh, my gosh, you *are* prettier than me. I can't stand it."

Anna assumed this was a joke of some kind, but she wasn't entirely sure. LaRue sounded genuinely upset.

But then she smiled, wide, and she had something of Alex in her, too, those lovely eyes and her dark eyelashes. "You're beautiful, Anna. As pretty as the pictures."

"I've been on the train with the baby. I feel like such a mess."

"No, no. You're gorgeous." Now LaRue did embrace Anna. "I'm your sister," she said. "I'm LaRue. I love you already. Where's Gene?"

"I've got him," Grandma called out. "You leave him alone for now. He's just getting used to me."

"She's the only one he's gone to so far," Bea was saying.

"He likes my bracelets," Grandma said. "He hears the sound of money in them."

But all this was so confusing. Anna looked about at her own family, and somehow they seemed like stiff poles in the middle of all this movement, this talk, this easy flow of things. How could they ever fit in? And yet she loved it; it was all so informal, so fun, so noisy and good.

"I want you all to relax," Bea was saying. "Talk to everyone. Get acquainted, and I'm going to get some dinner on. Wally and Lorraine are coming over in a little while, and we'll eat, and then we'll take you up to your place and you can get a little peace and quiet. I'm afraid we've scared you half to death—all coming at you so fast."

"It's good the way you are," Frieda said. "You're so nice to us. But let me help you. I want to do this."

"Good. Good. Come in the kitchen with me. That'll give us a chance to talk a little."

"Is it possible that you have any diapers here?" Anna asked.

"Oh, yes, I think so. I kept the ones that weren't worn right out. I knew I'd need them someday." And so she ran upstairs, and Anna took Gene. Bea found the diapers, and Anna changed him while his grandma talked to him, and he seemed to like that. When they walked back downstairs, Great-Grandma wanted him again, and Gene didn't mind.

When Bea and Frieda went to the kitchen, LaRue dropped onto the couch next to Grandma, with Beverly on the other side, and they entertained Gene, who had begun to laugh at

them. Brother Stoltz and President Thomas had sat down at
the big table in the dining room, and Anna could hear them
talking about the Church, about the many members in Utah.

"Sit down, Anna," Beverly whispered to her. She pointed at
a big chair near the couch. "We don't mean to be impolite.
We're just excited to meet our nephew."

"You have such beautiful furniture," Anna said as she sat
down. "And this is such a big house."

"This isn't *really* very big, and it's old as the hills," LaRue
said. "Dad wants to build a new house, up in the foothills above
here, but Mom keeps saying that she doesn't want to move.
We're all waiting to see who wins that fight."

"It's not really a fight," Beverly said.

Anna realized that Peter had remained standing, caught
somewhere between his father in the dining room and all the
women in the living room.

Beverly had apparently noticed at the same time. "Would
you like to sit down?" she asked him.

The only place left was at the end of the couch, next to
LaRue. Anna saw how uncomfortable he was with the idea.
"I . . ." But he obviously couldn't think how to say what he
wanted to say, and he merely pointed to the men.

He began to turn that way when LaRue suddenly stood up.
"Peter, I haven't met you," she said. "We've been hearing about
you *forever.* Nice to meet you."

She stepped toward him and stuck out her hand. He shook
it, bowed his head quickly.

"Hey, that's what Germans always do in the movies," LaRue
said. "Do you click your heels, too?"

Peter clearly hadn't understood, and he blushed. Anna
didn't know whether he was embarrassed that he hadn't understood or because he had understood just enough to be
conscious of the way he was acting—compared to everyone
else. "Some German men still do click their heels when they

shake hands," Anna said, and she laughed. "It's a little old-fashioned now."

"Oh, is it? I think it's neat." Then she looked back at Peter. "How's your English?" she asked. "Have you learned much yet?"

"A little," he said. And then he got away, retreating to the men.

"But Anna, you speak really well," LaRue said. "You sound sort of British though. You've been hanging around with too many limeys."

Anna laughed because she knew that LaRue was teasing, but she wondered that LaRue would be so familiar already. It hardly seemed proper. She wasn't sure she could be that way herself—wasn't sure that she wanted to. But she liked LaRue, and sweet Beverly, and she even liked Grandma, who was nothing like any other elderly woman she had ever known. And before long Wally and Lorraine arrived. They were warm and kind and both embraced Anna too, and they took Gene for a time, laughing with him. Gene kept looking about to find his mother, but as long as she was within sight, he seemed quite happy with all the attention. It was as though he were saying, "This is fun. I like these people."

Dinner was overwhelming, with more food on one table than Anna remembered ever seeing: a large ham, mashed potatoes and gravy, a green salad, fresh peas and carrots, hot rolls and butter, pickled beats and cucumbers, black olives, and a wonderful cherry *Kuchen* that Sister Thomas called a "pie." And with it came lots of talk, lots of laughing, lots of questions for the Stoltzes. By the time President Thomas drove the family to the "little house" he had promised them, Anna was exhausted. But the house was anything but small. It was a wonderful brick home with three bedrooms, a nice kitchen, and a big living room. It was like a palace compared to the little flat they had lived in in London.

Anna and her parents thanked President Thomas over and over, but he seemed embarrassed about that. He kept changing the subject and showing them around the house, into the spacious basement, and out into the garage. And then he said, "You're going to need a car, and that's something I can get easier than anything. I'll figure something out and get one up to you."

"But President Thomas, I don't drive," Brother Stoltz said.

"You've never driven a car?"

"Perhaps a little, a long time ago. But wouldn't I need a permit of some sort? I hardly dare drive on these streets with so many cars about."

"That won't be a problem. You'll learn fast, and it's not difficult to get a driver's license. Don't worry about that. I'll see to it." And he was off.

After, when the Stoltzes were finally alone, they all looked at each other as though they still didn't believe what had been happening all afternoon. "Can we do this?" Sister Stoltz asked. "Can we live in a house like this and not pay them anything?"

"We will pay," Brother Stoltz said. "We'll work, and we'll pay."

"They are so rich. They have so many cars. And such a house. I don't know what they will think of us."

"They love us," Anna said. "They're just trying to help us."

"Sister Thomas is wonderful," Sister Stoltz said. "I never had such a close friend in Germany, and I've only known this woman for one afternoon."

"They are very rich, but they are very good," Brother Stoltz said.

Anna looked at Peter, who still looked nervous, concerned. "Are you all right?" she asked.

He sat down on a chair, a large comfortable upholstered chair that was clearly new. "Yes. I'm fine," he said.

"Will you be happy here?"

He looked confused by the question, but he seemed to consider it for a time. "They're very noisy," he said.

Everyone laughed. "But it's a good noise," Brother Stoltz

said. "They're our brothers and sisters, and our in-laws too. They have already accepted us into their family."

Peter nodded. "I like them," he said. "But how can we be like them?"

"We can't. But it doesn't matter," Brother Stoltz said. "Think of what we have here. In Germany we would have *nothing* now. We are blessed to be here with jobs, with a house, with everything." When Peter didn't answer, he asked, "Isn't it so, Peter?"

"Yes. Of course."

"What's the matter then? Are you homesick?"

"I've never had a home," he said. "Not since I was a boy."

Brother Stoltz said softly, "I know, Son. I'm sorry."

"It's not that. It couldn't be helped. But still—I don't know where I belong."

Anna understood, of course, and she worried about Peter. "You must try," she said. "You can make a home now, finally."

But he didn't respond.

"You'll be all right in time," Anna told him. "Everything will be good for you here."

Anna wanted to believe that, but she also knew that Peter was going to have to find his own way through his doubts.

In bed that night, when Gene had settled down next to Anna and was breathing steadily, still too wary to go off to a crib, Anna tried to think about her own future. She loved the Thomases and she liked Salt Lake City, and she felt blessed beyond belief to have this house to live in. Alex would be here before long, and she would have everything she had dreamed of. She held Gene close, trying to bask in this joy, but it all made her rather nervous. Was it really possible for life to be so perfect?

16

Wally was sitting at his office desk, trying to make some headway with his paperwork. He looked up when one of his foremen stepped to the door. "Wally, we've got a problem," he said.

Wally looked back at his desk for a moment. He entered the last number in a column, pulled the arm on his adding machine, and then wrote the results on the form he was filling out. "What's the matter, Ken?" he finally asked.

"We've been making casings all morning for those Bendix motors, but they're out of tolerance, every one of them."

"Did you check all the settings?"

"Yes. And they're all exactly right. I can't figure out what's going on."

Wally nodded. "Let's go have a look at it." He was glad Ken had had the good sense to check with him before he started fussing with the gauges. Ken was new, and he was a good man, but he had served in the navy all during the war, and sometimes, on ship, sailors learned to keep engines going any way they could—with a hunk of wire or a matchstick. This fine-tuned machinery couldn't be handled that way.

The truth was, Wally especially liked getting away from his office. He always felt satisfied when he cleared his desk—

processed all the paper and got rid of it—but he didn't like the tedium of the work itself. He really liked being out on the floor, and he liked seeing the actual parts come off the line, buffed and ready to ship. He liked talking to the workers, too, and above all he loved to solve problems. This new one sounded interesting, something that would be a challenge to figure out.

In recent months the work force in the plant had changed drastically. Wally was hiring lots of men who were home from the war, and they were happy to get the work. More and more of the young women who had worked there were getting married, or the married ones were shyly announcing to him that they were expecting and needed to stay home now. But some wanted to stay, and Wally was glad they did. These women had been running the machines longer, had the experience, and he didn't need a whole shop full of novices. He noticed that men who returned from something as sloppy and haphazard as war had a tendency to say "That looks close enough" rather than understand the tiny tolerances allowed in making interchangeable parts.

Wally spent an hour down on the line, and as usual, when he found the problem, it was actually a simple one. The machinist had read the spec sheet incorrectly. It took Wally a few minutes to explain the problem, but he loved that moment when the machinist, a young fellow named Monte Payne, and Ken Horsley, the foreman, both saw the point at the same time. "Oh, yeah, I was looking at the wrong drawing," Monte said, and Ken nodded and said, "Now I got ya."

"Well, it's an easy mistake to make. We're making parts for several different-sized motors. You'll get used to these spec sheets when you've worked with them more."

"Yeah, I think I will. I'm sorry I messed up all them casings this morning."

"It happens," Wally said, but he didn't want to be *too* easy. "Ken, you do need to keep on top of that. We really should have caught that right off—before we made up a whole batch of bad ones."

"I know. I had some things come up, and I didn't get back to the line for a little while."

For a time the three talked about the inspection process. Wally liked the decision that came out of the little talk, and he liked the way Monte and Ken reached an agreement without his saying too much. He even liked the way the men called him Wally, thanked him, joked a little as they began to reset the machinery. By the time Wally left the floor he was feeling that he was getting pretty good at what he did, and mostly that he liked it—liked solving the problems, liked dealing with the workers, liked being a crucial part of a well-run operation.

He walked back to his office—and then on by. He stepped to his mother's door. "How are you doing?" he asked.

"Not too bad. At least I don't feel like I'm in over my head all the time, now that you're around here."

"We had a little problem on the line, got some motor casings off-sized, but I figured out what was going wrong."

"See. Now that's the kind of thing I just had to leave to the foremen. I never have been much help with things like that."

"The difference was, you had a crew of foremen you could rely on. Since we started expanding, we've got way too many new guys around here."

Bea was wearing her reading glasses. She took them off now and leaned back in her chair, smiling. "Wally, I just never get over how much I like having you around here. Every time I hear your voice in the hallway, I think, 'That's my boy, and he's home.'"

"It's funny. I don't think about that so much anymore. It's all starting to seem normal to me—even having a *girl* in bed with me." He laughed.

"Hey, that wife of yours is nothing less than a dream come true. Don't you forget it."

"You don't know the true Lorraine, Mom. When I get

home, she's still got her hair up in curlers, and all she does is cuss me out and nag at me."

"She doesn't either. Don't you even *say* such a thing."

"How do you know?"

"Because she's the sweetest girl in the world—except for dear Anna. I've fallen in love with her already. Isn't she wonderful?"

"I haven't been around her as much as you have, but I sure like her, Mom. And that little Gene, he's a spitfire."

"He's so much like our Gene was at that age," Mom said, and Wally saw her glance away for a moment. But then she added, quickly, "They're all such good people. How are Heinrich and Peter doing with their jobs?"

"I don't see Peter much. He's down in the shipping department all the time. But Richard says he works really hard, and he's starting to relax a little. He tries to speak some English once in a while now."

"What about Heinrich?"

"Well . . . I don't know. I'm not sure he's cut out for machinist work. But he sure tries hard."

Mom usually wore an old gray cardigan over her dress when she worked in her office. She pulled it together now and began to button the front. It was April, but the weather had turned cold and rainy. There was even some new snow in the mountains. "I just wish we could get Alex home now," she said. "Now that Bobbi's getting married, I feel better about her. But I won't feel like the war is really over until we get Alex back."

"When is it going to be over for you, Mom? I thought you'd quit working down here by now."

But Wally thought he saw a bit of a reaction, maybe a little spark of annoyance. Mom glanced away from him and shrugged. "If I dropped all this paperwork on you right now, you'd be screaming for mercy in a week," she said.

"I know that. But we could get someone hired, and you could start training him."

"Or her."

Wally smiled. "Yes. Or her." And then he had a thought. "What about Heinrich? Could he do it?"

"I don't know, Wally. Would his English be good enough to handle all the technical words he'd have to know?"

"He could learn that fast enough, I would think."

"Well, maybe. But there's so much to it—all the government regulations and the way you have to word everything."

"So what are you saying, Mom? That no one else could ever learn your job?" He asked the question in a serious voice, but then, after he gave her a moment to think, he smiled.

Slowly, Mom let herself smile too. "I think maybe that's it, Wally. I want to think that no one else could do it—that I really am *needed* around here." She leaned back in her chair, as though she had decided, for just a moment, to separate herself from her work.

"I doubt that anyone else will do it as well, Mom. But that doesn't mean that you don't deserve to get out of here."

Suddenly she leaned forward again. She pointed her finger at Wally and said, more seriously than he expected, "You sound just like your dad."

"What do you mean?" Wally stepped inside the door and shut it behind him to block out some of the noise. In a softer voice, he asked, "Did I say the wrong thing?" She really had seemed a little upset with him.

"You just can't imagine that I might enjoy the work and want to stick around. What's so great about knocking around my big old house—especially when the girls are gone? And that won't be much longer now."

"But a lot of times you sound like you're really tired of this place."

"Who doesn't? All the men around here complain, and no one tells them they ought to go home and do housework."

Wally laughed. He sat down on a chair near the door. The old building always smelled of grease and sweat and metal

shavings; he couldn't imagine how his mom had stood it for all
these years. "I think I"d better stay out of this one," he said. "All
I know is, as long as you want to stay, this company is better
off."

"But is our family better off if I stay home? I could tend
Gene more often—and any other grandchildren we might get
some time." She cocked her head a little and looked at Wally
with a question in her eyes.

"Don't look at me. I can't have a baby. Lorraine has to do
that."

"Maybe somebody hasn't told you about the birds and the
bees yet. You have something to do with getting those babies,
you know."

"Really? Tell me how that works."

"Shush. But tell me the truth. Would we be better off at
home if I quit down here?"

"I don't know. I really have no idea. But I think it's your
decision and no one else's."

"Thanks for that. I don't think your dad looks at it that
way."

"Does he want you to stay home?"

"You know he does. He doesn't say it to me, but I know he
thinks it's wrong for me to be down here when *men* need work.
What he does tell me is that it 'looks bad' for his wife to keep
working."

"Well, like I said, I'll leave that up to you. But I wouldn't let
Dad decide for you."

"Do you decide things for Lorraine?"

Wally laughed. "I occasionally submit my recommenda-
tions, and then she gets back to me with the right answer. But
she retains all the veto power."

"How does that happen, Wally? How do girls know how
to do that now? When I was her age, I thought I had to do
whatever Al thought was right."

"Mom, Lorraine has been out making her own way for a

long time. She has a mind of her own, and she doesn't even stop to think that she shouldn't have. That's just what she's used to. I'm just kidding about her being bossy. She's not like that. But I don't *tell* her what to do. We talk everything over."

"And do you like that?"

"Of course I do. I don't want to be her boss; I want to be her partner."

"Do you think most men your age feel that way?"

"I don't know. Not most, maybe. But a lot do—especially all the ones who've married someone like Lorraine." He laughed. "They don't have much choice."

Mom smiled. "I like the way Lorraine does it," she said. "She's so soft-spoken, and she loves you so much I can see it every time she looks at you. But she's Lorraine, at the same time, and not just 'Wally's wife.'"

"Well . . . I will admit she loves me. But I can't say I blame her." He grinned.

"Don't sit here and brag about that, young man. You get busy and produce a grandchild for me."

"Okay. Should I run home right now?"

But now Wally had gone one step too far. Mom was blushing. And Wally thought maybe he was too. "You'd better get back to work," she said, "or I'll fire you for goofing around."

Wally laughed, and he headed back to his own office, but it was an interesting little joke his mom had made. In some ways, she did like to think that she was in charge. And Wally rather liked to think *he* was the boss. He hoped that wouldn't lead to problems somewhere down the line.

Later that day, Dad came by. Wally hadn't seen him for a few days. The dealership was getting busier now, with more new cars coming in all the time. New Hudsons and Nashes had been introduced at the first of the year, but few had actually reached Utah until lately. Now, in May, more were arriving, and buyers were waiting. Dad had been putting in some long hours. He walked briskly into Wally's office, looking like he was in a hurry, and said, "Wally, I had another man ask me today if you'd be willing to talk to his club. The Rotarians, I think it was."

Wally had gotten used to that. A lot of people seemed to be interested in hearing about his experiences in prison camp. Wally didn't mind; in fact, he was getting pretty good at it, but he sometimes felt as though people wanted to hear what devils all Japanese were. When Wally talked about all people being essentially the same, as he liked to do, he seemed to get a good response, but as soon as he allowed questions, people wanted to hear about the torture, about the inhuman treatment the POWs had received, and there was plenty of that to report. It just wasn't what Wally wanted to emphasize. Still, Wally said, "Sure, Dad. I can do that. Just have him give me a call."

"Well, actually, I already did. I gave him your number. I just wanted you to know he'd be getting in touch with you." He stepped toward the door, as though he were about to leave. He was holding his hat in his hand.

"Okay, Dad," Wally said. "I'll do my round of talks, and then Alex can come home and take over. He'll do a better job anyway. He always was a better speaker than me."

"Well, he's always been relaxed in front of a group. Not many of us feel that way."

Wally nodded, but he was a little surprised at the response. He had half expected a compliment for his own skills. What he couldn't resist asking was, "What do you think Alex will do when he gets back?"

"I know he wants to go back to college, but I hope he'll do like you—put that off just a little and then maybe start part-time. I could sure use him in the business."

"Where?"

"Well . . . I'm not sure." And now Dad walked to the desk and sat down on the chair across from Wally. "I'll tell you one thing I've thought of. You always used to tell me that you'd like to work at the dealership. What if you went over there when

Alex gets back? Alex started this whole operation back when it was running on a shoestring. He could probably fit in pretty fast around here. If you were with me, I'd start looking to a day when I could get out of there once in a while. I'd like to cut back my hours."

"So what would I do exactly?"

"Learn the whole operation. I'd love to see you lead up the sales team and get some of those guys in the showroom in line. Then come up in the office and start learning the ropes there. When I get ready to retire, you'd be in a perfect spot to take over the whole place."

"Are you really going to retire, Dad? I can't see you sitting around the house."

"I can't either. But I can get more involved with the Republican party, and Mom and I, we might decide we want to see what the world looks like. You kids have been all over, and we've never been out of the States."

"I can tell you all the nicest places to see in the Philippine jungles—or in the coal mines of Japan."

"I think I'll pass on that." Dad laughed. "Look, I've got to skedaddle." He stood up. "You think that over, though. Anna got a letter from Alex this week, and he really thinks he's going to get a discharge in the next few weeks. So if you think you'd like to come over and work with me, let's start talking seriously about it."

"Okay."

"Okay, you want to come over? Or okay, you want to think about it?"

"Uh . . . think about it for now."

"Good. You're sure doing a good job here. Your mom says you're a natural. The men on the line all tell her how much they like working with you. And Richard is a big help too. I feel like I don't have to worry about the place now, and I can concentrate on rebuilding things at the dealership."

"Good."

"What's wrong?"

"Nothing. What do you mean?"

"Well . . . okay. You think about it. I'll see you later." And Dad left. But Wally couldn't get the conversation out of his mind the rest of the day.

That night, when Wally got home, Lorraine was dressed up a little more than usual. She was wearing a pretty blue-green spring dress with a white collar—not one of the house dresses she usually wore. "What's the occasion?" he asked.

"So has it come to that already? You ask me why I want to look nice for you, and you don't even give me a kiss? Next you'll be sticking your head in a newspaper and telling me not to bother you."

"*Never!*" Wally took her in his arms and kissed her.

It was no peck either, but a slow, romantic kiss, and when he finally stopped and held her in his arms, she said, "Wow. You got any more of those?"

"One more of those and I might forget all about dinner."

"Then don't kiss me anymore," she said, stepping back from him and pushing against his chest. Wally found himself a little disappointed by her retreat, but at the same time pleased by the way she was smiling. "I have a special dinner for you. And I baked a cake."

"Wait a minute. Is it my birthday, and I forgot?"

"No."

"Then whose birthday is it? I hope it's not yours."

Lorraine was standing near their little kitchen table. She was gripping the top slat in one of their ladder-back chairs, and she was looking at him with delight in her eyes. And then Wally knew. "Does this have something to do with a birthday to come?"

"Yes."

"My little son?"

"Son? Why not a daughter?"

"Are you really pregnant, Lorraine?"

"Yes." And now her face was alight.

For the past couple of weeks she had been feeling rather sick, so this was not a surprise, but it was wonderful news to Wally. "Oh, that's so great," he said, and he took her into his arms again. "Today Mom said she wanted another grandchild. She'll think we're very efficient."

"Wally!"

"Well, you know what I mean."

Lorraine pulled back a little again and looked into his eyes. "First of all, I don't want you to tell her yet."

"Why not?"

"I don't know. It's still early. I don't want everyone making a fuss yet. A lot of girls miscarry with their first baby. That's what the doctor told me, and I don't want to announce it and then have something go wrong."

"Okay."

"But Wally, you shouldn't be telling your mother about . . . us. That embarrasses me."

"I didn't. She just told me that she wanted us to have a baby, and I made a joke. I told her I'd run home and get to work on it."

"Wally! I won't be able to look your mother in the eye."

"Lorraine, she knows where babies come from. I told her a long time ago."

"Hush."

"That's her favorite word—when she talks to me."

"That's because you have a smart mouth."

Wally laughed, but then he said, "Stop a second. I want to think about this."

"About what?"

"I'm going to be a daddy." He leaned back his head and laughed harder. "That's terrific, Lorraine. Good job."

"But Wally, you will be happy with a girl, won't you?"

"Hey, I was just joking about that. If we get a little girl, pretty as her mother, she'll have me wrapped right around her little finger."

"Oh, I know. I'm not sure I want the competition. It's been so nice, just the two of us, and *everything* is going to change now. I'll be fat as a sow in a few months, and you won't *want* to kiss me anymore."

"Let's check and see whether I'm losing my interest yet." He kissed her again, even longer than before, and then he held her close, smelled her wonderful perfume, felt the long curves of her against his body. "You're going to look great with a big belly," he told her. "Perfect."

"I vomited this morning, after you left. I hope I don't stay sick for the whole nine months."

He gripped her a little tighter. "Rainey, thanks. I know it makes you sick. And I know it's going to get uncomfortable. And I know it hurts to have a baby. But thanks. Okay? Thanks for doing it for us. We're going to have swell kids."

"I'm a little frightened by it all."

"About being pregnant or being a mom?"

"Both."

"Don't be. You're going to be the best. And I'm going to knock myself out to be a good dad."

"Don't spend your life at the plant, okay?"

"Do you worry about that?"

"A little. I do."

Wally released his hold on her, but he took hold of her hands. "That's interesting you would say that. I was thinking today that I don't want to be like my dad—at least in that way. His business, along with his Church jobs, kept him away from home so much when I was growing up."

"You'll be a bishop, Wally. Or a stake president or something. I already know that."

"Well . . . I don't know. But I want to be close to my kids. Dad was always one step removed from us, and Mom was pretty much the parent we could go to. I don't want that to happen. I want my kids to feel like they can talk to me."

"That's what I'm going to need, Wally. I'm not wise, and I don't know how to get that way." Suddenly she took a step back. "Oh, Wally, what am I doing? I've got to get this dinner on before it's cold."

She walked to the oven. Wally loved seeing her play this role, being a wife, fussing about dinner being cold. And their house was much nicer than Wally ever could have expected at this point in his life. Dad had found an older home in Sugar House, only a few blocks east of where the Thomases lived. Someone in the stake was moving, and when Dad heard about it, he had made a down payment on the place, and then told Wally that if he wanted to take over the payments, it was his. Wally and Lorraine had lived in an apartment for a couple of months and had been calculating how long it would be before they could get into a house, and then, suddenly, this place was theirs. It wasn't fancy, but it had lots of room, and Wally and Lorraine had plans about how they could fix it up in time.

Wally appreciated the way his dad was opening doors for him, making life so comfortable, but he also felt a little strange about it. Some of his friends were working hard, and they had almost nothing to show for it. Chuck didn't have parents who could do such things for him. He had finally found a job, and he was planning to go to college on the GI bill that fall, but he had years to go to be in the position Wally was. In some ways, that was embarrassing to Wally. He almost envied Chuck for being able to work his own way up and not get things so easily.

There was also something else bothering Wally. "Dad said something today that worries me a little," he told Lorraine.

"What was that?" Lorraine had roasted a whole chicken, and she was taking it from the oven. Wally loved the smell of it.

"He asked me if I wanted to change jobs—move over to the dealership when Alex gets home."

"Why is that strange?"

Wally pulled a chair out and sat down at the table. "He said that Alex used to run the plant, and he could move back into that. It just made me wonder whether he doesn't think Alex will do a better job."

"If he wants you working with him, that's quite a compliment, I would say."

"I know. But he talked about having me learn the ropes, selling cars for a while. It sort of sounds like Alex is getting promoted to the top, and I'm going to get knocked down a few rungs for a while."

"But isn't he saying that you would become the head of the dealership at some point?"

"Yeah. He said that, right out. But not for quite a while, and in the meantime, he would be in charge and telling me what to do all the time. He doesn't say much about what I do at the plant, but that's because he's so busy at the dealership. I just don't know whether I want to be right under his thumb like that."

"Either way, he's giving you a great opportunity." Lorraine's back was to Wally. She was using two forks to set the chicken on a platter.

"I know." Wally hadn't said it yet, and he told himself that he wouldn't, but then the words came out. "Dad has always thought that Alex was his smartest son, the one who would do the most. I told him today that Alex could take over the speaking for me, once he got home, and Dad seemed to think that made sense, like he *would* do a better job."

Lorraine glanced around at him. "He didn't say that."

"No. Not exactly. But I said he was a better speaker than me. And he seemed to agree with me."

"Wally, you're putting words into his mouth."

"Maybe. But I can picture what's going to happen. I may end up working with Dad a long time, and that might be fine. But Alex will be the head of Dad's many enterprises, in one way or another."

"Are you sure?"

Actually, Wally wasn't sure. And he didn't like what he was doing to himself. For so many years he had been in the habit of being jealous of his big brother, the star athlete, the student-body president, the missionary. Wally didn't want to do that again, to go back to that kind of attitude, but it was hard not to see Dad's extra pride when he spoke to people about Alex's war record. Wally had been a survivor—a victim—but Alex had won a bunch of medals, had received a battlefield commission, had dropped behind enemy lines as a spy. What a story he was—what a great man. And Wally didn't care about competing with all that. He was even happy to let Alex be the speaker, the hero. But he wanted his father's respect, and when he had first come home, he had thought he had it. Now what he was feeling was that Dad was pleased with him but still held him in a second position to the star of the family.

All that was wrongheaded, though. "Lorraine, I never should have brought this up. It's all my old teenage worries coming back, and it's stupid. Dad has shown me so much love since I've been home—more than he ever knew how to show when I was younger."

Lorraine brought the chicken to the table and set it down between their two plates. She had set the table earlier, had used their nice china and pretty lace tablecloth. "Wally, I just don't think you're in any kind of competition with your brother. You've always seemed to feel that you were."

"I know. He is better than me at most things, and that's just how it is. It's not his fault, and not Dad's either."

"That's still making a comparison, and it just isn't necessary."

"I know. What I want, this time, is just to love my brother. If I had Gene back, I'd be happy to have him. I wouldn't be worrying about who got the better job, or something like that."

"But it's hard, isn't it?" She put her hand on his shoulder.

"What is?"

"Just to live life and love it. And not think you have to be better at it than someone else."

"I thought you said that you weren't wise."

"That's not wisdom; that's just a question." She walked back to the cabinet.

"No. It's a lot more than that. It's the attitude I ought to have. A few months ago I got up every morning and thanked the Lord for my toothbrush, and now I'm already worrying about things that don't matter. I need to spend more time thanking the Lord for what I have—and not worrying about the rest."

She walked back to the table with a bowl of peas and new potatoes. "Now we're both wise. Let's eat."

17

Bobbi and Richard were getting married. At first, Bobbi had committed to a wedding date mostly out of resolve to move forward, as her grandmother—and almost everyone else—had advised her to do. But spending time with Richard had also reassured her. She could feel his commitment to her, and she was touched by his attempts to express more of his feelings. Added to that, he never seemed to tire of listening to Bobbi talk about her own dreams and wishes. What surprised Bobbi, however, and pleased her more than anything, was that those intense feelings she had known in Hawaii had gradually returned. She felt a powerful attraction to Richard, and at the same time, a deepened awareness of his goodness. In spite of that, she was often aware that he wasn't exactly the same man he had been when she had first met him. He had been shocked by the war back then, disappointed with people, but he hadn't been hurt personally. What she saw now were little hints of sadness that would show up in him when he was unguarded. Still, she loved Richard—she had no doubt about that now—and she had to accept all of him, even the wounds he carried, and she had to hope that her love could serve as one of the influences that would heal him.

The wedding ceremony was sacred and warm—with both

families together in the temple—and the first night with
Richard more lovely than Bobbi had dared to hope. She and
Richard also had great fun on their drive to California, with lots
of time to laugh and talk. Richard had arranged for a room in a
nice little motel close to the beach, north of San Diego, and
the two spent plenty of time near the water, and in it, and lots
of lovely time alone in the room. Bobbi loved being close to
this strong man who held her so gently, and she loved the
openness she felt in this new intimacy. What she wanted now
was to forget about the war, the past, the scars, and she wanted
to embrace, with Richard, this new beginning.

The two were lying on the beach one afternoon when
Bobbi asked him, "So, Mr. Hammond, are you happy?"

He was lying face down, with his back to the sun, but his
skin was already deep brown and wonderfully tight over
his muscles. His head was on his arms, and sideways, so that
he could look at her. His right hand, his better hand, lay close
to her face, and she could see the scar tissue, the pale, hairless
skin across the back. "You know I am," he said, and he smiled.

"It's strange to me to think that I've been with a man now—
after all these years of waiting."

His eyes went shut. He didn't say anything.

"Do you like it as much as you thought you would?" Bobbi
asked.

"What?"

"You know."

"Of course I do."

"Don't say it like that. You sound like you're saying, 'Yes,
and the sunsets are also very pretty in southern California.'"

"They are."

"I know. But tell me how *much* you like it."

He opened his eyes—those wonderful pale blue eyes—and
raised himself to his elbows. "Bobbi, you must have noticed my
. . . how should I say? . . . my enthusiasm. Let's just leave it at
that. Let's not try to put it into words."

"I'm embarrassing you, huh?"

"Yes. I'm still a blushing groom."

Bobbi laughed, and she ran her arm over his back, his hot skin. Then she leaned toward him and kissed his ear. "So do you want to go back across the street now—to the motel?"

"Sure."

"Oooh. That's better than pretty words. That's *enthusiasm*."

"But sometimes, let me think of it first. Okay?"

The words *stung*. "Excuse me. I certainly will," Bobbi said. She turned away and lay on her back. Not only was her ardor gone, but she was humiliated. She was never going to ask him again, if that's how he felt. In fact, the next time he did show some interest, she would let *him* wait.

She only told herself that for a minute or so, however, and then she admitted that she was being petty. She couldn't ruin her honeymoon by acting like a dumb kid. She would cool off a little more, and then she would try to make things right. But he had to know she was angry. Why didn't he say something? Couldn't *he* apologize?

She waited, wondered who should speak first, waited a little longer, and then couldn't stand it. She didn't want bad feelings between them, not now. "Richard, I'm sorry. I guess a man does like to be the one to take the first step."

"Not necessarily, Bobbi. It's not a problem. Don't worry about it." But he didn't say, "So let's go across the street anyway." He continued to lie in the same position, his eyes shut. Bobbi couldn't help but wonder whether the differences between them were starting to show themselves already. Would she always drive him crazy with her frankness, and would she always frustrate her with his reticence?

"Why don't we go in for a swim?" he said.

Bobbi had no idea how to read that. Was it a little dip he wanted *before* they went across the street? Was he merely hesitant to say that? Or did he mean "I've got a better idea than the one you had. I don't want to go to the motel right now."

"Okay." Bobbi got up.

Richard pulled himself up slowly, and then he walked alongside her to the water, but he didn't take her hand, didn't touch her. They waded into the water, and then without warning, he dove in and started to swim. She thought for a moment that he was challenging her, that he would call back with an invitation to race, but he didn't say anything; he simply kept swimming into the surf, taking powerful strokes.

Bobbi plunged in too, and she swam with all her strength, but she couldn't keep up. She raised her head from time to time, watched him move away from her until so many waves were between them that she could get a glance only once in a while. Finally, she was exhausted, and she had no idea where he was going. She doubted he could hear, but she called out, "I'm turning back."

She turned as a wave took her. She tried to ride it as far as she could, to rest. She was carried back to the shore much faster than she had gone out, however, and she crashed awkwardly onto the beach. She came up spitting and coughing, but she hurried to get her balance and trotted out of the water. Then she spun around and looked back. She scanned the water as far as she could see, but he had disappeared.

Richard was wearing dark blue swimming trunks, and she watched for that blotch of color on the water, for his arms splashing, but she saw nothing. He simply wasn't out there. She knew that she must be missing him somehow, that he had changed his angle or that she was not looking in the right direction at the right moment, when the waves lifted him into view. But nothing was there, no swimmer, not a break in the water except for the constant waves. She looked up the shoreline to the lifeguard who was seated on a high lookout. He was relaxing, apparently unconcerned. Had he seen Richard go out and still had him spotted, or had he not been paying attention?

She kept forcing down her fear, telling herself what a good swimmer Richard was, but she was trying to swallow away the salt in her mouth and couldn't seem to get it down. Her heart was still pounding much harder than it should have been. Where was he?

She spun toward the lifeguard, decided to run to him, changed her mind, looked back at the water, took a long, sweeping gaze across the waves, and then changed her mind again. She suddenly took off, trying to run hard in the loose sand. She was about to scream at the lifeguard when she glanced ahead and spotted Richard, farther north in the water than she had expected, closer to the shore, and riding a wave toward the beach.

She kept running—to him now—but her panic had too much inertia to give way so immediately, and suddenly what she felt was anger. She angled into the water, stumbled as a wave caught her ankle, and had to put a hand down to catch herself. Just then Richard raised up, stood in the water, which was waist high on him. He didn't smile, didn't say anything. He merely took a long breath and then wiped his hand over his hair, smoothing it back.

Bobbi was standing in front of him now, her feet in the water. "Richard, why did you go out so far? I couldn't see you."

He shrugged, looking confused—probably more at the passion in her voice than at her words.

"I couldn't *see* you, Richard," she shouted. "I looked and looked. I thought you had gone under."

"I . . ." But clearly, he didn't know what to say.

"Why did you keep going? Why did you leave me?"

"I was just swimming. I thought you were behind me."

"I can't swim that fast. We should stay together." But now—stupidly—she was crying.

"I'm sorry," he said, and she heard some kind of capitulation in his voice, as though he were saying, "So is this one more thing I have to do to please you?"

"It scared me, Richard. *Really* scared me."

He walked toward her in the water and tried to take her

into his arms. But she put her hands on his chest and said, "Why do you do things like that?"

"Like what?"

"In Hawaii we swam together and came back in together."

He raised his hands, palms open, and said, "I'd just started to swim again. I was weak then."

"But this is our honeymoon."

"What does that mean, Bobbi? That we never let each other out of sight?"

Bobbi heard his anger. She knew it was time to let up, to think before she spoke, but she never had been good at stopping once the words started to roll. "You swam away from me, Richard. You *wanted* to get away from me." She hesitated and took a breath, tried to stop again, but added, "I don't think you're happy, Richard."

"Bobbi, what in the world are you talking about?"

But Bobbi didn't answer. She had told herself a thousand times that she wasn't going to say this to him. She was going to make him happy, not demand it of him.

Richard's eyes went shut. He rubbed his hand over his face again, his hair. "Bobbi, let's calm down. All right? I'm sorry I swam out farther than you thought I was going to, and I'm sorry . . . that I seem unhappy to you. But I'm not. Can we sit down for a minute and just talk this out?"

"Is that what you want to do? Talk to me?" And suddenly she started to sob. "I thought you wanted to drown."

He pulled her into his arms. "Drown? Why would I want that?"

"I don't know, Richard. Because of the things I say. I'm driving you crazy already, and we just got married."

Her face was pressed against him, and she heard him laugh, inside his chest. Then he took hold of her shoulders and pushed her back far enough to look at her. He smiled. It was that tender, slow smile that always made her want to curl up with him, think of nothing but how much she loved him. "Trust me," he said. "I don't want to drown. What I want to do is walk across the street with you and . . . stay at the motel for a little while. But first we need to talk. Okay?"

"Really? Do you want to talk?"

"No. I want to go back to the motel. But we need to talk."

"Let's just go to the motel, then. We can talk later."

"Okay," he said, and he smiled again.

"But I did it again. I made it my idea."

"No, it was my idea. You just bumped it up a notch on our priority list."

"Is that all right?"

"Certainly."

"Oh, Richard, I'm not like this. I'm not a stupid little girl. I don't get all out of sorts and fuss and cry about silly things. You know me better than that, don't you?"

He was still smiling. "I thought I did," he said, "but that was before I tried to drown myself."

"I'm sorry, Richard. It scared me so bad." And she took hold of him, was so glad to have his strength around her again—glad to walk across the street with him.

Later that afternoon Richard was reading, sitting in a big chair in the motel room. Bobbi had made some sandwiches in the little kitchenette, but before they ate, she wanted to have that talk. She went to Richard and knelt by his knees. "Can we talk now?" she asked.

"Sure."

"Okay. Here's what I want to say." She took hold of his legs, wrapping her arms around them. She was wearing the old plaid robe she loved, not the new, nicer one she'd gotten for Christmas. "I shouldn't have said that about you not being happy. But it's what I feel sometimes."

"You don't need to worry about that. I'm fine."

"But there's something I *do* worry about."

"What?"

"I think you took the job with my dad so we could go ahead and get married. It's not what you really want to do."

He reached down and took hold of her, under the arms, and he pulled her up onto his lap. "Listen to me," he said. "Your dad gave me a great opportunity. I thought it through and decided I would grab it. It solved a lot of problems, and it opened up the chance for me to make a good living. Every man has to work, and I don't think the average guy gets up in the morning and says, 'Oh, boy, I love my job.' What I'm doing is a whole lot better than what most men do. And I don't mind it at all."

"I'm sorry, Richard, but I don't like the sound of that."

"Why?"

"It's going to be such a long life for you if you have to face a job you don't really get any satisfaction from. You're doing it for me, and I appreciate it, but I'm afraid something like that will gradually sap the life out of you."

"Bobbi, we talked at one time about my going back to college and becoming some kind of professor, but I didn't even know what I might want to teach. So it's not like I'm giving something up. And think about it—doesn't a professor wake up some mornings and wish he didn't have lectures to prepare or a bunch of research papers to read?"

"I want you to be happy, Richard. I want you to do something you're excited about. You're smart, and when we were in Hawaii you were always talking about reading all the books in the library, learning everything."

"I still read a lot."

"I know. But only after a long day at work. I don't think you care about washing-machine parts."

"Of course I don't. Who does? But—"

"Wally does."

"Oh, come on, Bobbi. Who can look at a little hunk of metal and get excited?"

"Wally gets excited about making things work right at the

plant. He told me that. But he also told me that he didn't think you liked what you were doing."

Richard was silent for a time, and she could feel the tension return, his chest muscles tightening. "Bobbi, I don't know what else to tell you," he said. "I want you. I want to provide for you and our family. I found a good way to do that, and I feel lucky for that."

"Now tell me you're happy. Really happy."

"These few days with you have been the best of my whole life, Bobbi. How can you ask me whether I'm happy? I've never been happier."

She liked that, but she didn't trust it. She kissed his neck. "Why don't you start taking classes at the U, the way Wally plans to do? You could study psychology or history. Then, gradually, you could break away from Dad's company, and you could do something that really excites you."

"Maybe, Bobbi. I mean, I wouldn't mind taking some classes, but there's no way that I would ever make the same kind of money at anything else—especially teaching."

"That's not important to me."

"It's more important than you think, Bobbi. You've never known anything else. And it matters to me. I want to provide our family with a nice house and all those other things you're accustomed to."

"And sacrifice your own life to do it?"

"That's what a man does, Bobbi. He goes to work. He makes a living. If he doesn't make washing-machine parts, he makes something else. It's all more or less the same."

But there was something plaintive in the words, as though Richard were acceding to a force he hated but couldn't change.

"What if I go to college?"

"I think you should. I've always told you that."

"What if I become a college professor?" She leaned away from him so she could look him in the face.

"Sure. Why not? I want you to be a mother first—and soon—but the day could come when you could do that."

"I mean, what if we were both professors? Couldn't we do all right financially that way?"

"And what happens to our kids? Do they get lost in the shuffle somewhere? I don't see how that could work."

Bobbi didn't either, really, but it was what David Stinson had pictured, and he had always made it seem possible.

"Will you at least sign up for a class or two this next fall?"

"Sure. I've been thinking about doing that all along."

"Okay." She took a long breath and tried to decide whether she would let this all drop now. But maybe this was the right time to ask. "There's one other thing I think you should tell me."

"What?"

She twisted, so she could look straight into his face. "You told me that something happened to you after your ship sank—but that you didn't want to talk about it. You wanted to forget it. But you haven't forgotten. It's still bothering you, isn't it?"

"What makes you think so?"

"I see you staring off at nothing sometimes, and you look like a broken-hearted little boy. Then you see me looking at you, and you try to cover up—like you're afraid I'm going to ask you what's wrong."

"Everybody sits and thinks sometimes. That's nothing to make a big thing of."

"Come on. You know there's more to it than that. What could it hurt for you to share with me what's on your mind?"

But Richard only glanced away.

"You're going to tell me that you don't *ever* want to talk about it, Richard. But I think we should. I think this is a good time—right now, at the beginning of our marriage—for you to let me share some of the burden. I really think that talking about it would help. You wouldn't have to—"

"No. Talking *won't* help."

"But if you shared it with me, it wouldn't be inside you, working on you."

"Bobbi, that doesn't even make sense. Telling *you* doesn't take it out of *my* head."

"Sometimes when you talk about something, get it out in the open, it doesn't turn out to be so bad as you thought."

"Bobbi, bad things happen in a war. *Horrible* things. And when the war is over, a guy has two choices: He can keep thinking about all that, and let it bother him forever, or he can put it behind him and go on. A man with any sense moves ahead and lets the past die."

"You're not doing that, Richard. I feel it in you sometimes. It's like a little bit of life has gone out of you. You're ninety percent of who you always were, but the missing ten percent makes all the difference. I see it in your eyes, your voice, everything. You're making do, but you're not fully Richard, the way I knew you at first."

"Then why did you marry me?"

"Because I love you." She slid off his lap, took hold of his hands, and looked up at him. "All I'm saying is that you aren't as happy as you were when I first met you, and I want to help."

"I am happy, Bobbi. I do have some devils I'm dealing with. I admit that. But they'll disappear and I'll be fine. I've made my choices, and I feel they're right."

"And you're not going to tell me what happened?"

"I've told you a lot of things."

"But nothing more?"

"Let's remember Hawaii and be happy that the war brought us together, but let's forget the rest."

"I don't have to forget the war. I saw some bad things, but they aren't plaguing me now."

"I'm not so 'plagued' as you seem to think I am. I'm fine." But he wasn't looking at her, not directly.

"So we just go on from there?"

"Don't say it that way, Bobbi." He slid off his chair and sat next to her on the floor. He took hold of her arms, just above the elbows. "I was going to wait until we got back to surprise you, but I just decided—I want to tell you now."

"What?"

"While we're gone, a contractor is going to dig the basement and start setting the footings for our new house. By fall, we're going to be living up on that hill I promised you, looking down on the valley. Providing you with that house is going to make me happier than anything else I can think of. That's what I'll be going to work for every day. A goal like that can make washing-machine parts look pretty good."

"Are you sure?"

"The only thing I ask of you is that you start making us a little baby, so we can start filling up the house."

"I want a baby, too, Richard, but—"

"Don't say 'but.' Let's just be happy. I will if you will. I promise."

Bobbi agreed. She thanked him, kissed him. But she didn't believe it. Things just weren't that simple. The problem wouldn't disappear just because they had said the words.

Alex was almost home. He had expected a slow voyage and then a long train ride, but a friend had pulled a few strings and gotten him air passage all the way. On a Monday morning early in May, he had learned that he was being discharged, and now it was Friday afternoon, and already he was on the last leg of his flight. He had spent a mostly sleepless night in a dump of a hotel room in New York City and had come within a few minutes of missing his connection in Chicago, but the airplane was crossing the Rockies now. He would soon see the Salt Lake Valley. He kept thinking about those numbing nights he had spent in foxholes in the Ardennes, and how he had dreamed of this day, above all other days. He would soon see Anna, and he would finally meet his son, who was nearing his first birthday. What made all this even better was that Anna and Gene were in Salt Lake now, and coming home really meant coming home.

But Alex was nervous. He had been gone for four years. When he had left, he had thought of doing his part in the war and then returning to college. He hadn't known he would come home a different person, and he certainly had never imagined that he would marry while he was gone. He was

returning to some big responsibilities, and his future was anything but clear to him.

Alex also hated the feeling that he had left a lot of unfin-
ished business in Germany. He had tried to make certain that
Gestapo Agent Kellerman paid for his crimes, but Kellerman's
sentence had been a mere two years, and that hardly seemed
adequate. The man was small potatoes compared to the leading Nazis, but Alex felt that somehow he should have made a
better case, that he had let the Stoltzes down. Alex had also
intended to return to Brünen to check on the Rietz family, who
had protected him and Otto Lang from the Gestapo during
their mission behind the enemy lines. But Alex had never found
the opportunity to go there, and finally he had learned that
Werner Rietz had been beaten to death by the Gestapo on the
same day that Alex and Otto had made their escape. This was
one more ghost to haunt Alex. He knew he would always
wonder about Werner's wife, Margarita, and her boys, and
about his own mistakes that might have caused Werner's death.

Ghosts. So many were hanging over Alex, but it was time
to move on with his life. As the airplane crossed over the
Wasatch Mountains and then made a wide turn across the Salt
Lake Valley, he was able to look out and see the temple, the
capitol building, and the broad streets. He counted blocks,
thought he could see Twenty-First South, and could guess
about where his parents' house was. Anna had written to him
that she was living with her parents in a rental house that Alex's
dad had made available to them. She had also spoken of
arrangements for another house, one where he and Anna could
live. But Alex didn't know how he was going to pay the rent,
and that concerned him.

Still, he told himself that he would figure everything out.
The important thing was that he had what he had longed for
in those dark days in France and Holland, Belgium and
Germany. He would spend his nights between clean sheets,
next to Anna. He liked the gradual descent of the airplane,

didn't even mind when the wheels jarred onto the runway, rather hard—after all, he didn't have to jump with a parachute. As the big propellers kept whirring and the airplane taxied toward the terminal, he watched the windows, hoping for some glimpse of Anna. He had telephoned her from New York to tell her his flight plans, and even though the airplane was a little late, he had no doubt that she would be waiting. It was strange to think of Anna in Utah, here where he had never seen her. He could tell from her letters that her English was improving, that she was picking up American—and LDS— expressions. She had been thrilled to attend general conference in April, and Alex had smiled when she had written what a "choice blessing" it had been.

When the airplane came to a stop, Alex waited as people ahead of him collected their belongings and worked their way up the aisle. He tried to be patient as he followed an older man slowly down the stairs outside the airplane. But once on the ground, he broke the line and walked much faster than the others. He made it to the terminal first, and as he entered the building, he looked frantically for Anna. Then, suddenly, there she was, off to his left and coming toward him, reaching with one arm, Gene in the other. Alex turned and grabbed both of them, but his movement was too forceful, and little Gene screeched. Before Alex could kiss Anna, she was already pulling back. "Oh, I'm sorry," Alex told her.

At the same time, Anna was saying, "Gene, it's okay. It's okay. It's only Daddy"—all in English.

"I'm your daddy," Alex said, and he took Gene by the sides, lifted him out of Anna's arms, but this only set the child off again. He cried even louder than before and twisted to reach for his mother.

Anna didn't take him back. "It's Daddy," she kept saying. "I told you about Daddy." But Gene was hearing none of that. He was stretching so hard that Alex could hardly keep hold of him. He had gotten hold of his mother's blouse and was pulling at it desperately.

"It's all right. Take him," Alex said. "He'll get to know me before long." And then he added, "Anna, he's so beautiful."

"He's sweet, too, Alex. I think it's your uniform that scares him."

Gene was clinging to his mother's neck now, crying, taking a peek from time to time at Alex. Alex glanced to see people watching, some smiling, understanding what was happening. It was a scene that had surely been repeated many times in airports, in bus and train stations, all over the world. That's what Alex told himself, but he still wanted to kiss his wife, and he wanted his little boy to come to him.

"Wait just a minute. Let him calm down, and then I'll kiss you," Anna said, and Alex was amazed at how natural her English was sounding now. "I'm sorry."

"It's fine. It's fine. Anna, you look so good." She was wearing a pale blue blouse and a gray skirt. She looked classy, better dressed than she had ever been in England. Alex wondered who had bought the clothes for her.

"Oh, no—I don't look my best. I still haven't lost all the weight I put on before Gene was born."

"I don't see that."

"You will." She smiled.

"I can't wait."

"I believe you'll have to."

And, of course, that was true, but Alex hadn't thought much about that—how life would be now with a baby in the middle of everything. He found himself wishing that the two of them might have had just a little time together. Since they had been married, they had only shared a few weeks, and those had always been under the shadow of Alex's return to action. "Where do we get my luggage?" he asked.

Anna pointed down the hall, and the two walked in that direction. "Alex, your mom said she'll take Gene for a few days, some time soon, and we can get away. I want to see Yellowstone Park, or maybe even California."

"Will Gene be all right with that?"

"I think so. He loves your mother." She reached out and patted his arm. "He'll love you, too."

"Is that right, Gene?" Alex asked, and he smiled at his son. But Gene twisted his head back against his mother's neck. His crying had almost stopped, but now it picked up again.

Alex was surprised to learn that Anna had driven to the airport. She had been practicing, she said, and so had her father. They had both obtained their driver's licenses just a few days before. President Thomas had given them a car "to use for now" but hadn't charged them anything for it. "It's wonderful how much he does for us," Anna told Alex.

"He's good that way," Alex said, and he meant it, but he told himself he wanted to pay for the car. He was relieved just a little when they reached the parking lot and he saw a pre-war Ford, not a fancy new Nash or Hudson.

"You drive," Anna said, and she handed him her keys. "I'll hold Gene."

"Where are we going?"

"To your parents' house. Everyone will be there. Your dad told Wally and Richard to take off work early and come over for a nice dinner. It's the first time all your family will be together at the same time since 1940."

"Not all," Alex said softly. He opened the trunk of the Ford, but then he looked at Anna. "Up there in the air a few minutes ago, I was thinking about walking into my house, and it hit me—my little brother won't be there. I thought I was used to that idea, but I guess I'm not."

"I know. I understand. For so long, I thought I had lost Peter."

He hoisted his duffel bag into the trunk. "What's Wally like?"

"I don't know what he was like before, Alex. But he seems

happy. He and Lorraine have been so kind to me and my parents."

"And what about Richard? Do you like him?"

"He's nice too. But he's quiet. It's not as easy to get to know him. Your mom has us over for Sunday dinner almost every week, and Wally's the center of all the talk, all the laughing."

Alex opened the door for Anna, but his getting that close seemed to alarm Gene again. He watched Alex with a careful eye, and he gripped his mother around the neck. Alex walked around the car, got in, and started it before he said, "I hope Wally and I can be good friends now. There's always been a certain amount of competition between us. But that should all be gone."

"He wants to be close to you, Alex. He's told me that. I guess your dad is talking about you going back to the parts plant, and Wally moving over to the dealership, but I'm sure you'll see each other a lot."

"Is that what Dad said?"

"He's mentioned it. And Wally talked about it."

"Do I get to have an opinion?"

Anna's head turned quickly. Alex was surprised by the tone of his own voice, by the force behind it. Anna switched to German and said, "Alex, it was only something he talked about. It wasn't a decision. I'm sure he wants to discuss it with you."

"I'm sorry, Anna. But I've never told Dad that I was going to work for him. That's all his idea."

She nodded, but Alex saw the concern in her face. "Alex, are you all right?" she asked.

"Oh, sure. But I hope this doesn't last too long today. Are the cousins coming, and everyone?"

"No, no. Just your family. I think your grandparents on the Thomas side might come, but your mother's parents aren't doing well, Alex. We'll have to go see them one of these first days. No one thinks Grandfather Snow will live much longer."

Alex knew this, had actually expected that Grandpa wouldn't last until he made it home.

"I've sort of pictured going home, bouncing Gene on my knee a little, and the three of us having some time together."

"That's what I want, too. I told my family we would see them all tomorrow." And then she said to the baby, "Is this Daddy? Do you like Daddy?"

Alex glanced to see Gene looking toward him. "Hi, Son," he said. "I love you." Gene leaned back against his mother, but he seemed a little more accepting now. Alex laughed, and he looked at Anna. "He's got your hair and eyes, just like I always hoped he would."

"I think he looks more like you. He's got that strong Thomas jaw."

Alex had spoken English, Anna German. "Are you speaking both languages with him?" Alex asked.

"Oh, yes. He hears mostly German now, around my family, but I speak English to him a lot. I hope he'll learn both."

"We'll keep speaking both. Kids can pick up two languages at the same time."

"We're going to be happy now, Alex. This is what we've been waiting for." She smiled, and he saw that dimple by her mouth that he loved so much. When she reached out to him, touched his shoulder, he longed to take her into his arms. He put his hand on top of hers for a moment, and at least Gene didn't protest.

"We *will* be happy now, Anna. I guess that's why I want to go home and just have an evening together, like a regular little family." What he didn't admit was that he was feeling strangely nervous about seeing everyone. He didn't exactly know why.

But Alex did like seeing the streets he remembered, the mountains, and as he got closer to his home, he loved driving through the old neighborhood in Sugar House. When he pulled up in front of the house and parked, he saw Beverly watching at the front window. He knew her mostly from pictures now; she hardly seemed the same little girl. But suddenly he felt his spirits lift, felt the excitement he had been missing.

Beverly was the first to burst from the house and run toward him, but Bobbi soon followed, and then everyone came outside. Alex grabbed Beverly in one arm and Bobbi in the other, and then he released them as Mom hurried toward him. He embraced her, then Dad, and then LaRue. And finally, there was Wally, waiting, looking different—older and somehow more complete, as though the change had come from inside out. His motions seemed calmer, more under control. He stepped to Alex and said, "Hello, Brother," and the two grabbed each other by the arms, looked into one another's faces.

"Man, oh, man," Alex said, "I can't believe this is happening." And then they embraced. "There were so many times when I thought I'd never see you again."

"I know. I know."

And now Alex knew what he had feared about this moment. He was letting go, releasing himself to his emotions, letting himself cry. He had been holding back so long, keeping himself under control, always believing that emotions were his enemy, some path to instability. So many times during the war—and since—he had tried, more than anything, not to feel.

But he cried hard now, and so did his brother, and the two held one another a long time. Around him, Alex could hear everyone sniffling, even sobbing. When the brothers finally stepped back and looked at one another again, Wally said, "While I was gone, I always tried to imagine this moment, when all of us would be back together. It seemed like the joy would just bust me wide open if it ever happened."

"Well, don't bust," Alex said. "We don't need that." He wanted to laugh.

"I won't. Not quite. But I'll tell you, I feel pretty close to it—awful close." Tears were still running down his cheeks.

"Yeah. Me too," Alex said, and he meant it. This was more

healing than anything he had experienced. He felt a little of his *self* coming back, settling in like warmth, like quiet. He looked around at everyone again, all of them still collected close to him. Mom took hold of his arm and put her face against his shoulder, her wet cheek, and Beverly grasped him around the waist. Dad had moved out of the way, but he was beaming, overjoyed, and so was LaRue, who was standing next to Dad.

"You remember Lorraine, don't you?" Wally said.

Alex did, but she looked older, looked wonderful. She greeted him quietly and stepped forward. He hugged her, too. "I'm so glad for Wally—so glad this worked out. I want you and Anna to be good friends."

"We already are," Lorraine told her. "And Bobbi too. We're all three best of friends now."

Bobbi was edging back toward Alex again. "Bobbi, you look so great," Alex told her.

"How can I look great when my brothers marry such beautiful women? I feel like a petunia in a rose garden." Alex laughed, but before he could argue with her, she said, "I want you to meet Richard." She grabbed her husband's arm and pulled him closer. Richard was a tall fellow, handsome, dressed in a perfectly pressed blue suit. There was something commanding, secure about him. Alex's first reaction was that he seemed wrong for Bobbi, almost too polished.

"Hey, it's nice to finally meet you," Richard said. His tone seemed lighter than Alex had expected, and the generosity in his smile forced Alex to make a quick adjustment to his first assessment.

"Hey, we just appreciate your marrying Bobbi," Alex said. "We weren't sure anyone ever would." Bobbi made a face, like a little girl, and then stuck her tongue out at Alex. He stepped toward her and grabbed hold of her. "We didn't think there was anyone in the world good enough for you. That's why." He picked her up and spun around. "Sis, you look so pretty—and happy. You must like being married."

"Who wouldn't—married to a guy who looks like *that?*" LaRue said.

"And speaking of pretty, look at these two little sisters of mine," Alex said. He grabbed the girls, one under each arm. "I can't believe this is happening," he said. "I just can't believe I'm here." He looked up at the porch. Grandma and Grandpa Thomas had come outside and were still waiting their turn. Alex climbed the steps onto the porch and hugged his grandma first.

"It's about time you got around to me," Grandma Thomas told him. "I was getting ready to cut you out of my will."

"I'd better be careful then," Alex said, "because I do want your money."

But Grandma was crying and saying, "Oh, Alex, I'm so glad to have you back. I can't tell you how much I've worried about you all these years."

Grandpa tried to get away with a handshake, but Alex wouldn't allow that. He hugged him, too, told him how happy he was to see him.

Everyone finally moved into the house. Alex was struck by the fancy new furniture, the new wallpaper. He looked around, trying to remember it all as it had been, but the new couch and chair were flowered, in reds and greens, and the living room hardly seemed the same place. "We're going to start with a little ceremony," Dad said. "You don't see many stars in people's windows anymore, but I told your mom we wouldn't take ours down until everyone really had come home." He had spoken loudly, with a sort of announcer's tone, but his voice softened when he said, "Of course, we don't have Gene back, but at least we have our *little* Gene—and that little boy has brought a lot of new happiness to this house."

Alex looked around to see that Anna had given the baby to

his grandma, and Gene seemed content with her. Alex smiled at him, but Gene immediately turned his head away.

"What we want," Dad said, "is for Alex to take the flag down, and then we're going to have a family prayer of thanksgiving."

So Alex stepped to the front window. The flag was tied with a couple of strands of fishing line to little nails up above. He reached high and unwound the line, first on one side and then the other. When the second line came loose, he took the flag and looked at it. He saw how faded the silk was, how long the fabric had hung in that window. Three blue stars and a gold one. What he wished was that Gene could be there, even if just for this moment, that they could have one grand reunion before the long wait to see him began. But Alex didn't say that, knew that everyone was thinking the same thing and that the words would only make things harder.

"Now the war is over," Dad said.

Everyone found a spot to kneel. "Alex," Dad said, "we'd like you to say the prayer, too."

"I think I'd rather hear you say it, Dad. While I've been gone, I've thought a lot about your prayers."

"Yes, Dad, you say it," Bobbi said.

"All right. I'd be happy to." But some time passed before his deep voice sounded. "Our Father in Heaven, we bow before thee to give thee thanks."

A sense of rightness surged in Alex. It was stronger than anything he had felt since his mission days. This was home: this voice, this family, this feeling.

But Dad couldn't speak. His voice cracked and he began to sob. Alex had never heard his father cry so openly. He was crying himself by then, shaking and clinging to Anna.

Dad couldn't add anything, never did. He finally muttered, "In the name of Jesus Christ, amen." And yet no one moved. Everyone remained bowed, and everyone was crying.

Without anyone asking him, Alex said, "Father in Heaven,

thanks for those, at home, who prayed for those of us who needed their prayers so desperately. We thank thee that we made it back. In the name of Jesus Christ, amen."

And then Bobbi said, "Father in Heaven, we thank thee for Mom and Dad, who taught us the things that kept us going. In the name of Jesus Christ, amen."

There was a long pause, and Alex thought of getting up, but Wally finally said, "Father in Heaven, we thank thee for our heritage, for Grandma and Grandpa Thomas and Grandma and Grandpa Snow, and for all the great people who came before them. In the name of Jesus Christ, amen."

Immediately, Mom said, "Father in Heaven, we thank thee for these good children we've been allowed to raise, and for Anna and Lorraine and Richard, who have joined our family. And for our grandson, Gene. In the name of the Jesus Christ, amen."

It was little Beverly who surprised Alex the most. Quivering and crying, she said, "Father in Heaven, tell our brother Gene how much we love him. We still miss him so much."

When everyone finally stood, no one could talk. Family members turned to each other in pairs, or in groups of three or four, and they embraced. Richard and Lorraine and Anna joined in, seeming to be as moved as the others, and just as much a part of the feeling. "This is the celestial kingdom. This is how it must feel," Alex heard Mom say, and he was sure that was true.

But after a few minutes a kind of embarrassment set in, as though everyone realized that life had to come back to prosaic reality, and no one knew how to bridge the gap. LaRue said something about everyone being boobs, and Grandma joked about her makeup—looking like a scary old lady. She went off to fix herself up.

Alex hadn't felt this good for a long time. He didn't want to end what was happening, but there was nothing to say now, no way to hold on.

Mom finally said, "Everyone just sit down and visit for a while. I've got dinner mostly ready, and I'll get it on in just a few minutes. Maybe the girls can help me."

Alex thought "the girls" probably meant LaRue and Beverly, but all the married women moved toward the kitchen too, and they took Gene with them. Dad and Grandpa, Alex and Wally and Richard all sat down in the living room. They began, rather self-consciously, to chat about the weather, about East High sports, but they didn't ask one another about the war. In fact, Alex was afraid one of them might raise the topic, and above all he didn't want to get into any of that. He was relieved when the women started bringing food out to the dining-room table.

"Come on, fellows," Mom said. "Let's eat."

So everyone sat down at the big table. Dad asked Richard to bless the food, since no one had remembered to do that during the prayers. And then everyone passed the serving bowls around.

"Alex, we have a lot to talk about," Dad said from the other end of the table, his voice booming over everyone else's. "Things are going great here. Richard and Wally have been a big help to me. They've stepped right in and taken over some of our departments. We've been expanding fast, and they haven't missed a beat. What we've talked about is moving you into Wally's spot, since you were there before and you know something about the parts business. Then Wally would be freed up to help me at the dealership. That's something he's always had some interest in."

For a moment Alex thought of avoiding the subject, but he didn't want to give his father the wrong idea. He knew he needed to say something now. "Dad, you've written about my working for you," he said, "and I wasn't sure what I would do about that. But I've pretty well made up my mind that I want to go back to school. I'm not really interested in a business career."

"But what will you do?"

"I'm not sure. I need to talk with Anna about that."

"That's fine. But you'll need an income. You can go to work with us and start back to college, a class or two at a time. Wally and Richard are both planning to do that this fall."

"Well . . . I don't know, Dad. I don't think so. I don't mean to sound ungrateful, but I'd kind of like to do things on my own."

The room was suddenly quiet.

"We can talk about all this later, Son," Dad said. "But you'll need work, no matter what, and we can start you just as soon as you'd like. I can certainly pay you more than you would make anywhere else—and trust me, you'll earn it."

"Al, leave the boy alone for a minute," Mom finally said. "Give him time to take a breath before he has to make all those decisions."

Alex laughed, and so did Dad. "I'm sorry. I don't mean to do that. But I've got to tell you, I'm excited about the future. If you don't want to be at the plant very long, I'll tell you what you ought to do: You ought to think about politics. If that's something you have even the slightest interest in, I think you have a real future there."

"Politics? Not me."

"Don't be so quick to say that. There's no one more loved in this country right now than a war hero. You've won all those medals and—"

"Dad, don't call me that!"

All the motion in the room seemed to stop. Alex realized that he had raised his voice, that he had almost shouted, and he was humiliated. He didn't know where so much emotion had come from, seemingly out of nowhere.

The old wall clock was ticking, the loudest sound in the room, and everyone was looking at Alex. "I'm sorry," he said. "I . . ." But he didn't know how to explain.

"Son, I'm sorry too. I know how soldiers are. You feel like you did your job, and you don't want a lot of glory. That's fine."

"That isn't it, Dad," Alex said, quietly now. "I'm just not a hero. And I don't want anyone to think I am."

Again the silence. And Alex knew what everyone was thinking. Alex was home, all right, but something was wrong with him.

"I'm really sorry. I'm tired, I think, and . . . I don't know . . . I didn't mean to sound like that."

Alex and Anna left soon after dinner. Alex told everyone how tired he was again, apologized one more time, and then drove to his new home. It was a nice little place, and Anna had fixed everything so it was neat and pretty. Alex didn't ask about the furniture, the pots and pans, the silverware. He knew that everything had come from his dad, and he knew that it would be hard to stop the flow of all that, but he also knew he had to do it somehow.

For a time Gene seemed especially alarmed that Alex had come home with him and his mother, and he clung to Anna jealously. But when he finally settled down enough to play with a toy on the floor, Alex had his chance. He took Anna in his arms and kissed her, then held her as he had wanted to do since the moment he had seen her.

"We'll be okay," she told him.

"I know. I'm sorry. I didn't mean to make trouble like that."

"It's okay. Everyone understood."

"Anna, I don't want to work for my dad."

"He just wants to help, Alex. He doesn't—"

"We'll owe him for everything. I'll get stuck in that plant my whole life. I can't do that."

"No, you can't. I understand. We'll find another way. But all the worst things are behind us now. "

Alex told her that was true, but he wondered why his hands were shaking, why he couldn't seem to concentrate. And now Gene was upset again, pushing between the two of them and screeching as though he had been hurt. They stepped apart, and it was Gene whom Anna took into her arms.

19

Alex and Anna talked a great deal over the weekend. What Alex had seen immediately was that he was living in a house he couldn't afford, furnished much too nicely for his means. If he was going to be a student, he needed to start thinking about GI Bill money, part-time work, and maybe a little apartment close to the U.

"Your dad hasn't charged me any rent, Alex," Anna had said. "He told me that we could buy the house later, but we could live here for free while we're getting started."

They were sitting at the kitchen table on Saturday afternoon. Gene was taking a nap. "But Anna, " Alex said, "don't you see what that will mean? We'll owe him for everything—and then he has right to make our decisions for us."

"Alex, how can you say that? I've never met such a generous man. He's just trying to help us."

Alex sat and looked at the table for a long time. It was true. Dad *was* generous, and he *was* trying to help. But he also wanted Alex to help build the family businesses, and the more Alex took from his father, the more he would feel bound to stay part of all that. What he didn't want to do was force Anna to give up this nice house. He had come home from the army with a little money, but it wasn't enough to last for more than a month or two. He could go out looking for work, but a good job was not easy to find—or so he was hearing. It was a lot to ask of Anna, to give all this up, when maybe it was only a point of pride for Alex. "Well," he finally said, "I guess I could work for my dad for the summer and build up a little nest egg. I can't start school until fall quarter anyway."

"Whatever you think, Alex. The house doesn't matter to me. You have to do the things that will make you happy."

"If I stay with my father, I could be rich someday. How will you feel if I throw that away?"

"It doesn't matter to me."

"It might. Someday, it might." But for now he couldn't think that far ahead. He had to get out of bed on Monday morning with something to do. The thought of knocking around town, looking for work, maybe finding nothing for quite some time— all that terrified him. He needed to be busy, needed to have his mind occupied. He'd make his break when the time was right, but for now he could stand to put in a few months at the plant.

So on Sunday, Alex and Anna went to the Thomas home for dinner, and Alex was careful not to make another scene. He told his dad that he would work for him "just for the summer." Dad said that was fine, but it wasn't long until he was talking again about "the advantages" of his taking over the whole oper- ation, and Alex knew he would have to be strong not to get pulled into things so deeply that there was no getting out.

On Monday morning Alex drove to the plant and went straight to Wally's office. "I'm not sure what Dad wants me to do," he told Wally, "but I might as well get started. He said that you had some work you could hand over to me."

"I sure do," Wally said. "Sit down. We need to talk."

Alex chose the seat near the door, across the room from Wally. He felt a little as though he had just reported to his commanding officer, but he told himself not to think that way. He wanted to feel the way he had when he had first seen Wally.

Wally got up and came around the desk. He turned the chair in front of his desk around so it faced Alex. "How are you feeling?" he asked, as he sat down.

"I'm fine."

"Alex, the other day you seemed a little . . . upset, or something. Coming back is strange at first. If you want to take another week and just—"

"No, no. I'm all right." He looked down at himself, his sport shirt and slacks, and he laughed. "I'm sorry to show up like this. I bought a suit on Saturday, but it isn't ready yet. I tried on my old clothes, from before the war, and I couldn't get into any of them."

"You've added some bulk to your shoulders, Alex. You're a big man now. You're looking more like Dad all the time."

"I guess so."

Alex looked away, looked down at the dreary old carpet, worn in a path from the door to the desk. The building had been expanded, some offices added, but the old rooms were as poorly lit as ever, and the smell of the building hadn't changed at all. It all reminded him of those dark days when he had been here before.

"Dad tells me you only want to work until school starts in the fall."

"That's right. So let me take some of the load off your shoulders, if I can, but don't give me anything that's long term."

"Do you feel like you've got to go to college full-time?"

"I do. I want to get on with it—not drag it out for years."

"Couldn't you work part-time for us?"

Alex wondered what "us" meant, and he smiled a little, but he didn't say anything about that. "I don't think I want to, Wally. I'm thinking I can save a little this summer, and then I've got the GI Bill. We should do all right as long as we move into a smaller place."

"But why do that, Alex? I'm sure Dad is happy to let you stay in that house for as long as you want."

Alex wasn't going to have that conversation with Wally. "Well . . . I'll probably want to live close to the university."

Alex saw Wally's reaction—the little movement of his head, his eyes. They both knew that Alex wasn't saying what he was really thinking. But Wally nodded, as if to say, "I won't push this matter. We'll leave it at that."

When Alex saw that, he suddenly felt a need to soften his stance, to clarify his feelings just a little. "Wally, I didn't like working in this place when I was here before. I think it's great that you and Richard enjoy it, but I want to go another way. I'm just not a businessman."

"I understand." Wally leaned forward and put his elbows on his knees. "But Alex, you were the one who got this plant started. Dad wouldn't be where he is now without your help. He told me that himself. So why not let him help you with the house for a while? That's what families are for. Richard is having a new house built, and so are Lorraine and I. We couldn't have done that without these good jobs. But Dad also gave us the building lots for next to nothing. If he can do that for us, he can certainly save you some rent while you're going to school."

Alex felt himself relax a little, ease off. "Well . . . maybe so. But Wally, when I told him I was only staying for the summer, right off he started talking, all over again, about how well it would work out if I took over here and you moved to the dealership."

Wally laughed. "I know. That's Dad. That's just how he is. He's got this vision in his head of all of us prospering from these businesses he started, and it's hard for him to understand when we don't get as excited about it as he is."

"But you do like it, don't you, Wally?"

"Yeah. I do. I like being responsible for an operation like this. It's fun for me—just to try to get the job done right."

"I never did feel that way when I was here. I just wasn't cut out for it, I guess."

"Alex, anything you choose to do, you'll do very well. I'm sure Dad would like to have you run all his operations someday."

"Are you serious?"

"Sure I am."

Alex shook his head. "No. You're the guy now. And you'll be great at it." Alex got up and walked across the little office. He looked at a picture on the wall—a photograph of the family right after Alex's mission. Everything was the way Alex remembered. Gene was a grinning teenager, and the little girls were just that—little girls. Wally was a softer version of himself, childlike in some ways, with more flesh on him. He had been so playful then that Alex had often found him annoying, but he was also the kid who had stood up to Dad, told him what he thought, and Alex had always wondered at that, maybe even envied Wally a little. "Well, anyway, what do you want me to do?"

"Alex, do you still think this place was built on blood money? Dad told me that's what might be bothering you. I guess you told him that once, back before you went into the army."

Alex turned around. He tried to think how he felt about that. Actually, he hadn't thought much about it for a long time. "Someone had to fight this war," he said. "And someone else had to make the weapons. I'm the last guy to accuse anyone of having blood on his hands."

"But soldiers didn't get rich."

"No."

"Does it bother you that Dad did?"

"I don't know, Wally. I guess it's just the way things work. I don't feel very idealistic about many things these days. If Dad hadn't made the money, someone else would have. At least he'll do better things with it than most people would."

"You're not happy, are you, Alex?"

Alex walked back to his chair and sat down; he was a little

surprised by the question. "I'm glad to be home, Wally. And I *want* to be happy. I think I will be."

"What's bothering you? Do you know?"

"I'm okay. Really. When Elder Benson came to Frankfurt, he told me not to plan too far into the future. He said I should get some education, then try to do something well. If I did that, opportunities would come along. So I'm trying to think that way, to take one step at a time, like he said. I just feel a little out of sorts right now, I guess mainly because I don't even know what the first step should be—except to work here for the summer."

"But what about the war? Did it bother you that—"

"Really, Wally, I just want to get to work. I'm a lot better off when I'm doing things and not sitting around feeling sorry for myself." Wally nodded, seemingly ready to let that be the end of the conversation. But Alex was sorry that he had been so curt. "I don't know exactly what's going on with me," he said. "I guess that's why I want to go to school. It was what I had planned before. I feel like I need to get back to the path I was walking and just start from there."

"Alex, all the paths are gone. We're all starting over."

"I know. But I need to find that feeling I had once—you know, just the desire, or the enthusiasm, or whatever it was, to make a go of things. Did you struggle with any of that when you got home?"

"Alex, they took *everything* away from us in those prison camps. And that made anything I got seem a blessing when I first got home. I didn't really have too much trouble."

"That's how I've got to look at life, Wally. I've got Anna and Gene now. How can I worry about things that are all in the past?"

"But some things don't go away just because you tell them to. My war was all about surviving. And I saw a lot of death around me. But I didn't have to go into battle."

Alex looked into Wally's eyes for a moment, liked the understanding, but he didn't want to talk anymore. "Well, anyway," he said, "I need to get moving ahead. Why don't you give me something to do."

"But sooner or later we need to talk some more, Alex. There are lots of things I've never told anyone, and it might be good to get some of that stuff off my chest. Maybe it's the same for you."

"That might be good, Wally. I've been trying not to say anything. But that might be good—you know, some time."

"All right." Wally grinned. "But not on Dad's time."

And so the brothers got busy. They spent all day together, and the truth was, Alex did feel better about the work by the end of the day. There was a lot to do, tracking orders and scheduling production, and it would occupy him, fill his head. On the way home, in the old Ford his dad had lent him and Anna, he told himself he could get through the summer just fine. What pleased him most was that he had enjoyed the time with Wally, finally in a situation where there was no competition. And that bit of shared understanding had been surprisingly comforting.

He found Anna in the kitchen. The house was full of the smell of baking bread and frying chicken. "I'm trying to be an American cook," she told Alex. "I wanted to have something nice for you at the end of your first day at work."

Alex walked up behind her, took hold of her shoulders and turned her around, away from the stove. He kissed her and said, "Now *that* is my idea of something nice for me."

"Ooh. That's something nice for me, too. It's so fun to have you here. This is what we've been waiting for, isn't it?"

"Yes, it is." Alex knew he had been entirely too somber over the weekend. He couldn't be like that all the time. He kissed her again, and then he laughed. "We need to make up for all those kisses we've missed the last couple of years."

"Good idea." But this time she only gave him a little peck and then turned back toward the stove.

Gene had been playing on the kitchen floor nearby. He

came to Alex now, stood and looked up at him. Alex picked him up, and Gene smiled. On Sunday afternoon Alex had held Gene on his lap and read some storybooks, but this was the first time that the little boy had initiated a connection between them, and Alex loved it. "How about a big kiss for Daddy?"

Gene wrapped his arms around Alex's neck, and he pressed his lips hard against his cheek. Then Alex hugged him tight. A few seconds later Gene squirmed and wanted down, but Alex felt that they had broken the ice a little. And Anna was especially pleased. "We love Daddy, don't we, Geney?" she said.

Gene was already busy with a metal dump truck and some wooden blocks. The boy was full of energy, always moving about the house like a windup toy, never settled in any one spot for very long. Alex wasn't used to such perpetual noise—or all the messes a little child could make.

Alex looked over Anna's shoulder at the frying chicken, took hold of her again. "So how was work?" she asked.

"Fine. Wally's trying to show me the ropes."

"The ropes?"

Alex laughed. "That just means 'show me how things are.'"

"Why ropes? What does it mean?"

"Actually, I don't know. But he's teaching me my duties, and he's a lot of help. You know, I like Wally. It's hard to think of him as the same kid I knew back before he left for the service."

"Is he still going to move over to the car place?"

"I don't know what they're going to do about that. I'm sure Dad is hoping I'll like the plant this time around—or at least the money—and stay."

"Is that possible?"

"Do you wish it were?"

"No. I just wondered."

Something hit the kitchen cabinets with a crack, and Alex turned from Anna to see that Gene had thrown a wooden block. He was standing now, smiling, as though he knew he had done something bad—and was proud of it.

"Gene," Anna said, "what has Mommy told you? We don't throw things. No, no."

Gene bent and picked up another block. He waited, as though wanting to get the full reaction, and then he threw it. The block struck the oven and then clattered onto the linoleum floor. Gene laughed.

"Son, that's enough of that," Alex said. He wasn't sure how much Gene understood sometimes—in either language—but the boy certainly knew he was being told to stop.

Slowly, Gene bent again, but this time Anna walked to him and took the block from his hand. "Mama is going to put your blocks away. You can't play with them if you throw them."

She began to gather up the blocks, dropping them into the little box she stored them in, but Gene set off a howl in response. Alex had still not gotten used to the volume of his shrieks.

"All right then," Anna said. "If you want to play with them, don't throw them." She set the box in front of him, and his screaming stopped instantly.

Alex wondered whether that was the right approach. Maybe she should have put the blocks away and let Gene learn his lesson. But Gene plopped down on the floor again and began to push his truck, seemingly uninterested in the blocks he had just screamed about. Alex said to Anna, "So what's been going on around here today?"

"I've tried to get some washing done, but Gene keeps me going. He didn't want to take a nap today. And then, when I finally got him down, he didn't sleep very long. That boy just never stops."

"Don't you need to have a set time for naps—and just keep the same schedule every day?"

Anna turned back around to look at Alex. "That's easy to say, but a one-year-old has a mind of his own—especially that boy of yours."

Alex had been a little annoyed in the evenings that Anna

seemed to let Gene stay up so late. He remembered in his own family that children all had to go to bed at eight whether they wanted to or not. "My parents were always pretty strict about things like that. Kids have to know you mean it. I think I would have taken those blocks away, after he threw them, and not given in just because he started to scream."

"Well, then, why didn't you do it?"

Alex heard the flash of anger, and that was something he had never experienced from Anna before. "I'm sorry, Anna," he said. "I don't mean to come in and start telling you how to do things. You've had to raise him by yourself up until now, and you've done a great job."

But Anna was turning the chicken in the frying pan now, looking away from Alex, and she didn't respond.

"Really, Anna. I'm sorry."

"Alex, I try to do my best, but maybe I don't do it right."

"No, no. I'm sure you do. What do I know about raising kids?"

Alex walked to the kitchen table and sat down. He didn't want this. He just wanted to relax and have some time with Anna. But now Gene was running his truck up against the corner of the cabinet, banging it over and over. It seemed such a stupid thing to do. "Gene, don't do that," he said. "You'll scuff up the cabinets."

Gene didn't even seem to hear. He simply continued the rhythmic banging of the truck against the wood corner. Alex knew he couldn't push things too far right now, not with Anna already upset, so he got up and walked to Gene, bent down and put his hand on the truck. "Gene," he said, in a careful, patient tone, "don't hit the cabinet. All right? No, no."

But Gene grabbed the truck with both hands, and he pushed it with all his force. The thrust took Alex by surprise. The truck slipped under his hand and banged into the cabinet again. "Gene!" Alex said, his voice suddenly hard. "No, no!"

Gene let out a scream and jumped up. Then he rushed to

his mother. He was crying furiously, as though he had been struck. Anna reached down and picked him up. "Daddy told you not to do that. You mustn't do it." But she was folding him into her arms, giving him the love he wanted, and Alex could only think what Gene was thinking—that his mother had to protect him from this evil "Daddy" who had come into his life.

Alex walked to the two of them. He patted Gene on the back. "Daddy loves you," he said, but Gene howled all the louder, held to his mom.

"You have to do what Daddy tells you," Anna said, but she was cooing this into his ear, all the while patting his back.

"I don't want him to think you love him and I don't," Alex said. "All I did was tell him to stop doing that."

"It's just a little difficult for him right now," Anna said. "He has to get used to you."

Alex nodded, but he stood stiff, afraid to touch either one of them. And during dinner, when Gene wouldn't eat, when he rubbed his food onto his shirt and dropped peas onto the floor, Alex didn't dare say anything about that either. Anna hardly seemed to notice as she questioned Alex about his day, and then, when eight o'clock came, she didn't put Gene to bed even though he was obviously getting tired and fussy. Alex didn't dare create problems again, but he wanted some quiet. He had waited all these years for this time with Anna, and now they could hardly talk with Gene demanding his mother's attention every second. Alex offered to read him a story for bedtime, but Gene took the book to his mother. Alex finally gave up and read the evening newspaper. By the time Anna got Gene to settle down, it was almost nine-thirty, and at that point, Anna told Alex, "I'm so tired. Do you care if I go to bed early?"

Alex did care, but he said he didn't. And then he talked to himself, admitted that family life was complicated, and he should have known that, with all his little brothers and sisters. He knew it was stupid to let a one-year-old, just a baby, feel like a rival, but the boy did seem to know what he was up to.

He wanted his mother's full attention, wanted to keep Alex away from her—and he was good at it. It was hard not to feel like the odd man out.

On the following day at work, Wally gave Alex more paperwork to handle, and Alex was glad for the sense of busyness it created. He sat at his desk, aware that he ought to ask certain questions, but he worked his way through the forms on his own anyway. Mom came in and chatted with him for a few minutes, and she explained certain parts of the papers better than Wally had, which helped, but she also—like everyone else—wanted to know how he liked being there. Alex told her with manufactured enthusiasm that he was happy to be "back in the harness."

"So what does Gene think about having a daddy around the house?" she asked.

Alex was tempted to talk to her about that, get her opinion on handling the situation, but he didn't want to hint that he had a problem, and so he merely laughed and said, "All in all, I think he wishes I'd stayed in Germany."

"That's only natural, Alex. I'm sure he's pretty jealous of you getting so much attention from his mother. It's going to take him a while to get used to that."

"What attention?" Alex wondered, but he wasn't about to say that. Instead, he passed off the whole matter, and then he put his mind back to the task at hand—the paperwork.

Later that morning Wally called Alex to a meeting of department heads. Wally explained to everyone that Alex would be helping out for a few months, looking after "some aspects of production." Alex actually had a lot of questions, but he kept his mouth shut. He didn't want to slow down the meeting, and he didn't want the department heads to know how little he really understood about the way the operation ran now. He knew a few of the men who worked out on the line, but he knew no one in this meeting.

Alex had learned the day before that Wally and Richard

often ate lunch together. It took too long to leave the plant to eat out, so they both usually brought a sandwich with them. This morning Alex had packed his own little lunch—stuck some of Anna's leftover fried chicken in a sack, along with a carrot and an apple. He actually planned to eat in his office, but Wally came by and said, "Why don't you walk over to Richard's office with me? We can eat lunch together and talk about a few things you two will end up working on together."

So Alex grabbed his sack lunch and walked with Wally down the hall. They found Richard bent over his desk, about the way Alex had been all morning, studying some sort of correspondence. "Oh, I'm glad to see you, Wally," he said. "I can't make heads or tails out of some of these Bendix letters. I swear, all I end up doing around here is shuffling paper."

Alex didn't feel that he had much sense of who Richard was. He was congenial but reserved. So far, Alex had the impression that Richard thought a great deal but rarely expressed those thoughts. That made for an intriguing combination, but it also made Alex a little nervous.

"So, Alex, how is it to be back?" Richard asked now.

Same question. "Fine. But everything has changed here at the plant, and I feel pretty stupid."

"Well, that's good to hear. I don't want to be the only stupid one." He smiled, and Alex was reminded of why Bobbi had fallen for him. He certainly was a good-looking man.

For the next ten minutes all the talk was between Richard and Wally. Richard had questions, and the two pored over a letter Richard had received. Alex had stolen one corner of Richard's old wooden desk—a relic from the early days—and had unfolded his waxed paper on it, with his chicken. He knew he ought to listen to the discussion, to pick up things he would need to know, but he couldn't get himself to concentrate on what they were saying. He was wishing that the afternoon would pass quickly and he could go home. He wanted to try harder tonight, to spend more time with Gene and see whether he couldn't start to break down some of the resistance he was getting.

And then Dad appeared at the office door. "So this is where you guys are all hiding out," he said. "There for a minute, I thought you had all gone to a picture show."

"What's playing? We might," Wally said, and everyone laughed, but Alex thought he saw Richard retreat just a little. He got out his lunch, and he let Wally do the talking. Wally chatted with his dad about meeting the next deadline, about problems with shipping that Richard must have known first-hand.

"Well, we'll be all right," Dad told the three of them, finally. "We've still got ten days or so, and they know, back in the main office, that they didn't get their specs to us on time. If we're late, it's their fault, not ours."

"I just like to keep up our reputation for always shipping on time," Wally said.

Alex thought of the Wally he had known long ago, the teenager who rarely did much of anything on time, who thought the main meaning of life could be found on the dance floor.

"I agree," Dad said. "I'm glad you boys feel the same way." Dad glanced at Alex, then seemed to think better of question-ing him. Instead he said, "Say, boys, while I've got you all here, I want to ask a favor. I know this thing is pretty far off, but I have to give an answer right away. Some people in the Republican party know that all three of you returned from the war and all have interesting experiences to relate, and they wanted you to share the time at a dinner we hold every spring—be the main speakers. It won't be until next May, but would it be all right if I go ahead and tell them you'll do that?"

"What would we talk about?" Wally asked.

"Well, it's one of those patriotic things. You could tell them what it feels like to come back to your home after serving your country—you know, that sort of thing. A lot of people are interested to know what it was like in prison camp, and Richard, you were in the Pacific, Alex in Europe. There's a lot you could say, but I'd just talk about your feelings about the country, more than anything."

"Dad, I think I'd rather not," Alex said. "I love my country, but I don't have anything new to say about that."

"Talk about Germany before and after the war. People would find that very interesting. You saw more of that than anyone."

But that's not what people wanted to hear, and Alex knew it. They wanted war stories.

"Well, listen, you don't have to give me an answer right this minute. Think it over. I have a meeting next week, and I do need an answer by then. I just think it's a real honor that they would think of you." He hesitated, looking at Alex. "I already told them that you don't want a lot of talk about being a hero. You are a hero, as far as I'm concerned, but I understand that you don't want a lot made of that."

Dad still didn't understand. He thought that Alex was only trying to be modest.

"Well, listen, I have to run," Dad said before anyone could respond. "But it would mean a lot to me if you boys would do that. So don't be too quick to say no. I respect the fact that all three of you don't like to pound your own chests, but you wouldn't have to do that. Anything you said would really please these people. They respect what you did—all three of you."

Dad left, and Alex ducked his head. He didn't want to give any speeches, but he didn't want to be the one to say so. He hoped Wally and Richard might feel the same way.

"What do you think?" Wally asked.

Alex waited for Richard to respond, but when he didn't, Alex finally said, "You know how they're going to introduce us—no matter what Dad says. And you know how I feel about that."

Richard was sitting across from Alex. He spoke softly. "Why does it bother you to be called a hero, Alex? You're the one who came home with a Distinguished Service Medal and a Silver Star."

Alex didn't want to talk about this. "Medals are more about politics than heroism; you know that."

"Sometimes they are. Sometimes, not."

"Well, I'm not a hero. I was actually a pretty sorry excuse for a soldier, if you want to know the truth. What I want more than anything is to forget that the war ever happened."

"That I can agree with," Richard said.

But Wally said, "Alex, you got a battlefield commission. You must have been a great soldier, so I don't know why you keep saying things like that."

"I spoke German, that was all. They needed someone to do a job."

"Don't do that, Alex. You can level with me and Richard. We were there too."

Alex took a long breath. Then he took a chance. "Wally, I fought Germans. I felt like I was fighting my own people. There was no way to do anything right. The better I soldiered, the worse person I felt I was."

Richard nodded, and Alex saw something solemn in his eyes, felt he did understand.

"The Germans sent young boys at us at the end. I killed kids who were Beverly's age. Then I went back to Germany and called everyone brother and sister."

"You couldn't help that."

"That doesn't change anything. Those boys are still dead. I don't care if someone says, 'Thanks for doing what you had to do,' but folks back home all want stories about killing the filthy krauts. And I'm not going to give them any of that. What do people mean when they call a guy a hero, Wally? They mean he killed, and he did it well."

"Not always."

"Well, that's the only thing I did to get my medals."

"Alex, you put your own life on the line. That's why people want to honor you."

"But those people don't know what war is. They think it's all a bunch of John Wayne movies: brave boys, fighting for home and country. I had kids in my squad who would curl up and bawl when the artillery started coming in. We weren't out there looking for a chance to die for our country. We just wanted to get home, all in one piece."

"Most people do know that, Alex. But they honor you, all the same, because you stayed with it, no matter how scared you were."

But that wasn't it. Alex didn't know how to say what he was feeling, never had known.

"There's more to it than that, Wally," Richard said. His voice was gentle, almost a whisper, but Alex heard some pain, too.

"What do you mean?" Wally asked.

"I saw things that I could *never* tell a bunch of people at a banquet. They'd stop waving their flags and just sit there in shock. The evil is never all on one side. War *makes* men evil."

No one spoke for a time, but Alex felt an immediate attachment to Richard. Without looking at him, he reached over and rested his hand on his shoulder.

"I know about that," Wally said. "The guards in the prison camps did everything they could to break us down. And it worked. When a man is hungry enough, he'll do almost anything. I can't tell you what it took just to stay human."

Richard spoke in that same quiet, troubled voice. "Most guys, when they face death, don't turn into heroes. They save themselves, if they can—even if someone else has to die."

Alex didn't know how Richard knew that, and he didn't ask. "People at home have no idea what goes on," he said. "Sometimes the men who fought the best were the worst guys over there. If you come back from a battle—*blooded*—and you can laugh about it, I've got to think there's something wrong with you. But I saw men like that get medals—lots of times. And that's what I think of when I hear the word *hero*. Maybe I had to kill, but I don't ever want to feel good about it."

"But Alex," Wally said, "I saw the other side, too. I saw guys give up their own lives to save their friends—and a lot more who would have done it, if it had come to that."

"I know. I saw that, too. But I don't want to honor war in any way. I don't want boys to grow up thinking that's the best way to show that they're men. I don't want *my* little boy to be a soldier, *ever*."

"Tell them that at the banquet."

"No. People don't understand. And if you try to tell them enough to make them understand, they don't want to hear it."

"I still say that we ought to come through for Dad. I think we owe it to him, and I think there are things we can say that we all believe, things we can be honest about."

"I'd really rather not," Alex said.

"I don't want to either," Richard said. But after a moment, he added, "But I guess I will—for your dad. I do love my country. I can say something about that."

"I love my country too," Alex said, "but I don't like all this 'we're better than everyone else' stuff that I'm hearing so much these days."

"Say that. Say what you want to say. By next spring you'll probably feel a lot better about doing that. I'll tell Dad we'll do it as long as we can say what we really feel. How's that?"

Richard nodded, and Alex didn't say no. What he really thought was that he wouldn't turn his dad down at the moment, but he would find some way out of the situation between now and then. Right now, he needed to be careful not to create any bad feelings. What he wished was that he could feel the way he had that first hour after he had arrived at his home and seen his family. He hated all this fuss, all these negative feelings—all this awkwardness with his dad.

Later, when Alex was back in his office, he thought about the conversation with his brother and brother-in-law, and he did feel good about that. He even felt some relief. They had understood—he was sure of that—and that made a difference to him. But it didn't exactly change anything. What he wanted was to be Alex again, and he had to wonder whether that boy he remembered as himself hadn't been lost in action.

2 0

Beverly was standing straight while LaRue fixed the back of her hair. "It's not going to work," Beverly kept saying. "My hair isn't thick like yours."

"Just stand still," LaRue told her. "It's going to look great."

LaRue had pinned Beverly's hair into parted, high waves in front and was trying now to make the ends roll under, tight against her neck. "I look like those girls who work the counters down at Walgreen's," Beverly said. "Let me just do it my normal way."

"No. This is a special night. You have to do something *dramatic.*"

"You mean *tragic,* I think." But the truth was, Beverly did like the way the hairdo made her look—older and more glamorous. She only wished that LaRue would hurry; she was getting nervous, standing so long. She was wearing only her slip now, and she wanted to put on the pretty blue-green dress that she and LaRue had picked out. But more than anything, she wished the night were already over. This was her first real date, her first time to spend an entire evening with one boy. Garner Manning was taking her to the spring dance, the last school dance of the year, and he was dreadfully cute. He was exactly the boy Beverly had wanted to flirt with—had even tried to flirt with.

But she had stumbled over her words, hadn't known what to say, and ended up seeming frightened, maybe even distant.

Somehow, however, he had seemed to understand. He had called the very next day and asked her, his brief invitation sounding coached and memorized, even shaky. Beverly had whooped with joy when she had hung up the phone, but now she was scared. "LaRue, help me think of some things I can talk about tonight."

"No."

"What?"

"Don't practice. Don't worry about it. Just be yourself. He wouldn't have asked you out if he didn't like you the way you are."

"LaRue, he's never been around me for more than a few minutes at a time. He doesn't know how boring I am."

"Boring? You're not boring. You read all the time. You know all kinds of things." She took hold of Beverly's shoulders, turned her a little, then looked over her shoulder at the mirror.

"Oh, sure, LaRue. He'd just love talking about books all night."

"Why wouldn't he?"

"LaRue, he's a boy. He's on the track team."

"Some boys read, Bev. Even the athletes." Now LaRue turned Beverly the opposite way and looked over her left shoulder. "If he doesn't read at all, I wouldn't bother to go out with him again."

Beverly tried to see LaRue's assessment of the hairdo in the mirror, but she couldn't decipher anything from her expression. "You don't know how cute he is," she said.

"Trust me, my dear. 'Cute' isn't everything. After about two hours with some guy you have nothing in common with, you don't care what he looks like."

"I'm the one who doesn't have anything in common, LaRue. Not him." Bev knew that was a stupid thing to say before the words were out. But that's how she felt. If the two had nothing to say, it was only because she wasn't what she wished she were: one of the really popular girls who knew everything that was going on at school.

LaRue did laugh, but she was merciful. She said, "He should talk about the things you're interested in just as much as the other way around."

"What can I say about track and stuff like that? And what does he care about Jane Austen?" She reached up and touched the hair just over her ear, but LaRue slapped her hand away.

"Hey, just ask him about track. And if he's a nice guy, he'll ask you what you like to do, and you can tell him about Jane Austen."

"LaRue, don't say anything else. You're making me too nervous. I would never know how to say things like that. I don't even know what all those different races are that they run—the four-forty and all that stuff. And what am I supposed to do? Tell him the plot to Pride and Prejudice?"

"Okay, never mind. But I'm just going to tell you one more time: you're a fun girl, and you're bright and interesting. So just be yourself."

Beverly liked hearing that, even if she wasn't sure it was true, and she suspected that she wasn't quite the dolt that she must seem sometimes. She could certainly talk to LaRue.

"It's okay to be quiet, Bev. That's a lot better than being one of these chatterbox girls who never shuts her mouth." She gave Beverly's hair a last little pat. Then she took hold of her shoulders again and this time turned her all the way around. "You look really cute, Bev. Honest. As sweet as you are."

"Boys don't like sweet girls. They like girls who kiss them goodnight."

Beverly knew she had taken a chance to say something so bold, but she wanted to know. What was she supposed to do about that? Mom always said not to be kissing every boy who came along, and Bev thought that sounded right—especially not to kiss on the first date—but LaRue would know more about it than Mom. Beverly just didn't want to ask, not directly.

"If a boy only likes you if you'll kiss him, forget him. He's not worth it."

"Really?"

"Really."

"But don't all the boys want to kiss?"

"Some boys want to do a lot more than kiss, Bev. Don't act so naive. But stay away from guys like that. And don't kiss this boy tonight. You'll just give him the wrong idea about yourself if you do."

Beverly turned back toward the mirror. She knew she was blushing. "Garner isn't like that. He's very nice."

"Well, that's good. But let me show you a little trick." LaRue hesitated and then said, "Look at me." Beverly turned toward her again. "When a boy walks up to the porch with you, he lets you give the signals. If he steps kind of close to you, and you just look up at him, that's the same as saying, 'Go ahead.' If you *want* a boy to kiss you, give him a straight path—take hold of his hand maybe, step even closer, and turn your head just a little so he can get past your nose."

"LaRue!"

"I'm not saying you should do that. I'm saying that's how you send smoke signals to these guys. They're not very smart, you know. But if you don't want to be kissed, you do the opposite. When he steps up, you step back just a little, and you say, 'Thanks for a wonderful time.' She spoke in falsetto, and then she acted out the motion as she said, "And you start opening the door. Not one guy in a dozen is going to come after you when you're in full retreat."

"What if you want him to know you do like him, but you don't want to kiss him?"

"Ah. Now that takes some art. That's a great question. I used to be very good at that." She took hold of Beverly's hand. "What you do is, you give him that little squeeze of the hand and make him think for a second that he might get that kiss, but then you move away, and in a really sincere voice you say, 'Irving, I've had such a great time. I hope you'll call me again.' That way, he knows you want to go out again, but he figures you're just not 'that kind of girl.'"

"I could say that." Bev tried to imitate LaRue's voice, but she ended up exaggerating. "I hope you'll call me again."

"Yeah. That's not too bad. But you know what? I don't do that anymore. I just tell them something honest. I say, 'I had fun. I'll see you at school, okay?' or something like that."

"Why don't you do it the way you used to? You said you were good at it."

LaRue walked over and sat down on Beverly's bed. "The next boy I go out with more than once is going to be smart enough to say something worth talking about."

"You're really a brain now, aren't you?"

"No. I wish I were. I do my homework now, that's all."

"How come you don't go with anyone? You don't even go around with Cecil as much as you used to."

"Cecil makes me mad. He's smart, but he thinks he's smarter than he is. He tries to tell me what's what, and I'm not sure he knows himself."

"LaRue, I worry about you. You're too serious anymore."

"I know I am. But don't pay any attention to me. Just relax and have fun. You're going to have a great night."

"I'll just be glad when it's over."

"Well, yeah. I know what you mean. But it's not anything worth worrying about. If Garter, or whatever his name is, doesn't like you, so what? There's lots more fish in the old East High fishing hole."

"His names is *Garner*, and I like that name. It sounds distinguished. Garner Manning."

"You've tried it out, haven't you? You've written it in your notebook: Beverly Manning. Just to see how it sounds—and looks."

"I have *not*." But Beverly was lying, and she was afraid LaRue could see it in her face. She had written it twenty times at least, and she liked the sound of it.

It was time to get her dress on, and so LaRue helped her slip it on without mussing her hair. And then LaRue distracted her, joked with her, until the doorbell rang, right on time. "Which way are you going to play it?" LaRue asked. "Are you going to stay up here for a while so he doesn't think you're ready and waiting for him?"

"No. I might as well just go down when Mom calls me."

"Good. Now see—that's you. That's the way you do things. Be that way the whole evening."

But Beverly doubted she could take the advice. She didn't *know* what was natural to her, not in this situation.

When Mom came to the top of the stairs and said, "Beverly, your young man is here," Bev almost died. Garner had heard that for sure. What would he think? He wasn't *her* 'young man.' But she hurried out, then stopped at the head of the stairs and took a deep breath. She knew she had to stop blushing. But after at least a minute, she could still feel the heat in her ears and cheeks, and so she decided there was nothing else to do but walk on down. She glanced back and saw LaRue, who was standing in the hall, just outside Bev's bedroom door.

LaRue nodded and smiled. "Thanks," Beverly whispered. Again LaRue nodded, and Beverly, amazed, noticed tears in her eyes. So Beverly went back and kissed her sister's cheek, and something in that filled her up, made her feel less self-conscious. She wasn't quite so nervous as she walked down the stairs.

Garner was waiting at the foot of the stairway. He was wearing a dark blue suit, a white shirt, and a striped tie, red and blue. He was a tall boy, slender, with brown hair that was neatly combed tonight, with a little wave at the front. He smiled and said something Beverly couldn't quite hear. "Excuse me?" she said.

"Oh. I just said you look nice." And he didn't sound at all the way he did at school. Bev could see how scared he was. He looked pale, and he had gripped his hands together into a knot.

Mom was still there. "Garner, I'd like you to meet Beverly's father," she said.

Al stood up. He had been reading a book, which he set face down on the table next to him. Then he walked toward Garner, who met him halfway. "Nice to meet you, President Thomas."

"Do you live in our stake?" Dad asked.

"No. I just know that you're a stake president."

"Well, I was. I've been released now."

"Yeah. I guess that's what my dad said."

"Who's your dad?"

Beverly couldn't believe her father would start into all this. But it was what he always did. She had watched him grill LaRue's dates a hundred times.

"His name is Arvin Manning."

"Oh, sure." And then Dad started off on a story about how he and Mr. Manning had had some business dealings with each other. Garner kept nodding, looking interested, but Bev could see that he was trying to act like a grown-up, and he seemed as stiff as a mannequin.

By the time Beverly got out the door, she was feeling relieved to be with Garner alone—which was the last thing she had expected. But the car was the next challenge. Garner's big brother was driving them to the dance—Garner wasn't old enough to drive.

Garner opened the door, and Beverly got in and started to slide over, only to discover that Garner was going around to the other side. As she slid back, Garner's brother said, "So you're Beverly. My name's Tom. Say, you're just as cute as Garner said you were," and then he laughed as though he had cracked a good one.

Beverly was blushing again, she knew. When Garner got

into the car, he obviously knew that his brother had said something, but he didn't know what, and he said, "Tom, lay off, all
right?" His voice was so full of warning that Beverly wondered
whether the brothers might not come to blows before they
reached East High.

Tom did lay off, didn't say another word, but he continued
to chuckle. And Garner was obviously too self-conscious to
talk to Beverly in front of him. Everyone rode in silence for a
couple of blocks, and finally Bev couldn't stand the awkwardness. "It sure was a pretty day today," she said.

"It was. It was real nice," Garner said.

Tom seemed to sputter for a moment, as though trying to
resist, and then he laughed out loud, hard.

And that was the end of the talk. Only when Tom pulled
up to the high school and swung a U-turn so he could let the
two out, did he say, "Mom says to pick you up at eleven-thirty.
Okay?"

"Okay," Garner said, and he slid out of the seat.

As he walked around the car, Tom said, "Good luck,
Beverly. This little brother of mine might tromp your feet into
bloody stubs."

"Oh, I doubt that," Beverly said, but she was greatly
relieved when the door came open and she was able to slip out.
And when she did, she was looking up into Garner's cute
face. "Sorry about all that," he said, and under the street light,
Beverly could see that he was the one blushing now.

Suddenly she felt more relaxed. "There's nothing to be
sorry about," she said. She took his arm and walked with him
into the school. And inside the gym, things went pretty well.
Garner wasn't such a terrible dancer as Tom had claimed—just
bad. And somehow that was rather pleasing. She liked to think
that Garner wasn't any better at this dating business than she
was. And when they traded dances, even though some of
the other boys danced better, she still liked returning to
Garner, who seemed a little protective of her, the way he led

her about, got her a drink of punch, asked how she was doing. They really didn't have to talk a whole lot, but subjects kept coming up, and Beverly didn't feel all that nervous.

But then the band leader announced a short break. "Hey, we'll be back in fifteen minutes," he said, "so keep your dancing shoes on." His voice, through the microphone, echoed around the gym, and then suddenly all the sound seemed to stop.

Garner went off and got cups of punch for the two of them again, and when he returned, they sat down side by side on the first row of the gymnasium bleachers. Beverly hoped that another couple would come over to them and chat a little, but no one did. And Garner wasn't saying a word.

"That's a good band, isn't it?" Beverly finally offered.

"I guess so. I don't think I have much rhythm, though. When my mom tries to teach me, she always says, 'Listen to the beat. Step to the music.' But I guess I don't hear it."

"You're doing fine."

"Not really."

And then there was nothing to say again. Beverly thought of commenting on the punch, but there was really nothing to say about it. And she wasn't going to bring up the weather again. Finally, when she just couldn't stand the silence, she asked, "What are your interests, Garner?"

He hesitated, thinking. "Well, I guess . . ." Then he burst out laughing. "That's what my mom told me to ask you, but I was afraid if I did, you'd ask me. And I couldn't think of anything. At least nothing . . . you know . . . *interesting*."

"That's how I am. My sister told me to talk about Jane Austen, but I didn't know what to say about her."

"I know something about Jane Austen. I read one of her books, cover to cover. I thought it would kill me, but here I am, alive and well."

"Which one was it?"

"I don't know. Tell me some of them."

"*Pride and Prejudice, Sense and Sensibility*—"

"I think it was one of those two, because it was like that—two words that sort of rhyme or whatever that is."

"Alliterate."

"What?"

"When the first letters are the same like that, it's called 'alliteration.'"

"Wow. You must be really smart."

"No, I just . . . happened to know that."

"But anyway, it was probably one of those. It was all about these English people who mostly go to parties and worry about who's going to marry who, and stuff like that."

"That could be either one of those two. Mostly, all of Jane Austen novels are like that."

"And you like them?"

"Uh huh."

"Why?"

"I don't know. I just like the girls, and I wonder what's going to happen to them. You didn't like the book at all?"

"Well . . . not really."

So that took care of Jane Austen. Beverly was thinking about asking about track, but she had only gone to one track meet in her life. That was back when Wally was running and she had been a little girl. She remembered long, boring delays, quick races, and then more delays.

She knew that Garner was surely trying to think what to say, so Bev decided to take a chance on whatever he came up with this time. But the seconds ticked by like hammer blows, and she could sense how nervous he was getting. Finally, he said, "My mom told me that your brother was a prisoner of war, over in the Philippines."

"Yes, he was."

"Was that pretty rough?"

"He lost about eighty pounds, I think it was. When we first

saw him, he looked all right, but he told us that he looked almost like a skeleton when they first let him go."

"Is he doing okay now?"

"He's doing great. He got married, and he's working for my dad. But the whole time he was gone we didn't know if he was alive or not. My parents always said they thought he was, but I worried about it every single minute, it seemed like. That's the best thing about the war being over—not worrying all the time."

"I thought the war would keep going on, and I would have to go. I always said I wanted to, but it scared me. I didn't want guys shooting at me. My brother went through that."

"Did he come home okay?"

"He came home. I wouldn't say he's okay."

"That wasn't Tom, was it?"

"No. An older brother. His name is Lawrence. He says his name is Larry now, but we never have called him that."

"Did he get wounded or something?"

"Well, yeah. He did. But that's not what's wrong. He came home a lot different from how he used to be. I didn't remember him all that well, he was gone so long, but my Mom, she cries all the time, just thinking about him. He smokes now, and he goes out every night, doesn't come in until almost morning, drunk and everything. And he swears really bad, right in front of my mom and dad."

"My dad always talks about that—how many boys are coming home like that. I guess being in the army does that to some people."

"I guess it's his own business if he doesn't want to go to church, but right now, he's just ruining our family. He's mad all the time. It doesn't matter what anybody says to him, he blows up about it. The bishop came over to talk to him, and Lawrence almost threw him out the door. He was cursing God, saying how he had seen too much bad stuff to think God loved anyone—and saying words that were the worst ones you can even think of. I went to my room and put a pillow over my head, and I could still hear him."

Garner wasn't looking at her. He was looking off across the room. Kids were standing around in little groups, talking, drinking punch, but Beverly didn't think he was seeing any of that. He was remembering, and she could see how sad he was.

"Maybe, after a while, he'll get over some of that, Garner. My dad says that some soldiers have to get things out of their systems for a while."

"Lawrence is too far gone. I don't know what's going to happen to him. Sometimes I think he would have been better off to die in the war. I don't think he's ever going to be happy."

"My brother *did* die. My brother Gene."

"Oh. I'm sorry. I didn't know that."

"That's all right. He was on the island of Saipan, and he died the very first day he was in battle. He went onto the beach and he got shot, right off. His sergeant wrote to us and said how brave he was and everything, but I don't see how he had time to do much of anything that was brave."

"It was brave to hit that beach."

"I know. But somebody made him do it. Gene never would have hurt anybody if there hadn't been a war. He was the nicest boy you can even imagine."

"I wish the war had never happened."

Beverly looked over at Garner. It was hardly a brilliant thing to say, but she felt how much he meant it, knew the feeling herself. "Sometimes I think we got cheated," she said. "We missed out on a lot of neat things, just because everything got changed so much."

"I don't care if we didn't have as many parties, or if we couldn't bake cakes as much—stuff like that. I just wish Lawrence was okay."

"I know. I wish I had Gene back."

"Yeah. I'll bet."

The silence returned. Beverly was pretty sure she had

nothing more to say on the subject, and Garner didn't either, but she felt close to him. They even danced a little closer when the band came back. When Tom picked them up and drove them home, they didn't say anything again, but Garner sat with his leg touching hers a little, and she didn't feel nearly so awkward. At the door, he stayed far away, seeming only too happy to say "Well, thanks a lot" and make his getaway. But Beverly liked him. She was pretty sure LaRue would think he was rough as a cob, and maybe he was, in a way, but he was nice, and he had talked to her about things she doubted he had told anyone else.

When Beverly walked inside, she was hoping that her parents were in bed, but she not only found her mother up but also Bobbi and Richard sitting in the living room. "I just wanted to see you in your pretty dress," Bobbi said.

And Richard stood up and said, "My goodness. You look so grown up, Bev. You're a knockout."

The truth was, Beverly still had a bigger crush on Richard than she did on Garner—or on anyone else. Richard was handsome and confident, and so nice. She wished there were boys more like him at the high school. But then, they probably wouldn't want to take her out; they would all be chasing after LaRue.

"Your hair is so cute," Bobbi said.

"LaRue did it for me."

"Didn't LaRue go to the dance?"

"No. She doesn't go to dances very often any more."

"Why not?"

"She's gone from chasing boys to running them off," Bea said. "I don't know which I worry about more."

Bobbi came to Beverly and took her into her arms. "Oh, honey, this is so fun for me to see you. I hate to watch you grow up, in a way, but it all reminds me of me—not so long ago as you might think."

Beverly thought she understood that, but she thought she would rather escape now, not be quite so admired.

"So how was this boy? Do you like him?"

"He can't dance at all," Beverly said, and she giggled. "But he was really nice to me."

"Did you think of anything to say?" Bea asked.

"I guess so—enough to get by." Everyone laughed, including Beverly. But the truth was, she thought she had done pretty well.

2 1

Wally and Lorraine were seated in a sealing room in the Salt Lake Temple. They watched as Don Cluff and his wife Marjorie knelt on opposite sides of the altar, reached across, and took one another's hand. Elder Spencer W. Kimball, one of the newest members of the Quorum of the Twelve, had agreed to perform the ceremony. He spoke the prayer gently, and Wally listened to the words, the promises, that he had received not so long ago himself. He could see Don's solemn face, how gratefully he looked at his wife. What Wally thought of, had thought of often these past few days, was that night near Clark Field in the Philippines when Don had asked Wally to pray. Wally had hardly felt worthy to do such a thing, but he had asked for the very thing that had happened, that Don would be spared so he could return to his family. What Wally never would have imagined then was that someday the two of them, with their wives, would be here in the temple together.

When the marriage sealing was complete, Elder Kimball stepped outside for a moment, and everyone waited until Don and Marjorie's daughters were brought to the room by a temple matron. Then the little girls joined their parents at the altar. Patty, who was nine now, knelt next to her father, and seven-year-old Joanne next to her mother, and the two rested their little hands on top of the joined hands of their parents. Both were dark-haired little girls, petite like their mother. They were busy kids, little live-wires, but they looked angelic now in their white dresses. Wally thought how often Don had talked of these two while he and Don had been in prison camp together, and how much Don had longed to see them. Now Marjorie was expecting her third baby in the fall, but this next child would be born in the covenant.

Again Elder Kimball pronounced the sealing quietly, slowly, in his mellow voice, and the children listened intently. Then, when he had finished and everyone was standing up, he said, "I want all of you to come around to this side of the altar and stand together, and I want you to look into that mirror." On either side of the altar were large mirrors, facing one another, the surfaces reflecting back and forth. Above the altar was a pretty glass chandelier whose image, in successive reflections, seemed to recede into nothingness. Don and Marjorie and the little girls stepped into that picture. "What you see there, children," Elder Kimball said, "should give you some idea of eternity. Can you see how those images of you seem to go on and on forever?"

The girls were obviously touched by this quiet, holy place, by the mood here, by Elder Kimball's mildness. They looked solemnly into the mirrors, and both nodded.

"You're joined to your family forever now. You'll be together in the next life. And you can create a link to them when you find mates someday and marry. You can be sealed to your husbands and to your own children. You can keep your family together throughout all eternity."

Wally had heard those words all his life, had thought he knew what they meant. But he glanced now at Lorraine's lovely roundness. He hadn't realized how he would feel about that, about a life coming from the two of them, about the connection not only to his child but also of the child's connection to his parents and grandparents. And then he tried to picture that chain into the future, like the images in the mirror, separate and yet overlaid upon each other, individual and still aggregate. Being one, being an agent unto himself, was important, and it carried responsibility, but this larger whole, his tie to something that had started long before him and would continue long after—that was so much more meaningful. His dad had tried so hard to tell him those things when he was a teenager, and Wally had grown weary of hearing about his "heritage," but he thought he understood now, hoped he could somehow get the idea across to his own children.

Wally and Lorraine hugged Don and Marjorie and the girls. Wally shook Elder Kimball's hand too. "Thanks so much," he told him.

"Oh, I'm glad to do it. We in the Twelve don't do so many as we used to, but I always enjoy doing sealings." Elder Kimball was much shorter than Wally, but he reached up and patted him on the shoulder. "You served a mission, as it turned out—to bring this family into the Church. Maybe, at the time, you didn't realize that that's what you were doing. I'm glad you remembered who you were, even in those terrible circumstances."

Wally had never thought of it that way, but the idea struck him as right.

"How's your father doing?" Elder Kimball asked. "Is he making the adjustment all right, not having quite so much to do?"

"I think he is. But it wasn't quite as easy as he thought it was going to be. It's taken him all this last year just to settle into a new routine."

"Well, we need to send him out as a mission president somewhere, just so he doesn't start feeling lazy." Elder Kimball smiled, almost playfully. He had been called to the Twelve during the war, so he was not one of the General Authorities Wally knew, but Wally liked the man already. He was natural and genial. What Wally liked, however, was that he didn't seem at all impressed with himself.

"Dad *would* make a good mission president," Wally said, and he meant it. He suspected that his father might be just a little too stern with the missionaries at times, but he would be a lot more understanding than he might have been a few years back.

"He's one of the stalwarts," Elder Kimball said. "People out in your part of town tell me all the time how much they love that man. I doubt you have any idea how many families he's helped. If someone was up against it during the war, he'd do whatever it took to get them through, and I happen to know that a lot of that came right out of his own pocket—not from the bishops' storehouse."

"Elder Kimball, I didn't know that. He never mentions anything like that to the rest of us."

"Well, that's just like him. I'm sure your mother knows, but he would never blow his own horn about the things he does."

"No, he wouldn't."

Elder Kimball took hold of Wally's arm, gripped it. "I had a long chat with your father one day, during the war, when he didn't know whether he would ever see you again. He told me some of his regrets—that he hadn't been as close to you as he wished he had been. He said that if he got the chance, he wanted to make up for that. I hope that you two are taking advantage of this second chance you have."

"I think we are." But Wally realized that he sounded hesitant, so he added quickly, "I appreciate my father more than I did when I was younger."

"Well, that happens to most of us. We grow up, and then we see things a little differently." He looked over at Lorraine and smiled. "Someday—maybe not so long from now—you two might have a child who tests *your* patience. That's when you'll really understand your father."

"I'm sure that's true," Wally said.

Lorraine laughed and said, "This one we're expecting has already made up its mind that it needs more room to move around in."

"Yes, yes. It starts from the very beginning." Elder Kimball turned then to the Cluffs and chatted with them. Wally looked again at the mirrors. It struck him how many times in the history of the world the same story had been told: parents teaching their children the things they believed, and the children trying on those ideas, sometimes throwing them off, sometimes grabbing hold. He wondered what it would be like if this baby he and Lorraine were expecting turned out to be the kind of teenager he had been himself.

But Wally saw something else in the mirror—in his own face. He had been lazy, certainly; irresolute about what he wanted out of life; and he had taken some experimental steps off the path. But his dad had been a little too impatient, a little too quick to compare him to Alex and Bobbi. Wally hoped he could learn from that. He loved his father, but he didn't want to be exactly like him.

Elder Kimball wished everyone well one last time, and then he left the room. The Cluffs followed, each holding a daughter's hand, and Lorraine walked after them. Wally, however, continued to look at himself in the mirror, and in those few seconds before he turned to catch up, he wondered what kind of a man he was becoming, whether he was measuring up, yet, to his father's expectations. He had been called, recently, to serve in his ward as president of the Young Men's Mutual Improvement Association, and he liked being around the young people in the ward. But he felt, as he looked at himself, a need to give those kids a little more of himself—to guide them away from some of the mistakes he had made.

Bea prepared lunch for the Cluffs after the temple ceremony, and then later in the afternoon she held a little reception so that everyone in the family could meet Don and his wife and celebrate with them. It was a Friday, so the men were all working, but Al took some time off, and Alex and Richard knocked off early for the day, and they brought Heinrich and Peter Stoltz along. Chuck Adair showed up too. The women in the family had all come a little earlier and had helped Bea get ready. LaRue was the only one who couldn't make it. She was working at Snelgrove's ice cream parlor and had to work an afternoon and evening shift.

It was a hot August day, but Dad had set up electric fans in both the living room and dining room, and the old house held the morning coolness pretty well. Everyone had a chance to get acquainted with the Cluffs and congratulate them, and there was lots of good food. But when Richard and Bobbi spoke of leaving, President Thomas spoke above the other voices. "Before people start heading home, let me just say a couple of things," he said. "I want to express our congratulations to Don and Marj and tell them how happy we are for them. I'm very impressed with their little family, and with the commitment they have to the gospel, even though they're still new in the Church." He hesitated, then put his hand on Don's shoulder. "But especially I wanted to thank you, Don, on behalf of our family, for all you did for Wally. He's told me what a strength you and Chuck were to him. He said he never would have made it if it hadn't been for his group of close friends. So God bless you. We have our son back, and—to no small degree—we have you to thank for it."

Wally stepped a little closer to Don and said softly, "That's right."

"Thanks, President Thomas," Don said, "but you've got it pretty much backward. The strength of our group was always in Wally and Chuck. Everyone in our camp respected those two. They were the ones who pulled *me* through."

"Chuck was actually the one who led the way," Wally said.

Don laughed. "Wally never will take credit for all he did, but he started changing my life right from the beginning, in the first few days of the war. He prayed for me—and that showed me how to pray for myself. Long before I met Chuck, Wally was the one who taught me how to survive. And he did the same for a lot of other guys. He deserves a medal—but I guess he'll never get one." Don's voice had gotten shaky. He turned toward Wally and gave him a little pat on the back, but then he ducked his head, obviously embarrassed by his own emotion.

Marjorie turned to Wally and hugged him. "Thank you so much," she said.

Wally didn't know what to say. He looked over Marjorie's shoulder at his father, and Dad gave Wally a little nod. It was the simplest of confirmations, but it touched Wally, made a difference, as though a medal had been pinned on his chest. But he heard someone climbing the steps, heading upstairs, and he realized that it had to be Alex, who had been standing on that side of the living room. Wally wondered what it meant that Alex would leave at that moment, and he feared that he knew the answer.

Wally waited for the conversation to drift away from such serious matters, and then he walked to the stairs, but Anna saw him and reached out for his arm. "Don't go after him. Just give him a little time," she said.

"Is he all right?"

"He will be."

"What can I do?"

"Talk to him. But not today."

Wally didn't want to wait, but he accepted Anna's judgment. He saw that Richard and Bobbi were leaving, so he went to them and said good-bye. The Stoltzes were getting ready to go too. They were talking to the Cluffs. As Wally returned to the living room, he noticed that Peter was standing back, waiting. So Wally stepped over to him. "Peter, I haven't had a chance to talk to you today. How are you doing?"

"Fine, thank you," Peter said.

"Hey, that was good. You're getting that 'th' sound better all the time."

Peter seemed pleased with that. "Now if I could learn to say my 'w' sounds, I wouldn't sound so much like those Germans in the movies."

Wally was glad to hear Peter laugh. In the past little while he seemed to be turning into the Peter that Anna had promised he would become. At work he had been a little more outgoing, a little more trusting of his language. Wally talked with him often enough to know that he was a bright young man, and witty when he relaxed around people.

"We didn't get a chance to meet your son," Wally heard Don say to the Stoltzes.

Brother Stoltz turned and said, "Peter, come. Shake hands with Brother and Sister Cluff."

Peter stepped forward and shook hands. Wally noticed that he was less formal about it than he had been when he had first arrived in Salt Lake City. He didn't bow his head, and in an almost American style, he said, "Nice to meet you."

"You know," Don said, "right after the war ended, us prisoners finally had a chance to meet some of the Japanese civilians. They turned out to be wonderful people. After all those years of thinking of the Japanese as my enemy, it was really good for me to have that experience. People still feel a lot of hatred—on all sides—and I hear the kinds of things they say, but to me, people are people. They're the same everywhere."

"Yes. I think that's true," Heinrich said. "We've been treated very well here."

"Wally told me that you resisted Hitler—that you fought against him."

"Only a little. When we could."

Wally saw the next sentence coming, but it was too late to interrupt. "Well," Don said, "I respect you for that. It would have been easy to go along with Hitler and just protect yourselves. But you put your lives on the line. That took a lot of courage. That's the trouble in this world: too many good people stand back and let the bad people run the show."

"Most people in Germany couldn't resist. It was far too dangerous."

"But that's what impresses me about you and your family, Heinrich. You didn't worry about your own lives. You took the chance."

Wally felt Peter straighten ever so little, saw him take a small step back, and then another. Heinrich was clearly trying to think of the right thing to say. "It's difficult," he mumbled. "It's different in every case." But he too was moving back, and by now Peter was retreating from the living room toward the front door. Wally didn't know the boy well enough to go after him, to say something—nor did he know what he could say—but he knew how Peter would take the words, how he would apply them to himself.

The Stoltzes left, and Alex came downstairs without saying anything about his own disappearance, and then he and Anna left too. Marjorie insisted at that point that she help Bea with the dishes, and Beverly took the little girls up to her room to entertain them. Maybe Dad sensed that this was the first opportunity for the old friends to talk by themselves; he excused himself to his office. That left Wally with Chuck and Don in the living room. Wally was still worried about Alex and Peter, but he didn't say anything, didn't want Don to feel bad about the things he had said so innocently.

Chuck and Don had not had much time to catch up, so they chatted with each other about their lives now. Chuck spoke with more confidence than Wally had heard from him since they had come home. He told Don about his early struggles, but he said, "I'm working now—even if it isn't a great job. Wally keeps telling me I ought to go to college. I've never figured I had the brains for that, but I guess I'm going to give it a try this fall. I figure, if Uncle Sam is willing to pay for it, it can't hurt to see what I can do."

"That's right, Chuck," Don said, "and don't worry about being smart enough. You'll do fine."

Chuck was sitting in Dad's new chair, with all the flowers on it. Wally never had grown accustomed to the idea of his father sitting there, and Chuck looked even more out of place. Wally had spent too many days with him in that crowded little barracks in Japan, sitting on the floor. "Well, we'll see what happens," Chuck said. "What I've got to do is get married. I envy you two guys when I see you with your wives."

"What about Louise?" Wally asked. "She seems awful nice to me."

"She is. I just don't move very fast, I guess. It scares me to get married right away, until I've got a little more to offer." But Wally and Lorraine had been out with Chuck and Louise a few times, and Wally was quite sure that Chuck would be getting engaged before long. Maybe that's why he changed the subject. "Have you been feeling all right, Don?" Chuck asked. And Wally understood the question. Don looked strange, all filled out again, the way Wally had first known him, but he seemed much older—even old for his age.

"Well . . . yes. Mostly. I'm eating fine, but I feel just a little sick to my stomach—almost all the time."

"Have you told a doctor about that?"

"Yeah. I've been to the veteran's hospital a couple of times. They can't find anything wrong with me. They say it's in my head, and it probably is." He hesitated, looked at Chuck and then Wally. "Do you guys ever have any trouble in your head? You know, just doing all the things you used to do?"

"I couldn't think straight for a while," Chuck said. "I felt like I was nuts or something. I didn't dare try anything. I didn't even want to leave the house."

"I was kind of like that too," Don said. "But now, my brain seems to get stuck on certain things—certain memories—and then I can't stop running everything back through my mind. Sometimes I can't sleep. Then other times I'm so tired I can hardly stay awake."

"I've been lucky," Wally said. "I haven't had those kinds of troubles. But I ache. My whole body aches—especially my knees. I don't say anything about it because I don't want Lorraine to worry, but sometimes I wake up in the night, and I feel like I'm coming down with one of those fevers again—like I got out in the jungle. My doctor says some of those diseases never really go away. They just stay in your system, and they could come back, full-blown, all over again. I probably worry too much about that."

"I talked to Eddie the other day," Don said. "He called long distance. He's doing pretty well, but he said that Bill Doherty killed himself."

"Killed himself? Why?"

"Nobody knows for sure. They said he got real depressed, wouldn't talk or anything, and started telling his family to leave him alone. Then one night they heard a gun fire and ran to his room and found him there, shot through the temple."

"How could a guy make it through everything we put up with and then do something like that?" Wally asked.

No one answered for a time, but then Chuck said, "I think I know how it happens."

"*You* do?"

"Sure. A guy hangs on any way he can through all those years, and he figures, 'If I can just make it home, everything will be all right,' and then he gets home and maybe everything isn't so great."

"Some guys had their wives divorce them. I know that," Don said. "And sometimes wives got involved with other guys. That'd be pretty rough to come back to."

"In prison camp everything was clear cut," Chuck said. "We ate what they gave us, we worked, and we stayed alive if we could. That's all there was. And then a guy gets home and everything starts to look complicated—way too complicated. For a while, that's how it looked to me."

"You did what you had to do, though," Wally said. "You forced yourself out of the house."

"But I don't know if I could've done it without you—and then you and Lorraine. You two have really helped me. Louise probably would have given up on me a long time ago if we hadn't had you two to run around with."

"Hey, we're friends."

"I'm glad you guys are sticking together," Don said. "When I first came home, I had my wife and kids, but I felt alone all the time. In Japan, I got used to us guys all looking out for each other—making sure a guy got help if he was sick and all that kind of stuff. That's the only time in my life when I felt like I had friends I could depend on, absolutely, without feeling like I was asking too much."

"But your wife looks after you now, doesn't she?" Chuck asked.

"Sure. But I can't tell her what we went through over there—not so she would ever understand. When I'm around you two, I know I don't have to *explain* anything. We don't even have to bring it up. We just know." He ducked his head and added, "I think I'll miss you guys the rest of my life."

"Sometimes," Chuck said, "I wake up in the morning, and the first thing I think is that I'm glad I'm home, not back in that camp, but then I'll think, 'But I'm alone here,' and I almost want to turn around and go back. That's how much you guys meant to me."

Everyone was looking down. Wally didn't want to look in their eyes; he was too embarrassed. But he knew what they meant, felt the same way. He was certainly happier to be home, to be married to Lorraine, but he also knew he would never experience anything quite like he had in the Philippines and Japan, where life hung in the balance every day, and the only lifeline was his group of friends.

"I've been telling Marj we might want to move up here," Don said. "If I could find a good job, I think we would. Marj likes the idea of being where there are more Church members, and I'd like to be where you guys are. I feel like we're brothers—and always will be."

"That's right," Chuck said. "What we should have told President Thomas was that we took turns saving each other's lives. Don't you forget that—ever."

Wally looked at Don, and then Chuck, and the three of them nodded.

"I wouldn't ever say it was worth it," Wally said. "That would be too much like thanking those guards for all the stuff they put us through. But if it had to happen, I'm glad for some of the things we learned. My brother told me a while back that war brings out the worst in people, and I'm sure it does, just about all the time. But I feel like what happened to us showed us the other side: what a guy can be, at his best."

Again, they all nodded.

2 2

Bea Thomas was about to leave her office and take the bus home when her husband showed up. "Hey, lady, need a ride?" he asked.

"Oh, yes. Thank you, Al," she said. "I was just thinking how much I hate waiting for that silly bus."

"Do you mind if we take a little detour on the way home? I want to show you something—and get your opinion."

Bea smiled. Al was careful these days to include her in virtually every decision. She knew that doing that actually ran against his instincts, but it pleased her that he was trying so hard to reform. "That's fine," Bea said. "But I hope it's not too far out of the way. I need to get dinner started."

"The girls could look after themselves for once, Bea. You spoil them."

"Oh, I do? And who has been telling me for twenty-nine years now that he likes to have his whole family sit down together for dinner?"

He grinned and shook his head. "I do like that. But the girls could at least get things started. They never think to do that unless you give them specific instructions."

"I know. But you also tell them to get busy on their

homework right after school, and both of them are really good about doing that."

Bea hadn't worn a hat that morning. The day was just too warm. She looked around on her desk to find a file folder she had promised herself to take home. She didn't carry work home as often as she used to, but sometimes it was still difficult to keep up with everything, especially since she had cut back on her hours. She never came in on Saturdays now, and most afternoons she tried to leave by three or four.

"The only reason LaRue studies," Al said, "is that she wants that scholarship—so she can run off to some eastern girls' college where they'll stuff her head with all kinds of apostate attitudes."

Bea found the folder under some papers she had stacked on her desk. She tucked it into the little valise she carried with her to work, and then she looked back up at Al. "Let's not talk about that again," she said.

"What do you mean? Why?"

"Because we usually get into an argument about it." She walked to the door, waited until Al stepped out, and then turned out the light.

As she stepped into the hallway, Al said, "I don't know why you say that. You don't want her going back east to college any more than I do."

"I don't, Al. You know that. But it also doesn't do any good to harp on her about it all the time. It only makes her more stubborn."

"*Harp* about it? I don't harp about it. I'd like to *talk* to the girl, but she won't discuss the matter without getting upset."

"Are you sure that *she* is the one who gets upset? It was *your* voice I could hear through your office door the last time you two tried to talk."

But this was the wrong thing to say. Al looked away, unwilling to argue the point, but obviously not pleased with Bea's little jab.

Bea didn't want that. She took hold of his arm. "So what are you going to show me?" she asked. She knew that he had come into her office excited about something, and now—as she did far too often—she had dampened his enthusiasm.

"We don't need to go today. It might be better some other time."

"No, no. That's fine."

But he didn't respond, and clearly he was deflated. The two walked to the parking lot without saying a word. But at the car, Bea apologized, told him she really did want to see whatever it was he had intended to show her. Some of the life did come back to his voice when he said, "It's something very exciting, if you'll take it right. But you can't make up your mind without hearing me out first. So maybe this isn't the right time, with you in a hurry to get home."

"Don't worry about it. Let's go."

Al drove as though he were heading home, south and then up Twenty-First South. But then he turned south again on Eleventh East, in the center of Sugar House, and drove out beyond the end of the pavement and the last houses, past some farms and orchards. Eventually he stopped the car on the side of the dirt road. "Let's get out of the car, where it's not so hot," he said, "and where we can see a little better." He opened the door on his side.

Bea didn't wait for him to come around to open her door even though he was on his way to do it. She got out and looked about. "I'll bet you want to buy this land, don't you?" she said.

"Bea, please. I asked you not to make up your mind until—"

"I'm not making up my mind. I'm just guessing what this is all about."

"All right. But give me a chance—okay?"

For the first time Bea was a little irritated. She knew what this was all about. He didn't have to "explain" anything. And this wasn't really about gaining her permission. She knew very well that he had already made up *his* mind. "Have your say. I won't speak a word."

He looked down for a moment, and she could see that he understood the same thing she did: that this was the wrong time for this conversation to take place. But there was also no stopping it now.

They stood on the west side of the road, in front of the car. "A man called me this morning and said this piece of land was coming on the market. It's not just this orchard. It's all the land stretching from here up toward the foothills and about half a mile farther south." He pointed east and then motioned with his hand in a big swinging motion. "It's two hundred acres, and there's a good chance we could get another big section next to it, which is about the same size. We could get our hands on an area that could turn into more than a thousand building lots."

"And cost us a fortune, Al. You've never bought land in such big parcels."

Al looked down at the ground again. He had left his hat and his suit coat in the car, and now he was standing there in his white shirt, his black suspenders, and his brown necktie, with his hands tucked into his trouser pockets. She watched the thinning hair on the top of his head stir in the breeze. "I can get a loan," he said. "That's not a problem."

"Did you check on that already?"

"Not officially, Bea. All I did was chat with my friend Nelford Backman. He's the one who worked out that last loan for me and Dad. He said he couldn't see a problem."

"But do you want to get into that much debt?"

"Bea, we could turn it over fast. Once we draw up the plans, clear the trees, and put in the sewer lines and streets, we could sell off those lots in no time. We can make more money in three or four years than we could the rest of our lives selling cars and making washing-machine parts."

"Why would we want that much money, Al?"

"I knew that's *exactly* what you would say."

"Then why did you bring me up here? You know what you're going to do. So just go ahead and do it. Don't pretend you want my opinion."

She watched him take a long breath, could feel that he was weighing his words carefully when he said, "Bea, what do you want from me? This is something I would like to do. But I won't do it if you're against it. You tell me that you want me to include you in these kinds of decisions, and then, when I do, you tell me I'm not really sincere about it. I don't know what else to do. You suspect me of the worst, no matter how I deal with it."

Now Bea was the one taking a breath. And it was she who considered for several painful seconds before she said, "I'm sorry, Al. You're right. But it scares me—such a huge debt."

"It's the surest thing in the world, Bea. This is where Salt Lake is going to grow. If we don't develop this land, someone else will. There's not even a question about that."

Bea told herself the truth. It wasn't really the debt she feared the most. "Al, I feel like our lives are changing too much. I don't want to be rich. I just want life to settle down and be a little more simple."

Al turned away, looked back toward the orchard, the land he wanted to buy. "I understand what you're saying, Bea. I really do. But I keep thinking about the depression years, when everyone had it so hard. I want to open the way for our kids— get them all on solid ground—so I won't have to worry about them if hard times come again."

"Is that the best thing, Al? Wouldn't our kids be better off making their own way, without us doing everything for them?"

Al pulled a folded white handkerchief from his back pocket and wiped the sweat off his forehead and then off the back of his neck. "I don't see that as a problem, Bea. I'm opening up some doors, but they still have to work hard to make a go of things. I just hope they can gradually take over, and that would simplify our lives more than anything."

"Is that the next step in this plan—to send me home to an empty house?"

"If that's what you want, that's fine, Bea, but that's not what I was thinking."

He still wouldn't look at her, and Bea tried to think what he meant. "So what do you want me to do?"

"Well, a couple of things." He stepped over to the Hudson and leaned back against the fender. He folded his arms across his chest and looked at Bea. "First off, if we did go into this, we'd need to reorganize the management of all of our businesses. I've been trying to develop the land we already own and keep the dealership going at the same time—and it's just too much. Someone has to be in charge of our land development projects, full-time."

"If you're thinking of Alex, I'd forget it. He's set on going to college, and he'll be starting in another couple of weeks."

"I know that. But maybe Richard could take over the plant, and Wally could move over to the dealership, the way we talked about before. I think Richard might finally get excited about the business if he was the man in charge. I've been thinking that Heinrich Stoltz could move into the office and do some of the accounting and paperwork you've done."

Bea was getting too much sun. She backed up to where she could feel the shade from a ragged old cottonwood tree behind her. "Al, I see where all this is leading. You're figuring out a way to send me home. I guess that's all right, but—"

"That's not what I was thinking." He shook his head firmly, his arms still tight across his chest.

"Then what?"

"Bea, I know better than to try to *send you* anywhere. It's your decision. I just have an idea that I want to run past you." He pointed over his shoulder with his thumb. "What if you took over this project—ran the development company?"

"Me?"

"Yes. You're the best manager in the family, better than I'll ever be, and way ahead of any of the kids. I don't say that to blow smoke at you. It's just true. If you ran this operation, I'd be able to sleep at night because I know you'd keep on top of everything, make sure that things happened right. I can't really hand the dealership over to Wally until he learns that business, and he's planning to go to school part-time, which will take a lot of his concentration. If I try to do both, I don't think it would work. I've thought about the three boys, and I just don't see any one of them taking over something this big. Not yet."

"Al, thank you. I really am pleased that you would put that much faith in me. But I don't want to do this." She came out of the shade, walked to him, and put her hand on his arm. "When I went to work at the plant, I felt like I was doing something that had to be done. But how can I get excited about clearing off all this pretty farmland and filling it up with houses?"

"Can't you think in terms of putting our family on a sound footing?"

"No. Because you're doing a lot more than that. You're the one who wants to build a big house up by the country club. It won't be long until the kids will think they're better than the people they grew up with. And what will our grandchildren think of themselves? I don't want all that."

"Bea, it doesn't have to be like that."

"Let's go home, Al. It's too hot out here."

She watched him prepare another argument, get set to speak, and then give it up. He stepped to the car door and opened it for Bea, and she got in. The car was like an oven inside, and Bea was frustrated. Why couldn't he understand? She didn't want life to change. She wanted things to be the way they had been before the war, before people started to think they had to have so much. All this time, since Al had shown up at her office, she had been holding back, but she was getting angrier by the minute. When he got into the car, she said, "Al, you want me and the boys to run everything so you can go off and play politics. That's your next move—to run for mayor or Congress or something like that. You're getting too big for your britches, making so much money."

Al didn't start the car. He put his arm over the steering wheel and turned and looked at Bea. "I'm not running for anything. I've made up my mind about that. I couldn't give a good political speech if I had to. I bored the people in my stake for almost a decade. They only listened to me because they had no choice."

There was something to that, and Bea knew it. He had always known how to call people to repentance, but he never had been one to grease them up and entertain them the way politicians did. The truth was, she was rather impressed to think that Al knew that much about himself, and she was softened a little by the discouragement she heard in his voice, but she was still angry. "It's one of our boys you'll try to send off to Congress."

"I'd love that, but the boys aren't interested." Al started the car, stepped on the clutch and shifted into first, and then drove forward to a place where he could angle into a little side road and get turned around.

Bea tried to stop herself, but she couldn't resist saying, "Why do we need all that power, Al? What's it good for?"

And now she finally heard his anger. "Bea, to hear you tell it, anyone who has success turns into some snooty socialite, and anyone who wants to run for office is only out for himself. I'm sure glad everyone doesn't think that way. I happen to think some things need to be changed in this country, and I'd like to see Alex lead the way—instead of moping around licking his wounds."

"Don't talk that way about him, Al. You know what he's been through."

"What I know is that it's time for him to get over it."

"That's easy for you to say. While he was ducking bullets, you were home making money off the war."

Suddenly Al veered off the road and stopped the car. He

twisted toward Bea and barked into her face, "That's what this is all about, isn't it? You've listened to Alex cry about the war. Maybe we should have *lost* it, and you'd both be happier."

"I *respect* the way Alex feels."

"And our money is blood money. Right?"

Bea almost said yes, almost shouted it, but she stopped herself, knew better than to stick that knife into him, even knew it wasn't fair. She waited a moment before she said, "No, Al. I'm not saying that. But so many people paid so much, and it just feels wrong that we came out so far ahead."

"I thought we built those weapons so America could *win* the war. And I thought that was what good Americans tried to do. But I guess I'm wrong."

"The war killed Gene, Al. And we got rich. How can you put those two facts together and not feel . . . *dirty?*"

"I see no logic in that, Bea. None whatsoever." But his anger was gone. He turned away, and then he shifted gears and drove back onto the road. Bea had won, had emptied the air out of him—but suddenly she felt sick. The car was so hot.

It took Bea a few minutes to understand her own regret, but she gradually admitted to herself that she had no right to act so pure and high minded. She had enjoyed the fruits of their newfound wealth as much as anyone in the family—loved all her new furniture. She had been thinking about remodeling the house, fixing up her kitchen. Was that so different from building a new house?

"I'm sorry, Al," she finally said. "I'm just mixed up about what's right and wrong these days. I see the paper every night, and I know that little children in Europe and Japan don't have enough to eat. And then I wonder why we have so much."

"Look, Bea, I think about that too. I'm not such a bad person as you think I am."

"Don't say that. I didn't mean it that way."

He drove for a minute or so, not saying a word, but when

he stopped at the light on Twenty-First South, he looked over at Bea. "Let's do something for those kids," he said.

"What kids?"

"The ones you were talking about. In Germany and Japan. We could make a bigger donation this year—through the Church. The Brethren have been asking for more help so they can carry out some of these relief projects they have going. We could certainly do more than we've done in the past."

Bea didn't respond immediately, but she thought about the idea all the way home. She didn't want to live like a princess and then salve her conscience by throwing scraps to the poor. What did appeal to her was the idea of using their resources to make a real difference somewhere in the world. As Al drove the car into the driveway, she said, "What if I managed the land development company and also managed our charitable giving—and we started to do a lot more for people in need? Not just in Europe but here in Salt Lake, too."

Bea was surprised by his quick response. "I like that idea, Bea."

"Why? Would we just be buying off our consciences?"

He opened his door but still sat behind the steering wheel, and he looked out the windshield, not at Bea. "A lot of people in this country made money off the war. Almost everyone is better off financially because of it. I don't know what to say about that, exactly, but I've known for a long time that we could be doing more good with our money than we've done so far. I told myself I had to worry about our family first, but I've had some of the same thoughts you've had, and I feel good about trying to do something for people who lost everything, through no fault of their own."

"If I develop that land, I want to create some beautiful neighborhoods, not some ugly row of houses, all alike, the way some of these new companies are doing."

"That's good. That's why we should do it. We care about this city."

Bea wondered. There were so many ways to justify the very things she had just said she didn't want to do. And yet she knew that Al was right. Someone was going to build houses on that land soon, and maybe she would do it right—and do something good with the profits. Or would she let the money change her? "Al, I sound like I think I'm better than you, and I'm not. You could probably build a new house and just enjoy it—and not worry what other people thought. I think of it as showing off because that's exactly what it would be for me."

"Oh, Bea, you've never shown off in your whole life. You hate wearing a new dress because you think someone might notice."

He got out of the car, and once again she got out before he could come around. "Al, that's not true," she said. "I've spent more money on clothes this last year than I ever thought I would in my life. And I like these nice things from ZCMI and Auerbach's. You never do that. You buy something plain and practical and you use it until it's worn out."

He tried to smile, but she could see that he was still disheartened. "Even your compliments sound like insults," he said.

"No, no. I'm sorry. Al, I'm way too hard on you. You're a good man, through and through, and I'm the one who puts a bad light on things that you do so innocently."

"The fact is, I just follow my instincts, and all too often they aren't the best. You're my conscience, Bea, and I need one."

"But you're the energy that keeps us moving forward. I'm glad I'm not married to some dud who never dreams."

They were standing in front of one another, looking into each other's eyes, and Bea was surprised by the thought that came to her mind. She loved this man more now than she ever had. She had put up quite a fight these past few years, taken her stand over and over, and what he had done was listen and learn. She told herself she needed to do a lot more of that herself.

That night Bea called Alex. When he came to the phone, he sounded tired, maybe even a little blue. "How are you doing?" she asked him.

"Oh, fine. I wish I knew a little better how to be a daddy. I think Gene is pretty mad at me tonight."

"You didn't spank him, did you? If you did, I'll be over there with a switch of my own."

"No. I didn't spank him. But I got after him. Anna says he's pretty good all day, and the minute I walk through the door, he starts acting up. He was jumping on our couch—and I've told him a hundred times he can't do that."

Bea pulled a chair away from the dining room table and sat down by the phone. She had gotten a new telephone with her new furniture and replaced the old wall phone with one of the new ones that sat on a shelf. At least she didn't need to stand up to the old phone anymore, but she hated the plastic smell of this one. "Alex, I shouldn't say this, but I enjoy watching you try to figure out this child-raising thing. It's not so easy, is it?"

"No. But I think Anna and I have to face some things you didn't. Gene never has adjusted to me the way I figured he would."

Bea laughed. "Oh, Alex. The adjustments never stop. It's just one thing after another. Your dad and I are still working things out."

"What an encouraging thought," Alex said, his voice sounding a little lighter now.

"You know what, though? It's worth it. I was just thinking this afternoon, I love Al more than I ever did when we were young."

"Really?"

"I know that sounds funny to you, but we've been through so many things together. I think back, and when we were newly married, like you and Anna, we hardly knew each other. There are all kinds of ways that two people blend together without knowing it, and all sorts of differences that have to be worked out. But newlyweds don't deal with most of those things. I was mad at your dad this afternoon—really mad—and a few minutes later I was thinking how much I love him."

"I can't imagine loving Anna any more than I already do, Mom, but I didn't know that everyday life would be so complicated. I didn't think I could ever be mad at her, but . . . well, you know how it is."

"Oh, yes. I know how it is."

"She's sitting here listening to this, and she just stuck her tongue out at me. She's learning American English, I guess." He chuckled softly. "But I'll tell you, Mom, I never stay mad at her very long." And then Bea heard some confusion, some shifting of the phone. "Oh, oh," Alex said. "Now she's kissing me."

"Well, I'd better get off the phone. It sounds like you two want to be alone."

"Wasn't there something you wanted to talk to me about?"

"Well, yes. I talked to your dad this afternoon about using some of the money we're making to get some help to people in Europe. I thought you might be able to give me some ideas about that."

"Mom, I'd love to help you work on that. I'm not going to have a lot of time once school starts, but I'll do whatever I can."

"Would it be best to work through the Church, or—"

"Yes, I think so. But we could also work with any of the organizations that are trying to help—the Red Cross as much as anyone."

"Well, let's get together tomorrow—or soon, anyway—and start to think it through."

"Okay. And I'm going to go in and kiss Gene. He's in bed, but he's still crying."

"Give him a couple of extra kisses from his grandma. I haven't seen that boy for at least three days. I miss him."

When Bea hung up the phone, she walked into the kitchen and found Al there. He was cutting himself a slice of banana cream pie. "Oh, oh," he said. "Caught in the act. You're going to tell me that I already had one dessert and I don't need another one."

Bea was knocked off guard. Those were exactly the words that had come to her mind. "I nag you about things like that too much, don't I?"

"I'm pretty sure the correct answer is, 'No, honey, not at all.'" He laughed. "Want some?"

"No, thanks." Bea paused. "I called Alex. He seemed excited about doing something to help in Europe. But I've been thinking more about the whole idea. I'd like to reach some people that maybe the Church can't. What we can do will only be a drop in the bucket compared to what is needed over there, but maybe I can enlist some other Salt Lake people who are doing well right now, and we can pool some of what we have."

"That would be good, Bea." He walked to the refrigerator and put the pie away, but as he returned to the table, he said, "I feel good about this too. It seems what Thomases and Snows ought to do."

Bea walked to the table, put her arms around her husband's neck, and kissed him on the cheek. "Life is harder than I thought it was going to be when I was young," she said.

"What makes you say that?"

"Oh, I don't know. I was just talking to Alex. He's really struggling with all the adjustments in his life." Bea moved around the table and sat down across from Al. "Have you ever noticed how you can love someone and most of the time never give it a thought?"

"Sure. That's the way I operate." He smiled.

"You know how much Alex loves Anna, but he's already surprised at how complicated married life is."

"We both understand that."

"Al, I love you. But I don't tell you that, and I'm not even sure you know it."

She watched her husband's eyes fill with tears. "Bea, something occurred to me a while back, and it knocked me for a loop when I thought of it." He lowered his head. "I always have the feeling that you're just a little disappointed in me. I'm not the man I ought to be, and no one knows it better than you do."

"Oh, Al, I'm sorry. I've pushed you so hard lately. But that's mostly because I doubt myself so much, and you get the spillover."

"I never doubt you."

"That's true. Or at least that's how you make me feel. Thank you for that." And now she was seeing through her own tears.

"It's okay. Just take good care of my money, and I'll remember to feel guilty for having it."

She laughed. "I'll give away so much you won't have to worry about it."

"It's a deal. That's just what I deserve."

"But Al, I'm not disappointed in you. I don't want you to think I am."

"Well, fine. I'll take over that part of the job myself."

Bea was touched by that. She knew he meant it. But she told herself she needed to be easier on him and take a little harder look at herself.

2 3

Alex had made a decision. He was going to keep working at his father's parts factory even though he was starting his first quarter at the University of Utah on Monday. Anna didn't think he should break with his father, nor did Wally, but finally, it had been Alex's decision. There was nothing wrong with his working part-time, the same as he might for someone else, and he didn't mind the work he had been doing. But mostly he felt that his dad would see it as an insult if he left the company and then found another job.

So on Friday morning, before Alex had to be at the plant, he drove to the dealership. He figured he could catch his father in his office early, before things got busy. As it turned out, he found him in the showroom in a meeting with some of his salespeople, but the meeting broke up soon after Alex arrived, and he and his dad walked to the office, upstairs. Alex didn't want to make a big deal of all this, so he said, rather casually, as they climbed the stairs, "Dad, I just came over to tell you that I'm going to stay on at the plant, part-time. Wally needs the help, and I appreciate the pay I'm getting. I thought about looking for a job on campus, which would have been a little more convenient, but nothing else would pay as well."

Alex had planned his words ahead of time. He wanted Dad

to know that he appreciated what he was getting, recognized that his father was being more than fair with him. But he hadn't expected his dad to be quite so pleased. "That's great, Alex. Great. We need you, and I'd like you to keep your hand in things just so you could move back into the company, if that's what you feel like you want to do, once you finish college."

"Well, that's not what I have in mind, Dad. But sure, who knows? I might feel different about things by then." It was a huge opening to give his dad but one Alex thought he could allow for the sake of peace. He just hoped Dad would let the whole matter end with that—a delay in the ultimate decision, but nothing more.

"Listen, that brings up something I want to talk to you about. I've got a whole new idea about what you could do— and it might change the way you look at all of this."

"I don't think so, Dad. I just—"

"Now, don't be like your mom. Let me tell you what I mean before you make up your mind. In fact, don't make up your mind at all. I just want to put something into your head to think about."

They had reached the door to Dad's office. He swung it open and let Alex walk in first. And then he came around Alex and grabbed one of the chairs in front of his desk, turned it, and motioned for Alex to sit down.

Alex was chafing just a little. He hadn't liked that little crack about being like his mom. It seemed a criticism of her, and not one that Alex thought she deserved. She might stand up to Dad at times, but overall she had shaped her will to his much more than the other way around. But Alex did sit down. He decided to listen, to say, "I'll think about it," and then go.

Dad took off his suit coat and hung it on a coat tree near the door. The days had remained warm this September, and the office was hot. Alex had left his own coat in his car. When his dad turned around, Alex was struck by the mirror image he saw. Both of them were wearing white shirts, dark trousers, and dark suspenders, but more than that, Dad's big frame, his thick shoulders, were shaped like Alex's. Dad was stouter, and he seemed to move with a little less authority than he once had, but as he turned his chair to face Alex's and took his seat, the movements reminded Alex of himself. There was a certain exaggerated force, a kind of boldness, not without a hint of grace, that Alex often saw in Dad and felt in himself. And Dad's face, under weightier cheeks, was Alex's: the bone structure, the eye color, the skin, even the blue shadow left by a good morning's shave.

"Mom talked to you about some of our plans, didn't she?"

"What plans?"

"To create a foundation of some kind and see what we can do to help some of the people suffering over in Europe and Japan."

"Yes. It's a great thing, Dad. I'm sure you can't do all that much, but anything will help."

"Don't be so quick to say that. The thing you might forget is that the wealthy people in our country are the ones who build the libraries, endow universities, set up soup kitchens—all kinds of things. And that's how it ought to be. The ones who succeed in our free market are the ones who can give something back. Roosevelt got it into his head that the government ought to step in and do everything, but that adds too much bureaucracy and waste. I may not be as rich as Rockefeller, but I can join with other people like myself, and we can make a real difference in this world."

"Sure. I know what you mean." But Alex saw another side to all that. A man could accumulate wealth by whatever means, profit off the work of simple people, and then, after living high, put his name on a university building or toss some of his wealth to the poor and tell himself that he was noble. But Alex wasn't going to say anything of that kind. He did admire his parents, who had accumulated only a little wealth and were already willing to start sharing it.

"Well, anyway, here is what I was thinking." Dad leaned on his elbows, his fingers threaded together. "I know you don't like making parts. You never did. And I don't want to get into a discussion of your feelings about that. But what if you worked with your mom on these land deals we've got going? You could help her make this south part of the valley the prettiest in Salt Lake, really see something beautiful take form out here—and at the same time help provide good, well-built houses for people who are just getting their families established. I think it's exciting to think about, and it's not at all like watching hunks of metal come off an assembly line—which I know you've never liked."

The truth was, Alex hadn't minded the plant so much lately. He had found satisfaction in having an order to fill and seeing the work get done. It had been the most calming thing in his life lately to watch for a few minutes as the parts came off the line, got packed into boxes, and moved away. It was something finished, accomplished, whereas his attempt at fatherhood was a work in progress and not one he was sure he was doing very well. But that was not something he wanted to talk about either. "Dad," he said, "what I'd like to do, if you don't mind, is just work on an hourly basis at the plant. Land development, at this stage, probably involves a lot of planning and thinking, and a lot of running around and dealing with people and offices. I want to concentrate primarily on school right now. If I can go down to the plant, put in a few hours, feel like I accomplished something, and then get back to my studies, I think that would work best."

"That's fine. I understand. But here's the one thing you might think about. Mom doesn't want to work too much longer. By the time you get out of school, what if you took over the land development part of our business? In the long run, you might like that a lot better than anything else we do, and it would be a much better opportunity than you'd probably get with anyone else. You come out of college and start teaching school, or something like that, and you're never going to make a decent living."

"But if that's what I decide to do, I guess it will have to be decent enough."

There had been an edge in Alex's voice, and the tone seemed to linger, as though a barrier had been raised between them. Alex hated the feeling, hadn't wanted it, but why couldn't Dad ever let up a little?

"Well, anyway . . . as I said before . . . it's just something for you to think about. That's all I had in mind."

"Okay, I'll think about it."

"No, you won't." And now it was Dad who had let some anger seep into his voice.

"What?"

"Never mind. Just go ahead and do what you want to do. I know you think I'm trying to interfere in your life again."

Alex took a big breath, exaggerated it, tried to show his dad how hard he was working not to fire back.

"Look, I'm sorry. I really am," Dad said. "I get carried away. But Alex, I see you withdrawing from the family, and it's hard for me. It just feels to me like the war ought to be over now, and you ought to move on and be yourself again."

"What do you mean by that?"

"You know very well what I mean. We all feel it. There's something seething in you. It's there every second I'm around you—like you're just waiting for an insult, looking for one. You're angry, and yet you walk around pretending that you're not, all stone-faced and emotionless. I know the war was troubling for you, but it just seems like enough time has passed now. You need to let all that go."

Alex was trying to keep his breathing even and calm. But he really wanted to give his father an answer, if he could. He waited for a few seconds, and then, in a restrained voice, he said, "Dad, you have no idea how hard I'm trying. But I spend every day of my life just fighting not to explode."

"Why, Alex?"

"I don't know. But I know that if I let go, just once, just a little, I'm going to break into a million pieces. You—everyone—tells me to put things in the past, and that's what I try to do, but I'm shaking inside almost all the time. It's been a year and a half, and I'm still not sleeping right, still waking up with terrible dreams. And you're right, I feel angry most of the time." He took a deeper breath, and then he added, "I'm sorry. I don't want to feel that way, but I do. I don't usually talk about it, because it doesn't do any good. But you raised the question."

"Alex, you need to get some help. I had no idea it was that bad for you."

"I've talked to the doctors at the veterans' hospital. It doesn't seem to make any difference."

"But you've got to do something."

"I am doing something. Elder Benson told me not to look back, to take a step forward, then pray and decide what the next step should be. That's the only thing that makes sense to me right now. My first step is to go to college. I feel like that's what I'm supposed to do. And I've prayed a lot about that."

"But what is it that bothers you, Son? Do you know?" Dad leaned forward, put his hand on the armrest, almost touching Alex's hand. "What is it you think about that gets you upset?"

"I don't know, Dad. I don't think about the war. But things pop into my mind—things I don't want to remember. When I try to push that stuff out of my head, I start sweating, and my heart starts to race."

"I think you need to admit yourself into the hospital, let the doctors there spend some time with you, and—"

"Into some pysch ward?" Alex pulled his hand back, and the two leaned away from each other.

"Sure. There's nothing wrong with that."

"Dad, I've seen those psychos at the hospital. They sit around talking to themselves, drooling on their shirts. And I'll tell you how that happens. I saw it in combat, lots of times. It

happens when you let go. A guy can put up with an awful lot, if
he just keeps hanging on, but all you have to do is give into it,
and then you're crazy. I'm not going to let that happen to me. I
can't let Anna down. Or Gene."

Alex was telling himself to stay calm, not to think about
this. He just needed to end the conversation, get to the plant,
bury himself in his work.

"Could you talk to Wally or maybe Richard—someone
who's been there? I'd like to help you, but I don't know how."

Alex could feel his hands shaking now, and he knew he was
on the edge. For so long he had been keeping everything con-
tained. He didn't need this kind of talk. He just needed to get
going, to get busy. "I've got to go, Dad," he managed to say. "I'll
be fine. Don't worry about me." He got up, but his head was
suddenly dizzy. He breathed, reminded himself to get lots of
air, pull it deep into his lungs.

"Alex, I'm worried to death about you. I don't think you
ought to drive right now. Couldn't I just take you over to the
hospital? What could it hurt to talk to someone for a little
while?"

"I've talked." He walked to the door. "I'm really all right,
Dad. Don't worry about me. Every time I get another day
behind me, I'm a little better off. I just need more time to pass,
so I'll forget."

"But you're not getting anywhere that way. Why not—"

But Alex left. He walked down the hallway and then downstairs. He sensed that Dad was following him, was watching,
but he kept going, and he got into his car and started it. He
would be fine. It was just a matter of getting his breath, of
calming down, going to work, and doing his job. He had been
to this point hundreds of times before, and he had always made
it through. He would keep getting through until he finally won
the battle, and all this nervousness, or whatever it was, finally
passed away. But he wasn't going to talk to anyone again; that
only made things worse.

* * *

Peter was out on the loading dock. A truck was backing in, and Peter, with a stack of boxes on a hand truck, was waiting to start loading. Richard had hired a couple of new guys and they were waiting too. The truck needed to be loaded before quitting time that afternoon so the driver could get on the road. The parts would make it on time, to a factory in Illinois, but only if the trucker got a good start on the trip that evening.

When the truck edged close enough to the dock, Peter signaled, and the driver shut the truck down, then hopped from the cab. "Before you start loading, let me see the paperwork, will you?" he said.

Peter struggled with some of the accents of these truckers, but this guy was not hard to understand. "Yes, yes. I'll bring it. Just one minute." He turned and walked toward the office. As he passed the other workers, Monte and Ross, he said, "A moment. I bring the paper. We must not load now."

Peter had almost reached the door to the office when he heard Monte's rough voice. "I brink za paper. We not load now." And then both men laughed.

Peter was taken by surprise. He had rather liked these two. They hadn't seemed bothered when Richard had asked Peter to teach them their duties, even though he was considerably younger. Peter had heard Monte say that he had fought in France, had been sent in as a replacement, after D-Day, and had been wounded in Normandy, but to Peter's relief, neither man had asked about his own background.

Peter decided to let it go. He could understand that his accent might sound funny to these men. Germans might do the same thing with an American learning their language. It wouldn't do any good to challenge them on something like that. But he felt an old sadness, one that had often returned to him since he had come to the States.

Peter got the paperwork he needed and headed back to the dock. But he didn't speak this time. He merely handed the papers to the truck driver, and then, when everything seemed to be in order, he rolled the first stack of boxes onto the truck. Monte and Ross clearly took that as a signal, and they went to work. For quite some time no one said anything. There were lots of boxes, a lot of work to do before five o'clock, and all three of the men kept a steady pace, passing each other as they walked back and forth.

At least an hour passed before Ross yelled to Peter, as they passed by each other, "Hey, do we get a break sometime? I need a cigarette, bad."

"Yes. It's good," Peter said. He continued into the back of the truck with his load, stacked the boxes, and then left his hand truck on the dock and walked inside. It was October now, but quite warm, and Peter had been sweating hard. He wanted a drink of water. When he walked back out to the dock, he saw Richard. Monte and Ross were sitting on the stairs at the end of the dock, and Richard was looking down at them. They had been talking, but they stopped as Peter approached. "Can you get this done by quitting time?" Richard asked Peter.

"Yes. We will." He wanted to explain the break, that the men had asked to stop for a smoke, but he didn't want to use that much English in front of Monte, not now.

Monte stood up, leaned against the metal railing on the stairs, and took a last puff on his cigarette. He was a big man, with fists the size of cobblestones, and a massive, round head. He tossed the cigarette away without crushing it. "Say, Mr. Hammond, I need to know one thing. Is Peter our boss or what?"

"No. He works on the dock and in the packing room, the same as you guys."

"Well, he's the one telling us what to do around here."

"I told him to teach you what we do. But he's not your boss. Marlin is. You know that."

"So where's Marlin?"

"He's keeping things going inside, in the packing room. I don't see what you're getting at."

"Well, my only point is, if Marlin sends us out here to load a truck, ain't no one in charge. We're just three guys loading a truck. Ain't that right."

"Yes."

"Fine. Just so we know."

There was something ugly in Monte's raspy voice, and Peter felt the challenge. Richard clearly heard it too. He stepped a little closer to the top of the stairs and looked down on Monte. "There's no reason to worry about who the boss is. Just work together and get the job done."

"That's fine. But tell him that. It ain't his decision when we have a smoke, or take a break, or anything like that. Not the way I understand it."

"Ross ask me," Peter said. "I tell him yes. That's all."

"Well maybe *zats* all, but from now on, we ain't going to ask."

"Hey, come on, Monte, don't start trouble," Richard said. "If you don't like this job, there are plenty of guys who'd like to have it. Peter knows what's going on around here, knows the paperwork and all that. I don't see what you're worried about."

"Hey," Monte said, and he grinned, "I ain't got no grief with nobody. I just wondered who my boss was."

Ross was smiling too. He was a smaller man, but tighter. He had rolled up the sleeves on his gray work shirt, showing his thick forearms and a "Semper Fi" tattoo. He gave his cigarette a toss and then looked at Peter with his head cocked back defiantly, as if to say, "We took care of you, didn't we?" Peter suspected that things would only get worse with these two.

But a couple of weeks went by and Peter didn't have any problems with Monte or Ross. Neither one was friendly, but they stayed mostly together and said almost nothing to Peter. The three worked in the same room most of the time, with other men around. They packed boxes, loaded trucks, and simply went about their business. But one day the three, along with a man named Ken Schmidt, ended up loading another truck together.

Monte and Ross were actually fairly hard workers, but they did like their cigarette breaks. The two of them had stopped for a smoke at one point that day even though Ken and Peter had kept on loading. Later, when they took a second break, Monte yelled to Ken, "Hey, come on. Stop a minute. Take a rest."

Ken stopped and wiped his forehead with his sleeve. "I don't smoke," he said.

"That's all right. Take a break." He looked at Peter, whose path to the truck was blocked by the men. "Come on, kid. Lay off for a minute. We don't have to kill ourselves." Then he grinned. "I'll be the boss today."

That was fair enough. Peter nodded and lifted his hand truck until it was resting on the dock. Then he stood next to it, hardly knowing what to do. "Schmidt, are you a German, like ol' Peter here?" Monte asked.

"Way back, I am," Ken said. He was a short fellow, rather slight. He would often work all day without saying more than a few words. Peter had never really gotten to know him, but he had wondered the same thing about his German heritage.

"So you can't speak any of Peter's lingo, huh?"

"Nope."

"*Nein?*" Ross asked. And then he broke up laughing, as though he had made a marvelous joke.

"Hey, Peter, speak a little German. Let us hear some of that."

Peter tried to smile. But he shook his head. He didn't know where this was heading, but he wasn't going to play any of Monte's games.

"How come they call you guys krauts?" Monte asked. "What's the meaning behind that word?" He was leaning on his hand truck, his shoulders hunched forward, and Peter could see in his steady eyes that this was a challenge, the beginning of something.

Ross was laughing.

Peter didn't answer. He turned to walk away. He had decided to go inside for a drink of water.

"Do you really like that sauerkraut stuff, Peter?" Monte asked. "It tastes like something gone bad to me. I can't eat it." He cursed.

"Lay off, Monte," Ken said, quietly, but Monte continued to laugh.

Peter turned back around. "Yes, I like it," he said, defiantly.

"Yeah. I thought maybe you would." Monte turned to Ross. "I probably told you, I killed a lot of krauts over in France."

"Yup. You did mention that."

"Did you know that when their bodies have been out there on the ground a few days, Germans smell just like sauerkraut?"

"No, I didn't know that," Ross said. He was looking at Peter, not Monte, and he was grinning, showing a missing tooth on one side.

"Well, they do. They have that same sour *stink*. I think that's how that got started, calling them krauts." He looked back at Peter. "Do you think that's how that happened?"

"Okay. That's enough," Ken said, with surprising force this time.

Peter turned and walked away again. He was halfway up the dock when Monte called out, "Hey, *Peter*, don't let me get you upset. I don't have nothing against you. The only kraut I hate is that Nazi kid who shot me through the leg." Peter kept going. He was almost to the door when Monte yelled, "I can see you know how to run away. That's what we taught you krauts to do during the war."

Peter stopped. He stood for a time, trying to think what he wanted to do. And then he turned and walked toward Monte. He had no idea what he was going to do when he got there, but he wasn't taking any more of this. He walked straight at

Monte's grin. He heard Ross laughing and Ken saying, "Don't start anything, boys," but he kept on. He didn't put his hands up, didn't double up his fists. He merely strode toward Monte until he was about to walk right into him, and it was then that Monte's big fist shot out and caught Peter flat in the forehead.

Peter fell backward, landing on his backside. Then he stood up, faced Monte, and stepped toward him, and Monte took another shot. This one hurt more, smashed his nose. He felt the blood spurt, felt the pain through his cheekbones and forehead. He stumbled back but stayed on his feet, caught his balance and stepped forward again. But now Ken was in the way. "No more," he was yelling.

Peter would have taken a hundred punches. He just wasn't going to raise his own fists. But it was Monte who was retreating now, saying, "Hey, he came at me. I was just joking with him a little. I didn't mean nothing by any of that."

And Ross kept saying, "He came after you. What could you do?"

Someone was running from the office by then, the fellow who processed the paperwork inside. He grabbed hold of Peter and yelled to Ken, "Get Mr. Hammond."

Ken ran inside, but by the time Richard reached the dock, a woman from the office had already come out with a wet towel. She had begun to wipe off Peter's face. "Take him inside," Richard said. But Peter was going to leave. He had quit his job—quit it in his mind. He would take a bus home, or maybe walk, but he was leaving, going back to Germany.

He took the towel with him and walked inside, but he kept going, on through the building and out the front door. Richard caught up with him in the parking lot and told him that he had fired those guys, both of them, and then he got Peter into his car and drove him home. And all the way he kept saying things that Peter already knew: that some guys were like that in any country; that Peter shouldn't let it bother him; that most people at the plant thought the world of him. Peter didn't say a word, didn't want to speak with his German accent, didn't want to discuss any of this.

At home, only his mother was there. Peter was still holding the towel to his face, and when she saw the blood, she hurried to him. "What's happened?" she asked, in German.

Richard told her, "A big guy down at the plant, one of these guys who can't forget the war, took into him. We fired the guy, him and his friend. It won't happen again."

But Peter looked at his mother. "It *won't* happen again. I'm going back to Germany."

"Oh, no, Peter. Don't say that," his mother pleaded.

"It's not what that stupid man did," he said in German. "It's not any of that. I just can't stay here. I don't belong."

Peter went to his room, and after a time he heard the door shut and knew that Richard had gone. His mother knocked soon after that. "Peter, let me look at you," she said. "Is your nose broken?"

"No. I'm fine. Just let me rest."

"All right. For now. But when your father comes home, I want to take you to a doctor."

"It won't be necessary."

He lay on his bed and looked at the ceiling. He tried to think how he could manage everything, how he could pay for a trip to Germany.

It was perhaps an hour later that his father came home. Peter knew he had left work early because of what had happened. He came to the door and knocked, and then opened the door. "Let me look at your nose, Peter," he said. "Richard said you might need to see a doctor."

"It's fine."

His father came in and sat down on the bed next to him. "It's swollen," he said, and he looked at it from several angles. "How badly does it hurt?"

"It doesn't hurt much."

"What happened?"

"That man—Monte—insulted me because I was a German."

"Ken told me that you didn't defend yourself, that you let him hit you. Why?"

"I don't know." Peter looked away. But after a time, he added, "He said that in the war Germans only learned how to run away."

"Oh, Peter. What a silly thing to listen to. How could you do this?"

Peter didn't answer. He looked at his father, who had aged so much in the past few years. His hair was gray now. His eyes looked tired. "How did all this happen?" Peter asked.

"What?"

"All this? Everything. We were happy in Frankfurt, and then everything went wrong. I want to go back and have my life. I never got it."

"I know," Papa said. He nodded, looking so solemn that Peter wished he hadn't said it.

"I'm going back to Germany," Peter said. "As soon as I can."

"But Peter, we have good jobs here, this nice house."

"It doesn't matter."

"We're together. If you go back, we may never see you again. That would be too much for your mother."

"Papa, how can you stay? We're not ourselves here."

His father nodded. "I know what you're saying, Peter. I miss my language. I miss our country. I miss our way of living. But it can't be helped. Anna will be here, our grandchildren. We can't leave them."

"I want to live in Germany and have grandchildren for you there."

"Oh, Peter, don't do this to us. Don't divide us that way."

Peter didn't want the separation either. He had been the one separated from the others during all those nightmarish months he had been at war. But he couldn't stay. He would go back to work at the plant long enough to earn the money he needed, but he just couldn't stay. "We'll see each other. I'll come back someday, for a visit. But I have nothing here—not one thing to look forward to."

"Is it Katrina? Is that what you have in Germany?"

"Yes. That's one thing."

"Then bring her here."

"No. I'm the enemy. I chose Germany when I chose the army. I didn't know it then, but I know it now."

Papa didn't tell him no again; he only sat on the edge of the bed and cried. And then his mother came in and knew what this meant, and she cried too.

* * *

Katrina had a job now. She worked for the British, the same as her mother. Her English was not as good, but language skills were not required. She worked every evening, late into the night, cleaning offices, scrubbing sinks and toilets, washing uniforms. She didn't mind the work; she only hated the routine of her life, the boredom. What she lived for were the letters that came once or twice a week, from Peter.

She got home very late each night and slept long into the day; then she had only the evening of work to look forward to again. And so she got up each day hoping that mail had come, that Peter might say a little more than he usually did in his noncommittal letters. When she got up this November day, she found a letter on the kitchen table, where Frau Heiner always left them. She sat down and opened it carefully, slowly, wanting to savor this time—always the best of her life. She read:

Dear Katrina,

I have decided. I'm coming home to Germany. But I don't know when. I have to earn the money to travel, and I have to save enough to live for a time. I don't know how I can do all this, but I have decided, and nothing will change my mind now. I'm coming back.

Katrina, you owe nothing to me. But when I get to Germany, I will come straight to you, and then we can talk about everything. I don't know how I can make a living. I have no idea how I could marry now, with no job, no future. But if I come to you, can we talk about all these things— maybe think of a way we can manage? Do you still want to think about me that way? If you do, please write back and tell me. I need something more in my life. I want you.

Love,
Peter

Katrina was more relieved than ecstatic, and she felt the reality of his concern. She didn't know how they would manage. But she got out her paper—her dear, costly paper—and she wrote:

Dear Peter,

Please don't wait. Come now. We'll find a way. I love you. Write again, and please say those words to me, finally, once.

She could think of nothing else to add, so she merely signed the letter and sent it.

blouse. LaRue seemed thankful for those, but it was the type-writer that got all her attention. She was learning touch-typing in school this year, and as far as Al could tell, she was already quite proficient. She rolled in a sheet of paper and tapped out some sentences, quickly and cleanly, without even looking at her fingers. He had typed for many years, but always with two fingers and always looking at the keys.

Al was baffled by LaRue these days. He could understand Beverly running upstairs to try on her new "outfits" and then bouncing back down to show everyone. In years past he had watched Bobbi do that, and then LaRue. He had always worried a little that the girls' love of clothing was too materialistic, too extravagant, but now he wished he could see at least a little of that girlish behavior left in LaRue. When she got something into her head, she rarely let it go, and she was still insisting that she was going away to college next fall. All the schools she talked about were in the east, and to Al it was almost as though she were saying that she wanted to go off and join another church. He had heard far too many stories about Mormon kids who had gone away from home for their education. Al was not even sure it was such a good idea to send kids all the way down to Provo, to the BYU, not when the University was practically around the corner, and a son or daughter could live at home where parents could still monitor the things they were taught by some of these young and rather too ardent professors.

Al was still fairly convinced that LaRue would back out when it actually came down to leaving her home at age eighteen, but he told himself not to bring it up, not to say anything that would ruin the day. He knew he had done that too many times in the past. But it was not easy for him to listen to her prattle on, describing her life at college and the great value of a student's having her very own typewriter. The talk only made the gray, cold morning seem longer, and as it turned out, even nine o'clock had been too ambitious a goal. Richard and Bobbi arrived shortly after nine, and Alex and Anna, with Gene, just a

few minutes later, but it was after nine-thirty before Wally and
Lorraine showed up. Al was watching from the big window in
the living room by then. A sprinkle of rain had begun to fall.
He saw Wally park out front, by the curb, and then get out and
hurry around the car. He had on his overcoat but no hat, no
gloves. Al couldn't believe that so many young men had begun
to run around that way, even in the very heart of winter. Wally
opened the car door for Lorraine, and then he reached in and
took the bundle from her arms—the pink blanket. He held the
baby in one arm and helped Lorraine from the car with
the other. Al could see the steam burst from Lorraine's lips as
she made the effort to step out of the car. The baby was three
weeks old now, and Lorraine was doing very well, Al was told,
but she looked flushed and still rather puffy in the cheeks.

A memory crossed Al's mind. He thought of the year that
little Alex had been born. He and Bea had been living in a tiny
house on the west side of town, and Bea had decorated for
Christmas as best she could. Al had bought a tree—a scrawny
thing that cost him seventy-five cents—and Bea had bought a
set of glass balls at a five-and-dime store—that, and a single
package of icicles. Al's mother had tried to get Bea to take some
of her old decorations, but Bea hadn't wanted to do that. "We
need to start our own traditions," she had said. Al hadn't
thought much about that at the time, but he had noticed those
clear glass balls this morning, and he knew that for nearly
thirty years now, Bea had been carefully packing them away
and protecting them. He suddenly felt a little guilty that he
had been impatient all morning. These married kids of his did
need to start something of their own, however left out it made
him feel.

"Wally and Lorraine are here," he called out to anyone who
could hear.

"You mean *Kathy*," Beverly shouted, and she ran for the
door.

But that was something Al didn't understand either. The

baby's name was Kathleen Beatrice, which was very nice, but everyone was calling her Kathy already, and Al was not aware of a Kathy—or a Kathleen, for that matter—in all their family line. Wally and Lorraine both said it was just a name they liked, but Al really thought that names ought to come from somewhere, not just pop out of parents' heads. Catherine would have been better; his mother's sister was named Catherine. But he did like to call the baby "Little Bea," since that name had some rhyme and reason to it.

All the same, he loved this little girl. When Beverly took her from Wally at the door and promptly ran off to the couch with her, everyone crowded around: Bea and Bobbi, LaRue, even Richard and Alex. Beverly carefully moved the blanket away from her face, and all the adults laughed. "Oh, what a big yawn," Bea said. "Let me take her, Bev."

"No. Not yet. She wants to say good morning to her Aunt Beverly."

"She wants to sleep," Wally said. "She loves to sleep all day and then stay awake half the night. It's her way of telling us that she's going to do things her own way—whether we like it or not."

"Good for her," Bea said. "Wally's going to get just what he deserves."

Little Gene had slipped between the legs of the adults, and suddenly there he was, reaching for Kathy's face, only intending to pat her cheeks, apparently, but causing Beverly to jerk in response.

"No, no. Don't touch the baby," Anna said.

But Kathy's eyes came open, and this caused new oohs and ahs.

"Baby," Gene said, and he turned his head and bent forward to touch his cheek to hers.

Al didn't want to overwhelm the poor little girl with so many people staring at her, breathing on her, but he did want a better look, and so he walked to the end of the couch and watched from a bit of distance. He would have his turn before long, he told himself. He knew he had never been all that wonderful with newborns. They scared him a little. But he told himself he was going to be a very good grandpa to this little girl, the way he was trying to be to Gene. He and Bea had finally agreed to break ground on their new house in the spring, and Al had already decided he would hold out a few acres from the area they were developing around it, and he would build a little barn. He had never told anyone, but he thought it would be fun to keep a pony or two for the grandchildren to ride. He liked to think of having all his kids close around—and all their kids. Everyone could gather at his place on holidays and weekends. The children could sleigh ride off the hillside in winter, or maybe skate on the pond that he also liked to imagine. He would plant the pond with trout, and in the summer he would take the kids out there, maybe even on a little boat, and they could catch fish with him. He had gone fishing with his grandfather, but it wasn't something he had done very often with his own kids. The family had fished on vacation now and then, especially on their trips to Yellowstone Park, but somehow life had gotten too busy, and he had never done as much with his kids as he had always intended.

Al was going to be better at this grandpa business than he had been at fatherhood. That was a promise he had made to himself. And some day little Bea would sit on a pony, and he would hold her up there on a little saddle, and he would lead her about the pasture. And then he would teach her to ride on her own. She and Gene, cousins—they would have a great time together, and Gene would look out for her, being older.

That was what he was thinking, and yet, almost in spite of himself, he found himself saying, "We'd better start opening these presents or the day will be over. The rest of the family is coming over this afternoon, you know."

"Oh, Dad, we've got time," Bobbi said, and she came over

and kissed him on the cheek. "We've even got time to hear you give us a speech."

"Oh, no. No meeting this year," Al said. "Let's just enjoy ourselves."

And he meant it. He had said enough to this family over the years—too much, actually. He didn't want to be teased about that again this year. He was sure that some of the resentment ran a little deeper than the jokes they all made about him. Besides, he had spent so much money on Christmas presents this year, he knew he would be nothing but a hypocrite if he brought up his concerns—although he still had them—about Christmas being too commercialized. The fact was, people were going crazy now buying for Christmas, and some of the holiday advertising had started clear back at Thanksgiving time. The whole thing was an annoyance to him, the way the radio ads blared out little jingles and songs, all to sell six-shooters at Woolworth's or dolls that wet their pants, down at the Emporium. Still, Al had gone out and bought gifts for everyone, and way too many things for the babies. So he was going to keep his mouth shut this year, and he had even told himself that he would laugh a little more, enter into the fun, the way Bea always did.

The opening of presents lasted over an hour, with everyone taking turns and showing off their gifts. Beverly balked when her gift was a box of panties, but her brothers invoked the family rule and made her show off her pretty things. Beverly turned red, but she held up the open box and said, "You naughty boys. You shouldn't look."

Wally was chanting, "I see London; I see France; I see someone's underpants."

There were lots of gifts. Al had bought Bea a double necklace of real pearls that he had paid more than two hundred dollars for. It was something she had always wanted, and he had enjoyed getting them for her—even though he had never really understood the idea of jewelry. Even as he had purchased

them, he had asked himself what good they were. They were
certainly pretty, but to hang something around your neck, just
for the decoration, had never made sense to him. He thought
too often of the scriptures: women in the last days adorning
themselves with "fine apparel," with rings and jewels. But he
loved to see Bea so pleased and so certain that he shouldn't
have spent so much. He even liked his daughters' praise. "Oh,
Daddy," Bobbi told him, "what a perfect gift. You're so *extravagant* these days."

He liked the word and hated it at the same time. He
wanted to give. He just didn't want to get the wrong idea
started in his family: that the kids should spend more than they
had, that they would perhaps not remember to *save* for nice
things. He made a point of telling Bobbi that he had never
once gone into debt for Christmas the way some silly people
were doing these days.

In the middle of all the talk and laughter and general confusion, Gene was having a grand time. He had gotten some
sort of toy from everyone in the family, and he seemed perplexed by all the little trucks and trains and toy horses, as
though overwhelmed by the choices. What he liked more than
the toys were the boxes and the wrapping paper. He would
open a present as if the tearing of paper were the real joy, and
as often as not, he would drop the toy and begin to play with
the box. He was a year and a half old now, and very tall for his
age. What Al could see was that he loved being among all
his uncles and aunts, his family. He had grown comfortable
with everyone, and he liked all the attention. All the same, he
seemed to sense at times that he was being forgotten in the
midst of all the fun, and he would run to the tree and grab one
of the decorations, or he would toss wrapping paper at
someone—things he seemed to know would bring about a rep-
rimand. Then he would laugh and look about, as though he
were daring someone to follow up on the little warnings.

When Gene opened a box and found a wooden train—a

gift from Al and Bea, but in reality purchased by Al—he didn't understand how it hooked together. "Bring it here," Al told him. "Let me show you."

Gene didn't respond. He ran the engine across the carpet, unconcerned with the other cars. So Al knelt on the floor next to him and said, "Look how it hooks up. Grandpa's going to show you."

He attached the little hooks, the five cars lining up behind the engine, a caboose on the back. And then Al pulled the engine along, tugging the cars after it. Gene laughed at that, but he wanted to do it himself, and when he turned the engine too sharply, the first car—a coal car—came loose. Gene was content to go ahead without the rest of the train, but Grandpa stopped him, linked the cars up again, and then said, "Choo, choo, choo—toot, toot. Here comes the train."

Gene laughed and tried to make the sound. "Toot, toot." And then he pulled the engine too fast and the cars fell over on their sides. Al set them right and told Gene to go more slowly, and the two started out again. "Choo, choo. Toot, toot, toot."

Finally Al realized that the room had fallen silent. He looked up and saw that everyone was smiling, that they were all watching him, and he was embarrassed by what he knew they were thinking: Is this *President* Thomas? He rather liked that, and he looked about at everyone without saying anything but smiling back.

LaRue said, "Dad, I've never seen you do anything like that in my entire life," and that stung a little.

But Alex said, "I have. We used to play on the floor together when I was little. I remember that."

And Wally said, "Me too."

It was such a little thing, but the memory—or the fact that *they* remembered—touched Al, reminded him of the young man he had once been. He wasn't so different, really, hadn't changed as much as everyone thought. But he had given the wrong impression at times, had maybe taken himself a little too seriously for some of the years of his life, and he was sorry about that.

Eventually Mom made her usual claim that everyone ought to have breakfast, late as it was, and she cooked up eggs and bacon. Some of the family ate in the kitchen, some at the dining-room table, and Bea liked what was happening. She loved to watch the way Bobbi and Anna and Lorraine ended up together, talking about babies and their new homes, but also about the world. They were all girls who read the newspaper, read books, had things they wanted to think about and share with their "sisters." And Bea liked the way LaRue joined in, had perhaps stronger opinions on some issues, but seemed to like sharing her ideas with the married women. She liked even better what Al was doing. He argued that he had eaten plenty earlier, and he just wanted to hold "Kathleen Beatrice." Bea found him, after she had served everyone, sitting in his big chair holding the sleeping baby, looking down on her and seeming quite content.

"All right, everyone," Bea said as loudly as she dared without startling the baby, "Al said he's not holding a meeting this year, so I've decided to conduct one myself." This got a good laugh, and it brought the "girls" from the kitchen, but no one seemed to take the idea seriously, so Bea had to say, rather forcefully, "I mean it. I want to have a meeting. I'm in charge. So sit down and quit your gabbing for a few minutes."

All the family managed to find places to sit. Richard and Wally gathered some chairs from the dining-room table and placed them near the opening between the dining room and living room. They let the wives take those seats, and the younger girls and some of the men sat on the floor. Gene was starting to get tired, and his mother took him onto her lap, but he soon squirmed away and went to his Aunt LaRue, who was sitting on the floor. She seemed more than pleased to hold him.

Bea was standing up in the living room, next to Al's chair.

Al was still holding the baby. "I'm sorry to say," Bea announced, "that your father, in his weary old age, has become less than diligent about keeping one of our family traditions. If he won't talk to us on Christmas day, then I guess I'll have to do it myself."

"Dad doesn't think it's Christmas," Wally said. "He had his Christmas in November."

Al grinned. "That's right," he said. And it had been a great year for Republicans. The '46 elections had been a landslide, both nationally and in Utah, with the power in the state legislature actually reversing.

"Wally knows Dad's talk," Bobbi said. "He could give it."

"No. I tried that once, a long time ago, and it didn't go over very well."

Bea remembered that Christmas, of course, but not with fondness, and she wasn't even comfortable joking about the days when tensions had been so high. "It's time for a new talk," she said. "After buying me pearls this year, your dad can never talk about spending too much money again."

Al laughed, and he nodded his head as if he agreed with her.

"Here's what I want to say." She looked around at everyone, motioned with her hand. "This, right here, is what we've all been dreaming about for seven years. And now that we have it, we need to pause just long enough to notice, so we won't forget how blessed we are."

Bea meant it. She was afraid that this day could pass, and everyone would be funny, even flippant, and never stop to think about the day and what it meant. But already she could see in her children's faces that they did understand, that they were ready to pause and take notice.

"The last time our family was all together on Christmas was in 1939—seven years ago. And since then, most of our Christmas Days have been sad and full of worry. On three of those Christmases we didn't know for sure whether Wally was alive, and in those same years we had to wonder whether Alex and Bobbi would be safe. We worried about Anna and her family, too, and then later about Richard. The worst was 1944, two years ago, when we had buried Gene and everyone else was in so much danger. I remember how the four of us here at home pleaded with the Lord that this day would come—that we'd all have a Christmas together again." She could see that everyone was remembering.

"That was the worst year of all," Anna whispered, glancing toward Alex.

"I want you all to tell me where you were that year," Bea said. "And what you were doing. What you were thinking about—and what you were hoping for. Bobbi, you start. And then let's go around the circle and say what we remember."

Bobbi nodded. Richard was sitting next to her, on the floor. She reached to touch his shoulder. "I had to work part of the day at the hospital, at Pearl Harbor, " she said. "And then I went to Ishi Aoki's house for dinner. Richard was at sea, and the last I had known he was safe, but I hadn't heard from him for a while. Ishi's husband, Daniel, was fighting in Italy, and he was in danger every day. So the four of us, Ishi and I and her two little children, spent the evening together." Bea saw Bobbi's eyes go shut. "It was a scary time. We made the best of it, but we were worried. I read in the papers about Alex's division in Bastogne, so I was terrified for him, and I was worried about Wally. It was a very hard day. I don't like to remember it, even now. But I remember I prayed all day—just little short prayers in my mind, over and over."

Richard hadn't looked at Bobbi. He was staring at the floor. But when Bea spoke his name, he said, "I was at sea—like Bobbi said. We had seen some action, but that day was quiet. We ate a nice dinner and relaxed a little, but everyone knew the hard days were still ahead. We were moving closer to Japan all the time. The truth is, it didn't seem very likely that I would get home. No one on our ship ever said that, but I knew we all felt that way."

"Did you pray that day that you *would* get home?" Bea asked him.

"Sure. I prayed every day about that."

Alex was sitting next to Richard. Mom looked at him and nodded. "Well," he said, softly, hesitantly, "that *was* the worst year. That Christmas Eve and Christmas Day, in Bastogne, were two of the worst days I can remember."

"We know that, Alex," Mom said. "But you've never really said much about it. What was going on?"

Bea saw Alex take one of his long breaths, the way he seemed to do so often anymore. "It was cold. Really cold. I thought I would never get warm again. We were in foxholes—two guys to a hole—and I was with a kid from Idaho named Howie Douglas. We made it through those nights by . . . I don't know . . . it's not something that's easy to talk about. We huddled up together like little puppies." He stopped for a moment. "Some guy started singing Christmas songs, and it almost killed us."

Alex took another breath and everyone waited. "We got through. That's all I can say. But then Howie got killed a few days later."

Bea hadn't known that. She knew about the cold, had even heard Alex mention Howie, but she didn't know about his being killed.

"Right after that, we got inside for a couple of nights. That's when my mail caught up to me, and I found out that Anna was expecting. That brought me back to life a little."

Bea kept watching Alex. She thought it was a good sign that he would talk about this, but she didn't like the way he was gripping his fingers together, squeezing so hard. "Alex," she said, "did you try to imagine this day, back then?"

"Not that much. I thought about Anna, in England, more than anything. I wanted to get back to her. But something like this seemed impossible. It just seemed like, sooner or later, we were all going to die. After Howie got hit, my friend Duncan took a bullet in the throat. I didn't know if he was alive or not. We'd been together from the beginning, and after he got knocked out, it just seemed like it was my turn."

Everyone in the room knew what it was costing Alex just to say this much. The silence seemed almost sacred.

Bobbi finally said, "Alex, are you okay now? We all worry so much about you, still."

It was a surprisingly open question, and simple, but Bea didn't like Alex's response. He looked at the floor. "I'm trying," he said.

"Are you still having bad dreams?"

He didn't answer, but Anna did. "Not as often, I don't think. But I still have to be careful about walking up behind him and touching him. He's almost knocked me down a couple of times."

"I'm doing all right," Alex said, not very convincingly. He didn't look all right. But Alex seemed to sense that that was what everyone was thinking. "It's been good to be back in college," he said. "I feel like I'm moving forward now." He glanced around, as though to reassure his family, but Bea didn't see his eyes focus on anyone.

"Anna," Bea said, "what do you remember from that Christmas?"

"I was pregnant, and sick, a little." She glanced at Alex and smiled, asking a question with a little nod of her head. He nodded back. "Just like I am again now," she said, and she let herself laugh.

"Oh, Anna, really?"

"Yes. We're expecting another baby."

Beverly let out a little screech, and then a whoop, and everyone laughed. "I'll tend the baby any time you want. And Gene too," she said. "I'm a very good aunt."

Anna reached to her and patted her hand. "Don't worry. We'll let you do that all you want."

Bea leaned down and whispered to Al, "Things just keep getting better and better for us."

He looked up from the baby, who was still asleep. "I know. But I always want more," he said. "I'm a greedy man."

"When is the baby due?" Bobbi wanted to know.

"In July—maybe for the twenty-fourth."

Gene slipped off Aunt LaRue's lap and walked to his mother. He climbed onto her lap and snuggled up against her, almost as though he understood this conversation and sensed a rival. But he looked tired now, his little eyelids seeming heavy.

"Oh, Anna, that's such wonderful news," Bea said, and from around the room, everyone was voicing their congratulations.

Lorraine took hold of Anna's hand. "That's so good," she said. "Gene needs a little brother or sister."

By then Bea had picked up on something else. Bobbi had turned to Richard and was whispering something in his ear.

Richard laughed and then said, loud enough for everyone to hear, "You're the one who wanted to wait a while before you told everyone."

"Oh, Bobbi, what?" Bea asked. "You too?"

"Yes. But not that soon. I'm just starting out. I shouldn't really say anything so early."

Beverly jumped up from the floor, ran to Bobbi, and grabbed her around the neck. "I'll tend your baby, too," she said. "Every night, if you want."

Bea was thrilled. She waited her turn, hugged her daughter, and felt a kind of kinship she didn't know how to express. She knew what a lifetime of change was coming for Bobbi, the little girl she had raised. For all Bea's joy, there was a sense of awe, even a touch of something like sorrow, that the cycle would now repeat itself, and Bobbi would take on this new responsibility—never be simply Bobbi again.

Somewhere in the middle of all the noise, LaRue said, "Well, I might as well break the news. I'm pregnant too." But only LaRue seemed to think that was funny.

Al said, "LaRue, don't joke about something like that."

But Bea saw more than a joke. LaRue certainly had to be saying, "Notice, everyone. I'm not the same as the rest of you. I'm the one who *doesn't* want to be a mother. I'm going a different direction." And the idea frightened Bea much more than Bobbi's new condition.

"I've been sick too," Bobbi was admitting. "I feel all right this morning, but yesterday I lost my breakfast and felt pretty sick all day."

For a time, all the talk was about morning sickness, about the births in the summer, but finally Anna said, "I think I got us on the wrong subject."

"That's all right. We liked the news," Bea said. "But do tell us about your Christmas that year."

"What I remember was that my father was in Germany, and we got word that he was alive. But we were very worried about him, and we had no idea where Peter was. He told us, later, that he was in a bombed-out building, in East Prussia, I think, and someone told him it was Christmas. He was so sick and so cold that he couldn't even think about it. He was expecting to die any day. But Mama and I, we prayed so hard that day—for Alex and Papa and Peter. I think the Lord had mercy on us."

"Think how much we all prayed that day," Bea said. "That's really what I want you all to remember. Where were you that day, Lorraine?"

"I was here in Salt Lake, and I came to see you that day. I wanted to know about Wally. I wanted him to come home— to you—and I told myself that's all I was praying for. But I wanted him for me, too, whether I said it in my prayers or not."

"And Wally, what did you pray for that day?" Bea asked.

"I worked in the mine that day—all day. I was in fairly good health right then, and I figured I could hang on for a while. But every Christmas we'd say that we'd be home by the next Christmas, and I remember feeling that day that I just couldn't hold out for another year. I'm glad I didn't have to. I went through some really bad times after that."

"Did you think about being here with everyone?"

"That's what POWs do for Christmas. We'd eat Christmas dinner—in our minds—and we'd live out the whole day at home, from memory. What I always wanted was everything that's here right now. Good food. All of us together. But a day like this always seemed too good to be true—like some dream that you didn't quite believe in anymore."

"Did you pray?"

"Oh, yes. I prayed." He laughed. "I also gave someone a present that day."

"Who?"

"Our guard, down in the mine." He laughed again. "Those guards loved to get a lot of work done. The more we accomplished, the more their superiors liked them. So that day, for a gift, I worked during the lunch break."

"You skipped lunch?"

"Well, not exactly. We would eat all our food in the morning so that we'd have enough energy to keep us going. So at noon there was nothing to eat. What I skipped was my resting time."

"Weren't you exhausted at the end of the day?"

"I was always exhausted. But I liked what I did. The guard didn't understand. He probably thought I was nuts. But I just liked the idea of giving someone something. That way, I felt like it was Christmas."

"I'm glad you told that, Wally," Bea said. "That's our Christmas speech. That says everything we need to say."

"What did you do here at home that day?" Wally asked.

"It was a quiet day," Bea said. "Kids, what do you remember?"

Beverly said, "When all the Thomases came over, they

were talking about Bastogne, and about Alex being surrounded. I didn't know about that until then. So I asked Dad about it, and I wanted Dad to say that everything would be all right. But he told me he didn't know for sure, because things looked pretty bad over there. I felt grown up because he would admit that to me, but I was scared. That whole day, I just remember being scared."

LaRue said, "I remember that Dad and I had a good talk. I'd been really mad at him, but he talked to me that day, and he listened to me, and I sort of even liked him a little—just not very much."

Al nodded. "Yes, I do remember that. But I'm like Beverly. What I remember more than anything was feeling that one of my sons was gone, and the other two were in mortal danger. And my daughter wasn't exactly safe. I remember feeling that if I lost everyone, I just couldn't deal with it, no matter how strong I had always tried to be. I kept thinking about my great-grandfather who lost his entire family, and I didn't want to find out whether I was as strong as he had been."

"That's how I was, too," Bea said. "And so we had a family prayer, and we asked for this day—a Christmas when we'd all be together. And we got more than we asked for. We couldn't have imagined that Lorraine would be part of us, and Anna would be here, with a grandson, and Bobbi and Richard together—and more babies on the way."

Bea had not wanted to cry, and she was fighting hard to smile now. "I just think we need to remember how hard we prayed, and stop and say to ourselves, 'We got what we asked for, and more.' We just can't forget to be thankful. Al, is there anything you want to add to that?"

"No. But I'm glad we stopped to think about all this. I just hope we can stand the prosperity. We can't let success ruin us any more than we let the hardship get us down."

"We got Dad's speech after all," Bobbi said, and everyone laughed.

It was time to end the meeting. Bea had made her point, and she didn't want to belabor it. Gene was asleep now and needed to be put down for a time, and some of the couples needed to go visit in-laws. So Dad, by popular demand, said a prayer for the family. He was not as eloquent as he sometimes had been, and he didn't say a great deal, perhaps because it had all been said, but he did thank the Lord in that strong voice of his, and to Bea, this was the voice of the family, the clear guide they had all depended on. She was glad she had called the little meeting, but she was even happier that Al had established the tradition long ago. She didn't want him to be ashamed of it, no matter how much teasing he had taken over the years.

But there was still one more thing to do that day. Bea had engaged a photographer to come to the home, and he arrived before the larger family gathering late in the afternoon. By then, all the children had returned. First, Bea asked the imme-diate family to sit together in the living room—she and Al and the five children. Then she invited the spouses to join them. But Bobbi said, "Mom, I was just thinking. Before we get every-one into the picture, why don't you have one with you and Dad and us kids—and with Gene?"

Everyone knew immediately what Bobbi meant. Anna brought Gene and gave him to his grandpa, who held him on his lap. And the photographer took the picture. But it was not easy. Gene was squirming, not sure he wanted his picture taken, and everyone else was struggling, trying to smile.

2 5

Bobbi was kneeling on the bathroom floor, her head over the toilet. She was hoping that she could vomit one more time, and that that might make her feel better. But it was never quite that simple. This was not an upset stomach that got better once she threw up. What Bobbi had wasn't going away for a long time.

She finally did vomit one more time, and she did feel a little better for the moment, but it was 5:30 in the morning, and she was deeply tired. She cupped her hand under the faucet in the sink, washed out her mouth, and then trudged back to bed, where she fell instantly asleep. But twenty minutes later everything started again, and she jumped up and hurried to the bathroom. The only problem was, there was nothing left inside her, and even though she gagged, nothing came up. After a time Richard came into the bathroom, knelt down beside her, and put his arm around her shoulders. "Is there anything I can do?" he asked.

"Yes. But you already did it. Now get away from me."

Bobbi had intended some humor in that, but it didn't sound that way, and the truth was, she really didn't want him fawning over her at the moment. She just wanted to be left alone. But she wasn't prepared for his quick retreat, and now she wondered whether she hadn't hurt his feelings.

This time, when Bobbi made it back to the bed, Richard immediately rolled out. "Where are you going?" Bobbi asked.

"To take a bath. I've got to get going." It was January 2, and the plant had been shut down the day before. Bobbi and Richard had spent part of New Year's Day with her family, and the men had talked about how much they had to do to keep up with the orders that were coming in faster all the time.

"This early?"

"I've got a big day ahead of me."

"Richard, I'm sorry."

"What are you sorry about?" he said. It didn't exactly sound like a question. And he certainly didn't wait for an answer. He merely walked on into the bathroom and shut the door. In a moment, the bath water began to run.

Had she insulted him with that little jibe? Or was he just tired? Most mornings he seemed not just quiet but depressed, even cranky. He was perfectly willing to fix his own breakfast, to express pity for Bobbi, but he would give her a little smack of a kiss and then leave with a look on his face and sound in his voice that seemed to say, "I hate what I'm doing; hate where I'm going to spend my day."

By evening he was always much more pleasant to be around, but Bobbi was now seeing some of what she had always feared from him. He was quiet, sometimes silent, for long stretches of time, even in the evenings. He liked to come home to his newspaper, and he liked to read, after supper. What he didn't seem to understand was that Bobbi was spending a great deal of time alone these days. She couldn't visit her mother, since Bea was working, and while she spent a certain amount of time trying to prepare baby clothes, diapers, and the like, she really wasn't much of a seamstress. She had borrowed her mother's old treadle machine, which she had finally learned to coordinate, but she could never sew a seam quite straight, never get anything to turn out the way it looked on the pattern cover.

Nor did she like to sew. She tried to busy herself around her pretty new house, but there was nothing to clean—except for a few breakfast dishes and a bed to make. So what she did most often was lose herself in Victorian novels—Dickens, Thackeray, Trollope. There was a certain addiction in this kind of escape, especially during the hours when her stomach wasn't rolling, but the reading usually led to little afternoon naps, and that to difficulty sleeping at night, and then again to the round of nausea in the morning. She had spent too many years working hard, involved with people, busy. This life was becoming not just tedious but almost frightening. She felt as though she were losing contact with the world, even with herself. Maybe it was the nausea and the tiredness that made her feel so detached, but she also wondered what she was doing home all the time. "Don't worry, you'll have plenty to do once the baby comes," Richard liked to tell her. But Bobbi still wondered. What would she say to a baby, or even a little child, all day? And why was it that when Richard got home he seemed so uninterested in the things she had to say to him?

But then, why not? What did she have to say? What new things ever happened to her now? And when she asked him about his day, Richard especially lost interest. "Just the usual things," he would say. Or, "We're behind schedule, and one of our trucks broke down. I hope it'll be running in the morning."

It was nothing that Bobbi could even think how to comment about.

And so the "how was your day?" talk ended quickly, usually soon after Richard came through the door, and the dinner talk seemed to fall into already familiar patterns: the weather, Bobbi's sickness, Thomas family events. Bobbi could have taken all that, and maybe even could have concluded that this quiet little interlude in her life was rather pleasant after all the years of intensity in the navy, but she wondered whether this state of things wasn't a taste of her life from now on. Maybe Richard was turning out to be the man she feared he might be: uncommunicative and eventually downright dull. Right now he seemed to show no passion for anything, even for her, and she was certainly less than exciting in her emotional state, her "illness." Every now and then, though she tried not to do it, she found herself wondering about David—what life might have been like with him. She couldn't imagine him ever reading all evening, as much as he loved books, without having something more fun, more interesting to say to her. She couldn't imagine that he ever would have let life become bland. He would have thought of something, done something crazy, just to lighten things up. He had always been that way. And he would have had so many thoughts in his head, so many things he was wondering about, reading, teaching, that he surely would have talked to her about all of it.

Maybe. But she knew she shouldn't think that way. Even if it was true, it wasn't healthy to imagine. And it probably wasn't true. David could be self-centered, and he might have expected her to satisfy his ego in too many ways. Maybe he would have stayed late at the office, devoted more to his books and his ideas—and to his young students—than to her. Maybe every woman became less exciting to a man once she became domesticated, once she lost her shape, once she was a mother. Maybe David would have dazzled his young students, thrived on the attention of pretty twenty-year old girls. Maybe he would have . . .

But none of that mattered. Bobbi had made a choice, even before she had known that David had died. Richard was a good man, and really sweet to her, except for his moodiness in the mornings. She had a nice home already, and Richard had a steady, good-paying job. She had what every girl dreamed of, and she wasn't going to indulge herself in a lot of self-pity and regret. What she needed to do was think less of herself and concentrate on making Richard as happy as she could.

So when Richard returned to the bedroom and was slipping on his trousers, she whispered, "Richard, I love you."

"I love you too, honey. Are you feeling any better?"

"A little."

"Stay in bed for a while. You need some rest. I'll make some toast and—"

"No. I'll fry you some eggs. Once you're gone, I won't have anyone to talk to all day." She sat up in bed and made sure she wasn't dizzy. Then she stepped to him and pressed herself against him, so that he put his arms around her. "Don't kiss me. My breath stinks," she said, and they both laughed.

But he held her for a time, and then he said, more convincingly than the time before, "I do love you, Bobbi, and I'm sorry you have to be sick. If you want, I'll have the next baby."

"I wish you could."

"It might be worth it if I could stay home and read."

Bobbi was angry, in a flash. She pulled away and walked to the bathroom. She washed her face and hands, and then she brushed her teeth. She ran a brush through her hair a few strokes and then came back and slipped on a robe. By then Richard was putting a couple of slices of bread in the toaster. What he didn't seem to notice was that he had upset her.

"It's not so great as you think," she said, finally, with some tension in her voice.

"What?"

But she saw his look of recognition—that "Oh, no, I've made her mad again" look. It was almost like panic. "Honey, I know I wouldn't really like it. I was just teasing."

"I don't see anyone, Richard. And I feel so terrible most of the time." But Bobbi couldn't believe she was doing this. Her emotions were all so strong these days. She cried about nothing at all. She was trying not to do that now, but tears were in her eyes, blurring her vision.

"Maybe I'll take you out to dinner tonight, if you feel like it. We need to get out a little more."

"Okay. That would be good. I'm sorry, Richard. I don't know why I react that way. I hardly feel like myself these days." She opened the refrigerator and got out a carton of eggs.

"You're PG—that's what's going on. My mom told me that's what happens to women."

So he had been talking to his mother about her? Bobbi was suddenly angry all over again. "Okay, we've explained my problem," she said. "Now, what's yours?"

"What problem?"

"Oh, nothing much. Just that you're miserable."

"That's not true, Bobbi. I'm fine."

"If this is fine, I just hope you never get depressed."

"What's that supposed to mean?"

Bobbi was going to shut up. She got a bowl down from her pretty birch cupboards and cracked an egg, dropped the insides into the bowl, then broke another one. "Do you want these scrambled?"

"Sure. It doesn't matter. Bobbi, you know me. I don't create a lot of excitement, I'm afraid. Maybe you're just beginning to see how uninteresting I really am. But I'm doing fine. I don't know why you always tell me that I'm not."

"Richard, you're not happy. You're going through the motions, doing what you have to do, but you're not happy. I don't want to live with you a whole lifetime and watch you sleepwalk your way through it. You weren't this way when I first met you. You weren't this way even when you first came home from the war."

"Bobbi, I'm doing what I need to do for our family. Apparently, I also need to improve my personality. Is there anything else you don't like about me? I'll work on that, too."

"Don't do that, Richard. It's not fair. I watch you walk out of here every morning, and you look like you're heading to the gallows to meet your death. I can't stand to see you doing that to yourself. You know we have to do something about it."

"I told you, I'm not going to have this conversation again.

I need to get to work." He opened the toaster, grabbed the hot toast, and headed for the door, where he picked up his leather briefcase. And then he was gone, and Bobbi was left alone for another long day. She sat down at the kitchen table and thought about crying, but she was entirely too devastated. She had always assumed that she would have a good marriage, that she would find someone wonderful, and that she would be a good wife. And now what? Divorce? A standoff? A long life with someone she didn't know how to talk to? Would she be one of those women who filled her life with her children and church work, PTA and all the rest—but shared next to nothing with the man she had married forever?

Other people's lives turned into tragedies, long miserable acts of courage, but not hers—certainly not hers. The nausea was back, and Bobbi couldn't stand to think of the eggs, not even toast. She went back to bed and lay there waiting for the sickness to pass, wondering whether it was possible that life was going to turn out as bad as it now looked.

Bobbi couldn't sleep, couldn't even vomit, and she couldn't settle her mind enough to read. She stayed on the bed until she was too restless for that, and then she went back to the kitchen in her robe. She knew she needed to clean up, brighten up, get busy, and then life would start to feel normal. But she also knew she would be kidding herself. If Richard came home that night, apologized, and then simply went back to his routine, she couldn't stand it. Somehow, she had to break through all this distance that was growing between them before it was too late. Maybe she could take a bus to the plant, walk into his office, and say, "We're going to talk." But she knew better. He would be upset and wouldn't respond.

She walked to the phone, picked it up, and dialed her home phone. Her mother answered. "Hi, Mom," Bobbi said, "I thought you might be gone by now."

"Well, I am about ready to head out."

"Are you planning to work all day?"

"Right now, I would say no, but I say that every morning, and then I usually end up staying around the place longer than I should. Why?"

"Oh, nothing. I just thought I'd come over for a few minutes, if you were going to be around."

"Are you lonely, Bobbi?"

"Sure. A little." But Bobbi was crying and fighting desperately to stifle the sound so her mother wouldn't know.

"Honey, what's wrong? Are you sick this morning?"

"Yes. A little."

"What else is it?"

"I don't know, Mom. I don't know how to tell you this, but I don't know if my marriage is going to work out." And now she was crying hard.

"Oh, Bobbi, don't say that. It seems that way sometimes, but every couple can work things out. Did you have a fight?"

Bobbi was sobbing. When she got herself under control a little, she said, "No, Mom. We don't fight. That would be exciting. Richard just wanders around like all the life has drained from his heart, and then he tells me he's not unhappy."

"I know what you mean, Bobbi. I watch him sometimes. I'll see him sitting in a meeting, and he's really not listening to the conversation. His head isn't really in the work, and I don't think it ever will be."

"So what do I do, Mom?"

"Get him away from the plant. He's got to do something he cares about."

"He thinks he has to work there for *us*—for me and the baby."

"That's good that he wants to do what he thinks is right. But it's not going to work. You need to get this all out in the open, Bobbi."

"He won't *talk*, Mom."

"Well, it's time you have a really good fight. I didn't fight with your dad for twenty-five years, and I was always proud of that. But I also let things keep going along in ways I really didn't like. When I finally challenged him, he responded, and we've made some headway since then."

"Have you, Mom? Can you work things out when they go wrong?"

"Oh, Bobbi, you're just getting started. Marriage lasts a long time—sometimes it seems like an eternity." She laughed. "Don't be nasty and sarcastic, though, and don't take pot shots at him. Come at him straight, tell him what you think, and don't let him run from you. Have it out—find out what he's really feeling."

"I'll try."

"Remember, though, if you challenge him, be ready to listen. I've had to make some changes too. I feel better about your dad than I ever have, and I think he feels the same way about me. We've been going out lately, doing more together. He's even remembered how to kiss."

Bobbi certainly didn't want to know about that part. But she was pretty sure her mother was right. It was time to force the issue.

When Richard got home that night, he seemed tentative. He wasn't the sort to bring home flowers as a peace offering, but that was all right with Bobbi. She didn't want a gift; she wanted a connection. She had taken a bath and washed her hair after the conversation with her mother that morning, and now she had slipped on a pretty dress and put on some lipstick. "Say, honey, I'm glad you dressed up a little," Richard said. "It looks like you're going to take me up on my offer. Shall we go out for dinner?"

"Yes. But not yet. We need to talk. Let's sit down here at the table."

"Why don't we go into the living room?"

"No. I want to look you straight in the face."

He smiled a little, but she could see the nervousness in his eyes, the way he refused to look at her directly. The two sat down opposite each other, and then Bobbi said what she had practiced all day. "Richard, you have to quit working for my dad. You know it as well as I do."

He looked down at the table, at his hands, which were gripped together. "And how do you propose I would do that?" he asked. "How do we make house payments? How do we pay for our baby?"

"So what you're telling me is that you plan to be unhappy all your life, do a job you hate, in order to create a *happy* family life. Is that the idea? Does that make even the slightest bit of sense?"

"Bobbi, you exaggerate everything. The job isn't that bad."

"Then what's wrong? Does it have something to do with the war?"

"Bobbi, I've told you a thousand times, there are things I'm not going to talk to you about. I thought we had an understanding about that."

"No. We never did. I always told you I wanted you to be open with me. And I'm telling you right now, I'm not going to do this for my entire life. Something is wrong, and you're going to tell me what it is. That's the only option."

She saw a splotch of red forming on his throat. He held firm for a few seconds, swallowed, and then said in a rigid, governed voice, "Don't start giving me ultimatums, Bobbi. You might not like the result."

"What does that mean, Richard? What are you going to do?" She leaned across the table and grabbed his forearms, making him look back at her. "Are you talking about a divorce? Are you going to beat me up? Yell and scream at me? Go back to your silence? If you're going to threaten me, at least be specific."

"Don't do this, Bobbi. I love you, but I won't let you browbeat me. I just won't. There are some things I have to do my own way."

"No!" Bobbi was standing up now, leaning over the table.

"You don't have that right," she shouted into his face. "You can do things your own way when they don't affect me. But when you make choices that are ruining our marriage, making us both miserable, you *lose* that right. I want to know, right now, what's going on in your head."

"You don't know what you're trying to get me to do, Bobbi. There's no way you can. Can't you just let me be the judge on this?"

"No. It can't be that bad, if we just talk about it. It's *not* talking about it that is so terrible."

He was sitting still now, and she thought maybe she had won. But for the first time, she wondered whether she was wrong. What was it he didn't want to tell her?

He leaned forward, his elbows on the table, and he sat that way for a long time. When he finally spoke, the anger was gone. "Bobbi, as you know, something did happen to me. I try to put it out of my mind, but it seems to have changed me. I can't even say why. But I think it's temporary. I feel like I can get over it."

"Just tell me. Then we'll go from there. You don't have to do this alone anymore."

He still didn't speak. She didn't know whether he was looking for the words to explain or the strength to tell her no one more time. But finally he said, "All right. Maybe I do need to tell you. I guess it is only fair."

Bobbi waited, but Richard still wouldn't look at her.

"As you know, a kamikaze hit our ship. I was trying to help the men get hoses over to the fire, and that's when I got hit by a secondary explosion. When it went off, I threw my hands over my face, and I felt the flash at the same time. It knocked me down, knocked me out for a while—maybe a minute or two. That much I've told you before."

"Sort of. But that's more detail than you ever gave me."

"When I woke up, people were dragging me, and I don't remember much of what happened at first. Someone had apparently given me a shot of morphine before I even came around. The first thing I clearly remember is that some guys were handing me down into a rubber life raft. I was in pain, even with the morphine, and I was still pretty confused about what was happening."

He paused, looking at the table. All his words had been in monotone, without emotion.

"I've tried to remember what happened after that, but I must have gone unconscious again for a while. At some point I remember that I was across some guys' laps, and they were hanging onto me. I could feel the raft roll in the waves, and the sun was in my eyes. I tried to turn, to avoid the sun, and men were yelling for me to hold still. But there was some sort of commotion going on, and I didn't understand for a minute what was happening. Then I got a look at the water, and it was full of men from our ship—dozens of them out there in the water with life jackets on. The ones who were close to us were swimming toward the boat, or they were grabbing at us, reaching out for help."

Richard put his hands over his face, covered his eyes the way he must have done during the explosion, and it struck Bobbi how rarely he showed the backs of his hands, even to her.

"The guys in the water were frantic. They were trying to get onto our boat. But the men in the boat wouldn't let them on. They were swinging their oars at the ones in the water, knocking their hands away, even hitting them over the head, and they were screaming like crazy people. 'Let go. Let go. There's no room. You'll sink us all.'"

Bobbi felt the sickness return to her stomach. "Oh, Richard," she said. "What a terrible thing to witness. But they *would* have sunk the boat. And what good would that do? Then you'd all be in the water."

"I know that."

"Then no one did anything wrong."

"It was wrong, Bobbi. Hitting those guys was wrong."

"Did all the men in the water die?"

"More than half of them did."

"Richard, you can't blame yourself for something like that."

"I don't blame myself."

"Then what?"

Richard lowered his head and rested his forehead on his arms. "I don't know. I just keep remembering it. And I feel . . . empty . . . most of the time. I feel like someone pulled the solid ground out from under me."

"Do you think people are evil, or something like that?"

Richard sat for a long time, his head still down. "I don't know, Bobbi," he finally said. "I just see those guys in my mind, reaching toward us, wanting our help. I see their faces, how scared they were. I thought I would forget it after a while, but it keeps getting worse, not better."

"You feel guilty that you lived and they died, don't you?"

Richard raised his head and looked at her. Tears began to drip onto his cheeks and run down his face. "Sure I do," he said. "If I hadn't gotten hurt *I* would have been one of the guys in the water. I probably would have died. But one more guy could have gotten on that boat."

"Richard, it wasn't your fault. None of this was your fault."

"Tell my spirit that, Bobbi. It doesn't believe me."

Now Bobbi was crying. She hadn't realized what he had been living with all this time.

"I keep telling myself that I have to buckle down and live a good life—you know, be worthy of the blessing I got. I always think that if I do my best on the job, provide for my family, work in the Church, sooner or later this will go away."

"But you have to be true to your own heart. I don't think those washing-machine parts are important enough to you. You need something that feels significant to you, Richard."

"No. I need something that *is* significant. I want to give

something to this world, since I got to stay. But I have no idea what that is."

"Well . . . it's not washing-machine parts.

"How would we make it, Bobbi? If I went back to school, or something like that, we'd have to sell this house and maybe—"

"That doesn't matter. You're trying to sacrifice yourself, Richard. And it's a noble thing to do. But you just can't do it. It won't make either one of us happy."

"Are you sure we could—"

"Yes. We'll figure something out. But we can't go on the way we've been lately."

He was looking at her curiously, and he seemed frightened, but Bobbi also thought she saw some relief in his eyes.

2 6

Cecil Broadbent had come home for the holidays. He'd been attending MIT that fall, and this was his first trip back to Salt Lake City. East High was back in school now, after the New Year, but Cecil's holiday extended longer into January. He had called a couple of times, only to be put off by LaRue, but today he showed up at the Thomas home just after LaRue arrived home from school. "Do you feel like going for a walk?" he asked.

"Are you kidding?" LaRue said. "I just walked home. It's freezing out there." She grabbed his arm and pulled him inside so she could close the door.

"That's what I thought you'd say. So let's go get a cup of coffee or something. I've got Dad's car."

"Coffee?"

"Well, whatever you want. I didn't mean you had to drink coffee."

She let that go, but she said, "Cecil, I don't have a lot of time. I have a test in chemistry tomorrow."

"Ooooh. Those high-school chemistry tests—they're real killers." He grasped his chest, on top of his big overcoat, pretending that he was having a heart attack.

"Hey, go back to *Cambridge*. Okay?"

"No, no. I'm just kidding. Come on. We'll go down to Fred and Kelly's and get you a nice glass of milk, and we'll catch up a little. You only wrote me one crummy letter since I left."

"You only wrote two. So I'm just one behind." LaRue had taken off her coat and hung it on the coat rack by the door, but she put it back on now, and the two headed out to Cecil's car. No one was home yet, but Beverly was walking down the street with some friends. LaRue yelled to her, "I'm going with Cecil for half an hour or so. Don't worry about supper. I know it's my turn."

"What's this?" Cecil said. "Have you become domesticated?"

There was something going on with Cecil. He had taken on a new style. His hair was combed straight back, slick, and his voice was stronger, more confident. He actually looked better, a little more grown up, his skin finally clear, and he was wearing expensive shoes—wingtips—and gray flannel dress slacks under his black overcoat. But LaRue was already annoyed with his condescension. "Bev and I take turns cooking," LaRue said. "My mom is running one of our family businesses, and she puts in long hours some days."

"She's still at the plant?"

"No. She and Dad are buying land and developing it. They have a big housing project going. They're going to start selling lots in the spring."

"Your family keeps climbing a little higher up the bourgeois ladder all the time. Your father might get himself appointed to the Quorum of the Twelve if he continues on the rise."

"What's that supposed to mean?"

Cecil opened the door for LaRue, and then he walked around the car and got in. "Nothing at all," he said. "I just know how things operate around here."

"Well, then, you mean something. But I don't understand what you're trying to say."

"Never mind. But if you get away from here next year, and

then take a good look back, you'll see a lot of things you never noticed when you were growing up."

"Okay. So enlighten me, great traveler from the east." She turned in her seat, leaned against the door, and waited for him to respond.

"Look, I'm not being critical of your father. All I'm saying is, one of the best ways to get into leadership in the Church is to make a lot of money." He started his father's old car, an ancient Chevy. The engine muttered and strained and then fell silent. On the second try, it caught, then continued to gurgle, so Cecil fed it a little more gas and waited, without shifting into gear.

"Let's see," LaRue said. "President Smith. Now there's a wealthy man. He's spent his whole life in Church positions. And there's President McKay. A teacher. He's a rich guy. President Clark worked in the government all his life. That's a good way to get rich."

"He's got a big cattle ranch."

"Now there's royalty for you. A rancher."

"I'm not saying they're all rich. I'm just saying that you have to become prominent in Salt Lake circles before they call you in."

"Oh, that's certainly true. Like Elder Brown. He came down from Canada. And Elder Kimball. They brought him up from Arizona."

Cecil laughed and shook his head. "Wow. I'd better keep my mouth shut. You know all these guys."

"Ah—finally, some wisdom."

"Since when did you become the defender of the faith?" The engine was finally smoothing out a little, running steady, and so he shifted into first gear and pulled away from the curb.

"I didn't know I was. But if you're going to make accusations, you ought to know what you're talking about."

"The truth is, I'm not that interested in any of that stuff."

Cecil didn't say what "that stuff" was, and LaRue decided
to let it go. She did want to hear about college. "So tell me
about MIT. What's it like out there?"

"It's beautiful. I live right by the Charles River. All during
the fall I would look out my window onto a row of chestnut
trees, all in color, and just beyond that, the river. There's
almost always a crew or two out on the water in the afternoon,
training."

"What do you mean, a crew?"

"Rowing. It's the big sport out there."

"Oh."

"We go into Boston all the time, see all the historical sites,
take in a concert."

"Have you ever gone to the Commons, where they have
those swan boats?"

"Of course. It's right in the middle of the city. That's our
subway stop when we ride in from Cambridge."

Cecil slowed, rolled down his window, and signaled, then
made a left-hand turn. LaRue felt the rush of cold air just when
the heater was starting to take the chill off the air. "What are
the people like in Boston?"

"That depends on what you mean. Boston's very ethnic,
very divided. There's a big Italian section, and Irish and Jewish
and Negro parts of town. But I don't see much of that in
Cambridge. The students are mostly from the east, the largest
share of them from excellent prep schools and well-off families. They're nothing at all like people here."

"They sound like snobs."

"Well . . . they know who they are. They're not trying to
prove anything. Not everyone is quite as brilliant as I thought
they might be, but no one looks down on me for my intelli-
gence either. I'm very well accepted there."

Cecil had tried to speak this last with an easy nonchalance,
but it didn't work. LaRue could sense how delighted he was
with himself. And when they arrived at Fred and Kelly's and

LaRue ordered a root beer, Cecil said, "I'll just have a cup of coffee. I don't suppose you could slip a little shot of whiskey in it?"

"No, sir," the waitress said, and she laughed. LaRue had the feeling she was laughing at Cecil more than she was at the idea. She waited and tapped her pencil on the little notepad she was carrying. Johnny Mercer was singing his new hit song, "Ac-Cent-Tchu-Ate the Positive," on the jukebox, and some girls in the next booth were singing along. The place was packed, mostly with high-school kids.

"Oh, well. Just the coffee then," Cecil said, and then, as soon as the waitress was gone, he told LaRue, "I'll have to admit that I've gotten so I do like my coffee with a little shot of whiskey. Almost anywhere in Boston you can ask a waitress, and she'll fix you up."

"So you're a big whiskey drinker now, are you?"

"Not really. But we do have some *feverish* parties around the dorms on weekends. I guess I have indulged a little too much at times—and I've learned to enjoy a good cigar once in a while."

"Why don't you just lay off, okay?"

"What?"

"I don't want to go away to school and come back a big *phony*. That's what you're acting like."

Cecil turned in the booth and leaned against the wall at the end of the seat. He smiled. He looked strange with his hair out of his eyes. "I guess I have changed in some ways. I hardly realize it."

"You realize it, all right. You've been gone three months, and now you're trying to act like you're some 'man of the world.' Can't you be in a place like that and still be a Mormon?"

LaRue watched Cecil. She could see his confusion, his attempt to keep up this new manner of his, and yet to handle the challenge. "I don't know about that, LaRue. I don't suppose that was the main goal I was trying to achieve."

"What you mean is, you didn't try. Did you even go to church?"

"I heard there's a branch in Boston, but no, I didn't ever go over to it."

"You knew you wouldn't before you ever got there. That's one of the reasons you left."

"LaRue, you really won't have any idea what it's like until you go away yourself. All the things that people make such a big thing of here just aren't that important to me now. I haven't turned into a drunk, if that's what you think, but for a man to take a drink once in a while is hardly a matter of any great importance. Around here we've almost made a religion of a few silly little health rules."

"And you're above that now?"

"LaRue, please. You sound like your dad. What does a cup of coffee have to do with theology? I can't imagine that God, if there is such a fellow, cares one way or the other about it."

"So you've made up your mind about that? You don't believe in God now?"

He let his hand swing, as if to dismiss the matter, but LaRue could hear a certain tightness in his voice now. "I haven't known what to believe about that for a long time. If there is a God, I certainly don't think he's some man in the sky."

"At least you weren't making fun of such things last year."

"I'm not making fun of God. I'm making fun of the way people think around here. Mormons act like they have the corner on truth, and yet, when you get to the east coast, no one has even heard of them. Or when people have, the only thing they know is that it's some weird little cult that used to practice polygamy, and probably still does."

"So what do you say about that? Do you tell them that's not how it is, or do you let them go on thinking it?"

"I really don't talk about it. I'm not out there to do missionary work."

"I don't like you anymore, Cecil."

"Oh, come on, LaRue. Don't be so adolescent." The waitress brought the coffee and the root beer, set them down, and left a little check next to Cecil's coffee at the same time. As soon as she walked away, Cecil shifted in his seat to face his coffee. "Talk to me in a year, when you've been away for a while," he said. "See how you feel about things then."

"If I'm going to come back acting like you, I don't want to leave."

"LaRue, listen to me. This place is a strange little aberration. No one thinks like people here. No one is so close-minded and so cocksure that they have *all* the truth. Once you get away from here, Utah seems mostly just comic: all these people out here in the middle of nowhere, talking about the world as though Salt Lake is the center of the universe and everyone else is in outer darkness. This is just an ugly little sagebrush valley, and Mormons pretend it's God's green earth. In Boston or New York or London no one even knows that Salt Lake exists, and they wouldn't care if they did."

"So that means the Church isn't true? Is that what you're saying?"

Cecil had poured a couple of spoonfuls of sugar into his coffee and now was stirring it in, the spoon making little scraping noises against the cup. "True? Oh come on, LaRue. If some little sect claims itself to be God's true religion, what does that matter to Catholicism or Buddhism or Judaism—or any of the other great religions of the world? It's like an anthill proclaiming itself a mountain and then never going to see what a real mountain looks like."

"So the bigger a religion is, the more likely it is to be true?"

"No. The truth is there is no *one* truth. There are all sorts of truths to all sorts of people. Or better put, all sorts of superstitions, each designed for its own culture. And that's fine. I just think it becomes laughable when some little tribe proclaims itself the pipeline from God for the entire universe."

Cecil was back on top now. His voice had taken back its

full, deep authority. LaRue was angry, but even more, frustrated by his assumption that *he* had all the answers. But she said, softly, "Cecil, Christ only taught a few people. That's how it all started—just a little flock of followers who had to take the truth to the rest of the world. Don't you believe in Christ?"

She watched the air go out of him, and then he said, much more meekly, "LaRue, I don't know right now. He taught good things. But I don't know whether he was the Son of God. I suppose I don't believe that right now. But I'm not saying I've made up my mind forever."

"I like you when you sound like yourself, Cecil. So don't try to act like a big shot. It's ugly."

He took a long breath, and as he exhaled, his shoulders slumped a little. "I don't mean to do that. It's just . . . I don't know, LaRue. All those years, growing up here, I felt like an outsider. Out there, I have friends; I'm accepted. I just wanted you to know that I'm not a *nobody* anymore."

"Just remember, Cecil, no matter what happens, or what you do, you'll *always* be a nobody to me."

He laughed, but the old sadness had returned to his eyes. "Actually, I know that, LaRue. I know it better than anything." Bing Crosby and the Andrews Sisters were singing their big hit, "Don't Fence Me In," only just audible over all the noise, the laughing and talking.

LaRue thought of saying she was sorry, but she didn't know what the words would imply. She couldn't help it that she didn't love him. But she did like the Cecil she remembered, and all the things he had said today were filling her head, scaring her much more than he could have realized. She was afraid to leave this valley. Maybe she couldn't leave and come back as LaRue. And yet, what frightened her just as much was the idea of not leaving. What if she spent her whole life wondering what the world might have done to her if only she had let herself experience it?

When LaRue got home, she wanted to be alone. She

wanted to go up to her room and do some thinking. The last thing she wanted was to find Beverly standing at the front window, looking upset, and then running out to the front porch. "LaRue," she shouted, "Bobbi's in the hospital. Something's wrong. She's losing her baby. She might have to have an operation."

"How do you know?"

"Mom called. She's gone to the hospital. I want to go too."

"Which hospital?"

"LDS."

"How would we get there, Beverly? The bus would take forever. Does Dad know?"

But LaRue saw a car approaching, and she realized it was Wally's. She and Beverly ran down the steps and out toward the curb. Wally stepped from his car quickly and said, "Did Mom call you?"

"Yes," Beverly said. "Are you going to the hospital?"

"Yes, I am." He hurried around the car, his overcoat open and spreading like a cape. "Richard called at the dealership. He wanted Dad to go over and help him give Bobbi a blessing. But Dad wasn't there, so I'm going. I just stopped by to get some consecrated oil."

"Can we go with you?" Beverly asked.

"I don't think you can see Bobbi, Bev, but if you want to ride over, that's fine with me."

"Yes, I want to go."

"How bad is this?" LaRue asked. "Is this dangerous to Bobbi?"

"It might be, LaRue. She's lost the baby already, and now the doctors can't get the bleeding stopped."

"She couldn't die, could she?" Beverly asked.

"I don't know." Wally kept walking, fast, heading into the house. "Richard said they might have to operate, and if they do, she might not be able to have children."

Beverly had started to cry, and LaRue turned to her. "Don't do that, Bev. That's stupid. Think about Bobbi, not yourself."

"I am thinking about Bobbi," Beverly sobbed.

LaRue hated it when Beverly acted like a little girl, but she felt some of the same panic. "We'll go with you," LaRue said. "We can sit with Mom. She's going to be scared. But can't you find Dad?"

Wally had reached the front door. He looked back as he pushed his way in. "I put a couple of calls in and left word for him to call his secretary. I don't know what else to do for now." He disappeared into the house.

LaRue thought about grabbing her homework and then decided she wouldn't. She would stay up late if she had to, but she didn't want to carry her books to the hospital. She couldn't concentrate anyway, not with Bobbi in trouble.

Wally was back quickly, and the three got into the car. Beverly had stopped crying now, but she continued to ask questions, virtually all of them questions that Wally had no answer for. "Let's say a prayer," she finally said.

"That's a good idea," Wally told her. "You say it."

Instantly Beverly began to pray, and the words came out easily, as though she had already been repeating them in her head. "Heavenly Father," she said, "please take care of our dear Bobbi. Don't let her die. And make her well, so she can have a baby someday." She closed in the name of Jesus Christ. And then, only a few seconds later, as though she had hesitated long enough to get her answer, she said, "She'll be all right."

LaRue was touched. She didn't know whether that was true, but she had no doubt at all that Beverly believed it. The three were close to one another, all in the front seat, and now LaRue put her arm around Bev and pulled her even closer. But Wally was driving much too fast, and that frightened LaRue, seemed to cancel Beverly's words, seemed to say that Wally wasn't nearly so sure.

At the hospital, Wally stopped at the information desk,

asked some quick questions, and then told the girls they would
have to wait downstairs while he went up to see Bobbi. "I'll
come back down and let you know what's happening just as
soon as I can. But they don't want a lot of people in the room.
They're only letting me in long enough to give her the blessing."

Wally walked to the elevator and disappeared, and LaRue
and Beverly sat on a little couch in the waiting area. An elderly
man was sitting in an upholstered chair across from them, but
he was leaning back, breathing deeply, seeming asleep except
for his eyes, which were not quite shut. No one else was
around. Beverly wasn't talking now, but she seemed under control. LaRue suspected that she was repeating her little prayer.
LaRue picked up a *Look* magazine from the table in front of
them, but she didn't open it. She was trying to think what this
could mean—for Richard, for everyone.

Before long the elevator door opened and Mom got off. As
she began to look around, LaRue stood up. "Mom," she said,
and then she walked toward her mother. "Is she all right?"

Mom met LaRue halfway and then waited until Beverly
came to them as well. "I don't think her life is in danger," she
said. "She lost a lot of blood, but they've got that pretty well
stopped, and they're giving her a transfusion right now. I just
don't know what's happened to her, inside. The doctor doesn't
know either. He's trying to get her stabilized and get her blood
pressure back up. Then he might have to operate."

"Wally and Richard will bless her. She'll be all right,"
Beverly said.

"Well, that's what we're all praying for, Bev. But things happen sometimes, no matter what we ask for." Mom sounded a
little irritated, as though Beverly's confidence felt a little too
naive, too trusting, at such a difficult moment.

And LaRue let her old question run through her head, the
one she had thought of so many times before: why *ask* God if
he was just going to do whatever he wanted to anyway?

But Beverly whispered, as if to herself, "I know she'll be all right."

The three of them walked back to the couch and sat down. Bea said that she had left while the men gave the blessing, to avoid having too many in the room at once, but she planned to go back up as soon as Wally came down. "I thought our worries would all be over when the war ended," she told the girls, "but I guess there are always problems in life."

"How's Richard doing?" LaRue asked.

"He's upset. When I first got here, she was still hemorrhaging. They'd made him stay outside. I found him in a corner, crying, and I know he was praying. He's feeling a lot better now, since the doctor told him Bobbi was out of serious danger."

"How did Bobbi get here?"

"In an ambulance. She was home when the pain hit her, and then she started to bleed really hard. She called Richard, but he didn't take any chances. He called for an ambulance. When he got home, they were already taking her away. By then she had passed out, so it's good he didn't try to run home first."

"God won't let any more of us die," Beverly said. "He just won't."

"Beverly, you don't know that," Mom said, and now her voice was taut, almost angry.

LaRue looked at Beverly, who didn't say a word, didn't react, but LaRue could see that Bev's confidence hadn't cracked. She nodded, ever so slightly, as though she were offering reassurance to herself. Whatever whispers she had heard, she wasn't doubting.

In a few minutes Wally came down. "She's awake," he said. "Her color is coming back. She feels bad about the baby, and I think she's worried about what's happened to her—but she was smiling, even joking with us."

"That's good," Mom said, but the idea of it seemed a little

much for her. She bent forward and put her face in her hands, gathering herself for a few seconds. "I'm going back up to see her," she said, but she didn't get up.

"The doctor wants us all to stay out so she'll sleep for a while," Wally said. "Richard is going to sit in her room with her, and the doctor said that was all right as long as he didn't talk to her and keep her awake."

"Will they let the girls go up to see her after a while?"

"I think so. I'm not sure."

"Well, let's wait for a while. I want to be close . . . you know, if something should go wrong."

LaRue could hardly stand to hear those words. She wanted this all to be over. She stood up. "I think I'll walk outside and get some air for a few minutes. It's hot in here."

"I've got to get back to the office," Wally said. "I'm going to see what I can do to find Dad."

So Bea and Beverly stayed in the waiting area, and LaRue walked outside with Wally. As they reached the car, she asked him, "How did you feel when you gave the blessing, Wally? Did you feel like everything would be all right?"

"Yes, I did," he said. He tucked his hands into his coat pockets and nodded a couple of times. "I anointed her, and Richard gave her the blessing. He put those scarred hands on her head, and he told her how much he loved her." Wally stopped and cleared his throat. "It was heartbreaking, LaRue. He told her how sorry he was that he didn't have all the qualities she wanted in a husband. He cried so hard he couldn't even talk for a while, but when he got his voice back, he told Bobbi that she was a 'pure vessel' and he knew God loved her. He promised her that the Lord would grant her another chance to bear a child."

"Did you believe it? I mean, do you think it was just what Richard wanted, or was that what the Spirit told him?"

"LaRue, you're asking the same kinds of questions I've

always asked. But that's good. There's not one thing wrong with asking."

"So answer me." She pulled her coat around her face. The wind was blowing in gusts, cutting through her clothes.

"I did feel the Spirit, LaRue. And I've gotten so I trust my feelings about things like that."

"How?"

"LaRue, you and I have talked about that a lot of times. I told you what happened to me when I finally humbled myself and really prayed."

LaRue was trying to think, trying to sort out what she felt. "Wally, I talked to my friend Cecil this afternoon. He says that it's stupid to think that one church—one little church—has the corner on all truth."

"Obviously, we don't."

"But don't we believe that Joseph Smith brought back the *whole* truth?"

"Not exactly. God gave him the authority to reestablish Christ's church, but Joseph kept learning more all his life. We have to do the same thing."

LaRue stamped her feet and shivered. "Cecil says we shouldn't be trying to tell the rest of the world how to think— that it's like a little tribe off in some corner of the world telling everyone else what's what."

"But LaRue, we *do* have something. Chuck and I didn't do a lot of preaching in our camps, but guys came to us, and when they heard what we believed, it rang true to them. And that was really helpful to me, to tell a man what I had been taught and see him begin to grow because of what I could give him. We really do know things that the world needs to hear."

"I told him that Christ's followers, when he was on earth, were just a small group too."

"That's right. That's a good answer. But now you need your own answer. You need to read about that little group. I doubt you've ever read the New Testament all the way through."

"No. I haven't."

"I hadn't either when I left home. But you need to do that, LaRue. You're asking hard questions. You need to humble yourself and really look for the answers."

"Beverly doesn't have to. She just believes."

"That's good for her. And don't make fun of her for it. But you're going to have to work harder." Wally finally pulled his coat shut. His cheeks were red, and his nose.

"Would it be a mistake for me to go away to college? Will I lose what faith I have?"

"That's another answer you're going to have to get for yourself."

LaRue nodded, thankful in a way that Wally thought so. She had expected him to tell her to stay home and play it safe. "I'm freezing," she said.

"I know. I am too. Go back in. But talk to me again. I can't give you all the answers, but I can tell you what I've thought about some of the same questions."

"Okay. I will." She turned to walk away and then twisted back and said, "If I find out anything new about Bobbi, I'll call you at your office."

"Great. I'll see you later." But then he reached out and took her into his arms. That wasn't something he had done very often in their lives, and LaRue was touched by the closeness she felt. She liked the spirit about him—liked it so much more than the one she had felt from Cecil.

She walked back inside to Mom and Beverly. There, in the waiting area, she found Richard, looking pale and tired. He got up and hugged her. "Thanks for coming over," he said. "I told Bobbi that you were here, and she joked about it, but I know it meant a lot to her."

"Do you feel bad about the baby?"

"Sure I do. But as long as Bobbi is all right, we'll be okay."

"If I stay for a while, can I go up and see Bobbi?"

"I don't know, LaRue. Maybe."

But LaRue wanted to do that, and so she waited, and later that evening, after Dad had come and Bobbi had rested quite some time, the doctor said that each family member could come in for a minute, one at a time, and say goodnight. When LaRue got her turn, she found Bobbi looking weary, her hair loose and messy, her lips still almost blue. "You don't look so hot," she told Bobbi, and she bent and kissed her cheek.

"Thanks a lot," Bobbi said.

"I love you, Bobbi."

"Really? I don't think you've ever told me that, not since you were a little girl."

"I know. I don't say things I ought to say. I'm too busy saying all the things I shouldn't. But all this time, down in the lobby, I've been thinking how much I love you."

"LaRue, don't start being sweet. I couldn't take it. I'd be crying all the time." She was crying now.

"Don't worry. You've seen the last of it." But LaRue took her hand and said, "Are you worried, Bobbi?"

"Not right now. I just feel so blessed. Richard was wonderful to me, and Wally, and now all of you. I think things will be okay. I'm just glad all of us are together now."

"Bobbi, did you feel the Spirit when they blessed you?"

"I don't know. I felt comfortable—and the fear left me. I guess that's the Spirit."

"But aren't you sure?"

"LaRue, I don't think life allows us many chances to be sure."

LaRue nodded. It was such a terrible answer, not at all what she wanted. But it was also the perfect answer because it rang with such honesty. Bobbi was someone LaRue could trust. So was Wally. And so were Mom and Dad. Even Beverly, as much as anyone. LaRue had to remember that.

27

Alex arrived at work after his morning classes at the university. It was a cold February day. He wished that he didn't have to come in on a day like this, when he had a test coming up in a biology class and a paper in Early American History. But he needed the money. Dad refused to take any rent for the house he and Anna lived in, but there were still plenty of bills to pay. For one thing, Gene had been sick a number of times that winter, and Anna was rather quick to run to the doctor, or at least it seemed so to Alex. In fact, he and Anna had quarreled about that, had quarreled a good deal lately. He loved her so much, but she was not feeling all that well, with the new baby coming, and she seemed exhausted every day when he got home from work. He sometimes blamed their problems on that, but Alex knew the truth: he was grouchy much of the time and not easy to get along with. He told himself every day that he had to be more patient with Gene, kinder to Anna—the way he always thought he would be if he ever got back to them—but the nervousness that plagued him hadn't abated at all. Going to school—having a new goal—was supposed to help, but in fact, the intensity of his life, working and studying, coming home to a noisy toddler when he needed to study, seemed to keep him on edge almost all the time. He felt a malaise, a discouragement, that he didn't know how to deal with. He knew how tired Anna was of his moods, his caustic remarks, his advice about Gene, but he couldn't seem to stop himself.

Alex sat at his desk and tried to think what he needed to do today. He opened a file that was in front of him, wondered for a moment what it was, but then realized why he had left it out. He needed to get a letter off to a supplier. He would work on that now. But as he read through the file, he couldn't think what it was that he needed to say in the letter. His eyes were taking in the words, but his mind wasn't letting them register. This kept happening lately—this confusion, this lack of concentration. He decided to walk down and see what was happening on the line. After he did that, he would come back, settle down, and get to work.

He strode through the hall and down the stairs. When he reached the floor, he saw Oscar, the foreman, talking to a machinist. Alex started toward him and was walking along the conveyor belt when something flashed, some spark of light— bright, intense. At the same instant, he heard a crash.

Alex dove flat on his chest onto the hard concrete, but he saw no cover, no foxhole. He rolled under something, tried to hide . . . but he *knew* where he was. He couldn't do this. "Take cover!" he screamed. "Take cover!" And even as he shouted, he knew he had to stop. He was acting crazy. People would think he *was* crazy.

But the sound cracked through the building again, and he pulled his legs up against his chest and grabbed his knees. "Don't shoot. Don't shoot," he yelled. He wasn't in the war. He knew that. But someone was shooting. Why were they shooting?

By then, someone was on the floor with him. Oscar. "Alex, you're okay," he was saying. "You're okay."

"I know. I know," Alex screamed into his face. "But make them stop shooting."

When Alex awoke the next morning, most of the previous day was a muddle to him. He knew he was at the veterans'

hospital in a ward for the mentally ill, and in all the initial confusion, he had let others make decisions for him. His father had
come to the plant and told Alex, "I'm taking you to a hospital.
You've got to talk to someone about this," and Alex had let
himself be driven there. But he told his father, told the doctor,
that he understood what had happened. Even when he had
heard the sounds and had lunged to the floor, he had realized
that no one was shooting—no matter what he had been shouting. He had only reacted to the sound; he hadn't gone crazy.
This had happened to him before, once long ago in London,
at the train station. It had happened to lots of soldiers. "I'm
okay now," he told the doctor, and he tried to explain to Anna
when she got there. "I'm not losing my mind. You know how
noises do that to me sometimes."

"It was worse this time," she told him, and she cupped her
hand behind his head and kissed his eyes, as though he were
wounded in some way.

But it hadn't been worse, not much anyway. He was all
right. Alex needed to get out of this ward and get back to
work. If he accepted everyone's idea of him, assumed that he
really was going crazy, then he wasn't far away. People should
understand that. Being crazy wasn't as hard as most people
thought; it was mostly a matter of accepting.

At least the doctor seemed to understand more than the
others did. He came in after breakfast and told Alex he could
get dressed and go home. But he wanted to see Alex later that
week, and every week for a while. His name was Kowallis. He
was a rough-looking guy with dark teeth, a day's growth of
beard, and hair that was matted on one side, as though he had
slept at the hospital and had just gotten up. "Look, Thomas,"
he said, and he sounded like the officers Alex had known in the
army, "I was in England during the war. I worked with the boys
they brought back from the front, the ones with battle fatigue.
You've been keeping your finger in the dyke for a long time,
but if you don't work some things out—and I mean right

away—you're going to get caught in the flood you've been holding back. I can guarantee that."

"I'll meet with you. I'm happy to," Alex said. "But I'm not as far gone as you think. I was doing a lot better, and then that loud noise caught me off guard. That's all."

"I'll tell you what, Thomas. You know just as well as I do that there's more to it than that. Don't you?"

Alex had gotten off his bed. He had grabbed his trousers from the little closet, but then he turned around. "Well, sure," he said. "I mean, I know I get nervous. But—"

"You gotta stop lying to yourself. That's the first thing."

Alex bent over, stepped into his pants, pulled up one leg, and then stepped into the other. He pulled the trousers up, under the flimsy robe he had been told to wear. He finally looked at Doctor Kowallis. "I'm not crazy," he said.

"I didn't say you were. But you've got problems, and you need to deal with them."

Alex nodded. He just wasn't sure that "dealing with them" meant meeting with this guy. But he agreed to do it so he could get out of this ward, where half the people mumbled to themselves or stared at the walls. What bothered Alex most was that so many of them were young men.

Alex finished getting dressed and then sat on his bed and waited, but he was surprised when he saw Wally at his door, not Anna, and Richard standing behind Wally. "Anna had to leave Gene with Mom most of the day yesterday," Wally explained. "I just thought it might be easier if I ran over to get you. I asked Richard to come along." But there was something unnatural in Wally's voice, a hint of tension. "And actually," he admitted, "the two of us wanted to talk to you."

"Dad sent you over, didn't he?"

"Not exactly. But he did think it might be a good idea."

"Wally, everyone's making too much out of this. I'm just fine."

Wally stepped all the way into the room, and so did

Richard, and then Wally shut the door. "Could we just sit down and talk for a little while?"

"No. I don't want to stay in this nut house another minute." He stood up and walked to his closet. "I know Dad's got it in his head that you two were in the war, so you understand what's going on with me, but we were all in different situations. I don't think our experiences were much alike." He got his coat down and put it on.

"That's probably true, Alex. But we understand better than other people do. You'll have to admit that."

"Let's go. I think what I'd like to do is go down to the plant. I was supposed to get a letter off yesterday, and I—"

"No, Alex. You're not going down there today. We're taking you home. I'll take care of the letter myself."

But that was the worst thing Wally could say. Didn't he think Alex could take care of something as simple as that? What had everyone decided about him? He glanced at Richard, who hadn't said a word and was standing with his hands tucked into his overcoat pockets, looking grim and worried. They were all giving up, assuming the worst, but Alex wasn't going to let them do that to him. He had to keep pushing forward.

"Fine. Take me home," Alex said. "Then I'll head back over to the U. I don't want to miss my ten o'clock class." But Alex couldn't remember what day it was and whether he really had a class at ten today. How was he going to get that paper done and study for his test when he couldn't seem to think straight?

"Alex, the doctor told Anna that you need to take it easy for a few days. He wrote up a prescription for something that will help you relax. How about if we just take the long way home and go for a ride. Richard and I feel like we do have some things we want to talk to you about, and then you can rest tomorrow, and over the weekend, and start fresh at school on Monday."

But Alex knew better. His paper was due next week. He

needed to put in more time at the library before he finished it, and the test was . . . but he couldn't think about that now. He could feel that his breathing was coming in hard gusts, and his heart had begun to pound, the sound filling up his ears. Wally had seen that something was wrong, and Richard. They were staring at him, and then Wally stepped to him and took hold of his arm. "Alex, are you all right?"

"Sure. Sure. Let's just go."

But by the time they had stopped at the hospital office, signed some papers, and made it out to the parking lot, Alex was feeling frantic. Maybe he could call his professors, tell them he had been in the hospital, and get a little delay on his paper and take the test late, but they would only want to know what was wrong. He didn't want to tell them that. And what about work? Alex needed to get some more hours in before the next paycheck. If he didn't, he wouldn't have enough to cover his bills. He had figured that out very carefully, just a few days before. Dad, of course, would cover him on anything like that, but he didn't want that—didn't want that—didn't want that. He was breathing in gasps again when he sat down in the back seat of the car.

As Wally backed the car out of the parking spot, Richard, who was also sitting in the front, twisted and looked at Alex. "There's something I wanted to tell you," he said.

Alex didn't care. He told himself he would let these guys talk, but he wouldn't let them tell him how nuts he was.

"I think you know I've had a rough time since I got home. Maybe not as bad as you—I'm not sure—but bad enough. Something happened to me that I didn't want to talk to anyone about. But Bobbi finally just wouldn't put up with it anymore, and she made me tell her. I've got to tell you, Alex, that's helped me a lot more than I ever thought it would. It didn't change anything, but I feel better than I have for a long time."

"Tell him what you and Bobbi decided," Wally said.

Richard looked back at Alex again. "I'm going back to

school next fall. We're saving until then, but then I'm going to do what you're doing—go to school full-time and work part-time. I really don't like working at the plant, and I guess I felt trapped down there. I know you're ahead of me on that one, but I just think talking things out, figuring out what's best for me, *and* for Bobbi, that's been really a good step forward."

Alex nodded. But he knew what Richard didn't know. He was walking into a pressure cooker, trying to go to school, work, and raise a family all at once. That wasn't going to be as great as Richard thought.

Maybe he could get the paper done if he didn't go to work at all for a few days, and maybe he could delay a bill or two and catch up next month. But by then finals would be coming on, and how would he find extra time to work then?

"Alex, would it help you to get some things off your chest?" Wally asked. "Are you holding some feelings inside, like Richard was doing, that you ought to tell someone? You could tell us, if you don't feel like telling Anna. We certainly know the kinds of things that go on in a war."

Alex waited for a time, not wanting to answer, but he knew he had to say something. "No," he said. "I'd just rather leave it alone."

"But maybe you can't, Alex. You told us once that you had to kill young boys. Is that what keeps eating at you?"

"Nothing's eating at me exactly, Wally. It's not like that."

"Something's wrong, Alex."

"Look, Wally, don't do this. I've been nervous, I know that. But I have a lot going on in my life, that's all. And loud noises still scare me. A lot of soldiers have that problem. It's no reason to stick me away in a loony bin."

He wasn't going to say anything else. He couldn't get into this kind of conversation. He felt like the top of his head was going to blow off. Wally was driving west, down Broadway. He wasn't taking Alex home. But Alex didn't protest. He would let them have their say, and then maybe that would be the end of it.

Out the window, Alex saw two little boys, brothers probably, both too young for school. They were bundled up in
matching wool coats and hats with ear flaps. The weather
wasn't quite *that* cold, but he was sure some mother had made
them put all that stuff on. He remembered that, of course,
remembered himself out there with Wally and Gene. He liked
how simple it looked, the two boys playing together, there in
that nice neighborhood.

Richard was still looking back. "Alex, I think you know," he
said, quietly, "I was on a ship that was sunk in the Leyte Gulf. I
was one of the guys who ended up on a life raft—mainly
because I had gotten burned. But most of our crew went into
the water with only their life jackets on, and I'm sure they knew
they didn't have much chance of surviving that way. A lot of
them saw our boat and swam toward us. But the boat couldn't
take any more weight without swamping."

Alex was looking up now, listening. He thought he knew
what Richard was going to say.

"The men on the boat kept screaming for the ones in the
water to stay away, but those poor guys were terrified, and they
kept grabbing at us. Guys started using oars to knock away all
the reaching arms. Some of them even hit those guys over the
head." Richard hesitated and then added, even more quietly,
"All the men in the boat lived—except for two who were
burned real bad, worse than me. The biggest share of the guys
in the water died."

Alex had lost his breath. "Richard, that's . . . rough."

No one tried to explain it, discuss it. But Alex understood.
He knew what Richard had been carrying around with him all
this time.

Wally kept driving west and then turned north on
Highway 89, heading out of Salt Lake toward Bountiful, and all
this time no one spoke. But eventually, in the same kind of quiet
voice, Wally said, "I had two friends who got me through the
death march: Warren Hicks, a Mormon guy, and another friend

from my unit, a kid named Jack Norland. We stuck together in our first camp, shared any food we could scrounge, and just tried to keep each other going. You get real close to guys in a situation like that. But one day those two got sent out on a one-day detail, and while they were gone, I got shipped off on a long-term job. I got trucked into a jungle with a lot of other POWs. The Japs made us cut a road through all that dense growth out there. Men started dying, almost from the beginning, and they kept dying every day. We would work long hours, with hardly anything to eat, and then come back and bury our friends every night. Almost everyone on that job died—something like three hundred men. Only forty or fifty of us lived. I got really sick too, and there wasn't much left of me by the end. But I made it out and got taken to another prison, back in Manila. After a while, I got a chance to talk to some guys from Camp O'Donnell, where I'd been at first. That's when I found out that Warren and Jack had both died while I was out there. I've never told anyone that—not even Lorraine. But I think about those guys every single day of my life."

"How'd you stay alive, Wally?" Alex asked.

"I don't know. Some of it was being able to pray and think about my family. Some of it was finding some other good buddies who helped me. A lot of it was luck—or maybe God looking out for me. But I don't like to say that, because that makes it sound like God didn't care about the guys who died."

"I know. I used to think about that too," Alex said. "Guys kept going down, and bullets kept flying right on by me."

Alex was breathing better, even feeling a little better.

"I think every soldier comes home wondering about that," Wally said. "Why did I live when guys all around me died?"

"Toward the end of the war," Alex said, "I got dropped into Germany, behind the lines. I was with a German guy named Otto. A couple of military cops picked us up, and we had no choice but to kill them. That got people looking for us, and we ended up blowing the cover for our underground contact man over there. I found out later that because of us, this guy was tortured and killed by the Gestapo. He had a wife and two little boys, too. And then, after we'd made it through the whole thing, and we were getting out, some quick-trigger GI shot Otto—even though he had his hands in the air. Our own guys killed him, after I thought we'd made it through. There I was standing right next to Otto, but they killed him and not me."

Wally and Richard told Alex how hard they thought that would be, but Alex knew that wasn't the whole thing. "A lot of things have stayed in my mind," he said. "I try not to think about them, but all of a sudden, they're just there. When Otto killed one of those MPs, he got behind him and cut his throat. The blood spurted from his neck, just like it was coming out of a hose. It got all over my clothes. Sometimes now, when I dream, I see that blood squirting, and I try to run from it, but it keeps flowing, just covering me all up. It's all crazy, you know—it doesn't make any sense. But I wake up . . . I don't know . . . all upset. A lot of times I can't go back to sleep after that."

Alex didn't want to let go of his emotions, but he felt himself beginning to shake. He turned, curled up a little, and leaned his head against the seat, and only then did he realize that he had begun to weep.

"You were out there in the battle so long," Richard said. "We got attacked a few times, but I never had to face all those days in combat. And I never had to kill anyone."

"It was the same with me," Wally said. "We suffered, but we never had to kill."

"It's part of war. It's something you have to do," Alex said. He was trying to tell that to himself, mostly, had been trying for such a long time.

"Maybe it's part of war," Wally said. "But that doesn't make it part of *you*."

Alex knew there was something else he wanted to tell. He gritted his teeth and tried to get his control. "On the first morning after we dropped into Normandy, on D-Day, we took some German prisoners. I talked to this one young German. He said he was from Mannheim. I'd spent some time in Heidelberg on my mission, not far from there, so I'd been to Mannheim, and I said something to him about that. He was a nice kid, you know—scared, hoping we wouldn't kill him. We only talked a little, but he told me I spoke good German—a couple of things like that. It was just enough to feel like I knew him a little. And then we got caught in an ambush. Somewhere in the middle of everything, I looked over, and that boy was reaching for a rifle. So I had to shoot him. That was the first guy I killed—this nice kid I'd been talking with. I've never forgotten his face. It comes back to me. I dream about it, or suddenly, for no reason, I'll see his face in my mind, right when I'm trying to do my work, or study, or something like that."

"Alex, bad dreams are really common," Wally said. "I dream that the Japs are beating us, that I'm still back there shoveling coal and getting nothing to eat."

"I saw a whole sea full of dead Japanese soldiers one night, floating in the water, out behind our ship," Richard said. "I've had dreams about them ever since."

Wally glanced back at Alex. "I guess if *you're* nuts, then so are we, Alex." Wally tried to laugh. "Does that make you feel any better?"

Alex took the question seriously. It did make a difference to know they had some of the same problems, and he hadn't thought it would.

Wally said, "Alex, most guys who went to war didn't really see combat, or at least not much, the way you did. I think the guys who went through as much as you did are having a lot of the same kind of struggles. You're not crazy, but you do need to keep talking. You need to see a doctor who understands how to deal with some of this stuff, and you need to stop hiding what you feel from yourself."

Alex took a long, smooth breath, one that felt deep and

satisfying. "Maybe so, Wally. But I'd like to talk to you guys more. This has helped more than anything ever has."

"Sure."

And so they kept driving north, all the way to Ogden, and Alex told more of what he had seen and done. He told about the men in his squad, what they had meant to him, and how almost all of them had gone down sooner or later, dead or badly wounded, and how he assumed that he would have to die too, before he got out—and never see Anna again. He told about the mud and rain in Holland, the day he huddled in a foxhole as the Germans attacked with tanks, and how certain death had seemed. And then about Bastogne and the cold, and he told them more about Howie. "I promised Howie I would keep him alive, and I thought I could do it," he said. "But I let him down. I never should have made him that promise." And finally he told about the boy in the snow, the German boy lying in the field of white with the half-circle of blood around him—the boy who had become Christ, in his mind, slaughtered and forsaken.

Wally told more too, about hunger and disease, and eventually about forgiveness, and Richard told about losing a friend to a fighter attack, right before his eyes. And at one time or another, all three of the men cried. When they finally pulled up in front of Alex's house, Alex said, "Thanks, you guys. I guess I've been needing to say some of these things—ever since the war ended."

"The truth is, the war doesn't end," Richard said.

"No, I guess it doesn't. That's the problem. I guess I have to stop thinking that it will." But it was good to admit that—more important than he ever could have suspected. He thanked them again, and after he had gotten out of the car, he leaned back in and said, "I think I'd like to talk to you guys again."

"That's what we were thinking, too," Wally said. "I think it will help all three of us."

"It doesn't exactly solve the problems, though, does it?"

"No. It doesn't. The memories don't go away. But they don't go away when you try to hide from them either."

"Yeah."

Alex walked to his house. He found Anna in the living room. She was picking up some toys Gene had scattered there. She stood straight and came toward him hesitantly, looking worried, and it struck him how difficult he had made her life lately. "Wally and Richard took me for a ride," he said.

She nodded her understanding.

"They have a lot of the same problems—dreams and bad memories, all of that. And they went through some of the same kind of stuff."

She only nodded again.

"Where's Gene?"

"He's down for his nap."

Alex was the one nodding now, waiting, wondering what he could say to her. "Anna, I'll be okay. I've told you that before. But I'm going back to that doctor this time. And I'm going to talk more with Wally and Richard. I thought it would make things worse to talk about everything, but it seemed to help."

"Peter needs help too, Alex. Mama is so worried about him."

"I'll talk to him. We talked in Germany a little but not since then—not much."

"That would be so good. I don't think he would say anything to anyone else, but he might with you." She moved a little closer and touched his hand. He took hold of her and pulled her closer, wrapped his arms around her.

"Anna, why do some men come home and not have all these problems? That's how I wanted to be. I didn't want to act like a baby about all this."

"Alex, no one who went through as much as you did can come home and just go back to normal. But you're all so much the same. You try to hide what you're feeling—think that's the manly thing to do."

"Anna, I thought I'd be all right once I had you and Gene— and look what I've been doing to the two of you."

She had her arms around him, gripped against his back. He felt her squeeze tighter. "Alex, we've all asked too much of you. You've asked too much of yourself. But you are a good husband and a good father. And you'll be even better. You're going to be okay."

He took a long breath, wanting to believe that the struggle was almost over, that the air around him would be easier now. "I love you," he told Anna. "Thanks for not giving up on me."

"Alex, you know me better than that. I never will. And God won't either. He knows your heart. He knows what you tried to do."

"The war must have broken God's heart, Anna. How could he stand to watch what we did to each other?"

One day in April Wally left the dealership in the hands of his salesmen, and he drove to Mat Nakashima's farm. He had known for a long time that he needed to talk to Mat, but he just hadn't been able to get himself to do it. He was not surprised when he found Ike there, with Mat. Wally had heard that Ike was back in Utah and that he was working with his brother. They had even bought more land and were increasing the size of their farm.

Wally found the two of them in front of the barn. They were leaning over a tractor, peering at the engine. "Are you two trying to use the power of prayer on that tractor?" Wally asked as he walked toward them.

Mat turned around and smiled when he saw Wally. They had seen each other a couple of times since Wally had come home, but they had never had a chance to talk at any length. "That's actually not a bad idea," Mat said. "Nothing else we've tried has worked." He pulled a glove off and reached toward Wally, shook his hand. "Do you know my brother Ike?"

"Yes. I met him a long time ago—before the war." He shook hands with Ike, too.

"You look good, Wally," Mat said. "You've filled out. The last time I saw you, you were still awfully thin."

But Wally felt a little strange talking about that with these two. "Yeah, I'm pretty much back to normal," he said.

Mat leaned against the tractor and pulled off his other glove, as though he were relieved to forget about the engine trouble for the moment. "President Thomas told me that you're working for him. He said you're doing a great job."

"Really?" Wally asked. "Did he say that?"

"I'll tell you what he told me, exactly. He said, 'Wally's not the same boy he was before the war. He's the best man I've got working for me now.'"

Wally liked that, actually, but he laughed and said, "I sure hope I'm doing a better job for him than I did for you."

Mat smiled and tucked his hands into the pockets of his overalls. It was a nice afternoon, after a couple of showery days, and the sun on Wally's back felt good. Mat seemed content, relaxed, more so than Wally remembered. "You were young back then," Mat said. "Just a kid."

"Wally," Ike said, "I heard you got some pretty rough treatment in the Philippines. How'd you get through all that?" Ike was a little taller than his brother, bigger through the neck and shoulders, but the two sounded just alike, even had the same mannerisms. And neither of them seemed self-conscious about Ike's question.

"I don't know. A guy just does what he has to do. But it sure wasn't easy." Wally had thought ahead of time what he wanted to say, at least to Mat, but he had trouble now thinking of a way to introduce the topic. So he only said, "I'm just trying to get on with my life now."

"That's good, Wally," Mat said. "It could have made you bitter."

Again Wally hesitated. He had left his suit coat in the car and was wearing a dark pair of slacks with a white shirt and tie. He took hold of his suspenders, grasped them a little too tight, set his feet a little wider apart, and then said, "Mat and Ike, I just want you to know I don't hold any sort of grudge."

"Grudge?"

"I don't just mean against those guards who put us through so much. I'm saying I don't hold any hard feelings against anyone. I don't connect you two with any of that. Some guys came home from the war hating all Japanese, but I don't feel that way at all. I feel kind of bad that I've never stopped by to say hello or anything, but it wasn't out of hard feelings. It was just that I've been . . ." He had come close to saying something that wasn't true, that he had been too busy. He stopped himself and said instead, "What I mean is, I've tried not to think about the war and the prison camps since I got back, and maybe I avoided you some—just because it seemed like it might be a little awkward."

Mat didn't respond for a moment. He looked back at Wally, studying him, as though he were a little confused. "Well, it was good of you to come by," he said. He stood straight, leaned away from the tractor, and Wally felt the tension, felt as though he were being dismissed.

"That's right, Wally," Ike said. "It was good of you to come over here. You're a nice guy. You're not like Mat's dentist."

"What?"

Ike stepped forward a little and pulled his hands out of his pockets. "During the war," he said, "Mat couldn't find anyone to fix his teeth. Him, nor his kids."

Wally saw what was coming, and he had no idea how to respond.

"Don't get into that all that," Mat told his brother. "Let's just—"

"This dentist told him he wouldn't put his hands into a *Jap's* mouth. Our family had gone to that same dentist since we were little kids. Our money had always been as good as anyone else's—until the war broke out."

"Look," Wally said, "I know how things have been. I didn't mean to . . . you know . . ." But he couldn't think what to say.

"There were signs in store windows—all over this country: 'Japs, stay out.'"

"I know. I've heard about that."

"I spent the war in an internment camp, Wally."

"Look, Ike, I'm sorry. I said the wrong thing. I just didn't know quite what to say. All I wanted to do was put the war in the past and tell you that I hope we're still friends."

Ike chuckled and was about to say something else, but Mat said, "Wally, I do appreciate it. Thanks for stopping by." But the words were terse, almost hard. Once again, Wally was being dismissed.

"Hey, don't mind me," Ike said. "I don't mean to be like that. Your dad worked hard to get me out of that camp. He's one of the best men I know—and I'm sure you're just like him. But I'll tell you what. You ought to drive down to Delta some time before the Topaz camp totally disappears. You ought to have a look at that desert land out there, see where Japanese families had to live. We're *Americans*, Wally—the same as you. And a lot of us were held like prisoners, guarded by men with rifles."

Wally was trying not to be defensive, but his impulse was to describe some of the conditions he had lived in, to tell Ike what his guards had done.

"Sometimes, in those camps, eight or ten families would end up in one barracks, and there were no partitions. People would hang up blankets if they had any. But there was no privacy. If a man and his wife wanted to be together, you can imagine what it was like."

"It must have been humiliating," Wally said. It was something he hadn't known, and he sensed how deeply Ike still felt the shame of it.

"I'll tell you something else most people still don't know. Our people weren't given a proper diet, weren't fed enough. A lot of them got sick. And these were people who could have been home on their farms, feeding this country."

"It was wrong, Ike. There's no doubt about it."

"What do you think it did to our children, Wally? How would you like to be told, as a kid, that because your ancestors came from a certain country, you had to be placed in a camp like that? No one stuck Germans in those places. Or Italians."

"I know."

"The people who mistreated you were enemies—soldiers from another country. The ones who rounded us up and stuck us away were our own neighbors."

"Ike, that's enough," Mat said. "What good does it do to talk about all this now?" He turned halfway around, toward the tractor.

"That's fine," Ike said, "I only brought it up because there's something I want to say to Wally."

Wally nodded. "What's that?" he asked.

"We don't hold a grudge."

Wally looked at the ground. "I see what you mean," he said. "I'm sorry I said it that way."

But Mat said, "Wally, the war is over. Let's just forget about all of that."

"That's what I *did* want to say," Wally told him.

* * *

LaRue had the letter in her hand. She had been accepted to Radcliffe College in Massachusetts, and she had been awarded a scholarship that would cover her tuition. What the scholarship didn't cover was her living expenses. She believed she could earn enough money to add to her savings, at least to get by the first year, but that was not her biggest worry. The problem was, she didn't know what her dad was going to say. She planned to go, even if he told her she couldn't, but she didn't want a fight. She had fought with her father enough in her life. If she was going to leave home this fall, she wanted to go in peace and feel that she could come back in the same way.

She had walked the few blocks down to the dealership and asked Dad's secretary whether it would be all right to see him. "Just wait about five minutes," Gloria had told her. "He's in with a customer, but they've been 'almost finished' for about half an hour."

Actually, nearly fifteen minutes passed before Dad finally walked out, shook hands, and said good-bye to a big bald-headed man in a gray suit. But then Dad looked at LaRue and said, "My goodness, what are you doing here?"

"I need to talk to you," she told him.

"All right," he said, but he sounded concerned, as though he expected a problem. He held the door for LaRue and let her into his office ahead of him. He had her sit in a chair in front of his desk, but he turned it before he motioned for her to sit down, and then he pulled another chair close, facing hers. All this unnerved LaRue a little. In a way, it was easier to deal with his power with the expanse of his big desk between them.

"Read this," she said, and she pulled her letter from the envelope and handed it to him.

He unfolded the letter and read it very slowly. She had the feeling that he was delaying a little, probably preparing his response. Finally, he said, "And I suppose you want to accept this?"

"Of course I do."

He nodded and then seemed to consider for a time. "Could you explain just a little of your thinking?" he said. "Why would you rather go back to Massachusetts than stay here at the University?"

"It's a really good school, Dad. One of the best. It's an honor to get in."

"I'm not sure I understand who decides those kinds of things, but I still wonder why you would rather go to school back east than around here."

"Dad, we've been talking about this for almost two years. I think it'll be good for me. I want to meet other people and have a chance to be on my own."

"You could do that down at the Y, couldn't you?"

"No. I don't think so. People in Provo are exactly the same

as here in Salt Lake. I want to know how other people live—the way Bobbi had a chance to do when she lived in Hawaii all that time."

"Bobbi was a lot older when she left."

LaRue could see what was coming. He was going to force her to justify everything, and she didn't want to do that. She had made her choice, she was almost eighteen, and she had won the scholarship on her own. She had earned her right to make this decision. "Dad, I'm planning to go."

"I know," he said, and he was surprisingly quick to respond. LaRue had the feeling that he had accepted that she was leaving whether he liked it or not. That was something; it just wasn't what she wanted. Why couldn't he trust her for once, just assume that she could make a wise decision?

"I only asked what you're thinking—why you want to go away." His voice was calm, but she saw how stiff he was, his chin set, his breath drawn in.

"Dad, I've talked to Wally a lot about this. It seems like, living here with my family all around me, and surrounded by people who believe the same things I do, I can't really find out how deep my faith is—or what the other choices are. I feel like I need to get away to really get my own testimony."

"So is that what you're going away to look for—a deeper testimony?"

"In a way. That's one of the things." But that didn't ring true, not even to LaRue, and she knew it.

"It seems to me that you want to get out from under my thumb as much as anything." He laughed, and a little more ease seemed to come over him. He put his elbows on the arms of his chair and leaned forward a bit.

"Dad, you're so strong. You're so clear about everything. Half of what I do is to please you, and the other half is to get your goat. Do you know what I mean?"

"Oh, yes."

"It's like I'm not me. I'm just a reaction to *you*."

"Is that what you think? Or has someone said that to you?"

"Dad, why do you—"

"It's just that I think your friend Cecil felt that way, and he said a lot of those things to you. I'm not sure you'd feel the need to run off if he hadn't pushed that idea."

In the old days LaRue would have erupted. She would have denied the accusation, announced what she was going to do, and stomped out of the office. But she knew, in fact, that Cecil had had a big influence on her. So she took a breath and said, "Dad, Cecil got me thinking seriously about myself and what I believed. I'd never worried about those kinds of things until the two of us started talking. So in a way, he was a help to me. But I didn't like the way he acted when he came home for Christmas. He had his nose in the air, and he was saying all kinds of negative things about the Church. I won't ever be like that—I promise you. But I still want this experience. I've worked hard for it."

"But I still don't understand. Why is it you want to go? So you can think for yourself?"

"Yes. And experience something new. I want to know other people and live in another place. Don't you ever feel like you want to do that?"

"No, I guess I don't. The Saints struggled too hard to get to this valley and to build this city. I want to stay right here and try to protect it. It's becoming way too much like other towns."

"But when you were younger, didn't you feel like you wanted to get away for a while?"

"No. It never even occurred to me."

"But Dad, the world has changed. It's gotten smaller."

"I don't know what that means, LaRue."

She didn't either, and she knew it. It was just something she heard people saying lately. She sat back in her chair and tried to sort her thoughts out for real. "Dad, when did you first know that you believed in the Church?"

"I don't know. I don't remember ever doubting it. But I

didn't just 'go along' with it, if that's what you're thinking. The Spirit has borne testimony to me many times, very powerfully. I have no reason to doubt."

"But I'm not like that. I doubt *everything*. I know I want the excitement of going away, and I guess I like the idea of being on my own. But I really do want to see what happens when no one else does my thinking for me."

"Will you do that? Or will you let a bunch of eastern professors make fun of everything you've been taught?" He stopped and stared into her eyes. "And lead you carefully down to hell?"

LaRue was the one becoming nervous. She looked away. "I don't want *anyone* to lead me. I want to find my own path."

"Well, fine. I know it's what you feel you have to do, and if I tried to stop you, it would be a big mistake. But I'm scared to death, LaRue. I don't know whether you're as strong as you think you are. I do believe you're a good person, and you've grown up about ten years in the last two, but there's something defiant in you, and that could be your downfall. It's entirely possible that you'll resist everyone else's guidance—and make some very poor decisions on your own."

She looked at the carpet, calmed herself a little, and then looked back up and smiled. "This is where I'm supposed to start yelling, 'See, you still don't trust me.'"

"Aren't you going to do that?"

"No. I haven't given you many reasons to trust me, and I'm not sure you're wrong. Maybe I will mess everything up."

"Well, I'll tell you this much: I feel a lot better when you admit that it's a danger. That shows me you really are growing up. Do you still want to major in business and then start your own company?"

"They don't have a business major at Radcliffe. It's all liberal arts. But I do want to start my own company someday. I just don't care so much about money as I used to."

"That's a good sign, too. I've had to learn a little about that myself."

"Mom's getting tough these days, Dad. You're the one who's getting *led*."

"I know. But she's a better person than I am. At least I recognize that."

"Maybe I'll come back someday and run a business in Utah."

He smiled, waited for a moment, and then asked, "How about one of mine?"

"Really?"

"Sure. Why not?"

"Maybe I'll do that, Dad. We'd knock 'em dead together, don't you think?"

Now he grinned much wider. "I think we would, little girl. And I think I'd like to invest in that possibility. Since you earned your tuition on your own, how about if I pay your dorm bills, your books and food and that sort of thing?"

"Wow. Really?"

"Sure."

"This *is* a trick, isn't it?"

"Not at all. What do you mean?"

"You figure I won't stray quite so far away if you still have some financial control over me."

"LaRue, you're just like everyone else in the family. You always think I have ulterior motives."

"That's because you always do."

He gripped his hands together and looked down at them for a time, and when he raised his head, he seemed much more serious. "I suppose I do, LaRue. I want you kids to do good things with your lives. I want you to be righteous. And I don't know how to make that happen."

"You've already done what you can, Dad. Now you just have to wait and see how it all turns out."

"Maybe so. But that doesn't mean I have to like letting go of each one of you. It's hard for me, every single time."

"Then how come you're moving? We won't even have the old house to come home to."

"You'll have a nice new one—with a couple more bedrooms so you can all come home at the same time."

In recent weeks the builder had finally broken ground for the house Dad had been talking about for a couple of years now. Mom still didn't seem all that excited about it, but she had approved the plans, and Dad kept saying how great it would be, with more land for the grandkids to run on, a modern kitchen, a better furnace, and all those kinds of things. But it all seemed very strange to LaRue. "I like the house we have," she said.

"You'll like the new one even better."

"I hope," LaRue said, and then she got up, leaned toward her dad, and kissed him on the cheek. "Dad, thanks. Really. Thanks so much. And don't worry. I'm going to be all right. Honest."

He stood up and took hold of her shoulders. "You have no idea what you're going to face, LaRue. I almost wish we had the war back. It didn't scare me nearly so much as Radcliffe College does."

"I know what you mean, Dad. I'm scared to go."

"Well, good. That might help." He took her into his arms. "But I still wish you'd stay home a while yet."

* * *

Alex, Wally, and Richard, with their wives, were seated at the head table. Al and Bea were also there, along with Hyrum Christensen, head of the state Republican party, and his wife, Merla. Alex had dreaded this night for almost a year, but he had never found the nerve to tell his dad he wouldn't do it. The ballroom at the Newhouse Hotel was packed with people who had paid handsomely for their dinners, most of them people who could easily afford it, and now desserts had been served and the three speakers were about to be introduced. Mr. Christensen tapped on the microphone, then cleared his throat to get the attention of the audience. When the voices quieted a little, he said, "Could I have your attention please?" People began shifting in their chairs to look toward him.

"We have a great treat tonight—some wonderful speakers. Three truly great young men. These men—Al and Bea Thomas's sons and son-in-law—each fought in a different branch of the service: Alex Thomas in the army; Wally Thomas in the air corps; and Richard Hammond in the navy. Al Thomas has warned me that these boys don't like to be called heroes, and asked me not to call them that." Mr. Christensen hesitated, chuckling. "Here's what I want to say about that. I'd be disappointed if they *did* want me to call them heroes. But I would also be dead wrong if I called them anything else. These are young men who served our country and served it well. They defeated the devil himself, as far as I'm concerned, and preserved the peace for all of us. I will thank these boys—and millions more like them—until the day I die. I'm sure every one here feels the same way."

Someone began to applaud, and then everyone else joined in. Someone else, at the back of the ballroom, stood up, and that set the room in motion—people setting down their forks and napkins, pushing back their chairs, standing in their colorful gowns and dark suits. But Alex didn't watch long. He trained his eyes on the tablecloth, hoping that all of this would end soon. He also hoped that the order of the names, the way Mr. Christensen had mentioned them, would be the order of the talks. But when calm finally settled in and the guests took their seats again, Mr. Christensen announced the speakers in the opposite order. And Alex heard, in the descriptions, the levels of priority: Richard had survived the sinking of his ship, which was interesting, but Wally had survived the Bataan Death March—even better. What Alex heard about himself was that he had won the Distinguished Service Medal, a Silver

Star, and a Purple Heart. He had parachuted into Normandy on D-Day, had been surrounded at Bastogne with the famous 101st Airborne Division, had received a battlefield commission, and had been sent behind enemy lines to help the Allies cross the Rhine. It was the ultimate set of credentials for a hero, the sort every soldier longed for—now that the war was over.

Bobbi patted Richard's hand and whispered, "You'll do fine," as he slid his chair back. He walked to the podium, pulled his tie straight, and buttoned his double-breasted blue suit. But then he leaned a little too close to the microphone, and his first words sent a deep-voiced blast through the ballroom. He laughed, backed off a little, and said, "Sorry about that." He smiled and waited as the audience laughed, and Alex was sure that all these middle-aged women had just fallen in love. Richard looked the part of a hero with those crystalline eyes and that sculpted jaw.

"What I want to say tonight won't take long," Richard said, softly this time. "I love my country, and I'm glad the war turned out the way it did. But I really was *not* a hero. I was a guy like so many others who would have just as soon *not* gone off to war. I joined the navy before the war, and I didn't really bargain on the things that I ended up doing. But that's how most soldiers and sailors were. Americans aren't warlike people. We don't go looking for a fight. What we did in this war was what we *had* to do—and now we're glad it's over."

Alex had planned to say something of the same sort. He wondered whether he could say just a few sentences, agree with the others, and sit down. Maybe that was the best way to avoid some of the things that he found himself wanting to say. For over a month now, he had been meeting with Doctor Kowallis. He had told the man some things that he had never told anyone before, and he did find some hard-earned relief in doing that, but he wasn't sure that the talks accomplished as much as he would have liked. He hadn't been as nervous lately, and that was certainly a good sign, but just when he had decided he was doing much better, he had had a terrible dream one night, had rolled out of bed screaming and flailing at an enemy that had jumped at him in the dark. Anna had called to him from the bed, afraid to come near him until he had calmed down.

"My ship was hit by a kamikaze during the Battle of the Philippine Sea," Richard was saying. "It sank in the Leyte Gulf, and it went down fast. Many of the men went into the water with nothing but life jackets. These men were in the water for the better part of three days, and more than half of them died. Some were eaten by sharks. Some couldn't stand the thirst and drank the seawater. But most died of starvation and exposure. I was one of the lucky ones. I was able to board a life raft, and I'm alive. And for that I'm very thankful."

Alex, of course, knew how much more Richard might have said about all that, but he was glad that he didn't.

"All of us who came home from the war wonder why some died and some didn't. We wonder whether we deserved to be the survivors when so many good men were lost. I didn't want to die. No one did. In the movies, men die gladly, and I suppose that happens in some cases, but I saw how afraid most of us were. Some men panicked. Others worried more about themselves than about their friends—and that's understandable—but most of us just did our best, and some of us were luckier than others.

"So here's what I feel. A lot of young men gave their lives for the rest of us. And we must never cease to pay honor to them. They are the heroes. We are their benefactors. I feel like we have to live worthy of them and their sacrifice. I want to spend every day of my life making this country, this world, a better place to live. I can't do much. I'm not an important man. But all of us together—we can do plenty. Thank you."

Richard walked back to the table and sat down next to Bobbi. She put her arm around his neck and kissed him. "That was wonderful," she said.

Alex heard Richard whisper, "Maybe I should have told them the rest."

"No," Bobbi said. "That was just right. You told the truth. Every word of it was perfect."

Alex thought so too.

Wally had already reached the podium. "I ought to pull this microphone down an inch or two," he said, "but I don't want to admit that my brother-in-law is taller than I am. It's bad enough that he's better looking."

There was probably some truth to that, but Alex thought Wally looked great. In the last year, since Alex had come home, Wally had become so much stronger, his face getting back its old color, his chest filling out. And there was more to it than that. He always looked to Alex as if he knew something most people didn't, as though satisfaction was a natural state for him.

"One thing Richard didn't mention," he said, "is that he was badly burned before his ship sank, and that's why he was placed on that lifeboat. He has done his own share of suffering." Wally smiled then and said, "I started the war by surrendering. I doubt that qualifies me for a statue down on State Street, up next to Brigham Young."

People laughed again, but with a certain reserve. Alex knew—and of course, Wally did—that that wasn't exactly the right thing to say.

"I suppose we had no choice but to surrender in the Philippines, and the brass—not us soldiers—made the decision. But for a long time I worried that if I lived to see this place, you people would consider me a coward. My captors often told me how despicable my behavior had been. They said I should have fought to the death. But one of the greatest experiences of my life was to reach the Golden Gate Bridge and to be greeted by signs that called me a hero. The only thing I ever did to earn that title was to survive, but I will say, there's nothing I'll ever do in my life that will take more effort.

I'm just glad that Americans have been willing to grant us POWs respect for what we were able to do—stay alive."

The applause was quick in coming this time. People obviously wanted Wally to know that they understood what he was saying.

"I feel like Richard. I don't know why I lived and others died. Over half the men in my squadron died, and they weren't cowards or weaklings. Much of getting through was luck, but everyone who did get through had to find strength he didn't even know he had. There were many times I thought I was finished. What seems so strange to me now is that I can sit down to a meal like this and think it's just a normal thing. For three and a half years, I dreamed every day that I would someday have a chance to eat like this again. On most days we ate two cups of rice, and little else."

Alex heard the stir in the crowd, and he wondered whether this was what Wally ought to tell these people. They knew all this, and they often used this kind of information to cling to their anger over the war.

"I recently had a conversation with a friend of mine. He was held in a camp during the war, just as I was. I told him that I had no grudge against the Japanese, and I want to tell you, tonight, how that came about. When the war ended, and I was released from prison camp, I had an experience that changed my life. I had been badly mistreated by a man—the Japanese commander of our camp. He had come within an inch of taking my life. He had tortured me almost to the breaking point. And yet, when he announced our release, a change of heart came over me. In a matter of seconds I went from hating him to understanding him, and then forgiving him. I've never held any hatred toward him or any of the Japanese since that day. The war is over for me—truly over. But I couldn't have changed my own heart that way. God granted me the capacity to forgive, and I believe there is no greater gift I could have received. I know men who are trying to live with the bitterness they still harbor, and that is a curse I wouldn't want to deal with."

Wally paused, looked down at the podium, and then spoke quietly. "I mentioned my friend, who was also held in a camp. He has been able to do the same thing. He has forgiven those who held him during the war. He holds no grudge. His name is Ike Nakashima. He was raised here in this valley. He's a good man, a good American, and he spent the war in the Manzanar internment camp in California. He's like me. He wants to work hard and prosper and share with all Americans the good times that have followed this war. He and his brother, Mat—I'm sure some of you know them—love this country just as much as any of us."

Wally hesitated, and Alex could feel the nervous quiet in the room. "I would hope that this group gathered here tonight—people who care about the future of our country— would think about the Japanese Americans who helped get us through the war. No one fought more valiantly than the 100th Battalion and the 442nd Regimental Combat Team—made up almost entirely of Japanese Americans. Personally, I think it's time to heal all the wounds of the war, including those at home. We need to accept everyone—Americans of every background—into the circle of our brother and sisterhood."

Wally glanced quickly around the room. "I hope I haven't said the wrong thing. I don't want to create bad feelings on a night like this. I just think the greatest heroes are people who love their neighbors. That's something I don't think we should forget even during a war, and certainly not after one. Political parties can only solve so many problems. We have to solve the rest of them in our own hearts."

Alex was surprised by the volume of the applause. When Wally sat down, he said, "I'm sorry, Dad. I shouldn't have gotten into that."

"No, don't apologize. You're exactly right. And people need

to think about the very things you just brought up. Listen to them. They agree with you."

Alex was getting up. The only trouble was, he had no idea what he was going to say. He had prepared some ideas, but Richard and Wally had said most of what he had thought of, and some of his other thoughts now seemed inappropriate. There was a good feeling in the room, and he really didn't want to ruin that—especially for his dad.

When Alex stepped up to the podium, he found that he couldn't see very well. Lights were shining in his eyes, and the people were mostly just shadows, heads and shoulders in silhouette. He felt disconnected from them. "I would have preferred not to speak tonight," he said. "It's really hard for me to know what to say to you. I do want you to know that I think highly of people who are willing to commit their time to our country. I know how much it matters to my father to elect good people and to see the country move in the right direction. I haven't been very political so far in my life, but my interest is growing. I think citizens ought to be involved, and I want to be a problem-solver, not just a critic, the way so many people are. In fact, this just might be my first political speech." He stopped and laughed. "Except . . . I'm not entirely sure I'm not a Democrat."

Alex hoped for a laugh, but he got only a chuckle, mostly from the head table, and now he was really scared.

"Richard and Wally have both said they are not heroes. My father once called me a hero and I almost took his head off. I told him never to call me that again. I'm not exactly sure why I reacted so strongly, but one of the things I was feeling, back then, was that we shouldn't make heroes of people who are forced to take someone's life. We should make heroes of people who find ways not to kill, who bring goodness to our world. I agree with Richard that we should appreciate those who fought for our country, and I'm certainly not ashamed that I did my part. But right before I was a soldier, I was a missionary. And

I was never once called a hero for my missionary work—even though I believe that work was far greater than what I did in the war."

These were things Alex *had* planned to say, but he was saying them because they were the words he had put into his head. He still felt a gulf between him and the shadows.

"We should honor our warriors. I believe that. But we must never honor war. This was the most bloody, horrifying war in history. Some say that more than fifty million people are dead, many of them women and children. In many lands, more civilians died than soldiers. People are still starving and dying in Europe. In this country, we have many reasons to be happy: we won the war and some evil philosophies were defeated. But at what cost? Those of us who fought in this war will spend our lives trying to forget what we saw—trying to empty our minds of the pictures that are left there: the broken bodies, the demolished cities, the scarred earth."

This was not anything Alex had planned, but he felt his voice becoming more intense as the words came to him.

"Let me tell you what makes me proud. Most of the men who won this war were just kids. They would rather have stayed home. They didn't go into battle as career soldiers. They just did what they had to do. I saw kids hunker down in their foxholes and cry. I heard wounded guys beg for their mothers. I saw plenty of seasoned soldiers vomit when they walked across a battlefield, after a battle, and saw what they had done. These were just young guys who hated what they were doing but felt they had to do it.

"So that's what I want to say. Let's honor our soldiers—for doing a dirty, stinking job. But let's not honor war. I wish we would just stop all this talk about glory and honor and spend a little more time feeling disgusted that humans can't come up with any better way to solve problems.

"I was a missionary in Germany, and then I returned to that land with a dark purpose—one I didn't choose, but still, one that I did believe in. But I wish that it had been otherwise. I wish I had been able to finish my mission. I wish I had never had to kill. I've struggled for two years since this war ended just to live with myself. That's what war is to me: a black chapter of my life, a time I hope to overcome and put behind me. What I pray is that future heroes will find better answers. That's what I want to work for. I hope you do too."

The applause was more than polite, and it built as people seemed to realize that they were not alone in their enthusiasm for what they had heard.

Alex was especially pleased when Mr. Christensen said, "These young men have given us more than I expected. I put them in a position where they might have voiced a few platitudes and sat down. Instead, each one has tried to make us think. My hope is that Richard and Wally and Alex, each in his own way, will use his wisdom to make this country better. And I'm going to talk like a Dutch uncle to try to make Republicans of all three of them. We made tremendous strides in this last election, but to move forward, as we want to do, we need the best of our young people to join us."

This, too, brought on more applause.

Anna had hold of Alex by then. She was whispering in his ear, "You said what you really believe. That's what you need to keep doing. That's one of the things that will help you get better."

Alex was surprised to find himself thinking the same thing.

2 9

The dinner ended early. Richard, Wally, and Alex had kept
their remarks so brief that the event was over before nine
o'clock. As all the Thomases walked out together, Bea asked,
"Would you like to come over to the house for a little while?
We need a little time just to chat, by ourselves."

"Oh, good idea," Anna said. "I want Gene to be sound
asleep when we get home, so I don't have to put him down, for
once."

Bea saw Anna glance at Alex; he smiled and nodded. Bea
was pleased. Alex did seem a lot better tonight.

"Don't complain, Anna," Lorraine said. "At least Gene
sleeps through the night, once he does go down. Our little
Kathy will probably wake up and want to play about the time
we get home."

"Then don't you want to come over?" Bea asked.

"Oh, I didn't say that."

And Bea was pleased again. It was harder for the kids to
find time to visit these days, what with babies and work and
school. She thought this would be a nice time tonight, with the
babies home with babysitters and everyone seeming to be in
good spirits.

So the four couples drove in two cars back to Sugar House,

and Bea got out some of her bottled grape juice and served it to everyone. They sat in the living room and talked about this and that—almost anything but what the boys had said in their speeches that night. The men talked about Joe Lewis's next fight and about the Utes winning the NIT basketball championship that spring.

No one was happier than Al. After a time, he couldn't seem to resist turning the subject back to the dinner. "I hope you know, boys, Hyrum wasn't joking about recruiting the three of you to the party. Expect to hear from him."

Wally laughed. "I'll tell him how much I like President Truman. That should scare him off."

"I hope you don't mean that."

"I do. The guy has guts. He's been a good president."

Bea knew she didn't want this to get started—not with the way Al felt about Truman. She was sitting on the arm of Al's chair, and she leaned over and said, emphatically, into his ear, "My, hasn't the weather been nice lately?"

Al managed to laugh, and he let the subject go, but he did look across at Alex and ask, "What was that you were saying tonight about getting interested in politics?"

Alex was sitting on one of the dining-room chairs, next to Anna, who was on the couch with Bobbi and Richard. "I've just found myself thinking lately that I'd like to do something that makes a difference," he said. "I thought I wanted to be a professor, but I've watched those guys at the university this year, and I don't know, it just seems like they do a lot of talking, pushing ideas around, without ever *doing* anything."

"There's a lot of frustration in politics," Wally said. "You try to make changes, but everything ends up a compromise. You have to vote for this guy's bill, whether you agree with it or not, just so he'll vote for yours."

"Yeah, I know. And maybe I wouldn't like it. But it's the one thing that gets my blood pumping a little. I listened to George Marshall's talk the other day—about how important it is that we help rebuild Europe—and I just thought I'd like to help make things like that happen."

Bea knew that Al was less enthusiastic about the Marshall Plan, or at least had lots of questions about how it would take place. She put her hand on his shoulder and gave it a quick squeeze. He didn't say a thing.

"I don't think you can come out of school and just start running for office, Alex," Lorraine said. "You have to build a reputation one way or another."

"And usually you have to make some *money*," Bobbi said.

"I know," Alex said. "I've thought about that, too. Dad's going to fall right off his chair, but it's crossed my mind lately that I might want to come back to one of his businesses after I get out of school. Or maybe work for the foundation Mom is setting up. I wish that could even become a lifelong work."

"You can't give your money away faster than you make it, Alex," Al said.

"I know. I can't have it both ways. But I do want to do some good on this earth from now on. Most people don't think of politics as the best way to do that. But I think it could be. It *should* be."

Al was nodding, and Bea knew he was elated to hear such talk. "Alex," she said, "I don't care what you do. But the last couple of weeks, I've watched you come back to life. You seem like Alex now, and that means you can do anything you set your mind to."

Alex looked down. "I'm not doing as well as you might think," he said. "I don't feel much light inside me. But I'm trying to figure out what it's going to take."

There was quiet for a time, and then Richard, in his usual soft voice said, "I guess I'm searching around the same way. But it's leading me in the opposite direction. I'd rather be at a university, where the questions can be asked without all the political rhetoric. We need some people who think but don't have anything to sell."

"Maybe," Alex said. "But I think it takes both—the theoretical and the practical. Somebody has to try to find a way to put the ideas into action."

Bobbi patted her husband's hand. "I'm just happy that you're both starting to figure out what you want out of life."

"Well, that's fine, honey," Richard said, and he laughed, "as long as you can live with the vow of poverty I've taken."

"You won't ever be poor," Dad said.

Everyone looked at him.

"Our businesses will be handed down to everyone. Those who work for the companies will get salaries, but all of you will earn money from your share in the ownership. I want all of you to choose what you want to do—without worrying about money all that much. I don't want some of you rich and some poor."

"I couldn't take your money that way, Dad," Richard said.

"You won't. If you become a professor, you won't get a red cent from me, but in time, Bobbi will own twenty percent of everything. If these other lugs don't run the businesses into the ground, there should be plenty for all of you."

"Yes, but—"

"Hush, Richard," Bobbi said. "It's my money, so don't try to give it away."

Everyone laughed, but Bea was now patting her husband's shoulder, not squeezing it to keep him quiet. She had been worried these past few years about having too much money, not too little, but she had also worried about those who worked with Al having so much more than those who didn't.

"I agree with what Alex was saying," Al said. "I want all of you to do things that make a difference. Selling cars, making washing-machine parts, developing land—all those things are fine. But what matters to me is that you serve the Church, and you do things to make this valley—even the whole nation, if you can—better places. That's our heritage. That's what we do."

Bea was moved by that. Al had a bigger vision than she sometimes gave him credit for. But life still looked complicated to her: five children starting five families, if LaRue and Bev both married, and then another generation to follow. How did everyone keep the vision, understand that heritage, keep it going? And there were always so many problems, so many evils. Money could do plenty of good, but more often it seemed to do harm. She hoped her grandchildren wouldn't have too much of it.

* * *

When Alex and Anna got home, Alex walked the babysitter down the street, paid her, and then came back to find Anna in Gene's bedroom. She was looking down at him, in his crib. Alex walked over and stood next to her. The light from the hallway, through the door, allowed only a dim picture, but Gene's long eyelashes rested gently over his cheekbones, and his fine blond hair swirled about his ears. Alex thought he was the prettiest little boy he had ever seen. "I love you, Gene," he whispered.

Anna turned and wrapped her arms around Alex's waist. They watched the baby for a time, listened to him breathe, and then finally walked out quietly and into their own bedroom.

Anna sat down on the bed and took off her shoes. "Oh, Alex, I'm so tired," she said.

That's not what Alex had wanted to hear. He sat down next to her and loosened his tie. "I'll get up with Gene in the morning," he said. "You can sleep a little longer."

"I wake up anyway."

"I know. But rest a little longer tomorrow. You need it."

She turned and kissed him on the cheek. "Thank you."

"We need to get a bed for Gene, don't we?" Alex asked.

"Yes. I haven't wanted to say anything about that. He can stay in the crib for now, but certainly, when the new baby comes, we'll have to get one. Your father made it sound like we won't ever have any money worries. But that's only in the future."

Alex pulled off a shoe. "That's what I was thinking. But most young couples don't have as many resources as we do. All we'd have to do is tell Dad that we needed a bed, and he'd go buy one for us."

"I know. But I don't want that."

"I'm glad you don't." He pulled off the other shoe and then stood and pulled his shirt out of his trousers, began to unbutton it.

"Alex, I was surprised by what you said tonight. You've never said that to me, that you might go back to work for your dad. I never thought you would do that."

"I get different notions in my head every day, Anna. But right now, that seems to make the most sense. What do you think?"

"I don't know. I don't know what will make you happy." She lay back on the bed and shut her eyes. She cupped her hands over her round belly.

She was so like Gene, so beautiful, with her eyes shut the same way, her pretty hair around her face.

"I have to make me happy, Anna. That's what Doctor Kowallis and I talked about yesterday. A lot of it really is a choice."

Her eyes came open. "Maybe. But for so long, you just kept saying that you were all right—and I knew you weren't. It doesn't do any good to lie to yourself."

"That's what I'm trying to avoid now." He sat down by her again but turned so he could look into her face. "He introduced me to a couple of other vets yesterday. He wants to start a group and get us together once a month or so. He says there are hundreds of guys around this valley who are going through the same kind of stuff—but they never admit it to each other."

"What will you do when you get together?"

"Just talk about what happened to us. Maybe talk about things that bother us now. I'm not sure."

"And you'll do that?"

"I guess I will. I'd rather talk to Wally and Richard, but he said it's better to meet on a regular basis and talk to guys who aren't your relatives."

Anna sat up. She took hold of his hand. "Alex, I can hardly believe you're willing to do all that."

"I've got to do something. I've been making everyone so unhappy, the way I've been acting—especially you and Gene."

She rested her head against his shoulder. "Oh, Alex, this has all been so hard for you. But I love you. I always love you."

"I know you do, Anna. And sometimes this last year I haven't deserved it."

"Don't say that. I've been so awful lately. Tired all the time."

"Hey, you have to sleep for two."

She touched his chin, turned it gently, and kissed him more affectionately than she had for a time. "Thanks for trying so hard, Alex. I know you're going to be all right. I know who you are."

Alex took her into his arms and held her. "I don't know, Anna. The guy you remember is that young missionary you met, all those years ago. The doc says I can't keep worrying about that—getting back to being like him again. We all change, no matter what."

"I know, Alex. But there's something . . ." She switched to German and said, "I know your spirit. I know who *you* are, and you are good."

"I'm glad you still believe that," he said, also in German. "It heals me just to know you feel that way."

"I've loved you since I was sixteen years old, Alex."

"But I was easier to love when I was off at war, wasn't I?"

"I was easier to love when I wasn't pregnant and tired and worn out from putting up with a two-year-old all day."

"Life is hard, Anna. I didn't know that when I first met you."

"But it's good, too. It really is." And then she kissed him, this time with more interest.

"I thought you were tired," he said, and then he kissed her again.

"Not *that* tired. Especially if you're going to get up with Gene in the morning."

* * *

Bobbi was still wide awake when she got home. She didn't want to go to bed quite yet, so she went to the kitchen. "Do we have something sweet?" she asked Richard, who was in the bedroom, taking off his suit.

He appeared at the door in a minute, wearing his pajamas. He smiled. "We had that brick of ice cream. Did we eat it all?"

"Oh, good idea," Bobbi said. She walked to the freezer and got out what was left of the ice cream. "I've eaten so much tonight. I shouldn't be looking for more."

"You don't have anything to worry about."

In one sense, he was right. Bobbi knew that she had never gained back all the weight she had lost when the baby had miscarried. She really was as thin as she had been at any time since high school. But she also knew she couldn't get into the habit of eating too much. If she got pregnant again, she didn't want to be one of those women who gained a lot of weight and never lost it.

"Richard, does it bother you when everyone starts complaining about how their kids keep them up at night?" She had opened the carton of ice cream. It was Neapolitan, with stripes of vanilla, chocolate, and strawberry. She sliced it in half and then lifted the halves into two bowls.

"I guess what bothers me is that no one stops to think how it might make you feel."

"I'm sure they think I'll get pregnant before long." She got out spoons and then brought the ice cream to the table.

"And I think that will happen, Bobbi."

"What if it doesn't?"

"Worse things can happen. We'd be okay."

"I guess." She spooned in a mouthful of ice cream.

Richard began to eat too, and neither spoke for a time, but then Richard said, "Bobbi, I've been looking forward to being a dad for a long time. I want a baby as much as you do. In fact, I'd like to have quite a few kids—and do all the things with them that my dad never did."

"Why do you think your dad was like that?"

"I don't know. That's just the way he was. I think he figured women were supposed to raise the kids. It wasn't that he wasn't good to us. He'd tease and laugh, and he'd pile us into the car once a year and take us somewhere on vacation. But he never once talked to me about anything—you know, anything important. When I was growing up, if I had anything on my mind, it was my mom I always went to."

"Did you do that very often?"

"After a certain age, I didn't. By high school, I just figured things out for myself."

Bobbi ate some more of her ice cream. But she had kicked off her shoes, and now she reached across and rubbed her foot against Richard's.

"Sometimes, I think we try to do things different from our parents," Richard said, "but we're usually more like them than we think. Maybe I won't be one to talk with my kids either. I don't know."

"You'll be a good dad. I know that."

Richard smiled. "I hope so."

Bobbi continued to rub her foot across Richard's bare skin, over his foot and up his ankle. "You gave such a good talk tonight. Were you scared?"

"Did I seem scared?"

"No, you didn't. Not at all."

"I was—scared to death. My hands were shaking the whole time I was up there."

Again, they were quiet. There was only the clicking of their spoons in the bowls.

"What scares you, Bobbi? Anything?"

"Oh, wow. How can you say that? Lots of things scare me."

"What scares you most?"

"I don't know." She thought for a time. "Uncertainty, I guess. I always want to *know*, and I want to know right now. When you were lost at sea, I was scared of losing you, but I was even more scared that I would never know what had happened, and I would just have to live with that. And right now, I wish I *knew* whether I'll be able to have a baby or not. I wish the doctor would give us the go-ahead so we can start trying. If I can't have babies, I think I can get very strong—and deal with it. But waiting to find out is just so awful."

"Is that fear exactly, or is it . . . I don't know . . . worry, or something like that?"

"The two are all mixed up in my mind."

"Well, then, what's the scariest thing you can remember—just one moment of fear?"

"Oh, dear. Let's see." She rubbed his foot some more. "One night, when I was about thirteen or fourteen, I was home alone in my room upstairs. I can't remember where everyone was. But the wind was blowing, and I could hear all sorts of noises in our big old house. I built it all up in my mind until I thought there was someone downstairs breaking in or something."

"That's the most frightening thing in your life—*ever?*"

"Probably not. But that's what comes back to me. What scared you the most?"

"I was scared the whole time, out at sea. Several times we had Jap dive bombers, or fighters, drop out of the sky, right at us. Our guns would be firing away, but the closer they'd get, the more my heart would be right in my throat."

She wondered about that—what it would feel like to have someone attack you, try to kill you. "I didn't tell the truth a while ago."

"What do you mean?"

"I didn't know if I should say it, but that one day when I blew up at you, and you just got in the car and went off to work, I thought that day that we would end up getting a divorce, and I think that's the most frightened I've ever been."

"Why didn't you say that before?"

"I didn't want to tell you that I even thought about a divorce."

"I thought about it that day, too."

"Really?"

He nodded. But then he said, "But not for long."

Bobbi had finished her ice cream. She pushed the bowl out of the way and took hold of Richard's hand. "Let me ask you something else," she said.

"Okay."

"A while ago, when we stopped talking for a little while, I think you said to yourself, 'I need to talk. I shouldn't get quiet and let her carry the conversation. That's what she accuses me of all the time.'"

He smiled slowly, broadly. "When do you think I thought that?"

"First, when you started telling me about wanting to be a dad, and what you would do. And then, a little later, when you asked me what scared me. It isn't like you to talk about things in the war either, but you did it. I think you did that on purpose too."

He was still smiling.

"Well, am I right?"

"No. Nothing like that ever crossed my mind. I was just *gabbing*, like I always do."

"Come on. Tell the truth. You tried to think of things to talk about, didn't you?"

"You know I did."

"That's sweet, Richard. Really sweet." She pulled his hand to her lips and kissed it.

"I do like it when we talk, Bobbi. I just have to do it by the numbers more than you do. Maybe I won't always be like that."

"Do you think we'll ever know everything about each other?"

"No."

"I don't either. It's hard enough to know yourself without knowing someone else."

He nodded.

"Oh, Richard, I love you."

"I love you too, Bobbi. That's the one thing I got right since I came home from the war. I knew, somehow, I had to have you."

"But I drive you crazy; I force you to do things you don't really want to do."

"Sometimes we don't know what we want; we only know what we've always done. It's good when two people can lead each other to new things."

"Do you really mean that?"

"No. But it's the sort of thing you always say. It sounded good."

Bobbi laughed. "You're terrible, Richard. I'm even teaching you to be a smart aleck, just like me."

He was still smiling. She had fallen in love with that smile, and it still made her feel all liquid inside. But she was glad there was a lot more to him than just a smile. "I think we'll always be okay if we just try to make each other happy."

"We certainly will."

"You *smart aleck*. Now you're *mocking* me. Making *fun* of my opinions."

"Would I do that?"

She leaned back and grinned, loving him, and began to rub his feet again.

* * *

Wally and Lorraine went to bed quickly when they got home. But Kathy woke up a little after two o'clock. Wally woke up and felt Lorraine slip quietly from their bed and walk to the next room, where Kathy's crib was. In a moment the crying stopped, and Wally began to drift. But then he felt guilty. He knew how tired Lorraine was. So he slipped out of bed himself and walked out to the living room, where Lorraine was sitting on the couch, holding the baby and nursing her.

"Do you want me to do that?" he asked.

"I wish you had the right equipment. I'd love to take turns."

"No. I meant I could give her a bottle."

"She needs my milk, Wally. I'm just glad I have enough. Some women don't."

Wally walked over and sat down next to her on the couch.

"There's no reason for you to stay up, honey," she said. "Just go back to bed."

"I'll keep you company."

"Well . . . thanks."

He could hear the little squeaks and grunts the baby was making. "Doesn't that hurt?"

"No. Well . . . sometimes it does—a little."

"Do you like it?"

"Not right now." She sat for a moment, and then she added, "but it is nice sometimes. It makes you feel very close—when you're in the right mood."

"Do you think a dad can ever be as close to his kids as a mother?"

"In some ways you can be closer. Moms end up saying no a lot. Dads can be more fun."

"It depends on the family, I guess. I was always a lot closer to my mom."

"What about now?"

Wally thought for a time. "Even now," he finally said. "But Dad is like the stake that you drive into the ground to hold the tent firm. He never seems to forget who we are. I want to be like that too."

"You already are, Wally, but you're softer than your dad, and I like that side of you best."

"Dad's only hard on the outside."

"That's true. I've always known that. But you know how to show who you are better than he does. That's what I need."

Wally looked down at his little daughter again, trying to think what she would be like someday. He wanted to talk with her, listen to her, be around when she needed him. And he hoped he would have sons and could be the same with them.

"Wally, go to bed. Really. There's no reason for both of us to be up."

"I know." But he stayed. He put his arm around Lorraine, listening to the gentle sounds of his baby, and as he did so often, he offered a silent prayer of thanks.

* * *

Peter Stoltz was sitting up in bed. He had turned on the lamp nearby, and he was breathing now, gulping air, trying to calm down. He wasn't surprised when his door opened and his father was standing there. "Are you all right?" Papa asked.

Peter nodded, but he was still taking big breaths.

"I heard you."

"I know." Peter hated this, the way he would scream at night sometimes. He hated the fear and sleeplessness that would follow, but more than anything he hated the worry it caused his parents. "It's nothing, Papa. It's just the same thing. I'll be all right in a minute."

"Will you sleep?"

"I don't know."

Brother Stoltz walked to the bed and sat down. "I have bad memories too, Peter. I even dream about them sometimes."

"I know. But go to bed. I'm all right."

"What have you told Katrina?"

"That I'm coming back to Germany. I didn't say when."

"When are you thinking you'll go?"

"After I've saved some more money." He didn't want to say

more than that. All this only upset his parents. His heartbeat was settling down now, his breathing. He leaned back against the headboard of his bed.

"Peter, I think you should go. Maybe sooner. I have saved a little money, and you could have that. It would pay for your travel, I think."

"I can earn the money, Papa. And I need to give Mother time to get used to my going."

"She won't get used to it, Peter—not ever—but I do think you need to go."

"Why?"

"You know why—because you're so unhappy here."

Peter didn't like the words, even though they were true. He felt as though he were being accused of something. He shut his eyes and tried to relax. His father didn't know it, but this conversation would keep him up all night. It was just more to think about. "Are you happy here, Papa? Can you say that?"

"I'm happy enough. My English gets better all the time, and I like working in the office better than running the machines. It's more what I'm accustomed to. Sometimes I miss the food back home—our nice little apartment, our old neighborhood. " He laughed. "Our bad weather. Our bad temper. All those German things. But I have opportunities here. That means a good deal to me."

"I know what you think: I could be happy here. I could have opportunities too—if I would only try."

"I don't know, Peter. I thought that at one time. But I watch you every day and see how sad you are. And I know that your mother and I, we can't give you what you need. Maybe Kartrina can. Maybe Germany can."

"I don't want to leave you—especially not Gene. I'll miss everything, when he's growing up. But I can't stay."

"I know."

"Who knows? Maybe after I'm there for a while, I'll want to come back. And maybe then I can bring Katrina."

"I'll talk to your mother. I'll try to help her understand." Peter nodded. Papa got up and walked to the door. "Try to relax and sleep now."

"I will." But Peter left the light on. He wished there were music this time of night on the radio, but all the stations had signed off for the night. So he got up and got his German scriptures. He had read a great deal in them lately, and he was finding solace in that. He had spent some time talking to Alex, too, and that had also been good for him. But praying seemed to help him more than anything. He knew, when he was away from his family, that he would need the Church, and he would need God. Once before he had tried the separation, without the Lord, and he didn't want to do that again.

The Pioneer Day celebration in Salt Lake was huge this year. After all, it was 1947, the centennial celebration of Brigham Young's arrival in the valley. The traditional parade would actually march through downtown twice—once on the morning of the twenty-third and then again in the evening of the twenty-fourth of July. The morning of the twenty-fourth, the usual time for the parade, was reserved for the dedication of the new This Is the Place Monument at the mouth of Emigration Canyon. But all week things were happening. Al Thomas bought tickets for the entire family to attend the grand musical, *Promised Valley*, at the University of Utah stadium. He also took Bea to the Tabernacle Choir's performance of *The Restoration*, with the famous tenor Rulon Y. Robison. On Sunday, the twentieth, President Joseph F. Smith spoke on national radio, on the University of Chicago Roundtable, and that same day President David O. McKay, second counselor in the presidency, made a nationwide presentation on "Church of the Air." On July 22, a caravan of seventy-two automobiles, sponsored by the Sons of the Utah Pioneers and equipped with painted sideboards to look like covered wagons, arrived in the valley from Nauvoo, Illinois. These commemorative "trekkers" appeared that day at the dedication of the new Sugar House

Park and then paraded down Main Street. Added to all that, the Capitol Theatre, all refurbished, reopened on the twenty-second and was playing *I Wonder Who's Kissing Her Now*. Even the U.S. Postal Service had gotten involved by issuing a new "This Is the Place" three-cent stamp, and according to the newspapers, the fireworks show at the fairgrounds, going on every night that week, would be the "greatest show ever in the West."

Bea Thomas loved it all, and she wanted the whole family together at the parade, so she and Al got up early on the morning of the twenty-third, drove to town, and staked out a spot on State Street in an area where they would get some shade. Then they waited as the family gathered. LaRue and Beverly were the last to arrive, just in time for the parade, LaRue driving "Mom's car." This was an extravagance that amazed the older siblings. Dad had shocked everyone enough when, for Mother's Day, he had given Mom a car of her own, but the thought of driving two cars to the same place, when everyone could have fit into one—that was something Dad never would have considered in the past. "You wouldn't have let us do something like that when we were LaRue's age," Bobbi told her dad.

"Nobody had two cars in those days," Dad said.

"Nobody does now."

And that was almost true. But Bea was busy with the new land development project, and she actually had to run around more than Al did. The truth was, she was embarrassed to have the car, and she never told anyone it was "hers," but she found it more than useful, virtually necessary, the way her life ran these days.

"Here's what's amazing," LaRue told everyone. She plunked herself down in front of Bobbi on one of the blankets. "No matter how much Dad does for me and Beverly, we're not spoiled. We're still just as sweet as we ever were." She looked to Beverly for agreement.

"Even sweeter," Beverly said, and she giggled. She tried so

hard sometimes to be like LaRue, but Bea could see that Bev was actually blushing.

Everyone laughed, the teasing continued, and Bea enjoyed every bit of it. Al had bought little Gene a set of cap guns, with holsters, and a "cowboy suit": a little felt cowboy hat, a vest, and a neckerchief. The noise of the caps actually scared Gene a little, but he kept holding the guns well out in front of him and pulling the trigger, then flinching a little when the caps went off. Bea was surprised that Alex was willing to let him make such a racket, but Alex was trying very hard these days not to let things bother him. Al had picked up some sparklers, too, and before the parade arrived, Alex lit a few and let Gene hold them and wave them around. Gene kept insisting that baby Kathy needed to have her own sparklers, but "Little Bea" was asleep in Grandma Bea's arms.

Bea was sitting with the baby in a wooden folding chair at the back of this little Thomas section. There were only four chairs, so Al had insisted that Anna, Lorraine, and Bobbi take those, and he was sitting on the blankets with the men, and with Beverly and LaRue. In the middle of everything was a metal cooler, full of ice. Bea had bought it the week before at the big grand-opening sale at the new, enormous Sears store on Eighth South. She had also bought an entire case of soda water at Grand Central, on sale for ninety-eight cents, and a bunch of U-No candy bars, three for twelve cents. She hadn't seen a deal like that in a long time. Nickel candy bars seemed to get smaller all the time.

When the parade finally arrived, the beginning was impressive. A color guard of Marines marched by, followed by the famous U.S. Marine Band. The Thomases all stood in respect for the flag and then waved to Governor Maw, in the first car. Al and Bea knew the governor well, but Bea was still impressed that he noticed the family and waved back. Then the First Presidency came by in the second car, and the Brethren also smiled and waved. Bea loved these good men. The Centennial

Queen, Calleen Robinson, followed on a beautiful float, decked out in a jeweled gown. "Mom," Bobbi said, "I read in the paper that that dress cost a thousand dollars."

"I know," Bea said. "I talked to her mom. She said the thing weighs a ton. Calleen can hardly drag it around. She's only wearing it in the two parades."

"Seems a waste," Al said, but Bea laughed and gave him a little kick.

By then people had begun to throw out confetti from the windows of the buildings above, and it was floating down on everyone. Bea liked that. It made her think of the ticker-tape parades in New York City.

But now the Boy Scouts were marching by—five thousand of them. They looked nice in their uniforms, but it took a long time for all of them to pass by. Bea didn't mind, but LaRue, of course, had to fuss about it. And eventually Bea did begin to wonder whether the parade wasn't just a little too "grand." It lasted two hours, with something like eighty floats telling the history of Utah and all the cultures back to the early Indians and to Father Escalante. There were also trick riders on horseback, and clowns, the Tournament of Roses band—enough to catch Gene's interest now and then—but the heat kept rising, into the nineties, and poor little Kathy got very cranky before it was all over. Bea actually left with LaRue and Beverly, along with Lorraine and the baby, before it was quite over. And she wasn't sorry at all, at that point, that the girls had brought an extra car.

Bea actually enjoyed the next day much more. The couples with babies decided not to attend the dedication of the monument, and LaRue and Beverly didn't want to go, so Al and Bea took Richard and Bobbi with them, and they drove up early enough to get a good spot, close to the little speakers' platform. Eventually, the crowd was enormous—the *Deseret News* later estimated that 50,000 had shown up—but Bea was moved by the sentiments expressed and the pageantry as each of the five

sections of Mahonri H. Young's monument was unveiled sepa-
rately. The Marine Band was there again, and so were the Boy
Scouts. They sang "Home on the Range," and the sound of it,
up there against the mountains, was surprisingly rich. Mormon
leaders spoke, and so did Bishop Hunt from the Catholic
Church, Rabbi Luchs, and Reverend Moulton. Rabbi Luchs
spoke the words that lingered with Bea when the ceremony
was over: "We must stand for the granite and bronze virtues of
these pioneers." At the end, everyone sang "Come, Come, Ye
Saints," and the music seemed to fill up the whole valley.

After the ceremony, the family gathered at the new Sugar
House Park for a picnic. Wally went early to find a good spot,
and Grandma and Grandpa Thomas came this time. So did the
Stoltzes. Everyone ate fried chicken and potato salad, and then
Wally got a softball game going. He talked most of the males
in the family into playing, even his dad, along with Bev and
LaRue, and he recruited some friends and even a few strangers,
enough to have eight or ten on each side. Peter gave the sport
a try and turned out to have more of a knack for it than anyone could have expected. Brother Stoltz, who stayed at the picnic table and watched, told Bea, "Peter is a fine sportsman. He
missed his youth, for the most part—but he could have been
an excellent soccer player. That's what I would have enjoyed—
seeing him play."

"So many boys lost their chance to play," Bea told him.
Sometimes Bea thought she was forgetting the war, letting it
go, and then the enormity of it all would strike her again.

"Yes. So many boys," Brother Stoltz said.

The Stoltzes didn't like the heat, and they left sooner than
the others, as did Grandma and Grandpa Thomas. The game
continued, but Al got out rather quickly himself, and he took
Gene for a little walk, down to the swings. Eventually Bea was
left at the table in the shade of a young maple tree, with Bobbi,
Anna, and Lorraine. Kathy was content for the moment to play
with some little toys on a blanket in the shade.

Bea liked this, having her three "daughters" around her. They laughed about the softball game going on not far away, and they talked about this and that, nothing important. Anna was worried about Gene's wildness. "He never calms down. He can run all day. And he's *so* stubborn. He won't listen to me," she told Bea.

"It's the hardest thing I know of, raising kids," Bea told her. "You know what they ought to be learning, and you want so much to teach them—but they have their own will."

"At least you don't have to worry about *us* now," Bobbi said. "We all turned out just perfect—except for LaRue."

Bea laughed, but then she said, "You have turned out well—better than I dared to hope sometimes. But I still worry. Things are changing so fast these days, and I wonder what kind of world these little babies are going to grow up in."

"I worry about that too," Lorraine said. "I see the way some of the girls at the high school are dressing now, and I wonder what Kathy is going to face in another ten or fifteen years. There's almost no modesty left."

Bea laughed. "I love to hear you girls start to worry about the kinds of things I used to fuss about. Bobbi always told me I was getting upset about nothing at all."

"You were," Bobbi said. "It's this next generation *I'm* worried about."

Everyone was smiling, but Bea said, quite seriously, "So it always is." She picked up a paper plate—another new extravagance since the war—and used it to fan her face. She would have preferred to go on home, where the house was likely to be a little cooler, but she was willing to wait and let everyone enjoy themselves as long as they wished. "I'll say this. You girls have brought me more joy than I ever expected to have again in this life. I feel as close to you, Anna and Lorraine, as I do to my own daughters. And you're both so good for my sons. I watch the way you're healing them—I see them coming back to themselves—and I wonder what might have happened to

them if you hadn't been the ones they had chosen. Not every
girl would understand."

Bea watched as Beverly took a swing at the softball and
bounced it on the ground toward third base. She should have
been out, but a boy Bea didn't know muffed the ball and then
made a wild throw over the first baseman's head. Beverly's
teammates all screamed for her to run to second, but she
seemed relieved just to be on base. She stood with one foot on
the base—a brown paper bag held in place by a rock—and
fanned herself with her hand. She was wearing a tan cotton
skirt with a blue "boy's style" shirt, and her new saddle oxfords.
Bea could hardly believe how grown up she looked. In the past
year she had gained so much confidence, had become so much
more comfortable with herself. She was still dating Garner
from time to time, but she got asked to every dance, it seemed,
and by lots of different boys.

Anna was watching the game too, one hand resting on her
big middle. She waited until another girl hit the ball toward
second, and Beverly was forced out. As the players in the field
ran back toward home, she said, "I think I do understand
Alex—better now than I did last year. But he's not doing so well
as you might think. He's still so nervous. If he could, he would
just hide away from the world. I think he's braver now than
when he was in the war—just the way he makes himself keep
doing what he has to do."

"Do you think it was wise of him to accept this new
calling?"

"I do. He came home, after the stake president talked to
him, and he cried and cried. He kept telling me that he didn't
feel worthy. But it makes him feel better about himself to do it.
And he's doing a good job."

Bea worried about that. It had only been a month now
since he had been called to be second counselor to his bishop.
It was like Alex not to turn the calling down, but she had

sensed how worried he was about it. She hoped the pressure wouldn't be too much for him.

"He'll be all right," Bobbi said. "I've seen so much change in him lately. He's a lot more like the Alex I remember."

"He's better," Bea said, and tears came into her eyes. "He's deeper, more thoughtful. He's paid a price, but he's getting something from it."

"I think so too," Anna said. "Someday it will be worth it. But I wish everything wasn't so hard for him right now."

"It's the same for Richard," Bobbi said. "He's doing so much better, but I can feel, every day, that it's all such an effort for him."

Bea knew what the girls meant, and she wished too that there weren't always so many hard dues to pay in this life. But she heard Alex laugh, and she looked up to see that he had just hit the ball hard, knocking it way over Wally's head. Wally was chasing after it but not running hard. In fact, he eventually slowed to a walk and let a little boy toss him the ball. Alex was already loping toward home plate, but he was looking back at Wally. He yelled something Bea couldn't hear, and Wally laughed, then called back, "That was nothing. My little girl could hit the ball that far." And the joy of the moment—this day—struck Bea. How could she ever have hoped to see such a thing? Everyone there; everyone healthy; everyone having fun together. She looked across the park and saw Al pushing little Gene on the swing, Gene laughing, and then she looked down at Kathy on the blanket. She thought of these little cousins growing up together, along with Anna's next baby, soon to come: another generation. It was hard not to worry about that, about other wars, other hard times, but she told herself not to do that today. This was all too good.

Bea looked at Bobbi and Anna, across the table from her, and put her arm around Lorraine's shoulder. "I hope you girls know how much I love you—and these little grandbabies you've given me."

Anna reached across the table and patted Bea's hand. "We're glad they have such a good grandma."

Bobbi had begun to smile, seeming unexplainably delighted about something. "I wasn't going to say anything yet, but maybe this is a good time for me to make a little announcement," she said.

Bea knew immediately. In fact, she thought she'd known for a couple of weeks.

"Richard and I weren't going to say anything quite so soon this time—because of what happened last time. But I can't wait. He might be upset with me, but . . . well . . . I'm expecting again."

Bea got up and walked around the table. She sat down next to Bobbi and put her arms around her. "Oh, Bobbi, I've prayed so much about this. The best is just knowing for sure that you *can* have babies."

"I know," Bobbi said. "I know."

Bea clung to her daughter for a time, and then she got out of the way so her daughters-in-law could hug Bobbi too. All Bea could think was that the Lord was being good to her family. After all that had happened, all the nightmarish times she had been through, now the days seemed to bring one great blessing after another. She was still worried about Alex, concerned that Bobbi could carry this baby all right, and, mostly, fearful of what might lie ahead for LaRue. But troubles seemed to be part of life, and she had realized more than ever, these past few years, that she could never know the good of this world without experiencing some of the pain.

As the afternoon grew hotter, all the Thomases finally gathered their things together and moved the party back to the family home. Inside the house, with its good walls, and some fans going, the temperature wasn't quite so bad. Alex was pleased that everyone came—even the Stoltzes—and that no one, not even LaRue, made an excuse to run off. He liked having everyone around. During his years away from Utah, the

Twenty-Fourth of July had always been a little strange: a day most people didn't even notice on the calendar, and yet such a big day in the memory of a kid who had grown up among the Saints in Utah.

He and Wally and Richard ended up on the front porch together. Alex sat on the front steps, in the shade of the porch. Richard took the old love seat and left room for Wally, but Wally sat on the rail by the lilac bushes. He was chomping on a big slice of watermelon, then turning his head and spitting seeds into the lilacs. "Remember how we used to see who could spit a watermelon seed the farthest?" Wally asked Alex.

"Sure," Alex said. "But what I remember, when I think of watermelon, is that day we were up in the canyon, and our watermelon got away from us and went down the river."

"So you remember that too? I used to think about that when I was gone," Wally said. "Gene set up a howl, like his heart was going to break."

"Do you remember what Dad told him?"

"Sure. He told him it was going to make a good story—and a good memory was better than a watermelon. I don't know, though. *This* watermelon is awfully good." He bit into it again.

"But Dad was right. That's a good memory, still."

Wally spit out some seeds, worked his tongue around a little, and then spit one more. "It is. What I wish, though, is that I could have seen Gene at least one more time. My memory has to go too far back. I can only think of him as a little kid, and he grew up so much after I was gone."

"I saw him a little while later. But I feel the same way."

"Wouldn't that be something, if he could just be here today?"

But Alex didn't want to talk about that. He had never known Gene well enough, hadn't worked hard enough between his mission and his induction into the army to get close to him. It was one of the great regrets of his life. He never thought of the boy without feeling that he should have tried harder, should have said some things he never did. And it was that as much as anything that caused him to say, "I want to tell you guys something." He looked away from Wally and Richard when he continued. "I thought I'd never be so close to a group of guys as I was to the ones in my squad. But these last few weeks, since we've all kind of opened up with each other—I've felt just as close to you two. And there are a lot of things I can say to you that I never could have said to them."

"I feel the same way," Wally said.

"Yeah, me too," Richard said.

"You guys are saving my life," Alex said. "You really are."

After that they sat for a long time without talking. The sun was angling from deep in the valley now, over the Great Salt Lake, but the heat wasn't letting up yet. It seemed stuck under the roof of the porch, with no breeze to move it. A little flock of sparrows had landed on the front sidewalk. They were setting up a clatter, but that was the only sound. Then Richard said, "There's something I want to tell you. Bobbi and I agreed not to say anything yet, so I'll probably get in trouble—but I guess I'll take the chance." Alex looked around at Richard, saw him smile, and knew before he said it. "Bobbi's pregnant again."

"Oh, Richard, that's good," Alex said, and he felt the relief. "That's so good."

A little memory jumped into Alex's mind. He and Bobbi had gone for a walk one day, out in the cold, the winter before they had both left for the service. Alex had talked to Bobbi about Anna for the first time, and Bobbi was worrying about Glen, the guy she was engaged to. What struck Alex now was that both of them—he and Bobbi—had walked some long, hard roads, but they had ended up in the right places. Alex got up from the step and walked to Richard. Wally was already there, shaking Richard's hand, slapping him on the back. Alex shook his hand too, and then he asked, "Do you mind if we go in and say something to Bobbi?"

"No. That's fine," Richard said. "If she's going to chew me out, we might as well get it over with."

So the three walked into the house. Bobbi was in the living room, talking to Heinrich and Frieda, and to Peter. Dad was there, too, but he had his nose in the paper. The *Deseret News* had put out a big special edition, all about the history of Utah. As Alex walked toward Bobbi, smiling, she stood up and said, "He *told* you, didn't he? He wasn't supposed to do that."

But Alex paid no attention to that. He took Bobbi into his arms and said, "I was so worried that this couldn't happen, Bobbi. I'm so happy for you."

"I know," she said. "That's the best part." She hugged Wally, too, and then she went to Richard. "Don't worry. You're not in trouble. I spilled the beans to the girls already. And I told Dad."

Al looked up from his paper and smiled.

The Stoltzes now took their turn, shaking hands with Bobbi, congratulating her, and then Bea and Lorraine, LaRue and Beverly appeared from the kitchen. "Oh, that's old news now," LaRue said. "Bobbi told me and Bev an hour ago."

But Alex watched his mother. She walked over to Dad and looked down, and the two exchanged a little glance. "All this is what we've been waiting for," Alex heard his mom whisper.

Everyone was standing now, seeming unsure what to do. But after a moment, Heinrich said, "We have some news in our family, too. This might be a good time to tell you." He turned to Peter, who was standing off a little from the rest, near the couch where he had been sitting. "Peter, do you want to tell them?"

He nodded and said, "Yes. I'm going back soon to Germany."

"Really? Why?" Al asked.

Peter seemed to struggle for the right words. Finally, he said, simply, "It seems the best for me."

"But won't you miss your family?"

"Yes, I will. Certainly."

Everyone was quiet. A sort of circle had formed in the living room, and now no one moved. Alex knew that his family had heard this as bad news, and no one knew what to say.

"I want to build . . ." Peter began, but than he stopped and admitted, "I don't know how to say this in English."

Anna spoke for him. "He feels that he needs to help rebuild Germany, not leave it behind."

"Can you get work over there?" Al asked.

"Some kind of work. Yes."

"But what about college? You and I spoke about your going to college here. You'll never have that chance there, will you?"

"No. Probably not."

Brother Stoltz put his hand on Peter's shoulder. "We've talked about all those things," he said. "But love has something to do with all this too."

Alex saw Peter blush. "I write to a girl I know," he said. "But I don't know what happens to us now. That's not the only reason I go."

Alex knew it was a very big reason, and he understood. He also understood Peter's love of Germany, the desire to be there and help the people. He had suspected that Peter would decide to do this sooner or later. Alex stepped to Peter and put his arm around his shoulders. "I'm glad someone in our family will be there," he said. "Mom and I have been trying to send help, and it hasn't been easy. You can do something about that."

"Yes. I talked to Sister Thomas about this already."

Bea nodded.

"Couldn't you bring your girl over here?" Al asked.

"Maybe," Peter said. "But in Germany I have my language, and I want Germany to be . . . a good place again. Maybe you understand that."

"I do," LaRue said. "Are you leaving before me?" She dropped onto the couch. "Hey, sit down everyone. You look like statues."

"Yes. I think I leave first. Maybe in a month."

"Yup. That's before me. I won't be leaving until September."

Some people did begin to sit down, but Bea was still standing next to Al's chair. "LaRue, don't say it like that," she said. "You sound like you can't wait."

"Well, I am pretty excited about it. Who wouldn't want to get out of here?" But her voice didn't sound as arrogant as her words. Alex had talked to her quite a lot lately, and he knew she did have mixed feelings about the enormous change coming in her life.

"Aren't you scared at all?" Bobbi asked.

Alex could see that LaRue loved having the spotlight to herself. She always had. But she answered honestly. "I don't think it's real to me yet. When I try to really imagine getting on the train, then I feel kind of scared."

"I can promise you," Bobbi said, "you'll be a lot more scared when the day comes."

But Wally said, "She's thought a lot about this. I really think it's the right thing for her." He sat down next to LaRue.

"It's hard for me," Bea said. "We're finally together, and now some are leaving already."

"Well, that's how life is," Alex said, and he meant a lot of things. But he feared for Peter, and especially for LaRue. There were so many dangers she didn't understand yet.

* * *

Later that evening, after the sun had finally gone down, people began to head home. The Stoltzes left first, and then Lorraine and Wally, Richard and Bobbi. As the house quieted, little Gene had crawled up on his Grandpa's lap, and Al had read him a couple of storybooks. But somewhere in the middle of the second one, Al heard steady breathing, and he looked down to see Gene's long eyelashes resting shut. Al closed the book, tucked Gene a little closer to him, and simply sat there holding him.

When Anna came in to get him, Al held his finger to his

lips and said softly, "I'll carry him out to the car. You get your things together."

"No, no. Alex can carry him. You sit there until we're ready." Anna went off, and then Bea walked into the living room. She smiled down at Al. "That's a precious picture," she said. "I'd like to have a snapshot of you two."

But Al had some things on his mind by then. "Bea, we've been blessed," he said. But he didn't know how, exactly, to tell her what he was feeling.

"I know, Al," Bea said. "I've been thinking the same thing all day."

"We're going to be fine," he said. "This next generation is going to do all right."

"Even LaRue?"

"I think so."

"I think so, too. Or at least I hope so. It just seems like there will always be things to worry about."

"Well, sure. There will be."

Bea was still looking down at him, as though she understood that he had something else to say.

"Bea, I've been thinking a lot about the new house. When it gets right down to it, I'm not sure I want to leave this place."

"Well . . . you know how I feel about that."

"Maybe, when the house is finished, we could just go ahead and sell it."

"Are you sure?"

"Yes, I am. I want to stay here. This is home. The kids all say the same thing. They want to have this place to come back to."

"Thank you, Al," Bea said, and she bent and kissed him, and she kissed little Gene, too. "It's funny, but I've been feeling blue all day about that very thing. I just couldn't think of Christmas or Easter, or the next Twenty-Fourth, in some other place."

Al nodded, but he was surprised at how easy the decision

had been. What he knew was that it had come to him that morning, up there at the new monument.

"Let me help Anna gather up her things," Bea said, and she walked back to the kitchen.

Al leaned back and shut his eyes. He felt sleepy after such a long day. But he thought again of the ceremony that morning, of how much it had meant to him. He wondered what Brigham Young would think of everything now, if he could see what had been made of this valley that he and his little group had settled a hundred years before. Maybe Brigham would be surprised to see all the growth, to see what the Saints had become, but probably not. He'd probably known it all, even then, and known that some of that growth would bring disappointment. Surely he would have foreseen the mistakes, the sins, even the wars. The thing about life was to learn from it. Brigham had always known that.

Al thought too, as he often did, of his Grandpa Thomas, out on the plains, continuing on when his heart was broken. That was the beginning of this family trek.

In a few minutes he heard the front door open—that sticky front door. For just a moment he thought of how much he had wanted to get out of this old house and have something new. But he was content with the decision he and Bea had made. He even remembered exactly when he had reached his own decision. Father Hunt, the Catholic bishop, up at the ceremony, had talked about the victory of the "spiritual over the material." He had said that people in the Salt Lake Valley needed to "restore pioneer virtues." That had sounded so much like some of his own sermons, and suddenly the new house had not seemed right to him. There were things to keep, and there were things to let go. The house didn't matter so much, but the life he and Bea and the kids had shared there did. He had suddenly wondered whether that big new house might not change them in some way, cut them off from who they had always been. He didn't want to take that chance, and he had known all along that Bea didn't either.

So Al was content with all that. But what he wished was that he could have a few more minutes with Gene, that he could just sit there and hold him a little longer. Still, he wasn't about to complain. It had been long day for everyone. But it had been a good one.

This is the last book in the *Children of the Promise* series. What a strange feeling it is for me to say that. I've worked for seven years on these books and honestly never worked harder in my life. The research has been fun but time-consuming, and the writing and rewriting process has seemed endless. For five of those years, every time I finished a novel I immediately started the next one. So why am I feeling such a sense of loss? I suppose, in part, because I will miss the Thomases. I know that they exist only when I put words in their mouths or invent their actions, but it doesn't seem so to me. They seem like friends—or family—with all the complexities of real human beings. I may come back to the Thomases in some way, write about them in another era or from a different angle, but I believe this stopping place—July 24, 1947—is the right one for this series.

Writing these novels has deepened my respect for the generation that sent its sons and daughters off to set things right, who put aside personal goals "for the duration," who suffered immeasurable worry and loss. At the same time, I am disturbed by the romanticized version of the war that continues to be presented in movies and even in some of our patriotic messages. My greatest worry is that future generations will not understand the horror that was unleashed on the world during World War II. I hope my series has found a balance between the respect I feel for the soldiers and the distaste I feel for war.

I have worked hard to be accurate in my historical accounts, but to create fictional characters and give them life in history, I did alter some minor facts. The branch in Frankfurt, for example, actually met at the relatively undamaged mission home after the war. I needed a branch for the fictional President Meis, so I had his members meet in a *Gasthaus.* Many branches in Germany met in those or similar circumstances, so I felt that was representative, not misleading.

I want to clarify also that the words of Elder Ezra Taft Benson in his speech to the members in Frankfurt were actually delivered in Hannover. I would assume, however, that he said similar things in Frankfurt. Of course, the conversation Elder Benson had with Alex is also fictional, but I did not invent his sentiments. He actually expressed them to me. In 1965, when I was about to return from the South German Mission, President Benson (then president of the European Mission) interviewed me. I asked him whether he had any advice for a returning missionary. He surprised me by telling me not to plan too far into the future. Then he gave me the same advice that I had him give to Alex.

For this volume, the one "must read" book for those interested in LDS history is Frederick W. Babbel's *On Wings of Faith* (Bookcraft, 1972). This is the record of Brother Babbel's travels with Elder Benson throughout Europe in 1946.

I want to thank the people who have helped me so much in creating these novels. Sheri Dew was instrumental in conceiving and designing the series. Jack Lyon has been my editor. Jay Parry, Emily Watts, and Timothy Robinson have also read the manuscripts and given me excellent artistic and editorial advice. Ron Millett, president and CEO of Deseret Book Company, has amazingly made time in his demanding schedule to read them as well, and he has always been supportive.

Members of the board of directors at Deseret Book have taken unusual interest in the project; most of them have expressed their enthusiasm to me. A number of friends and family members have read the manuscripts and given me responses: my son Tom and his wife Kristen; my daughter Amy Russell and her husband Brad; my son Rob; my friends David and Shauna Weight, Sharon and Richard Jeppesen, Kathy Luke, Carolyn Rasmus, Pam Russell, and Cathryn Manning.

Of special help has been Horst A. Reschke, a native German who now lives in Utah. He wrote to me after the second book was published, complimented me for my overall accuracy, and then, with kindness and German directness, pointed out some mistakes. Since then, he has been willing to read the manuscripts and check my German language and history. He was in Hannover on the day in 1946 when Elder Benson spoke, and he allowed me to use a copy of that text along with other materials he has collected. He grew up in Germany during the war years and was able to give me insight into the challenges LDS families faced.

I dedicated the first book to my wife, Kathy, but that doesn't begin to express the thankfulness I feel for her assistance. She brainstormed with me all along the way and is responsible for the ideas behind some of the best scenes and plot lines. She's a busy woman (in Provo I'm known as "Kathy's husband"), but she has taken the time to read the manuscripts over and over, draft after draft. She has always made me feel that I was doing something wonderful even as she was raising hard questions and pointing out serious problems.

This last book is dedicated to my son Rob. He is a careful, intelligent reader, and he has read the drafts of all five novels. He catches my typos and writing errors, but he also raises wise questions about the content and artistry of the fiction. He, with the rest of my family, has enjoyed making suggestions for plot elements as the series has progressed. That is one of the losses

I will feel the most: the fun of having the Thomas family as part of *our* family.

I hope I have given readers an enjoyable and memorable reading experience, for they certainly deserve one. Their responses have been touching, and while the demand for the "next one" has kept me breathless at times, I've been moved by the interest and the expressions of appreciation. This has not been an easy time in my life, but I will always remember it as blessed. And for that, I thank you.